DISCARDED BY
MT LEBANON PUBLIC LIBRARY

Mt. Lebanon Public Library
16 Castle Shannon Blvd
Pittsburgh, PA 15228-2252
412-531-1912 |
www.mtlebanonlibrary.org

SAVING SUSY SWEETCHILD

Also by Barbara Hambly from Severn House

Silver Screen historical mysteries

SCANDAL IN BABYLON
ONE EXTRA CORPSE

The Benjamin January series

DEAD AND BURIED
THE SHIRT ON HIS BACK
RAN AWAY
GOOD MAN FRIDAY
CRIMSON ANGEL
DRINKING GOURD
MURDER IN JULY
COLD BAYOU
LADY OF PERDITION
HOUSE OF THE PATRIARCH
DEATH AND HARD CIDER
THE NUBIAN'S CURSE

The James Asher vampire novels

BLOOD MAIDENS
THE MAGISTRATES OF HELL
THE KINDRED OF DARKNESS
DARKNESS ON HIS BONES
PALE GUARDIAN
PRISONER OF MIDNIGHT

SAVING SUSY SWEETCHILD

Barbara Hambly

SEVERN HOUSE

First world edition published in Great Britain and the USA in 2024
by Severn House, an imprint of Canongate Books Ltd,
14 High Street, Edinburgh EH1 1TE.

severnhouse.com

Copyright © Barbara Hambly, 2024

All rights reserved including the right of
reproduction in whole or in part in any form.
The right of Barbara Hambly to be identified
as the author of this work has been asserted
in accordance with the Copyright,
Designs & Patents Act 1988.

British Library Cataloguing-in-Publication Data
A CIP catalogue record for this title is available from the British Library.

ISBN-13: 978-1-4483-1105-7 (cased)
ISBN-13: 978-1-4483-1106-4 (e-book)

This is a work of fiction. Names, characters, places and incidents are either the product of the author's imagination or are used fictitiously. Except where actual historical events and characters are being described for the storyline of this novel, all situations in this publication are fictitious and any resemblance to actual persons, living or dead, business establishments, events or locales is purely coincidental.

All Severn House titles are printed on acid-free paper.

Typeset by Palimpsest Book Production Ltd., Falkirk,
Stirlingshire, Scotland.
Printed and bound in Great Britain by TJ Books,
Padstow, Cornwall.

Praise for the Silver Screen historical mysteries

"Excellent"
Booklist Starred Review of *One Extra Corpse*

"Hambly's outstanding sequel to 2021's Scandal in Babylon showcases the author's wit and her compassion for the underdog"
Publishers Weekly Starred Review of *One Extra Corpse*

"Everything feels just right: the characters are abundantly human, the mystery is beautifully constructed, and the Hollywood milieu is vividly realized"
Booklist Starred Review of *One Extra Corpse*

"A wild lineup of possible killers mingles with historically accurate info in a fast-paced mystery"
Kirkus Reviews on *One Extra Corpse*

"This splendid romp is sure to win Hambly new fans"
Publishers Weekly Starred Review of *Scandal in Babylon*

"Exhilarating, exasperating, and dangerous . . . A sparkling series launch featuring Hollywood hijinks and a clever sleuth"
Kirkus Reviews on *Scandal in Babylon*

"Emma feels fresh: not merely another flapper-era amateur sleuth, but rather a vibrant, intelligent woman with whom readers will enjoy spending time"
Booklist on *Scandal in Babylon*

About the author

Barbara Hambly, though a native of Southern California, lived in New Orleans for a number of years while married to the late science fiction writer George Alec Effinger. Hambly holds a degree in medieval history from the University of California and has written novels in numerous genres.

www.barbarahambly.com

For

Sensei and Roger

And all the dojo family

ONE

The child stood in the baking glare of the desert sunlight, tears of terror streaming down her face. On the plank sidewalk behind her, a man lay dead, another sprawled in the dust of the street: every building in the gray little cow-town shut up and silent, no one daring to step forth. Clasping her tiny fists to her breast she screamed, 'Daddy! Daddy!' – hopeless, not seeing the rider pounding down the street behind her, leaning from his saddle, reaching down.

The little girl screamed again as the rider passed within inches of her, scooped her up at full gallop, the momentum of his passage causing one of her feet to catch on the edge of the wooden apple crate on which she'd been standing. The crate went spinning, nicked the back leg of the horse, which staggered, stumbled—

'CUT!!!' bellowed Laird Mullen.

Stuntman Vic Duffy yanked on the reins, but the liver-bay gelding he rode wasn't having any of it. The horse wheeled in a tight circle against the drag of the bit, kicked and bounced in a fog of street dust, while Duffy clinched his arm around Little Susy Sweetchild's waist and hauled the horse's head around, verbalizing his ire as only a cowboy can.

Emma Blackstone, just outside camera range, shoved the leashes of the three exquisitely groomed Pekinese she held into the hands of the nearest make-up man and took two long strides toward the tangle of hooves, flying gravel and invectives. But a slender hand shut vise-like around her wrist, yanked her back: 'Darling, don't!'

Camille de la Rose, gorgeous in the jeweled raiment of the Queen of the Crimson Desert (*What's she doing on this set?*), added urgently, 'You'll scare the horse!' even as Emma realized that danger herself. (And a part of her mind marveled that her usually scatter-brained sister-in-law would have that much sense . . .) There was, in fact, nothing that she could do but watch in helpless panic as the stuntman dragged his mount to a standstill, still gripping the child like a rag doll.

Second cameraman Alvy Turner rolled clear of the affray – he'd been lying almost in the animal's path to get a good shot of the snatch – cursing also, and one of the corpses in front of the saloon sat up and yelled, 'Fer Chrissake, Vic, can't you do nothin' right? That's six takes you fucked up!'

The horse juddered to a halt and stood panting like a bellows, flinging its head about. White gleamed all around the dark pupil of its eye. Emma shook off the Queen of the Desert's grip and stepped over the line of string that demarcated the shot, moving slowly and keeping where the beast could see her clearly. Even through the dust, she could see frozen terror on the child's face, and the death grip of those tiny hands on the rider's dark shirt. Behind her, she heard the Queen's Pekinese barking furiously, and the make-up man – the reptilian Herr Volmort – cursing in his native German.

Camille de la Rose – born Chava Blechstein and known to her many friends by her most recent married name of Kitty Flint – strode to catch up with her, dark eyes blazing and silken cloak billowing aside to reveal *déshabillé* that would have made a cooch-dancer blush, complete with a ruby-hilted dagger. *Crimson Desert*, currently being filmed on Stage One, was clearly between shots.

But as they reached horse and rider, director Laird Mullen overtook them, bellowing his opinion of events in words that would have peeled paint off the side of a barn. 'You (---) jackass Duffy, what the (---) you tryin' to (---)ing do—'

'You're the one who put that goddam box out.' With barely a glance at Emma, Vic Duffy shoved Little Susy into her arms, sprang from the saddle and closed with the director, dragging the horse behind him. Emma retreated at once toward the miniature encampment of parasols, pavilions, gramophones and folding chairs where Susy's mother – the beautiful Selina Sutton – sipped a gin fizz in casual disregard of the Eighteenth Amendment of the United States Constitution and didn't give her daughter so much as a glance. As she brushed the tangled curls from the child's face, Emma noted that Little Susy Sweetchild, though trembling like a frightened animal, had not shed a tear. Nor, she realized, had the little girl cried out after that first, scripted, scream of alarm.

'Are you all right, dear?'

Susy answered in a voice like crumbling chalk, 'I'm fine, ma'am, thank you for asking.' She wriggled politely, and Emma set her down, still holding the tiny hand in hers. In the shade of a canvas pavilion, protected from the grilling sun of a California July, Selina

Sutton leaned earnestly forward to say to columnist Thelma Turnbit of *Screen World*, 'From the moment I knew I would be a mother, I prayed every night that I would have a little girl. A little girl I could not only love, but teach, train, *instill* with everything *I* had learned before the cameras.'

Emma threw a glance behind her, aware that her beautiful sister-in-law was no longer at her heels. Kitty had stopped to fish a cigarette – God alone knew where she could have concealed such a thing in what there was of her costume – directly in front of the younger and more handsome of the two corpses outside the saloon: obediently and inevitably, the young man had revived and was now lighting it for her. Το τα αδύνατα διώκειν μανικόν, the Emperor Marcus Aurelius had written (and Emma's father had quoted, times without number): *It is insane to want the impossible.*

And it was impossible for Kitty to walk past any handsome young man without pausing to have her cigarette lit.

Oh, bother . . .

Nine months in Hollywood had taught Emma how likely it was that the mother of one of Foremost Productions' biggest money-makers (who had moreover been a star herself) would listen to a word from the mere sister-in-law who fetched and carried for Camille de la Rose and looked after her three Pekinese.

As they approached the pavilion, the child's hand tightened on hers. Looking down, Emma saw the little face schooled to a bright mask of cheerfulness, the great brown eyes now dry.

'It sounds silly' – Selina Sutton's ripple of laughter was like the fall of spring rain – 'but do you know, I did everything my mother and aunts all said I should? All the old wives' tales. I went to concerts, or the ballet, every week, sometimes twice a week, so that my precious baby would absorb the ambiance of good music even before she was born. And I kept up with my dancing— Not now, darling, Mother's talking.' Her eyes on the columnist's face, she didn't even turn her head. 'I kept up with my dancing for as long as I could. I was starring in *Pink Satin Angel* for Paramount that year, and *Moonless Sky* – with Francis Bushman, you know – for Magnum . . .'

'Mrs Sutton,' said Emma firmly, 'please excuse me, but there was – not exactly an accident, but—'

That at least made her look around. The flawless eyebrows lifted. Only a few years older than Emma herself – Kitty's age, Emma had heard, twenty-eight, but, like Kitty, Miss Sutton was exceedingly vague on the subject – Selina Sutton was still, like Kitty, heart-stoppingly beautiful. Those brown-velvet eyes that she had passed along to her daughter had stirred the hearts of America from 1916 to 1921. But at the word 'accident,' her attention went at once to Little Susy's torn calico dress, and she clicked her tongue dismissively.

'Well, go see Mrs Blanque and get another one, darling. And quickly – Mr Mullen needs to finish this scene and two more today.'

In glancing towards the director, she became aware of the commotion still in progress. 'Oh dear.' She looked again at Susy. 'Are you all right, dear?' Her tone could have applied to a skinned knee. 'She wasn't hurt, was she?' she asked, even as she turned her attention back towards the representative of the press.

Emma started to say, 'No, but she—'

With a convincing imitation of motherly tenderness – and a trace of exasperation in the set of her mouth – she turned again and put a hand under her daughter's chin. 'But nothing really happened, did it, dear?'

Susy whispered, 'No, Ma'am.'

'Speak up, darling. Children can be so shy sometimes, can't they?' She directed the full radiance of a rueful smile at Mrs Turnbit, a good-natured, rectangular journalist whose hair had been dyed to exactly the wrong shade of gold for her suit of purple-and-yellow linen checks. 'I know it sounds harsh, but one can't permit one's love – one's mothering heart – to indulge habits that will only harm a child in the long run. You *weren't* hurt, were you, darling?'

'No, Ma'am.' Susy squared her shoulders and smiled, the brisk, cheerful smile of a seven-year-old who knows her business and can defeat any number of villainous cowpokes.

'There.' Selina Sutton beamed. *Miss* Sutton, Emma had been instructed in the first days of her residence in Kitty's household last October. All actresses, even those who had been married three times and hadn't stepped before a camera in the past three years, were 'Miss.'

'Now, you may go pat Mr Gray before you go back to Mr Volmort, and then speak to Mrs Blanque. You'll need to change your dress . . . It literally tears my heart to pieces.' Maternal anguish throbbed once more in her voice as she addressed Mrs Turnbit, who was glancing from Little Susy to Emma, from the bloodbath of recriminations surrounding Vic Duffy, Laird Mullen and the liver-bay horse to the glittering goddess that was Camille de la Rose, still deep in flirtation with the cowpoke in the plaid shirt. 'I bleed inside – and I weep every night' – her hands clasped before her breast – 'for what I need to do, to raise my beautiful Susy to have the *courage* and the *skill*, to bring her stunning natural talent to its fullest promise . . .'

Emma opened her mouth to protest but knew it would do no good. Sheer politeness had refocused Mrs Turnbit's attention to the subject of her interview, though she would clearly rather have taken advantage of Miss Sutton's concern for her child (should she have displayed any) to excuse herself and go obtain a brief conversation with Kitty. ('When your correspondent spoke to her on the Foremost lot Monday about her upcoming masterpiece, *Crimson Desert*, Miss de la Rose said . . .') And Kitty would almost certainly have cut short her deepening passion for Mr Plaid Shirt to oblige her, despite the appearance of having already passed through emotions appropriate to the first five chapters of an Elinor Glyn novel at record speed.

No help there . . .

Tanto major famae stitis est quam virtutis. Her father, like most of the dons at Oxford, had tended to think in the terms of the classical authors, and she could almost hear his disapproving voice now: *How much greater is the taste for fame than for virtue . . .*

She knew in any case that the shooting would go on into the night. Even working through the previous weekend – which had encompassed American Independence Day – *Our Tiny Miracle* was weeks behind schedule owing to script changes, some demanded by Miss Sutton for her daughter and others necessitated by an accidental fire in the backlot. (Emma's dear friend, cameraman Zal Rokatansky, had captured the blaze on film, and studio chief Frank Pugh had ordered the script rewritten to include the burning-down of the home of Little Susy's parents by villainous ranchers.)

In the meantime, Miss Sutton's beautiful Susy retreated to the larger of the two pavilions which had been erected at the edge of the 'Western town' set (two streets of shabby board houses and a couple of dispirited-looking horses hitched in front of an ersatz bank). Beside a rack of duplicate costumes, the miniature tent housed half a dozen make-up boxes, a small rack of towels and a couple of wash-stations. There was also, tucked under a wash-station, a wicker cage, from which Susy carefully lifted an immense frost-gray Persian cat – wisely leashed to the tent pole – and cradled the animal in her arms like a fluffy doll. Her back was half turned towards Emma, revealing the handle of the leather harness strapped around the child's body under her dress, presumably to facilitate being snatched by the rider of a running horse. As the child's mother had pointed out, the projecting handle had indeed torn the cheap calico. Even though Little Susy's face was bent over her pet, Emma could see the heavy camera make-up was not only powdered with dust, but tracked with snot and soundless tears.

Emma's own mother had told her, again and again: Do not ever interfere in a mother's judgment of how to treat her child, unless the child is in obvious danger.

But she is*!* Emma's heart screamed back. *She* is *in danger . . .* obvious *danger!*

And deeper still in her heart: *How I wanted a little girl . . .*

She stepped into the shadows of the pavilion, hunkered to the girl's diminutive height. The child's eyes met hers across the cat's fluffy mane, schooling themselves once again to cheery fearlessness. 'What's your kitty's name, honey?' she asked, and Susy relaxed a little.

'Mr Gray.' The thin arms tightened protectively in soft oceans of fur. The formal title seemed absolutely appropriate: with his white shirt front, white muzzle and neat white gloves, the animal resembled nothing so much as the imperturbable butler out of a tale by P.G. Wodehouse.

'May I pet him? Or is he shy?'

From the sun-glare outside the tent, she heard Kitty's sweet, almost childlike laughter, and Selina's lovely voice: ' . . . dancing lessons from the time she was two and a half, and Mrs Padgett at the studio said she had never seen a child with such promise . . .'

'He likes people,' affirmed Little Susy. 'Are you really a duchess?'

'No.' Emma smiled. 'That's just what people here call me. I'm really just plain Mrs Blackstone.'

The child nodded, evidently well used to people being called all sorts of temporary names besides their real ones. She held out Mr Gray as well as she could – the magisterial Persian must have weighed fifteen pounds – and Emma took him carefully in her arms. He wore the same sort of businesslike leather harness that Kitty's three Pekes did (as in fact did Susy herself), but as Susy had claimed, he showed no inclination to bolt. Instead, he settled heavily into Emma's arms and with grave friendliness allowed his chin to be scritched. Only when Laird Mullen came striding into the pavilion with the make-up man Herr Volmort at his heels – still leading Chang Ming, Black Jasmine and Buttercreme – did the cat slip from her hold and retreat to the full extent of his tether.

'Come on, honey, let's have Herr Volmort get a look at you before the next take.' Mullen turned Susy briskly around. 'We're gonna do it without the box this time.'

That seemed to be a given, considering that the original apple crate, on which Little Susy had stood to raise her enough for the rancher's evil henchman to grab her easily, lay in flinders in the dust.

Herr Volmort – pallid, stooping and sinister with his heavy-lidded pale eyes and half-whispering accent – approached Emma to hand her the leashes of the Pekes, as Kitty and her admirer appeared to be in the planning stages of their honeymoon. Espying Mr Gray, Chang Ming's ears came forward and he trotted to investigate, and had his flat nose firmly batted by a white-gloved paw.

'He doesn't like dogs.' Little Susy picked up her pet (who was approximately Chang Ming's size and considerably larger than either Black Jasmine or Buttercreme) and replaced him in his wicker carry-box, then turned with professional aplomb to let Herr Volmort size up the damage to her make-up.

Mary Blanque entered the tent at that point with a replacement frock over one arm, and Emma led Kitty's three pets out into the hot sunlight outside.

Hollywood. After nine months in California, Emma understood that it was as much Volmort's job to get Little Susy ready to do another take of Scene 210 as it was Little Susy's – *HOW old is that poor child?* – to do it, this time without an apple crate to stand on. And, presumably, it was her mother's job to make sure Thelma Turnbit wrote up a glowing column about Little Susy Sweetchild's virtues, talents and beauty.

Vic Duffy had retreated to the far side of his still-nervous horse to refresh himself from a flat brown bottle. (Evidently, nobody in Hollywood had heard of Prohibition.) Gorgeous in her scanty finery as the Evil Zahar, Queen of the Crimson Desert, Kitty and this week's love of her life were glancingly visible in the alley beside the saloon, which, Emma knew, led to the dirt path behind the Roman forum in the direction of Stage One. She wondered if the young man (whatever his name was) was going to return, or if shooting would be further delayed by a runner sent to the casting office to arrange for a replacement corpse to finish the scene.

And if so, will the plaid of the new victim's shirt match that of his predecessor?

The older and less handsome Dead Cowboy was sitting on the plank sidewalk in the narrow shade of the saloon, smoking and waiting for things to get going again.

All this was better, Emma supposed – retreating to the shelter of the parasols that clustered around Miss Sutton's pavilion – than being a not-very-well-paid companion to a miserly manufacturer's widow in Manchester. For nearly four years, she had scrubbed the woman's chamber pots, rubbed her swollen feet and fended off the advances of her employer's son, who always expressed surprise that a woman who worked for her living would object to being groped in the pantry. ('How *dare* you tell such lies about my son? I know *your* sort, my girl!')

Rather to her own surprise, since coming to Hollywood last fall, Emma had found herself enjoying portions of the life on what sometimes felt like an alien planet. To her dear friend Zal Rokatansky (currently on Stage Two immortalizing the exquisite Darlene Golden in yet another bathtub scene), she had often likened the experience to running away with the gypsies – not that she would ever, in her well-regulated, well-bred, responsible life back in Oxford, have so much as considered so scandalous an activity. But the War, and the influenza, and (much as she shrank from admitting it) her father's ill-judged investments had left her, nine months ago, in the bleak October of 1923, with little choice. Husband dead, parents dead, family dead. When she had come out of hospital herself at the height of the epidemic in 1919, her parents' house on Holywell Street had already been sold. And after four years in Mrs Pendergast's household, she would have taken up an offer for work shoveling out stables, could she have found such a position that would pay enough to live on. Ζώμεν γαρ ού ως θέλομεν, αλλ' ως δυνάμεθα, the poet Menander had said. *We live not as we wish to, but as we can.*

But there were days when she deeply sympathized with Viola in *Twelfth Night*, cast ashore in an unknown land and forced to become a different person in order to survive. *What country, friends, is this?*

Hollywood.

Kitty and her Own True Love having reached an understanding, they emerged from the alleyway and headed in Emma's direction.

'Is it just me, Mrs Turnbit,' cooed Miss Sutton, laying a hand on the columnist's arm, 'or is the heat out here getting a little strong?' Mrs Turnbit had turned her eyes toward the dazzling figure of Foremost's top female star – who quite naturally trumped the mother of a child star (no matter how popular) any day of the week. 'They're going to be just *hours* setting up that same scene – I have *never* understood why they can't seem to get it right the first time . . . Shall we repair to the cafeteria?'

Or maybe, Emma reflected after a second glance at her sister-in-law, it was the militant glint in Kitty's eye that Miss Sutton wanted to get away from.

In either case, by the time Kitty and her Tom Mix hopeful reached Emma's side, Miss Sutton was steering Mrs Turnbit in the direction of another trail behind the town barbershop, which also led to the path behind the forum, and thence back to the crowding walls of the main lot.

Despite the Pekinese swarming adoringly around her feet, Kitty watched mother and journalist out of sight. Then, scooping little Buttercreme into her arms with baby-talk and kisses, she turned toward the make-up table, where Herr Volmort was smoothing Motion Picture Yellow on Little Susy's apple cheeks. 'Are you OK, honey?'

Again the perky smile. 'Uh-huh.' And Susy lowered her lids and held her head at the precise angle to permit the application of kohl and mascara. It was like watching Kitty's face when she applied her own make-up, or held herself, like an animate doll, for Herr Volmort's ministrations.

'Say, that Little Susy's a trooper, ain't she?' Laird Mullen pranced up, with the sort of rah-rah gesture that Emma had come to associate with American football cheers. 'Did you see her take that stunt in stride? You'd think she'd been doing this all her life!'

'She has,' muttered Herr Volmort, pale eyes sliding sidelong at the director. As if taking courage from this dissent, Black Jasmine – at five and a half pounds the smallest of the Pekes – advanced a step towards Mullen and emitted a piping growl.

'She could have been killed!' Emma protested.

'Nah.' Mullen waved the issue aside. 'Duffy's one of the best. You saw how he got that nag of his in hand. Susy couldn't have been safer in her mother's arms.'

Grimly, Emma had to agree with him there.

'Duffy's a goddam lush!' retorted the Love of Kitty's Life (*whatever his name is* . . . Emma wondered if Kitty knew yet). 'Gosh-*darn* lush,' he corrected himself quickly, with a glance at Emma. 'I meant gosh-darn. 'Scuse my French, Duchess.'

'Sometimes,' replied Emma quietly, 'one can only adequately express oneself in French.'

'Duffy's fine.' Mullen's reply came much too quickly. 'Nothing to worry about, Jack. He's sober today' – Handsome Jack opened his mouth to object – 'and anyways, he's been tapering off. He'll be fine. Duffy' – the director wheeled back towards Main Street, where Duffy was now sharing the contents of his bottle with the older Dead Cowboy – 'Duffy, you can grab the kid if she's standing on the ground, right?'

Duffy wiped his lips, called back, 'Sure thing, Laird.'

And, as Kitty started to speak again, Mullen added, ''Scuse me, Kitty – got to find Doc Larousse . . .' He was off in quest of the lighting chief in a cloud of self-important dust.

Little Susy Sweetchild pursed her lips to have lipstick applied, then lowered her eyes as powder was gently dusted over the whole masterpiece. Around the studio Emma had heard that the miniature star had made her first picture at the age of three – in 1920, when Emma herself had still been washing Mrs Pendergast's cotton drawers in Manchester.

To the handsome Jack, Kitty said, 'I thought Rog Clint was supposed do that stunt.' She handed the timid, flaxen Buttercreme to Emma, knelt to caress Black Jasmine and then big, rufous Chang Ming.

'Broke his wrist yesterday afternoon over at Paramount,' the cowboy reported.

'Balls. And they got *Duffy*?'

Emma began, 'Someone needs to report—'

'You can't.' Kitty stood and took back Buttercreme, who immediately tried to conceal herself in the folds of the Evil Queen's silken cloak.

'That poor child. Surely it's against the law . . .'

'Darling, no,' Kitty repeated firmly. 'For one thing, it won't do any good. Frank' – she named the studio head – and part owner – Frank Pugh, of Foremost Productions – 'pays a lot of money to keep the Gerry-men away.'

Seeing Emma frown, she explained, 'Men from the Gerry Society.

The Society for Prevention of Cruelty to Children, only I guess the only children they want to prevent cruelty to are the ones in the studios and the vaudeville houses. You don't see them out in Orange County doing anything about those little Mexican kids picking strawberries in the hot sun, or in New York defending the newsboys. And anyway,' she added, seeing that Emma was going to point out to her that being trampled by a panicky horse was a good deal more dangerous than picking strawberries in the agricultural fastnesses south of Los Angeles, 'the one time somebody from the school board came to ask Susy if she went to school, Susy said she did. She said she didn't work more than two hours a day – which is *complete* hooey – and that it was like playing make-believe. And I gotta say,' she added, stroking Buttercreme reassuringly as Jack held out a get-acquainted finger to the little dog, 'she sure looked like she meant it.'

'Looking like she means it,' returned Emma drily, 'is her job.'

Her mind went back to the first time that her parents had taken her to the Coliseum in London. It had been 1906, she recalled, and she had been only a few years older than Little Susy Sweetchild was now. She had seen children as young, or younger than, herself on the stage, dressed in bright costumes, dancing and singing. And though even at the age of eight she had absorbed far too much of her father's donnish reticence, combined with her mother's marrow-deep good breeding, to ever even *dream* of calling attention to herself in such a fashion, she had wondered what it was like.

Now, eighteen years later, she knew.

'Say, can we get rid of that harness?' Mullen came back with the wardrobe mistress, as Little Susy tried on various expressions – perky smiles, aghast distress (for others, never for herself), indignant childish consciousness of *Say, that's not right!* 'You can see it under her dress, God knows what it's going to look like in the dailies . . .'

If I had had a child by Jim . . . Even after six years, the thought of her late husband's slow smile could twist in Emma's heart like broken glass. *If he had left me with child, when he kissed me at the railway station, stepped on to the train with his unit, bound for the Front* – (the cold smell of coal smoke mingled with rain on the platform, the warmth of his mouth . . .) – *she would be almost Susy's age now.*

A young man in exaggerated plus-fours emerged from between

the saloon and the general store, panting with the news that the set-up was ready for the kidnapping scene and Miss de la Rose was needed on the set.

'Nertz,' said Kitty. 'Thank you, Herbie, darling. Jack, can you ride a camel? We leave for Seven Palms on Thursday and I'm sure Larry would hire you—'

'I can't and I don't want to learn. Them things spit. 'Sides, I start Monday for two weeks with Blue Star, in *Burning Gulch* . . . *You* ever ridden a camel, Miss Kitty?'

And a few feet away . . .

'You can grab her up without that handle, can't you, Duffy?'

'Hell, sure, easy as pie.'

There speaks a man who has never made pie crust . . .

As the wardrobe mistress led the child towards a makeshift changing pavilion ('Make it snappy, will you, Mary? We're trying to get Margie and Nick's stuff shot today as well'), Emma saw Susy turn her head in mute longing toward the tent's shady stillness and her silver-gray cat.

Hollywood . . .

Sometimes – sitting on the high porch of that ridiculous ersatz Moorish villa that the enamored Frank Pugh had purchased for Kitty, in the warm twilight of late spring with the air alive with desert dryness and the smell of sage – it was magic. Sometimes – driving up the California coast in Zal's Bearcat, or walking along the beaches watching the sun go down, or lying in his arms – it was more than magic. But sometimes she did indeed wonder what she was doing here. Kitty had rescued her from the Pendergast household last October simply because – while in England filming *Passion's Smoke* ('And we could have built that silly palace on the backlot for *half* what it cost to go there!' Kitty had protested) – Kitty had purchased three highly bred Pekinese only to belatedly realize that she needed someone to brush and look after them . . . and had remembered, just before sailing, that her brother Jim had married an English girl on his way to the Front in 1918.

Not everyone who ran away with the gypsies, Emma was well aware, ended up in the relatively comfortable position of handmaiden and dog-brusher to a flamboyant gypsy queen.

'. . . evil Queen of the Desert,' Kitty was saying to Jack, 'which if you ask me is *oodles* better than being some poor orphan who everybody suddenly discovers is the lost heiress to a millionaire. I mean, *really*, you don't just *lose* heiresses like that . . . You're sure you don't want to be one of my Evil Henchmen?'

'Jack!' yelled Benny Sherrod, Mullen's assistant. 'Let's get this show on the road! Louie, scootch over, you're about a foot away from the blood-stain.'

And beyond them . . . 'OK, honey, you come running out of the saloon and hit your mark, here, see? But this time Alvy'll be tracking you the whole way, 'cause there's no box. Don't worry, Duffy'll grab you up just the same.'

Emma turned, as Mullen hustled off to make sure Alvy Turner was in place – lying in the dust of the street with his camera angled where it would take in the saloon, the street and the terrified child in a single expressive frame. And she saw Susy Sweetchild pause in the act of stepping up on to the plank sidewalk, look back at the cameraman, the nervous horse and Vic Duffy taking a last quick drink from the bottle that the older Dead Cowboy sat up to offer him . . .

For one instant, the child's face was unguarded: like a rosy angel's in its frame of light-brown ringlets, those great brown eyes now sick with dread.

And she saw the little girl firmly put terror aside, square her shoulders and go into the saloon. Seven years old and absolutely alone.

Emma turned her steps towards the director, now instructing the second cameraman about the long shot.

'Duchess?'

It was Vinnie Lowder, one of the girls who worked the studio switchboard, stout and pretty and blonde beneath a big paper parasol and sweating like melting ice-cream in the July heat.

'There's a telephone call for you.' The operator sounded a little awed. 'She said she'd call back in fifteen minutes, if you can take it in Miss de la Rose's dressing room. She said her name was Professor Denham, from the university.'

TWO

'Mrs Blackstone?' The woman's voice, even through the tinny connection, was a pleasant alto, with the flat, slightly clipped accents of a long-time Californian. 'My name is Julia Denham; I'm an Associate Professor at the southern branch of the University of California, here in Los Angeles.'

'This is Mrs Blackstone.' *Why do I know that name?*

'Would you be the Emma Blackstone who is the daughter of Professor Edward Gracechurch of Exeter College, Oxford?'

Even at five years' distance, Emma's throat tightened. That tall, slightly stooped figure seemed for an instant to reappear, striding along the High with his gown flapping like a mainsail. She could smell again the scent of Sutliff tobacco that clung to the scuffed wool of his jumper. Hear his voice . . .

'Yes,' she said after a moment. 'I am his daughter.' *Is she about to tell me I'm the lost heiress of a millionaire?*

In spite of herself, she smiled at the thought of her father in the role . . .

The oracle is fulfilled, he would have quoted melodramatically, *the King's daughter is found* . . .

'First,' said Professor Denham, 'please let me tell you how sorry I was to hear of your father's passing. Along with everything else, a scholar of his erudition can never be easily spared.'

Emma said quietly, 'Thank you.'

'And it is about his work that I'd like to speak with you,' the woman went on. 'If this is a convenient time?'

'It is, yes.' She had closed the two tall French doors of Kitty's dressing room against the clamor of the 'plaza' that lay between Stage One – where Miss Golden was presumably still lolling in a marble-sided bathtub for the close-ups – the monolithic block of the properties department, the original 'hacienda' which included the stars' dressing rooms, and the wrought-iron gates that opened on to Sunset Boulevard. Despite two electric fans, the palatial chamber was stifling. Freed of their leashes, the Pekes had immediately lined up in the path of the gale, eyes shut and silky ears fluttering as they faced ecstatically into the blast. 'Thank you for asking.'

Kitty, she knew, would be spending the remainder of the afternoon and well into the evening supervising the kidnapping of the aforesaid lost heiress and, with luck, thrashing her servants in petty and terrifying wrath. *I really will have to get over there and watch . . .*

'In several of his later articles,' Professor Denham resumed, 'Professor Gracechurch acknowledges your assistance in organizing and cataloging his finds in the necropoli at Tarquinia and in Umbria. Did you work extensively with your father?'

Did I work extensively with my father?

How could you call the wonder of that giant golden jigsaw of space and time *work*?

The joy of being led by the hand through a kaleidoscopic wonderland of ten thousand pasts? The wonder of touching the things *they* had actually touched . . . People who'd had uncles in Babylon, in-laws in Pompeii . . .

Vixere fortes ante Agamemnona multi, her father had murmured, lifting shards of painted pottery from their wrappings in Italian newspapers, reverently fingering the lead votive of an owl that someone had offered to Athene twenty-five centuries before. *We only know of the trials of Agamemnon because Homer wrote of them. How many men – and women, too – had no Homer, and were not kings?*

'I did,' she answered. 'He needed someone to catalog all the bits of pottery and grave goods he'd found in Liguria, you see, once he got them home. Half the time, I think he forgot that I was only ten years old, or that I wasn't some Italian villager he was paying to keep track of his findings . . .'

But a thousand times better an Italian villager whom he talked to as he worked than a schoolgirl only seen at mealtimes – if then – like so many of her friends at the Misses Gibbs' Female Academy. She tasted as if it were yesterday – that proud, secret joy when he'd gotten so absorbed in his work that he'd addressed her in Italian.

'When I was done with school – when I started university,' she went on, 'I wanted to branch out. I was always fascinated by the work being done by Koldewey and the Germans in Babylon, though, of course, by the time I was ready to start university, it didn't do to say so. I had wanted to enroll in Paris or Berlin – Father had studied with Koldewey, and most of his investments were in Germany. But because of the War, I entered Somerville College and lived at home. So, one way and another, I continued to help Father until . . .' Her voice caught on the words. After a moment she finished, 'Through most of the War.'

Through all *of the War.*

Through all of the War, while the money disappeared with the ruin of Germany and the revolution in Russia. While Mother went from being a bright, thoughtful suffragist and pillar of the local Liberal Party to an exhausted drudge, trying to keep up a house too big without servants – often without bread or meat, as food stores in England dwindled with the German blockade.

Helped her father, through all that dazzling cocktail of wild joy and soul-deep peace in the eight weeks following the day she met Jim Blackstone ('It's really Blechstein,' he had confessed); through the numb shock after the letter came from his colonel at the Front ('Wait . . . What? We were supposed to be together, always . . .'). Then through all of that endless horror of caring for the eyeless, voiceless, unresponding automaton that had been her brother, shipped home like a parcel and never giving a single sign that he knew where he was or who any of them were, until he, too, died, an early case of the post-War influenza.

Long nights unpacking all those pottery fragments from boxes her father had gathered years ago in the Apennines: *Chart 12 – A) Frag. 953 found Well # 2, 6 cm below clay level. 7 x 4 cm lekythos pottery woman's hand portion of red/black bird. B) Frag. 954 found Well # 2, 9 cm below clay level, 6 x 9 cm red ware, white slip, geometric design. C) Frag. 955 . . .*

And the sound of her father coughing as he worked on his maps of the dig site.

Anything to keep from thinking.

She drew a deep breath, aware of how long she'd been silent.

'Would you be willing' – Professor Denham's voice was perfectly matter-of-fact, but deeply gentle, like the doctors at the VAD hospital at Bicester, explaining to the soldiers they brought in that *no, you'll never be able to do that again* – 'to assist us here with your expertise in the field? Doctor Leon Wright, who for years has taught Classics here, with a specialization in the Magna Graecia and the early Roman Republic, passed away suddenly last week. The papers he left on his work on Etruscan necropoli in Umbria are in a very confused state, and unfortunately, both Doctor Carmichael of the University of Southern California and Doctor Larson of the

University of Oregon – the closest scholars who have done any research specializing in ancient Italy – are on sabbatical. I've been given Professor Wright's summer session classes to finish, not that I know a single thing about the Etruscans. My own specialization—'

'Medieval Italy,' said Emma suddenly. 'You wrote that wonderful article on the eighth-century conflict between the bishops of Rome and Ravenna; it must have been in 1918 . . . I knew I knew your name from somewhere.'

'That was my first.' She tried, but she couldn't quite keep the shy pride from her voice. 'I'm glad you found it interesting.'

'Of course I'll be willing to help,' said Emma. 'I'm afraid I haven't set foot in a university – or even a library – in years.'

'You work at the studios, don't you?'

'I do "doctor" film scenarios, if changes need to be made and our regular scenarist is overwhelmed with work, as he often is. Mostly, I'm sort of an assistant to my sister-in-law, Camille de la Rose. I know she'd be willing to be flexible about my time, if it involves research.'

'It may,' agreed the historian. 'And I'm afraid we wouldn't be able to pay more than a small stipend – probably no more than seventy-five dollars, all told – but most of the work you could do at your home. Would you be willing to meet me to discuss the details over coffee? My office is in Millspaugh Hall – it's that ivy-covered barracks that thinks it looks like a Romanesque church – but there are a couple of nice cafés down on Melrose. I think we're fairly close to Foremost Studios – you're on Sunset, aren't you? You can take the streetcar to Vermont, then come south four blocks to the campus.'

'Would you be free tomorrow?' asked Emma.

'That'll be great. Thank you. It'll really help, having someone who knows something about the Etruscans going through these papers – and, of course, because this was all rough draft, he didn't do anything like number the pages or anything . . .'

'For nine months now,' responded Emma, 'I have collated and altered film scenarios. You address a woman inured to the name of fear.'

As she replaced the handpiece into the telephone's hook and set the instrument on the corner of Kitty's banquet-size dressing table, she found herself smiling, as if on a cold night she'd finally glimpsed the lights of home.

* * *

'How'd she find you?' asked Zal, later, over coffee and chili con carne at the studio commissary. (Chili con carne was another one of those things – like baseball, and 'blues,' and the American versions of Mexican and Chinese cuisine – which Emma hadn't even imagined existed twelve months previously.) It was ten fifteen on Monday night, and neither of them had the energy for an expedition to the Pacific Electric Buffet. Kitty – after seventeen takes of thrashing her servants with a whip ('C'mon, Kitty, hit 'em like you mean it!') and twelve gloating invasions, with henchmen, of poor innocent Rosebud Mary's Damascus hotel room, plus close-ups (and almost certainly a steamy *rencontre* in the prop warehouse with the handsome Jack Lee between takes) – had departed in Frank Pugh's black Pierce-Arrow for *poularde gratin* and *marchand de vin* with the studio chief at Fortunato's. ('You won't mind taking the car home for me, will you, darling? And my adorable little sweetnesses?')

Every door and window of the barracks-like dining hall stood open to the long-awaited cool of the California evening. Bare electric bulbs glared from the ceiling. Zal, as usual, looked like a bespectacled teddy bear, his red hair damp with sweat and his close-clipped rufous beard shaggier than usual. Emma doubted he'd been back to his cottage in Venice (California, not Italy) for more than a few hours at a time since Mr Pugh had commanded that all the non-location filming on *Crimson Desert* be completed by Thursday. Come hell or high water (per Mr Pugh), director Larry Palmer and the whole *Crimson Desert* company would be on the Thursday train for the desolate wastes to the east . . . or else.

She wanted to lean around and take his hand, but passed him the saltine crackers instead. Lunch (more chili con carne) had been a long, long time ago.

At the next table, the cast of *Boffo Boys!* clustered around Larry Davis and Jerry Stubbs, the studio's two resident slapstick comedians, working out tomorrow's gags amid a cloud of cigarette smoke and shouts of 'Wait, wait! How about if we do it on a hillside covered with mud?' and 'Can you set up a mirror under the car so it looks like he jumps in under the hood and then out the trunk?'

'I expect someone in the university's History department knows someone at Oxford,' said Emma. 'Someone at Exeter College may have mentioned to someone, at some time, that I had married an American and was supposed to be living in Los Angeles – with exclamations of horror, no doubt.' And she smiled at the thought of her father's fellow dons. Or would they even know such a place as Los Angeles existed? 'I shall ask her.'

'You like a ride down there?'

'It isn't far.' This time she did lay a hand on his wrist. Chubby, freckled and strong, it turned beneath her fingers and he gripped hers in return. 'And Mr Palmer would have a seizure if you disappeared from the set at eleven in the morning. Do you happen to know,' she went on more quietly, 'if Mr Pugh is going to be on the lot tomorrow? Kitty tells me that it isn't any of my business and that it will do no good to talk to him, but . . .'

She hesitated, then related the events she had witnessed that afternoon on the set of *Our Tiny Miracle*. 'That can't be right,' she concluded. 'I was inclined to try to speak to Mr Pugh after I finished talking with Professor Denham, but I . . .' She felt the flush of anger rise again to heat the tips of her ears. Her voice carefully level, she went on, 'I know that sometimes a complaint will only result in dismissal – not only of the troublemaker, but sometimes of that troublemaker's friends.' Her glance flicked to his face, and she saw the brown eyes behind the spectacles turn suddenly very hard with anger. 'Kitty warned me – and I'm glad she did. But I can't . . .' She shook her head, as if by doing so she could shoo away the dread in the little girl's eyes.

'Mullen had no goddam business hiring the first cowboy he could find who wasn't working yesterday morning,' he said after a moment in a level voice. 'He's lucky Duffy was sober enough to identify a horse at eight a.m., much less climb on to one.' He fell silent again for a time. Then, 'Kitty was right, though. It wouldn't do you any good.'

'She said the school authorities came on to the set to ask about Little Susy, and the child protested that she only worked two hours a day and had lessons at home with a tutor. And that she loved working. That it was like playtime to her.' Around her feet, the three Pekinese snored and twitched their paws in sleep, replete with the dinner she'd given them in Kitty's dressing room – chicken livers lightly grilled in butter by the well-tipped staff of the commissary. It crossed Emma's mind that she'd never seen Little Susy Sweetchild in the commissary, nor the child's beautiful mother. Did the staff get tipped to lightly grill chicken livers for *them*? Or for the dignified Mr Gray?

'That's horseshit.' Zal turned his attention to systematically mushing saltines into the concoction before him. 'The part about tutors, anyway. She may actually like dressing up and bossing grown-ups around. And I've never seen her cry, even when she's been working until ten at night and is just about asleep on her feet. She just sits there with her kitty-cat in her arms until it's time to go in front of the camera. Then she's spot on, letter perfect, button bright . . .'

'You've worked with her, then?'

'Three or four years ago, yeah, when I first came to Foremost. I usually work the features, now, but they start everybody out doing two-reelers.'

'Three or four *years*?' Emma was for a moment merely startled, then aghast. 'The poor child is only seven now!'

'Foremost isn't her first studio, either.' His voice had the hard note that it sometimes did, when he was keeping back rage that he knew would be pointless. 'When I started here in 1920, she was already doing fifteen two-reelers a year. Our little darling saves her mommy (or her daddy – or both of them) by loving them *so* much and being *so* brave.' He clasped his hands to his bosom in imitation of a thousand sentimental aunts and mothers in the audience.

'They had her in a whole string of tear-jerkers with Barry Shumacher – great big guy, bald as your elbow, used to be an enforcer for the City Hall Gang. She could sit on the palm of his hand. They'd always put her with big extras, like Berta Kelly – that woman who lifts weights down at the beach? Audiences eat it up.'

'I daresay.'

'Her mom was never much of an actress, but she's a hell of a coach. And the kid's got talent to burn. Her mom started out starring with her, back when they were at Magnum right after the War. But Selina Sutton usually played slinky man-eaters, like Kitty but with more talent – not that that's saying a lot. After about three pictures, they started putting in sweet types like Mona Robertson and Nelly Boardman to play Mom. They offered Selina the villainess in *Susy Plays the Palace*, and she turned it down. She hasn't worked since. Not that she needs to,' he added grimly. 'Parents have the legal right to every nickel their kid earns until Junior turns twenty-one. But I think it chaps her' – with barely a pause, he substituted '*delicate sensibilities*' for the more anatomical word Emma's husband had used in that particular simile – 'that her kid's making eight times as much as *she* ever did.'

He propped his spectacles more firmly on to his nose and stared out for a moment through the doorway, where prop men, plasterers, gaffers and riggers still moved through the warm darkness of the dusty plaza, finishing up the day's work and preparing for the morrow. Letting the anger pass through him, and away. At length, he said, 'But Frank knows which side the bread's buttered on. So does Selina. And so does the Los Angeles school board.' He made a gesture with his fingers, as if counting out money. 'Maybe Little Susy does, too. If she wasn't doing what she's doing, where would she be? Where could she go if she wasn't with Selina? I've met Selina's pop – he makes the average Dickens villain look like jolly old Saint Nick. And Susy's dad is the original crepe suzette: a soft pancake soaked with rum. She's not gonna get any help there.'

He glanced around him. The room had gone quiet. A white-aproned busboy was clearing up the jetsam of empty chili bowls, coffee cups and crumpled paper napkins scattered over the next table. From the kitchen came the clatter of washing-up.

'What you *can* do,' said Zal, as Emma reached over again and grasped his hand in thanks, 'is hit Frank up about Vic Duffy endangering his Tiny Miracle by drinking on the set. Come at him that way. But remember he's got Laird Mullen under contract for cheap and he won't take your side, or the kid's, against him. At least you can keep her out of one danger – if you don't mind Duffy bad-mouthing you all over town as a stuck-up witch after that.'

'*Ligna et lapides ut conteram ossa mea*,' replied Emma austerely. 'He's welcome to try.'

Zal grinned. 'Go get him, Your Grace. Go in with a stiletto, not a broadsword. Small victory, then watch for your next chance.'

She returned his smile. '*Victrix causa deis placuit.*'

'Let me know how it goes tomorrow.'

'If nothing else,' Emma sighed, 'I shall learn where in Los Angeles I can find a decent library.'

'I've seen that scenario for Emily Violet they want you to doctor,' said Zal. 'And I can tell you now, a library isn't going to do you any good.'

THREE

It wasn't Oxford. Vacant lots surrounded the southern branch-campus of the University of California on two sides, and despite a hopeful growth of ivy, its Romanesque red-brick buildings clearly stood on ground that ten years previously had been waving fields of barley. Emma had feared that setting foot on any college campus would awake in her lacerating memories of worn stone steps and iron-strapped doors, of small green quadrangles overlooked by lamplit windows in the spring dusk, and the voices of young men who had gone to the fields of Flanders and not returned. But, in fact, what she felt was exhilaration, and a sense of coming home.

Young men – and they looked *very* young, as everyone did, she thought, who had not been touched by the War – played at what Zal had told her was American football on one former bean field, clad in blue jerseys and close-fitting leather helmets. As she left the unbuilt spaces around the sides of the campus itself and drew closer to the plaza in the center, she saw only a few students: young men in linen sports jackets and girls in short, fashionable tube-shaped frocks of light cotton, sensibly sleeveless in the forenoon heat.

Summer term, she thought, observing not only the books in their arms but that half-worried, half-hopeful preoccupation in their faces.

And for the first time since she'd woken in the hospital to the news that her parents were dead and that the house on Holywell Street had already been sold for debts, she felt herself to be in a place she knew.

Professor Denham shook her hand firmly: a woman some ten years older than herself, wiry and dark-haired with the sun-browned complexion of one whose study of ancient civilizations was not confined to libraries. 'I'm afraid poor Professor Wright's office is still a mess.' She gestured Emma into her own small premises: crammed with books, scrupulously dusted, with barely floor space for a desk, a Windsor chair and a Baroque armchair for guests that wouldn't have looked out of place on a film set.

'He died sometime Wednesday night, and I think the police just wanted to finish up with the place Thursday, because the next day was the Fourth of July. They swear they didn't remove anything, but they just piled everything together, from the desk and from the floor.'

'The *floor*?'

'His body was lying cramped between the desk and the window, and most of his papers were scattered all over the carpet. That's kind of the problem. It looks like he fell face down on the desk, and swept what he was working on – and the stack of student papers – with his arm as he rolled over.' She demonstrated her theory with a gesture. 'The police just scooped everything up like a haystack in the middle of the desk. Then they got shuffled around again when the janitors came in to clean the blood off the corner of the—'

'*Blood?*'

'I'm sorry.' The historian put a hand briefly to her brow. 'I'm telling this backwards. Between the holiday and having to take over his classes . . . completely aside from what it's like to lose someone. I didn't know him well, but he was never anything but cordial to me – to everyone, I think, except Professor Partington, our Renaissance man. You can't work next to someone for three years and not feel it when something like this happens.'

'What *happened*?'

'Stroke, they think.' She cast a quick glance sidelong, in the direction, Emma guessed, of the deceased scholar's office. 'He was alone in this wing of the building Wednesday night – he often stayed till one or two in the morning, sometimes later. Or he'd come in to work early, before seven. His students were always griping about him scheduling lectures for eight a.m. It did make me wonder about his home life . . . Because of where he was lying, Frankie – the girl who does typing for the department – didn't find him till almost noon Thursday. Papers all over the floor and blood everywhere. It's an awful thing to say, but thank God it didn't happen over the weekend, in this heat. It looks like he fell and cracked his skull on the corner of his desk, hard enough to tear open one of those big veins in the back of the head. He must have just lain there unconscious and bled to death.'

'How awful!'

Professor Denham winced at the memory. 'His papers scattered clear to the wall, and the police and the coroner's men tracked all over them when they came. They said it didn't look like he knew anything about it,' she added. 'Because of the holiday, it wasn't until Sunday afternoon, when we were trying to sort out his Classics summer-term students, that anyone tried to have a look through the papers, and realized that not only were drafts of three separate research projects about pre-Roman Italy mixed up together – sixth century B.C. – but a bunch of student papers as well. Some sheets were partially typed, some handwritten, and only about a quarter of them numbered. There's a cafeteria over in the next building,' she added, 'if you want a soft drink, before I take you in to have a look at what was there. It's hot as Naples in August outside, but without the sea view.'

On the way back from the cafeteria, with green glass bottles of sweet, stinging Coca-Cola in hand – Emma wondered if Viola in *Twelfth Night* had been taken aback by unfamiliar Illyrian cuisine (to say nothing of the convenient fact that the inhabitants of Messina and Illyria all spoke the same language) – Emma asked the professor how she had located her. The answer was as she had thought.

'That was Professor Wright,' said Denham. 'When he heard about your father's passing – that must have been two or three years ago – he wrote to Exeter College to find out what had happened to your father's notes, artifacts and library. They didn't know at the college, and suggested that you might have them.'

Emma shook her head. 'I was very ill and in hospital for nearly a month. I knew my father was deeply in debt by that time – most of his investments were in Germany and Russia, and we were quite literally wiped out by the War and the revolutions that followed. The house was sold almost immediately to pay off the creditors, and since two of my mother's sisters also died of the influenza, and the third was with her husband in India, there were no family members in England to deal with the sale. I don't know where the things went. Into the rubbish bin, I'm afraid.'

She kept her voice light, but her companion – after an angry growl – looked up into her face and said, 'I'm sorry. Somebody said you'd married an American – he was listed as Captain Blackstone, in the Ninth Infantry – and I think Professor Wright tried to trace you through the Army. Finally, last year he heard from the hospital that you'd gone to Manchester to work. The woman you worked for there wrote that you hadn't had anything like notes when you were living in her house, much less books or boxes of "nasty broken crockery" – she underlined the words in her letter to him, like Queen Victoria. She sounded like she felt very ill-done-by, even being asked.'

'She always did.' Again, Emma kept her voice matter-of-fact with some effort, remembering all those nights of being woken at two in the morning and sent downstairs to fetch milk from the icebox – and the hectoring complaints about the time it took her to bring it, and the drink being too warm. 'She would go on about the War as if it had been specially designed to inconvenience her.' She pushed the older woman's nagging voice from her mind: *Stop sniveling as if you're the only girl who's ever lost a husband! It depresses me . . . At my age, the government should know I don't sleep properly if I don't have meat and sugar, and I think I'm entitled to some consideration . . .*

'She spent a good deal of money keeping her son out of the draft – something of which she reminded him, repeatedly. I'm surprised she took the trouble to answer Professor Wright.'

'It was just after you left her – "high and dry," she said – and "ran away to Hollywood with a *film person* . . ." She filled up about two pages with the effort it would cost her to look for your replacement.' The historian cocked an amused eye up at her, as if she understood perfectly well why anyone would flee the Pendergast household screaming, the moment they were offered someplace else – even Hollywood! – to go.

'Since she made it clear that whoever might have retrieved Professor Gracechurch's effects, it wasn't you, Leon – Professor Wright – let the inquiry drop. But in his desk he did have, along with this Mrs Pendergast's letter, an article someone had cut out of one of the film magazines about Camille de la Rose, which mentioned that she lived with a respectable English widow named Mrs Blackstone as a companion, and he'd ticked a mark in the margin by your name. So he probably meant to get in touch with you at some point, to ask if you knew who had all your father's work.'

They had reached Millspaugh Hall again by this time, and Denham got the key from the typist in the front office ('Thank you, Frankie . . .') and led Emma past her own door to another one further down the hall. This she unlocked, to loose into the corridor a clammy exhalation of overheated air, damp carpeting and carbolic soap. The curtains of the dead scholar's office were shut, blocking the view of the tennis courts, but the brownish-red light that filtered through was enough to show Emma that the desk which had – like that of Professor Denham – stood near the windows, had been dragged to one side and cleared of everything on it. The carpet had been taken up and the floor likewise scrubbed. A large cardboard box filled with papers stood in another corner of the room, and someone had clearly come in and helped themselves to about a third of the books in the shelves. *Probably other historians*, reflected Emma, having grown up with the breed. Another box, open, contained pottery fragments, some wrapped in newspaper and some simply dumped in on top of the heap. Emma shuddered to think what her father, or any of his colleagues, would have said of this. Aside from the damage to the artifacts themselves, it was like seeing someone hanging dirty washrags on the Venus of Knidos.

By itself in a third packing box, an exquisite modern reproduction of an Athenian red-figure krater lay half unwrapped, with a line of deer painted around the inside of its rim, so that when the vessel was full, they would appear to be drinking from a pond of wine.

The two women carried both boxes into Professor Denham's office, Emma glancing back at the disordered room where a man had bled out his life less than a week ago.

If he was sitting at his desk, how could he have cracked his skull in falling?

And if he was standing beside it, cluttered as the room is, he wouldn't have had room to pitch down on his head . . .

But such questions were chased away when she and her hostess began to look through the notes, lists and manuscript pages that the police had dumped in the larger box. (*And how could he have cracked the back of his head and still been lying so as to sweep his papers from the desk?*) She noted references to articles her father had written on his expeditions to the Apennines in 1908 and 1909, careful maps of minor excavations done in remote Umbrian fields, references to potsherds discovered in Rome and Naples – mixed in with pages of painful freshman prose on the subject of the Tarquins and Livy's *Ab Urbe Condita* and scribbled paragraphs of what appeared to be the tracks of a centipede in a fit. A sketch-plan of something that could have been either a village or a burial-site was pinned to a catalog of grave goods (*Good Heavens, did the man never publish this?*). Handwritten notes spoke of a place name she couldn't make out: *Corzo something-or-other*?

'I know just enough about ancient Italian history to see that this is important,' said Denham, after standing back and listening to Emma exclaim over every other page. 'I can have my husband bring them up to your apartment – or, no, you live with Miss de la Rose, don't you? If you'd care to give me the address – I promise I won't let anyone else see it. And Oscar – my husband – couldn't tell Mae Murray from Tony the Wonder Horse and doesn't care. Or I can hold it here until you can send someone with a car.'

She stepped forward and frowned around Emma's shoulder – her own hands conscientiously behind her back – at the two typed sheets Emma was holding up. Neither was numbered, but the ribbon of one typewriter was clearly new, the other faded almost to nothingness. The Gs on the machine with the new ribbon were worn away at the bottom, and its spacing was wider. Years of differentiating the rectilinear intricacy of ninth-century B.C. pottery from the more naturalistic shapes used a century later had given Emma an almost maniacal eye for tiny details. Both sheets were scrawled all over with barely decipherable comments in the same jagged hand.

'And any time you'd care to,' Julia Denham went on, 'you're welcome to come down here and check things – if you need to – either in the library or here in Professor Wright's office. Or you can use this office, if you believe in ghosts next door. There are only the three of us teaching here summer session – myself, Professor Partington and Professor Sanders. I've taken over Leon's classes, so I have my hands full.'

'Were these' – Emma held up another three pages of typescript, these numbered 6, 8 and 13 – 'from a student paper?' The ribbon on this one fitted badly – every capital letter was missing its top. 'I don't see anything that looks like a title page.'

The historian shook her head. 'He had a stack of student papers from this term, and two from last year's fall term. Leon was very generous about allowing students who weren't doing well to turn in papers late for an Incomplete grade. I never approved of it myself – one of the things you're here to teach young people is that some things need to get done on time – and it drove Hal Partington crazy. That's what I'd guess those are. You're welcome to look through his files from last term or last year. They should be in there somewhere.

'And you don't have to,' she added hastily, though Emma had made no comment. 'Half the late turn-ins are boys on the football team. Professor Wright bet heavily on those games – they're mostly against the local high schools, or sometimes the Trojans from over at USC on Hoover Street.'

She picked another couple of pages out of the box at random – these were handwritten – and frowned at the childish scribble. 'The official season won't start until September, but there's a big exhibition game coming up at the end of summer term. Partington swore that Professor Wright would pass members of the team because he had money on a game. But he never could prove anything. I should warn you, Partington may try to get hold of you and demand access to Wright's papers. If he does that, tell him to speak to me.'

'After dealing with directors,' sighed Emma, thumbing through the papers (the words 'ritual slaughter in the Colosseum' caught her eye), 'who want me to include scenes of Julius Caesar wrestling a tiger – in Britain, no less – and players who insist that the action be altered because they think another player is getting more close-ups than they are, the thought of repelling a mere bloodthirsty academic holds no terror for me. If your husband would be so good as to deliver this . . .'

She set the papers back in the box, which was some two feet by two and a half, and deep: more than she felt she could deal with, walking back up Vermont to the streetcar. With a fountain pen from the desk, she printed Kitty's address on Ivarene Street neatly on the cardboard flap.

'. . . I would most appreciate it, but only at his convenience. I expect' – she released the pen to Professor Denham, who proceeded to scribble her own telephone number on the back of a business card for her – 'the students whose papers are mixed up in the shuffle will be on tenterhooks to get them into your hands. I'll try to get those sorted out by at least the end of the week.'

Emma had intended to return to Foremost that afternoon, to seek out Frank Pugh and broach the subject, at least, of Vic Duffy. But as had befallen Adam in the garden, the woman tempted her, and she fell. After an excellent (and prolonged) lunch (plus milkshakes) at the Bear Cub Café on Melrose Avenue – talking of Livy and Herodotus, of ancient education and Plato's female students, of cabbages and kings – Emma returned to campus with Julia Denham for an extended tour of Professor Wright's boxed-up keepsakes from Italy and Greece. ('He found that one in a field in Perugia. It's got to be sixth-century B.C. – look at the way her hair's done . . .' 'Believe it or not, that cylinder seal was in an Etruscan tomb near Assisi – goodness knows what it was doing there; it's clearly Babylonian . . .' 'He had to keep *that* votive in a box so none of the students could see it.' 'Good *heavens*, I can see why!')

'Some of this came from a previously unknown necropolis Professor Wright discovered in the hills of Perugia.' The young professor held up a triangular shard of geometric ware, with strange, attenuated forms of warriors brandishing their spears. 'I'm no expert, but even I can see it was fantastic stuff: votives from Egypt and Nubia, and a fresco of what looked like a rhinoceros. Amazing. Professor Wright was fearfully secretive about it, since he was preparing an article on the finds. That's mostly what I hope you can sort out, because it would be a crime for that information to be lost!'

It was nearly twilight when Emma finally left the campus. Oscar Denham drove her, a sturdy and prematurely graying man with his wife's sun-browned complexion who worked as an accountant for the city ('The only digging she lets me do is in the garden . . .'), and carried the box of papers up the high, tiled steps and into Kitty's Moorish fairytale villa for her. She thanked him profusely, then walked the dogs and fed them, with a pang of guilt at having left them on their own all afternoon, despite her certainty that, in fact, they had slept the whole time.

Another pang assailed her as she bore the box of papers upstairs to her own room, aware that instead of doing a preliminary sort-through of the dead scholar's papers (*Was there anything he could have tripped over? But how could he have tripped and fallen between the desk and the window?*), she would be obliged to spend the rest of the evening rewriting Scenes 460–469 of *Toot-Toot-Tootsie* because Emily Violet refused to be depicted as swooning into Harry Garfield's arms upon first meeting (and be damned to Romeo's effect on Juliet . . .).

Her suitcase lay neatly open on her bed, reminding her that she still had to finish packing and make sure Kitty remembered such items as underclothing and toothpaste: the day after tomorrow, the whole production company for *Crimson Desert* was scheduled to be on a train for Seven Palms – camels, lions, Evil Queen Zahar and all.

I can at least take this along and sort it . . .

And is poor Zal still cranking away at sixteen frames per second hoping that Kitty won't catch her sleeve in the furniture (yet again) in the course of her quarrel with the Wicked Vizier, so everyone can get home in time to get a night's sleep?

But she could not keep her thoughts from returning to Susy

Sweetchild: to that single look of terror in the little girl's eyes as she headed into the saloon. What scenes had they been filming today? Presumably, a henchman having scooped the poor little darling up in the street outside the saloon where her mother (not Selina Sutton, but, for purposes of the plot, Eleanor Boardman) lay bleeding, an exciting horseback chase would follow. She shuddered to picture how that particular epic sequence would be shot.

I should have gone to the studio today, she thought, *and talked to Mr Pugh. I could have met Julia tomorrow.*

Scene 460 – Beth enters her bedroom, closes the door and leans against it as if to shut out the clamor of her family downstairs
Scene 461 – close on Beth as she shuts her eyes, clasps her hands in weariness. She hears a noise, ~~suddenly turns, her eyes wide with fright~~ the sound of birdsong from the open balcony door
Scene 462 – ~~Smokey stands in the balcony doorway, disheveled from the fight yet heedless in his passion for the girl he loves~~ Close on the nightingale in the roses that grow on the balcony
Scene 463 – ~~close on Beth as love overwhelms her~~ Beth crosses to the balcony, drawn by the beauty of the notes
    Scene 464 – ~~she crosses the room, falls into his arms~~ . . . On Smokey in the dark garden below, listening in rapture to the nightingale's sweet melody.

He's just gotten done with battling three of her uncle's ruffians; what's he doing lingering in the garden?

Scene 464-a – Beth appears on the balcony . . .

Is anybody in the audience not *going to think, 'But soft, what light through yonder window breaks'?*

Around her feet, the three Pekes raised their heads sharply, ears cocked at the sound of the front door. Then, in the darkness downstairs, Kitty's sensuous giggle mingled with Frank Pugh's deep, rather flat voice murmuring something about naughty little girls getting what was coming to them.

Emma sighed and laid down her pencil. Reaching down, she caught Chang Ming and Black Jasmine by their diamond-studded collars to keep them from rushing to the shut door of her bedroom in a barking paroxysm of welcome. (Buttercreme heard Pugh's voice and retreated under the bed.) From the first, it had been understood that when the studio head brought Kitty home late at night, he did not expect to see either Kitty's pets or Kitty's respectable sister-in-law. He had purchased the house as a love nest, not a home. The fact that Kitty had made a home of it – not only for herself, but for bold little Chang Ming, tiny Buttercreme and even tinier Black Jasmine, not to speak of her brother's widow – as far as Emma could determine, never crossed the man's mind.

Like a film set, it existed when he was there and vanished the moment he got in his car and drove away. When Frank was on the premises, Emma understood that neither she nor the Pekes were supposed to intrude . . . any more than the cameramen, the director and his assistant, Mrs Blanque from wardrobe and Herr Volmort and his minions existed outside the frame of the shot.

Which probably meant, she reflected, that, as usual when the company went on location Thursday, though she would share Kitty's hotel room in the resort town of Seven Palms (like a good chaperone for the benefit of the film magazines), she would be expected to find someplace else to be when Mr Pugh came out to visit the set.

Hollywood. ('Oh!' cried Kitty in ecstasy downstairs, 'Oh, my angel—!' For all her shortcomings before the cameras, Emma's sister-in-law could be tremendously convincing in an actual clinch.) Since she had begun doctoring scenarios for the studio – and being paid for her time – Emma found she minded her role as Peke-minder and Veil of Respectability a great deal less than she had at first. And glancing across the room now at the box of scholarly notes, she recalled the warm echo of what it had felt like that afternoon to be analyzing the significance of grave goods and the probable dates of pottery fragments. Remembered what it had felt like to talk about history for hours with someone who shared her interest in long-dead worlds, to read the words of those who'd actually walked those dusty streets . . .

(*Unless, of course, they were Etruscans* . . . The last records of *their* language had perished in the ashes of the Library of Alexandria.)

But she felt as if she'd gotten a postcard from her father: *Will you handle this for me, child? I know you can.* 'Some day may they say of him' – he paraphrased Homer's Hector – '*he's a better man than his father.*'

She sighed. *I suppose I can discreetly sneak some toast tomorrow morning, and 'encounter' Mr Pugh 'by chance' at the studio later in the day.* By the sound of things downstairs, he'd be in a good mood when she asked him not to endanger a little girl's life no matter how good it looked on-screen . . .

The boys throw stones at the frogs in sport, Bion of Borysthenes had said two centuries before Christ. *But the frogs do not die in sport. They die in earnest.*

As it happened, however, the entire question – at least in regard to *Our Tiny Miracle* – became moot. The following morning as Kitty maneuvered her daffodil-yellow Packard – an hour and a half late – out of the hectic traffic on Sunset Boulevard and through the gates of Foremost Productions, Floyd at the gate seemed half distracted in conversation with two of the studio guards. Emma saw at once that instead of moving purposefully across the plaza and among the studio's three stages and other barn-like, ramshackle buildings, the men who worked in the prop warehouse, the cutting and editing rooms, the nursery and the shops – the women from wardrobe and make-up – stood in tight clusters, glancing around them as they talked to make sure none of the Front Office gang saw them . . .

Kitty, who had been babbling all the way down Vine Street about her co-star Marsh Sloane's shortcomings as an actor ('Honestly, darling, if the Queen's guards didn't notice *something* fishy about the way he slinks into her tent, she should fire the lot of them!') seemed barely to notice. But when she paused to light another cigarette before driving on into the lot, Emma leaned over the door and asked the guard,

'What's going on? Has something happened?'

The man turned back to her, his craggy face perplexed. 'They're trying to keep it out of the papers,' he said in a low voice. 'Like *that's* gonna work! Selina Sutton's housekeeper just phoned with the news an hour ago, and Rhoda on the switchboard is already about half crazy, telling reporters it's no such thing.'

'What is?'

His voice turned hard. 'Little Susy Sweetchild,' he said, anger darkening his eyes. 'She was kidnapped last night. Stolen right out of her bed, it looks like. Her and her ma both. Ransom note says keep the cops out of it . . . or else.'

FOUR

'*D*arling—'
Emma startled as her sister-in-law's delicate hand closed on her elbow like a falcon's claw.

'You've got to go over and ask the switchboard about the hotel in Seven Palms!'

'The . . . What?' She turned from the French doors of Kitty's dressing room: she'd been observing Mary Blanque and Herr Volmort as they scattered a knot of gossiping extras and wardrobe ladies from the corner of Stage One. Wardrobe chief and head of make-up then strode across the plaza towards the dressing-room wing of the 'hacienda,' a line of assistants trotting in their wake like 'native bearers' behind white explorers in funny-paper cartoons. Instead of parcels on their heads, however, these 'bearers' carried armfuls of pale pink silk, fearsome-looking bejeweled belts and baldricks, Oriental pantaloons and three separate make-up kits.

(*Does life in fact imitate art?*)

A dark-blue saloon car momentarily blocked her view of the procession, as it deposited a tall, sour-faced man in a dirt-colored suit before the main block of the studio's original adobe farmhouse.

'Go!' Kitty urged her with a push. 'Now! That's Grandpa Snoach!'

'Who?'

'Selina Sutton's father! He's here to see Frank! Go talk to Vinnie at the switchboard so you can hear what he says to Frank when Frank comes in!' Resplendent in not very much underwear and a kimono gorgeous with copulating dragons, Kitty propelled her to the door and thrust the three loops of Russian leather into Emma's hand. 'Tell her I heard that the Araby Hotel doesn't take dogs and ask her to find out if it's true . . . there won't be anyone on their switchboard there who knows anything until nine at least . . . And, here, you better take our little celestial treasures, to make it look like it's a coincidence . . .'

Then despite her own admonitions of haste, she crouched to stroke each round silky head and croon words of love: 'It's OK, darlings, Mama loves you . . . you be good for Aunt Emma . . .'

Chang Ming and Black Jasmine threshed their ostrich-plume tails eagerly – an excursion of any kind anywhere in the studio was always welcome. Buttercreme, her pink tongue protruding its usual half inch, gazed reproachfully back as Emma led them along the walk to the hacienda's main doors. The booming voice of 'Grandpa Snoach' – *Snoach being Selina Sutton's maiden name?* – could be heard bullying the receptionist from ten feet down the walkway.

'What do you mean, he's not in? Don't you lie to me, girl.'

And, without waiting for Miss Daikin to reply: 'My granddaughter – Pugh's biggest moneymaker!' – (she wasn't) – 'was kidnapped last night and he hasn't bothered to show his face here yet? Nonsense!'

The reception lobby's heavy portal of Mexican oak stood open – even at eight in the morning, the day was growing hot – and from somewhere beyond the long chamber came the multiple shrilling of telephones.

'My daughter and her child in God knows what kind of danger . . . Or is he a drunk like that good-for-nothing Selina married? And get those goddam animals out of here!' he added, as Emma appeared in the doorway. 'Haven't any of you people heard about fleas? Over six hundred different kinds of germs live in a dog's mouth, for God's sake! Bad enough Selina tolerates that filthy cat of Susy's . . . Get those dirty little things out of here before I complain to the Department of Health.'

Emma – who bathed the Pekes weekly and brushed them daily – drew breath to protest, but Black Jasmine, who took that tone from nobody, forestalled her. Planting feet the size of demitasse spoons, the Peke quacked at his detractor like an infuriated duck, while Chang Ming stationed himself firmly before the perceived threat to Emma, and Buttercreme hid behind Emma's ankles. Miss Daikin – who also disapproved of Kitty's celestial treasures but was under strict orders not to permit any outsider to criticize them – could only purse her lips and fulminate, like a chameleon set upon a plaid. Emma, without a word, stepped back outside, drawing the dogs after her.

She had to drag Black Jasmine, who leaned against his jeweled collar to fling a final salvo at his foe: *And don't you forget it!*

Thereafter, she felt no compunction about stationing herself to one side of the door, out of the line of sight. Her one regret was that she didn't have a notebook on hand.

'Well, aren't you going to call janitorial? Or doesn't this place care about the filth that gets tracked indoors around here?'

'I'll call them,' came Vinnie's voice from the phone room beyond.

'It only proves what I've been saying for years!' Snoach stormed. 'That little girl has true genius, which was more than Selina ever had! As a father, I'm horrified, of course, but Selina has no more business being in charge of a talent like Susy's than she has being in charge of a lemonade stand, and for the same reason! Waste! Of talent, of opportunities . . .'

The appearance of a mop-bearing janitor coincided with the approach, from the Sunset Boulevard gate, of a dark-haired woman whose watered-down version of Selina Sutton's serpentine beauty marked her as a relative. A little older, Emma guessed, her wide crimson mouth harsh rather than sensual, bracketed with the marks of hard and constant bargaining for the good things of life. But she was as addicted as her – sister? – to lip-rouge and kohl, and arrayed in smart blue linen tailored – despite prevailing fashions – to make the most of her voluptuous lines. The woman paused only to raise a disparaging eyebrow at the Pekes – or possibly at Emma's outdated shirtwaist – before marching into the office: 'I must speak to Mr Pugh!' She had a voice like the trumpets of Judgment Day. 'Oh!' A pause. '*Dad.*'

It was the voice of a woman asking how that deceased fly came to be in the butter. After four years with Mrs Pendergast, Emma knew that inflection well.

'Mop the area around the door,' whispered Emma to Archie the janitor when that young man arrived. 'The gentleman in the brown suit feels that Miss de la Rose's pets contaminated it by sitting there – which they did *not*.'

'Oh, hell, no, Duchess,' murmured Archie. 'You ain't seen "contaminated" till you seen that cheetah of Gloria Swanson's throw up a hairball on the set of the Palace of Versailles.' He bestowed a valedictory ruffle upon Chang Ming and Black Jasmine – even Buttercreme peeked from behind Emma's ankles to dab his hand with her tongue – and then moved in respectful silence to cleanse away hypothetical germs.

'This *woman*' – Grandpa Snoach continued meanwhile at a volume that Kitty could probably have heard for herself, if she hadn't been (almost certainly) conferring with the wardrobe mistress about how much décolletage a villainous Queen of the Desert could get away with – '*claims* that Pugh isn't in.'

'So nothing is being done,' concluded the newcomer in a voice like a nutmeg grater. 'I could have told you *that*. And where's Burt? Drunk someplace, as usual?'

'I'd like to know what he was doing when poor Susy was carried away.'

The next several minutes were devoted to wholesale criticism of Selina Sutton ('Of course it's terrible that she's been taken, too, *but* . . .') by her father and sister (whose name appeared to be Mrs Ardiss Tinch), rivaled only by collaborative slander of Selina's husband Burt ('Why she tolerates the man anywhere near her at all is beyond me!') and the cacophony of the telephones in the room beyond. ('No, Mr Pugh isn't taking calls,' came Vinnie's sweet, patient voice. 'If you'll give me your name and number I'll be sure to tell him . . . No, I'm afraid Mr Pugh is in conference . . . I'm very sorry, I don't have that information . . .')

Four minutes into this sequence, another diversion occurred with the arrival of a bottle-green Bugatti and an extremely comely young man with a briefcase and a silk suit that Emma estimated at close to a hundred dollars. 'Frank in?' he demanded of Miss Daikin as he cleared the threshold. 'That stupid cow Lupe just got around to phoning me – if I told Miss Sutton once, I told her a thousand times to get rid of those wops and get some real Americans . . . Mrs Tinch.' He changed his voice mid-tirade. 'Mr Snoach. If Frank isn't in, is Fishy around?'

Miss Daikin denied knowledge of publicity chief Conrad Fishbein's current whereabouts.

'I think I'm entitled to a straight story from *somebody* . . .'

'What do you know about all this, Sandow?' demanded Grandpa. 'And why hasn't anyone called the police? Even a cretin like Pugh should know—'

'Don't be stupid, Dad, the ransom note said they'd kill her if anybody called the cops – isn't that so, Mitch?'

'Not in that many words, Ardiss.' Mitch Sandow's authoritative tenor gritted at the recollection. 'But the message was pretty clear. I can't imagine how kidnappers would be stupid enough to believe that the studio *isn't* going to call the cops, and we have to do something before somebody panics.'

'It only proves what I've been saying all along!' reiterated Snoach. 'You can talk all you like, Sandow, but when push comes to shove, Selina just isn't responsible.'

('I'm sorry, Mr Pugh is not on the lot today . . .' 'I'm afraid you'll have to call back later, Mr Pugh is in a meeting . . .' 'Mr Pugh isn't available for comment . . .')

'And where was that silly chippy Elena while all this was going on? That good-for-nothing greaser should have been sleeping right there in the room with our baby. Where was Burt, for that matter?'

'Where do you think?' retorted Sandow contemptuously. 'Burt was drunk, down in that cottage of his in the garden. He'd just waked up when I got there – he didn't know whether it was Tuesday or Thursday. Elena sleeps in the room next to the nursery and didn't hear a thing, so they must have been quiet as mice—'

'Or paid her!' Mrs Tinch almost shouted. 'Have the police thought about that? Oh, *I'm* sorry,' she added in accents of heavy sarcasm, 'the police aren't supposed to be told.'

'Elena was in hysterics,' snapped Sandow (*Whoever Mitch Sandow is*, reflected Emma . . .). 'She loves that little girl—'

'Like hell she does,' retorted Snoach. 'Loves what Selina pays her to keep our little girl safe, and you can see what *that's* worth. You can't trust those foreign bints,' he went on. 'Not one of 'em. And as for that gin-soaked rum-head – where the hell did he get the booze, anyway? From Lupe and that goombah she's got living with her, I bet. And was *Elena* sober?'

'How can you not hear?' Mrs Tinch was saying, as the studio gates yawned wide to admit Frank Pugh's sleek black Pierce-Arrow. The big car swung in a half-circle and came to a stop before the hacienda, and a guard jogged from the kiosk in time to take the wheel as the studio head himself climbed out: massive, obese and untidy in a wrinkled blue suit. Even as he climbed the steps to the building's shaded porch, a second vehicle rolled through the gate, a very shiny Ford coupe that Emma recognized as belonging to Colt Madison, the most photogenic private detective in Hollywood.

'You need to see me, Duchess?' demanded Pugh, even as Snoach, Sandow and Mrs Tinch all surged on to the porch to meet him. Emma shook her head. She had spent most of the night listening to his snores rattle the lampshades at the other end of the hall, but she could see her pretense that she hadn't been present pleased him.

'No, sir. I had a question for Vinnie, but it's not important, and she's been working like a hero sending callers about their business. It's nothing that can't wait.'

'I've been saying all along that Selina's no fit guardian.'

'You're not really going to call in the police.'

'Look here, Frank, as Miss Sutton's man of business, I have a right to know—'

Pugh waved them all towards the door of his office (Black Jasmine added his mite to the conversation by renewed imprecations directed at Snoach), and Colt Madison, springing up the steps in the studio chief's wake, tipped his hat to Emma with a breezy 'Hiya, Duchess' as he passed. ('And put out that damn cigarette,' ordered Snoach as the door closed. 'Don't you know . . . ?')

Guessing that poor Vinnie wouldn't have the time to pester hotels in Seven Palms about their feelings regarding furry guests (*with or without six hundred varieties of germs in their mouths*) – and that the clamor of telephones would preclude accurate eavesdropping in any case – Emma retreated back along the arcade that fronted the star dressing rooms. Already she could see Floyd at the gate arguing with the first of the reporters.

As Kitty had foreseen, Herr Volmort had finished his ministrations before Emma returned from her mission of espionage. Crossing the plaza towards Stage One, she observed only a few rumor-mongers remained at the corner of the properties warehouse. The crew and extras from *Our Tiny Miracle* had dispersed. Whatever blood oaths of silence their directors had exacted from them, the story of the kidnapping would be all over Los Angeles – all over California, the United States and the world – by lunchtime.

She shivered, thinking again of Susy's expression of dread. Was the child even with her mother now? Or were her kidnappers keeping them separate? She felt aghast even for Selina Sutton, whom she would cheerfully have slapped yesterday. What had been done – would be done – to *her*?

Whose name did Susy cry in the darkness?

On Stage One, young Lord Harlan Fairfax (Ken Elmore – né Elmore Perkins of Kenosha, Wisconsin), startled, rolled over on the silk-draped divan as the curtains of the tent were slashed aside.

'You!' he gasped.

Framed in the darkness and torchlight of the (silhouetted) encampment behind her, Queen Zahar glittered like a jeweled spider, fingers curled around the ruby-studded hilt of the dagger at her waist, a sneer of triumph twisting her beautiful face.

'Who'd ya expect, honey, Mary Pickford?'

The title card, Emma knew, would actually say, *Did you really think you could escape me?*

Just outside the line of string demarcating the limits of the shot, the Rothstein Boys throbbed out the ecstatic strains of Wagner's *Tannhäuser* on violin, cello and flute.

Knowing Scene 377 could go on all afternoon ('That was great, but Ken, could you sort of put your hand up in front of your face, like so?' – demonstration – 'Like you can't believe what you're seeing?'). Emma had collected the draft scenario of *Toot-Toot-Tootsie*, and now made her way through the semi-dark of the shooting stage to what she thought of as Kitty's 'base camp.' In the slot of waste space between the Evil Queen Zahar's tent interior and an elegant bedroom at Fairfax Manor – complete with topiary box-hedges outside its long windows and a painted view of the lawns beyond – a small circle of folding canvas camp chairs had been established. Like Little Susy's cluster of pavilions on the outskirts of the Wild West yesterday, it included a collapsible table bearing a full make-up kit and washstand. Smaller tables supported thermos bottles of coffee, a portable gramophone and records, a porcelain vase full of pink and white orchids, three mirrors, a manicure set, a stack of clean towels and another of astrology magazines ('Can Your Stars Warn of Catastrophe to Come?'). Emma shifted the manicure set and one of the mirrors to make room, and opened the school copybook she used for rough drafts: *How do I convey what a rotter Kincaid is without making Beth look like a complete imbecile for falling for him?*

But instead of devoting her attention to the innocent Beth, Emma's eye was drawn to the chiaroscuro of dark and brilliance beyond the chalked shot lines of the set, to the grotesque double circle of the main camera, and the gleam of round spectacle-lenses beyond it.

Zal. Sturdy in plain drill trousers, and the short shirt-sleeves that Emma still found slightly disconcerting on every American she'd ever met in Los Angeles. (No man back home, not even workmen, walked around with bare elbows and hairy forearms hanging out for all the world to see . . .)

Antipodal opposite of Jim's tall lankiness, but with the same sparkle in his eyes.

The same kindness. And the same deep sense of safety in his touch.

As always, it was a pleasure to watch Zal work, even if it was the fourteenth time those curtains had been slashed aside . . . 'You!' (Accompanied by the same twenty bars of the Venusberg Movement . . .)

It wasn't until lunch was called (at quarter to three) that he was able to walk over to the base camp and ask, 'How's the Perils of Miss Beth?' And then it was only for a moment, before Kitty scampered to join them . . .

'Darling, what *happened* over there? Ruby' – Ruby Saks was Kitty's stand-in – 'says that man-trap sister of Selina's turned up . . . If I don't get something to eat right this minute, I'm going to just *perish* . . . Did you hear anything?'

And Emma was obliged to deliver her report.

The brutal blue-white Klieg lights went down. Gaffers and prop men headed for the door ('Be back here three thirty!'); Eando Willers (Frank Pugh's private secretary) appeared, bearing the news that Scene 400 would not be shot that afternoon owing to the absence of animal trainer Gren Torley – this seemed to surprise nobody – and his furry minions. 'We'll go ahead with eighty to eighty-nine,' said Larry Palmer briskly. 'Ned, Doc – can you set me up with soft floods for a master shot over in the drawing room? Jeff, you guys got that Mozart stuff for eighty? Kitty, Ken – Mary's got your outfits for you ready in your dressing rooms . . .'

'Late night tonight,' opined Zal, as Emma got to her feet and went to collect leashes – in her own way, Kitty was as reliant on the comfort of her pets as Little Susy was.

'No, darling, Mary's going to help me dress.' Kitty straightened up, Buttercreme cradled in her arms. 'You go to the mess hall – poor Zallie's been an absolute *hero* and he deserves a real lunch . . . if you can call what they swill out in the commissary "real." Do you have a cigarette, Larry? I'm absolutely *dying* . . .'

'Benny!' yelled Larry, producing one. (One of the prop men leaped forward to light it for her). 'Somebody get Benny – oh, there you are. Where's . . . ?'

'He's kidding himself,' added Zal, as he and Emma joined the stream of crew headed for the stage's blanket-shrouded door, 'if he thinks he can get that whole sequence of Ken and his uncle meeting Kitty in London shot tonight.'

'Is Mr Torley well?' asked Emma, who liked the little animal trainer.

'Oh, hell, yeah. But Gren's probably the only person in town who'll speak to Burt Sutton today, especially if Mitch Sandow was right and Burt was on a bender last night. Burt swore off about six weeks ago,' he explained, to Emma's look of inquiry. 'All last week, Gren's had him out working at Sixth Morning – that's his ranch out in Chatsworth – just to keep him out of trouble and give him something to do.'

'Sixth Morning?'

'After the animals had been created,' said Zal, 'and before God made people. He said Burt was pretty much useless chopping up hay and shoveling by-products, but it was better than having him down at that cottage he's got behind Selina's place in Benedict Canyon. You can't blame him for wanting to stay down there, but—'

'That's very good of him.' Emma shook her head, a little wonderingly, thinking of the thick-set, wiry little man who would turn up on the set in company with elephants, lions, tigers, three trained vultures and (as Shylock had put it in *Merchant of Venice*) 'a wilderness of monkeys.' 'I don't think I've ever seen him talk with anyone on the set, not at any length.'

'He's got friends with the riding extras,' said Zal. 'Kitty's – uh – little friend Jack Lee is a pal of his.' And, seeing her still trying to piece together in her mind how that sturdy gnome had known the glamorous Selina Sutton's husband, added, 'Burt's his brother, you know.'

FIVE

Over sandwiches and lemonade (and three cups of coffee for Zal – it would indeed be a long evening) at the studio commissary, Zal provided what the ancient playwright Sophocles would have described as an analepsis and what Sam Wyatt, Foremost's principal scenarist, referred to as a 'flashback.'

'Burt Torley had Magnum Studios in Culver City at the end of the War. Selina Sutton was his big star – as big as you could get in a one-horse studio like Magnum back then.' He lifted the top slice of his meal, inspected the contents, shrugged, replaced the bread and devoured whatever it was like a starving wolf. 'When she married him was when the newspapers started calling him Burt Sutton. I think he bought the studio with his share of his father's dough when the old guy died, and his brother Gren bought ten square miles of a rancho at the feet of the Santa Susannas and started the critter farm. Magnum did OK until Burt's drinking got out of control. I shot a couple of two-reelers for Magnum when I first came to Hollywood, and I never did get paid.'

'Starring Miss – Mrs – Sutton?'

'Nah. She was too important by then to be in anything but a feature. She had Susy in a dance academy when the poor kid was barely out of diapers, and she was getting ready to make Burt star her in features when the studio folded. The only reason Selina didn't dump Burt at that point was because Pugh put Susy under contract, and he wasn't about to have the fan mags go around saying that the parents of America's Little Angel are divorced.'

Emma frowned, calculating the year of Susy Sweetchild's first picture for Foremost – 1920, *The Littlest Cowgirl*, according to one of Kitty's old issues of *Photoplay*. 'And she was how old?'

'Three and a half. And already pulling in dough hand over fist. I think she could have saved Magnum if Burt hadn't drunk half the profits and Selina hadn't blown the rest on six fur coats, a customized Vauxhall Velox and a jewelry-importing business set up by Chet Bovard – that was one of her sister's middle-period husbands.' He drank half a cup of commissary coffee at a gulp, as if it were medicine. Emma reflected that it probably was.

'So she put him in a cottage at the bottom of the garden.' Mitch Sandow's overheard words came back to her.

'The cottage was Frank's idea. I think he was scared Burt would make a stink in the papers if Selina went ahead with a legal split. Whatever else you can say about the poor sap, he adores Susy. By that time, Selina had dumped Frank for Marsh Sloane – or maybe Frank pushed her off on Sloane because he'd fallen for Kitty. So that would all come out in court as well.'

'*Marsh Sloane?*' Emma mentally tried to align the dignified, silver-maned actor with the curvaceous femme fatale . . . not to speak of adjusting to another of the studio head's divagations. She had deduced months earlier that Prohibition raised no difficulties for anyone who seriously wished to pursue a life of dipsomania.

'Didn't last.' Zal shrugged again. 'Frank bought her the house in Benedict Canyon as a goodbye present. Then about two years ago she damn near lost *that* over some cockamamie investment scheme to make radium toothpaste, and he hooked her up with Mitch Sandow as a financial manager. I think he was some connection of one of his in-laws. Again, mostly to keep her out of the papers.'

For all his obnoxious bullyragging, Emma reflected, Selina Sutton's father seemed to have a decent grasp of his daughter's likelihood of success in the lemonade business . . .

'I take it Mrs Sutton's maiden name was Snoach?'

'Enid Snoach. Chip Thaw' – he named another of the Foremost Productions cameramen – 'tells me Grandpa Snoach was part of the pow-wow in Frank's office this morning, along with Sister Ardiss, who's been sponging off Selina ever since her most recent husband turned out not to own land in Florida like he said he did. But the cottage idea seems to have been a good one. Since he's been out there, Burt's been on and off the wagon a couple of times, Gren tells me.'

He looked around quickly as the stooped, bearded form of Larry Palmer loped towards them among the tables, then glanced at his watch. According to the huge clock on the wall – even the toilets on the Foremost lot boasted prominent timepieces – it was twenty minutes past three, allowing for the fact that everything was set five minutes ahead . . .

'Duchess,' the director pleaded as he drew near, 'you gotta help me out . . .'

Emma had already recognized the shooting script of *Crimson Desert* under the man's tweedy arm. *Oh dear* . . .

'Looks like the trip out to location's been set back till Monday. We're three weeks behind schedule already, so we've got to move up the London and fox-hunt sequences to before we go. It's gonna be hot as hell's hinges out there now, and worse in a week. We don't have time to build exteriors in the Valley, so all the London stuff's got to take place indoors or on the backlot – I've got Big Ned putting together sets tonight. The Fairfax estate' – he ticked them off on his fingers, clutching the scenario to his side with his elbow – 'a terrace at night . . . we've already got Harlan's bedroom . . . plus a couple in front of the country house if we can get the façade set up.'

Zal wiped deposits of mayonnaise from his mustache, caught Emma's hand, pressed it to his lips. 'See you in the Tents of Turpitude.' He swept napkins, plates and his coffee cup on to his battered tin tray and deposited it at the end of the counter as he strode towards the door.

Larry Palmer – who as director had more leeway than he allowed his crew – barely turned his head. He laid the folder on the table before Emma and threw a coaxing note into his voice. 'If you can get me scenes in either Harlan's bedroom or on the terrace by tomorrow morning . . . Sam's handling all Darlene's stuff on the waterfront Friday and Saturday . . .'

Oh, good . . .

Sam Wyatt had been the principal writer on *Crimson Desert*. So far, Emma's sole appearance on a film title was the fleeting sight of her name at the beginning of an upcoming epic entitled *Hot Potato* . . . and an equally brief credit on the Foremost Productions version of *King Lear. Additional Dialog by Emma Blakeston* (sic). As she watched the director dart away in the direction of three prop men and an electrician, she earnestly hoped her Aunt Estelle would not be tempted to view it.

As Emma had foreseen, the attempted ravishment of poor Lord Harlan by the Evil Queen Zahar did indeed take until nearly ten o'clock that night, by which time every stage and dressing room at Foremost Productions was flooded with editions of the *Los Angeles Times*, the *Examiner*, the *Daily News*, the *Daily Citizen*, the *Express* and even the *Van Nuys News*, all of them proclaiming, by demonstration, publicity chief Conrad Fishbein's oft-stated belief that there is no such thing as bad publicity.

CHILD STAR ABDUCTED
SWEETCHILD SNATCHED
CITY-WIDE HUNT FOR INFANT STAR
REWARD FOR SWEETCHILD INFORMATION
BLACK FORD FLEES SCENE OF
SWEETCHILD KIDNAP

Sub-heads included 'Sweetchild Feature Halted,' 'Mother, Child, Sweetchild Kidnap,' 'Chaos at Foremost Productions' and 'Father Snored While Child Seized.'

The following evening, radio preacher Bushrod Pettinger vilified 'the bronze Moloch of Hollywood studios' for flinging the tiny innocent into the path of the juggernaut of Fame, while his sister begged listeners to pray for mother and child, and to boycott all products of so foul and soulless a machinery (and to contribute to the fund to rebuild their downtown Tabernacle of Grace).

'Not a word would have been said,' reflected Emma grimly, during one of the very brief dinner breaks that Thursday night, between takes of young Lord Harlan's quarrel with his father (now inexplicably moved from the garden to his bedroom), 'had the poor child been crippled for life in some stupid stunt involving a speeding car or a bonfire.'

'Papers would never even hear about it,' agreed Zal. During the explication of young Lord Harlan's family dynamics and the passionate analepsis of how, during his Oxford days, his lordship had spurned the Evil Zahar (now equally inexplicably invited to a Fairfax house party – *What were the servants all doing to let her sneak into the private family portions of the house?*), Emma had brought another sandwich and two bottles of Coca-Cola to Stage One for her friend. How long such a respite would last depended entirely on how quickly Doc Larousse and his crew could reset the lights.

Zal went on, 'I forget what picture it was over at Century, a couple years ago, that their kid-star Baby Peggy got knocked out of a pickup truck and damn near dragged to death behind it. And if you really want your hair to stand on end, get Buster Keaton to tell you sometime about the stuff his dad did to him in their vaudeville act.'

'Whether they find her and Selina or not' – the news that day had been filled with Frank Pugh's melodramatic oaths that the police were being begged not to take a hand – 'you know every one of her pictures is going to be back in the theaters inside a week. And there's forty of them.'

Hollywood. Over the past nine months, Emma had learned that the glare of the storied 'bright lights' threw shadows equally dark. But the anger she felt was new, and almost personal. Every single one of those one-reel and two-reel comedies and tear-jerkers – to say nothing of last spring's feature-length *Susy Goes to Town* – was, she knew, going to triple its original revenues, now that Susy was known to be in genuine peril.

'I know that,' she said softly, understanding that he was right. '*Nullumst iam dictum quod non dictum sit prius*, Terence said. He was a Roman playwright. *Nothing has been said that hasn't been said before*. Or done, somewhere at some time.'

She poured herself tea from her own thermos, and flinched as the reflectors flung a momentary glare over the base camp. Ruby Saks – buxom and motherly in a copy of Kitty's vampish finery – readjusted her lipstick and prepared to take her place on the set for a lights check.

'And I know it isn't just Hollywood. But there are times when it's hard not to hate humankind. Starting with Frank Pugh and Conrad Fishbein and going all the way down to those shopgirls and plumbers and mothers sitting out there in the theater seats, not asking how those scenes actually get filmed.'

Zal set his sandwich down, rubbed her back with the flat of his hand. 'Or who makes their clothes,' he pointed out gently. 'Which is what my mom did, and my sister, for two bits an hour before the War . . .'

'Zal, darling!' Kitty scurried over to them, silver lamé dress flashing in the reflector's glare.

'Is that a dress or a coat of paint?' Zal asked, straightening up.

'You *have* to talk some sense into Larry! He's talking about scrapping the whole scene in the library. Yes, Jazzums darling, I've missed you, too.' She crouched gracefully as the Pekes emerged from beneath the make-up table to surround her. 'He's talking about scrapping the whole scene and having it take place on the backlot, and that's going to mean we have to come in and shoot tomorrow, instead of having the crew go down to Venice Pier to shoot Darlene's stuff on the waterfront . . .'

While Zal soothed the Evil Zahar with the logistics of cinematography – and the Evil Zahar devoured the remainder of Zal's sandwich like a starving child – Emma sipped her tea and returned her attention to the compression of a rather spirited attempt at murder in the Leicestershire hunting field (*Was it Austin Freeman who first used that old trip-wire trope in a mystery, or was that someone else?*) to a narrative in Fairfax Manor's drawing room.

And how are we then going to plant the clues that Queen (then Princess) Zahar was behind it? Not to mention establishing the fact that she (or her stunt double) is in fact a skillful rider, contrary to the lies she's been spreading through the first reel and a half?

She was still puzzling over this the following morning at breakfast (*If Aeschylus could encompass the entire Battle of Salamis in a hundred and thirty-six lines, surely I can manage a simple attempted murder in six dialog cards . . .*) when, rather to her surprise, a tousled and sleepy (but newly and immaculately made-up) Kitty appeared in the kitchen door in a purple kimono refulgent with orchids.

'Oh, good, darling, you're up already!' (It was ten thirty). 'Could you run down to the garage and tell Mr Shang we'll want the car in' – Kitty glanced at the kitchen clock – 'half an hour? Thank *heavens* Zal talked Larry into letting that silly library scene alone . . . Look!'

She flopped a newspaper on to the table on top of Emma's scribbled drafts.

NO COPS FOR SUSY

At the urgent insistence of Foremost Productions studio chief Frank Pugh, the Los Angeles Police Department continues to hold off on the investigation of the kidnapping of child star Susy Sweetchild and her mother, actress Selina Sutton. Miss Sutton and her daughter disappeared from their Benedict Canyon home sometime between 8:15 p.m. on the night of Tuesday, July 8, and 8 a.m. the following morning. A note from the kidnappers found in the nursery stated, 'Don't call the cops if you know what's good for you. We'll be in touch.' It is assumed that the child was kidnapped for ransom from her studio – Foremost Productions, where she is currently starring in the frontier drama, *Our Tiny Miracle*, already praised by critics as her best work so far. Her previous films include *Little Susy Sweetchild*, *The Littlest Cowgirl*, *Susy Goes to Town*, *Susy and the Bad Men*, *Susy Steps Out*, *Susy's Big Night* . . .

(There followed four column inches of praise for Susy's films.)

The Los Angeles Police Department has issued a statement that no active investigation will be undertaken as of yet, but that the Los Angeles Police Department is keeping a close eye on the situation, and researching the background of similar cases against the eventual probability that they will be called in. The family has retained private detective Colt Madison, who is rumored to be pursuing his own contacts among the Los Angeles 'bootlegger' underworld for leads and possible assistance. 'A case like this puts the heat on everybody,' Madison was quoted as saying at a press conference at Foremost Productions yesterday. 'Even the hoods in this town know that this will double police activity against their own endeavors.'

Emma personally doubted this last assertion. In her months in Los Angeles, she had not noticed any police activity whatsoever against the endeavors of the local bootleggers, prostitutes, whoremasters or purveyors of heroin and cocaine – to say nothing of those in violation of the laws which said seven-year-olds should not be working twelve hours a day on film sets.

'Selling a little gin is one thing,' club owner Charlie Crawford said to reporters at his 'Maple Bar' when asked about the crime. 'But snatching a poor, helpless kid and her mom – that's over the line!'

(Emma had not been aware that anything was considered 'over the line' in Los Angeles. *Live and learn* . . .)

No ransom note has yet been delivered . . .

'Don't you see?' Kitty leaned across the newspaper, eyes sparkling. 'It's just a matter of time before they have cops all over the house, but this means that today, anyway, we can go up and have a look at the place!'

SIX

Qui audiunt, audita dicunt, Plautus had written in the second century B.C. *Qui vident, plane sciunt.*

Eyewitness evidence can be believed while a report is only a report of what someone heard said . . .

And whatever physical evidence might have existed at 1000 Shadygrove Terrace on the previous Wednesday morning, when Susy Sweetchild's 'nurse' had gone into the child's room and found her missing from her bed, nothing now remained that anyone could have observed, reported or believed. Emma wondered what possible clues the police would be able to use when they did finally get around to starting their investigation.

Once Kitty turned off Sunset Boulevard into the hills themselves, Emma glimpsed few houses in the dense tangles of scrub, oak trees and pale-trunked groves of exotic eucalyptus. They had left Hollywood, and the comfortable bungalows of Los Angeles, behind. South of the Boulevard, orange groves, barley and bean fields were punctuated by the stalky armatures of oil wells, like the Martian tripods in *War of the Worlds*, invading the Earth. The canyon itself, winding deep into the Santa Monica Mountains, was, Emma guessed – like the canyons to the east where Kitty's Moorish fantasy palace stood – what California must have looked like before the advent of Americans. In places, it reminded her of her father's descriptions of Liguria: scrub, oak trees, the smell of sage in the air.

In other places, it had its own magic.

No wonder people like Mary Pickford and Douglas Fairbanks (not to speak of Frank Pugh, whose Egyptian-style palace lay further up the other side of the canyon) came here to build houses. Wilderness peace with all the amenities (such as they were) of Los Angeles conveniently close by.

Shadygrove Terrace was an inconspicuous thread of asphalt leading back into a sheltered bay in the hills, barely more than a driveway to Shadygrove itself. Emma could see no other houses on the street. Having purchased the property, however, Frank Pugh could no more have resisted raising a palace on it than he'd resisted the urge to gift Kitty with a pink-tiled miniature Alhambra a few miles away.

'Well, of course, darling.' Kitty steered the Packard off the steep drive and bumped across the lawn, skirting more than a dozen other cars parked at random amid the topiary. The gate to the property stood open: Emma could already see gaggles of sightseers wandering around the house itself, trying to look in the windows, periodically banging (to no apparent effect) on the doors. Others pointed at a corner window on what Americans called the 'second' floor. '*Screen World*, and *Photo Play*, and *Picture Play*, and all the rest run features on our houses. *Motion Picture* did one on me about a month after you came, from pictures they took last summer.'

(*That must be the one Professor Wright had in his desk . . .*)

'Fishy told them all about how I lived with my widowed sister-in-law practically like a nun . . . Is there such a thing as a Jewish nun?'

'No,' said Emma, thinking about Frank's snores in the darkness.

Kitty steered carefully around a couple of beaten-looking Fords and braked between a marble fountain and a sparkling in-ground swimming pool. (*Great heavens, I hope someone is keeping an eye on all those children!*) A number of the families who'd come out to gawk at the 'Kidnap House' had brought their offspring with them, running unsupervised along the pavement at the water's edge and screaming with delight . . . It was only a matter of time before somebody got pushed in.

And clearly, the adult sightseers were far too absorbed in trying to get a look into the house itself to pay attention or care.

At least thirty separate parties from town appeared to have drawn the same conclusion as Kitty had, about the lack of police at the scene of Tuesday night's crime. Kitty said, 'Nertz,' and got out, and, skirting a family party (whose patriarch – in a garishly striped blazer – was attempting to force a ground-floor window with a penknife), led Emma into the long, stone-walled garden that stretched behind the house itself. The beds of roses, lemon trees and red-and-gold lantana extended for some fifty feet, and the cottage at the garden's end stood half hidden behind two enormous pepper trees. Only the first yard or two of the garden beds had been trampled, Emma noticed.

None of the unwelcome visitors surrounding the house had come down this far. The end of the garden was quiet.

'Burt?' Kitty tapped at the cottage door. 'Burt, honey, are you there? It's Kitty Flint.'

The sound of a bolt being drawn back. A slightly bent nose, a bloodshot blue-green eye and a long chin grimed with stubble appeared in the opening. By the smell of him, Burt Sutton had neither bathed nor sobered up since the disappearance of his wife and child two days before. 'Kit?'

Gently, she asked, 'Is there anything you need, Burt? Do you have food?'

He moved his head a little, as if not sure it was still attached to his neck. 'Not really hungry,' he said. He was not much like his older brother, Gren Torley. Taller than Emma had expected – she had formed a mental image of a downtrodden Caspar Milquetoast – and younger, not many years older than herself. Though, she reflected, they had been hard years. 'Can you get me some whiskey, Kit? I had some – can't find it now . . .' His voice was a light, scratchy tenor, and he spoke hesitantly, like a man who has come through a physical beating and expects another one soon.

Emma had to shut her mouth hard not to protest, but a second look at Burt's face, as he opened the door a little more and poured the entire contents of Kitty's flask down his throat, reminded her that this man had just lost his only, his beloved, child.

'Gren said he'd send me some food.' Burt handed back the empty flask. 'Yesterday? Wednesday? Told me I could come stay up at his place. But I couldn't stand it, Kit.' He looked vaguely around as if he expected to see his brother's dark-red Ford truck parked behind the salvias. 'They might bring the note here, see? Might leave it. I got some money . . .'

He stepped back, let them in, the stink of the place like a blow in the face: stale booze, food scraps rotting in the crawling horror of the kitchen sink, urine, unwashed clothing, unmopped vomit. As he pawed through the wilderness of crumpled newspapers that swamped the dark front room, he went on, 'Ardiss was here,' though Kitty had taken the telephone and retreated to the kitchen. He did not appear to notice. 'Brought me somethin' – bottle of somethin' . . . tried to get me to sign these papers. I wouldn't.' He straightened up, hands still full of newspapers, and faced Emma, his features working with impotent anger and disgust. 'Kept pourin' this booze, wantin' me to sign these papers sayin' Selina wasn't no fit mother an' I wasn't able to provide for Susy, so I give her my rights as a parent.'

He shook his head owlishly, blinked into Emma's face. 'I signed 'em *Calvin Coolidge*. She didn't even look, just crammed 'em into her bag an' left – took the bottle, too, the stingy bitch.' He giggled, horrifying at this close a range. 'Boy, she phoned up three hours later an' I never heard language like that since I worked the oil fields!'

As if forgetting what he was doing, he slumped down on the couch among the newspapers – *something* scuttled for safety over the back of the couch and up the curtain – and rubbed his hand on his soiled face. 'Her daddy was here by that time. Old Foy Snoach, tryin' to get me to sign *his* bunch of papers, sayin' Selina wasn't no fit mother an' when they was ransomed back *he* should get her . . . no mention of Selina . . .'

He licked his lips, trying to recall something he'd forgotten. From the hot gloom of the kitchen, with its roaring cloud of flies, Kitty's voice could be heard: 'Elena? This is Camille de la Rose.' She was using her smoky, languid 'Camille' voice, totally different from her off-camera, little-girl coo. 'Frank Pugh sent me to double-check what the nursery looks like – he has to be down in Venice today filming . . . Dearest, is there any chance you could let me in? I'll come to the side door, if you'll watch for me . . .'

'Ol' Foy was here when she called,' repeated Burt, with another drunken chuckle. 'He didn't bring no booze, you can be sure of that. Kept promisin' to write a check – maybe he woulda, too, if Ardiss hadn't phoned an' tore me a new one loud enough he could hear her screechin' – I never laughed so hard in my life!' But as he said the words, tears flowed down his face.

Kitty returned to the front room, held out her hand. 'Thank you,' she said. 'I'll send someone over with some groceries—'

Burt shook his head. 'Just a bottle of somethin',' he said. 'Little bottle.' His fingers measured something the size of a shot glass. 'Just to take away the shakes. Can't find the one I had. Gren'll bring me some food, or take me out to his ranch, or somethin'. You just send me a bottle, Kit, an' it'll be the last one, I swear it. I won't even drink it all. Just enough to set me up. Because I know it was my fault.' He closed trembling hands around Kitty's slender fingers. 'If I'd been sober, I coulda stopped 'em. They took the ladder, see, that was behind this cottage. You c'n see the dirt on its feet. I woulda seen 'em, comin' back, if I hadn't a been—.'

Tears leaked again from his reddened eyes, snot from his nose. 'It was all my fault and I know it. I don't know why I started in drinkin', Kit. I didn't have a bottle in the house, I swear it—'

'It's all right.' Emma laid her hands on his shoulders, aching with horror and at the same time fighting to keep her rage from lashing out: *Then why* did *you?* She saw again Vic Duffy slugging drinks from his flat brown bottle. Tasted on her mouth the booze-wet lips of Lawrence Pendergast the night he'd pushed his way into her attic room back in Manchester, felt again her panic as she'd fled.

You did it because you're a drunken lout would have been an unspeakable thing to say to this weeping man. Knowing that didn't stop her from almost choking on the words.

She knew that the anger she felt was not at him.

Burt followed them to the door. 'Please don't let 'em call the cops, Kitty,' he whispered. 'I'm beggin' you, don't let 'em call the cops. For all I know, they paid off the damn cops. Mitch Sandow came around sayin' how they're askin' the bootleggers for help, askin' all the crooks in this goddam city what they know . . . Goddam Pugh coulda set the whole thing up himself, him an' that publicity man, just to get in the papers! Or Hearst from the *Examiner* coulda done it, just to get everybody ginned up an' buyin' papers, like they did to poor Roscoe Arbuckle. Or . . .'

Emma followed Kitty from the cottage with the sensation of emerging from a badly neglected outhouse and a desperate longing to wash her hands – and bathe – at the earliest possible moment.

The former, at least, she was able to do within minutes in the spotless, pink-tiled kitchen of the main house. Lupe Santini, the stocky housekeeper, only shook her head and muttered, '*Borachio*,' as she glanced back in the direction of the garden and the cottage. But the nursemaid Elena Montoya sighed.

'He was doing so well, you know. And if I heard nothing that night, sleeping in the next room, how could he have heard anything, out in his *casita*?'

How indeed? Emma stood in the doorway of the second-floor nursery, biting her lip not to remind Kitty that nothing should be touched until the police could examine and fingerprint it – not that it mattered, at this point. She saw Kitty discreetly slip both women tightly folded bills. Who knew how many people, from poor Mr Sutton to the gentleman in the garish striped blazer outside, had managed to get in? Had picked and pawed at every toy, every doll, every inch of the window sill . . .

'Mr Sutton said they used the ladder to get in . . .' She put a question into her voice.

Elena – in her twenties, her round, creamy-brown face cheerful and friendly in a close-tied frame of thick black hair – nodded. 'There was scrapes in the dirt under the window and dirt on the bottom feet of the ladder. The ladder had been put back, though. I told the police,' she added. 'But they didn't send anybody out, because of the note, you know, and if there was any tracks or anything, they all got scuffed out by everybody coming around.'

Emma folded her arms, considering, while Kitty went on poking under the bed pillow and looking in the dresser drawers. 'Does the front door have a bolt?' she asked at length. 'And was it bolted the next morning – bolted from the inside, I mean?'

'It's got a bolt,' said Lupe Santini doubtfully. 'Half the time she doesn't bolt it, if she comes in late, or she's a little drunk. What with all the running around, and that note, and Mr Sandow yelling and cursing, I don't remember. I think it was bolted, 'cause Mr Sandow didn't ask about it.'

'Why would they have unbolted it?' Kitty held up a beautiful china-headed doll in a pink dress – a copy, Emma thought, of the one Susy was wearing on the poster for that spring's *Susy and the Bad Men*. 'They came in and out the window.'

'Think about it,' said Emma. 'You can carry an infant, or even a toddler, down a ladder whether she wants to go or not. But a girl of seven – even though she's very small for her age – is big enough to struggle. And if you're taking her mother along, wouldn't it make more sense to hold a gun on the child, and everybody go downstairs quietly and out the front door?'

'I can't imagine Selina going anywhere quietly,' Kitty sniffed.

'If they were holding a gun, or a knife, on her child?'

Kitty merely looked puzzled. Emma wondered if she were trying (and failing) to picture Selina Sutton's hypothetical emotions in the face of such a threat . . . or her own.

'They would have put the ladder back when they came out . . .' She turned to the nursemaid again. 'Were any of Miss Sutton's clothes gone?'

The young woman looked startled at the question. Evidently, reflected Emma, not something it had crossed private detective Colt Madison's mind to ask.

Lupe, who had come upstairs behind them, said, 'I'll look, Ma'am. It may take me a while – she had a lot of clothes, Miss Sutton. But I'll wash them, and iron them, and mend them – and give them to my nieces and sisters when Miss Sutton gets tired of them. I'll know if anything's gone.'

* * *

'You know,' remarked Kitty as the Packard whipped, without slowing, around the thicket of oaks that hid any glimpse of Benedict Canyon Drive from Shadygrove Terrace, 'now that I come to think of it, Burt may have a point. I wouldn't put it past Frank at that.'

'Would that actually work?' Emma clung grimly to the door handle of the big car and forced herself not to urge Kitty to look at the road instead of at her, as if they were sitting together on a couch. The last time she'd done so, her sister-in-law had let go of the wheel to explain how good her control of the vehicle actually was. 'As publicity, I mean?'

'You bet it would!' Kitty brightened at the idea. 'If it were me, I'd offer Selina a bonus to help me with it – except Frank's so cheap he wouldn't offer her more than a hundred, and Selina's so greedy she wouldn't take anything under five thousand.'

'Wouldn't he put himself in danger of being blackmailed?' inquired Emma, trying to look neither at the woodlands flashing past nor directly at Kitty for fear of causing her to feel that for the sake of good manners she needed to make eye contact. 'Either by Miss Sutton if she were in on it, or by whoever helped him if she wasn't.'

'Hmm.' Kitty swerved casually to miss a bottle-green Bugatti where the drive curved around a stand of eucalyptus: Emma wondered if that was the Sutton household's handsome 'financial manager', Mitch Sandow. And if so, what was *he* going to try to get poor Burt drunk enough to sign?

'But,' said Emma, as the road straightened out for its final drop towards Sunset Boulevard, 'wouldn't Mr Pugh have waited until after filming was done on *Tiny Miracle*? And on *Crimson Desert*?' The thought of Kitty taking it into her head to burgle her lover's quasi-Egyptian mansion further up the canyon in search of 'clues' some night made her shudder. '*Crimson Desert* is already weeks behind schedule. Further delays would interfere with the shooting schedules of *Toot-Toot-Tootsie* and *The Purgatoire Kid*.'

'I suppose you're right.' Kitty released the idea of a publicity conspiracy with a sigh, and veered on to Sunset across the nose of a yellow streetcar. 'Well, we'll know if Susy turns up before Monday when everybody's supposed to go out to the desert . . . But it would just *kill* Frank to cut the uproar short, you know, now when the newspapers are just getting started. Marsh Sloane told me yesterday the case made the headlines in the London *Times*!'

SEVEN

For Emma, the issue of whether Frank Pugh was behind his own child star's abduction was settled two days later – Sunday, after a marathon session of filming *Crimson Desert*'s 'England' sequences in the grassier portions of the studio backlot. Saturday evening had run into the early hours of Sunday morning, as the hastily rewritten scenario sought to explicate (rather than demonstrate) why the Evil Zahar would go to the trouble of later kidnapping poor Mr Fairfax and carrying him off to the depths of the Rub' al Khali in order to kill him. (*Oh, for a muse of fire!* Emma sighed.)

Filming on the non-Susy sequences of *Our Tiny Miracle* having been done over the previous weeks, Laird Mullen was re-assigned to immortalize the transformation of poor little Rosebud Mary – Darlene Golden as the lost heiress, apparently the only girl in the New York slums to actually sell enough flowers to permit her to retain both her innocence and a roof over her head – into a viable candidate for admission to Society's Four Hundred. Interior sets pertaining to this transformation had been hastily assembled at the other end of Stage One, and four extra musicians recruited to compete with the Rothstein Boys in 'setting the mood' for these new events. Emma had been urged to set up shop with her box of Professor Wright's papers at a folding table in the circle of Kitty's 'base camp,' to be on hand to quickly resolve issues in fitting together the two portions of what Conrad Fishbein insisted on referring to as the Epic Romance of the Sands.

'I?' Darlene pressed hands white as lilies to her swan-like throat. 'But my father was Jerry Marlon! He was a coal-heaver, who died when I was five! How could this be?'

'No, Miss Bellingham! Your father was Arthur Bellingham, who . . .'

'CUT! Fer Chrissake, Gully, look where you're goin'!'

* * *

'The Sant-Agnello necropolis' – (*Is that the same one referred to as the Corso? Corzo? discovery?*) – 'is laid out as an analog to a town, with seven streets, a village square and what appears to be a temple (see Map 1).' Emma shuffled for the third time through the papers, and found nothing labeled Map 1. Maps 4 and 11 – and anything after Map 13, if there *were* more than thirteen maps – were likewise missing, unless one counted those four plans that could have been either site maps of Etruscan burial grounds or plans of Roman towns. There were two maps labeled '3' and three more with no labels at all. Moreover, two other pages – neither of them superscribed or numbered – bore nearly identical wording, one of them in the typeface of Wright's office machine and the other – the Underwood (Emma guessed) with the very faded ribbon – followed by a disjointed passage of sophomoric prose concerning who the Etruscans had been, something Professor Wright would already have known.

From the other end of Stage One, Danny C. and the C-Notes crooned into 'It Had to Be You . . .'

Frowning, Emma drew out other pages to compare.

'It was me who set up that trap to trip his horse,' the Evil Zahar hissed, and smote the Louis XV boiseries of the Fairfax library (last seen in *Scandalous Lady*) with her beautiful little fist.

'Beware how you boast of it!' Marsh Sloane – in Arab robes and the most sinister pair of artificial eyebrows Emma had ever seen – flung up his hands in warning.

'Ha! No one spurns the Evil Zahar and lives!'

'Cut! That was great, Marsh, but Kitty, can you sort of draw yourself up as you say that? You need to really dominate the room. And can you actually call yourself the Lady of the Crimson Desert, so it'll match the dialog card?'

'I can see Frank arranging the kidnapping of Susy,' Zal had remarked, Friday night when, taking advantage of Pugh's absence on Venice Pier (and Kitty's consequent absence at Enyart's Café – and goodness knew where else – with the handsome Jack Lee), he had come to Ivarene Street for a quiet dinner in the kitchen. 'I can't see him snatching Selina because sooner or later she'd figure it out that it was him, and then where would he be?'

The remains of the meal had been cleared away – fish that Zal had bought on his way back from filming in Venice, a delicate Riesling acquired in the same locale from someone named Big Ole, a salad of the amazing variety of produce available in California, mashed avocado on toast . . . It was seldom these days that Emma cooked, and she relished the chance to do so for someone other than herself. They had made love, with slow leisure in the quiet house, all the windows open to the warm breezes off the hillslopes, then gone downstairs again for coffee and peaches and Mamie Smith on the phonograph, a magic evening of peace. Later Zal had helped her count and catalog Professor Wright's Etruscan fragments ('Boy, I wonder what they used *that* one for?'), and Emma had spoken of Kitty's theory.

'But why would kidnappers have taken Selina at all?' Emma set aside the broken piece of a Twenty-Fifth Dynasty Egyptian votive image that she was fairly certain her father would have killed a number of his professional colleagues to obtain: ebony and gold, fragile now with desiccation and time. 'If they came in through the window and left the same way, why burden themselves with a second victim?'

'She might have heard them. Might have surprised them. Maybe even recognized some of them, because the whole thing smells to me like an inside job. They'd *have* to take her with them at that point— Whoa, is that King Tut?' He took off his glasses to study the black-and-gold head – no bigger than a hazelnut – beside her hand. 'What's he doing in Italy?'

'The Etruscans were a trading people,' said Emma. 'They mined and smelted iron, which everybody wanted back then, including the Egyptians. And the Babylonians,' she added, holding up a cylinder seal about the size of a large spool of thread. 'Though this is neo-Babylonian, right before or right after they were taken over by Persia.'

'How can you tell?'

'By the crown the king is wearing: see here? It's characteristic of the later period, like the Kushite headdress on this votive. Which is one in the eye for Professor Partington at the university. Partington telephoned me yesterday morning to explain to me why I couldn't possibly interpret Professor Wright's findings because he – Partington – had conclusively proved that sixth-century trade in Italy came through the Greeks in Naples, because the Etruscans were too primitive to have conducted such a trade.'

'Yeah, I've heard that argument about the Aztecs in Mexico – the guys who built all those big cities – actually being Egyptians.' He turned the cylinder over in careful fingers. 'Would he have bumped off Wright over it?'

'More likely libeled him in the *Journal of Archaeology*. Or pulled his hair out in a tiff over the provenance of that seal. Mrs Pendergast – the woman I worked for in Manchester – claimed the Aztecs were actually from Atlantis. Or from unknown realms within the Earth – which is hollow, you know . . .'

'Oh, yeah, I heard about that,' said Zal gravely. 'And all I've got to say is, Edgar Rice Burroughs has a lot to answer for. I didn't know archaeology could be so exciting.'

'And I didn't know,' sighed Emma, recalling the previous week of takes, retakes, close-ups, continuity stills and long waits while the lights were shifted and costumes readjusted, 'that the movie business could be so dull.'

'Doc, can we get more light on Darlene's tits?'

Hollywood. Yesterday's *Examiner* and *Citizen* had both run front-page stories on how the intrepid Colt Madison had met with 'underworld figures' Tony 'the Hat' Cornero and Albert Marco – at great risk to his own life (said Madison) – to enlist their help in finding clues to the whereabouts of the stolen child. No ransom note had yet been received.

Page Two of the *Times* had featured a smaller notification that Mrs Ardiss Tinch, the aunt of Little Susy Sweetchild, had filed papers suing for custody of the child on the grounds that her sister, former actress Selina Sutton (Emma could just imagine Miss Sutton's reaction to that 'former'), was an unfit mother.

When Emma took the Pekes for their walk at ten, she made her way to the hacienda for a look at the morning's papers, which lay on a prop-department copy of a medieval refectory table in the tiled front hall. These contained nothing new on the search for the missing 'baby star,' though they did display another picture of Colt Madison looking intrepid, and an even larger picture of Little Susy looking adorable. These illustrated an article about the re-release of all four of Little Susy's feature films – each with a block-booked selection of her one- and two-reelers (and an assortment of other Foremost productions that had not yet earned back their expenses) – to the theatrical chain associated with Foremost.

Unfolding the sheets, Emma found on page two the information that Mr Foy Snoach, grandfather of Little Susy Sweetchild, was suing for custody of the child on the grounds that neither of his daughters – neither Miss Sutton nor Mrs Tinch – would be fit guardians (there followed copious evidence that bordered on the pornographic). It also claimed that the permissions entered by Mrs Tinch as having been signed by Little Susy's father were in fact forgeries. Mrs Tinch was counter-suing.

The studio was still requesting that no police investigation be made.

As she crossed back to Stage One – Chang Ming and Black Jasmine ceremoniously pausing at every pillar of the long arcade in front of the 'star' dressing rooms – Emma felt again the sick dread at the thought of the child, wherever they were keeping her . . . *She must be terrified.*

If she's still alive . . .

Against her will, she recalled the recent abduction of a millionaire's son named Bobby Franks, killed within a day of going missing in May. Once they got their hands on the ransom money, why would kidnappers risk leaving a witness alive?

'Duchess!' Director Madge Burdon barged from one of the dressing rooms at the end of the row, a sturdy block of a woman in a man's cotton shirt and a stout drill skirt, like someone about to set forth for the headwaters of the Amazon. Ominously, she had a file folder tucked under one arm. 'Hiya, Handsome,' she added, stooping to pat Chang Ming, then Black Jasmine, before asking, 'Any word on Susy?' She'd seen Emma emerge from the office. 'They got a note yet?'

And, when Emma shook her head: 'Crap. Listen, Duchess' – compassionate inquiry disposed of, she plunged on into business – 'I know Frank's got you trimming *Crimson Desert*, but Emily Violet's mother has been all over Frank about the script for *Toot-Toot-Tootsie* again. Is there any chance you can make a couple changes in the ocean-liner sequence?' She held out the script. 'We're two weeks behind schedule, and Sam just got handed that new Vane mystery to adapt.'

Emma refrained from expressing any opinion about Sam, Frank or Emily Violet's mother, and replied, 'I'll have a look at it, yes.' A schedule, she knew, was a schedule . . . 'But I can't guarantee—'

Miss Burdon smote her shoulder with comradely vigor. 'Aces! If you can get me something before you folks leave Monday' – today was Sunday – 'I'll sell my sister's first-born son to the Arabs and give you the money!' And she charged off like a whirlwind in the direction of Stage Two.

On Stage One, Rosebud Mary was weeping – to the tremulous strains of 'Meet Me Tonight in Dreamland' – over the Bellingham lawyer's insistence that there would be no room in her new life for her crippled younger sister (Delia Terry), and at the other end of the huge chamber, Kitty was still smiting the paneling in the Fairfax library and declaring, 'Ha! No one spurns the Lady of the Crimson Desert and lives!'

The passionate strains of *Le Rouet d'Omphale* chopped off midbar.

'No, honey, watch it with that dagger there. You look like you're about to stab Marsh . . .'

'I am not! I didn't get anywhere near him!'

Marsh Sloane clutched his breast like Juliet in Act Five and collapsed theatrically to the floor. Kitty kicked him.

Emma set *Toot-Toot-Tootsie* aside, took three deep breaths and reminded herself that nobody knew anything yet about the kidnapping. There was nothing she could do – except carry on, like Madge and Larry Palmer, like Kitty and Darlene and the Rothstein Boys and Zal who had to maintain a consistent sixteen frames per second no matter what was going on at the other end of the shooting stage . . . More puzzled than ever, she returned to the account of the Sant'Angello necropolis. One of the pages ended mid-sentence with an introduction to an 'interconnected series of painted tombs, with banqueting scenes painted along . . .' and nothing thereafter that could possibly be the series (*labyrinth? Gallery? Localized complexes?*) referred to. The fact that the typed pages, heavily interlined in Professor Wright's cramped hand, were not numbered didn't help. (*How did they know there was a ladder stored outside, on the back side of the cottage, easily accessible? Why kidnap the mother in the first place? How many people would it need to kidnap both a woman and a child and control them, either going down the stairs or down a ladder?*)

And not only did there seem to be a map missing – and the same block of text appeared in three different places, one of them weirdly out of context – but there were several shards and artifacts mentioned that, try as she might, she could not remember seeing in Friday night's count.

'Ha! No one spurns the Lady of the Crimson Desert and lives!'
'Cut! Marsh, don't duck like that.'
'Sir, I have had this nose for many years and I like it just the length it is.'
'Anyway, it's silly to think that I'll wear a dagger to some snooty tea party even if I *am* a princess! And who invites Arab princesses to tea parties? They won't even invite Jews!'
"Course it's silly, honey! This is the movies. But we've got to remind the audience you've got a dagger, 'cause that's the one you use to stab Ken with later . . .'

'. . . well tomb of the Villanovan period included votive statues of the goddess Leucothea (see fragment 20) and offerings of gold and onyx in the style of the Twenty-Fifth Dynasty of Egypt (see fragments 16–18) . . .'
Emma thumbed yet again through the unnumbered pages – this particular portion was handwritten into the bargain – seeking any page that contained a concluding sentence fragment pertaining to well tombs, or any page at all which contained a switch from typed to handwritten. Twice already she had encountered reference to the gold-and-ebony Egyptian votive of Osiris (*not* King Tut) being in three pieces, yet knew she had only seen the head. She had telephoned Professor Denham the previous day asking yet again if any search of the office had yielded further pages (no) or if the janitorial staff had disposed of any papers that might have been soiled with blood (no). Professor Denham was in the process of looking through every book in the office for stray sheets (in between collating assignments of her twenty-five new students from Classics 102) and had asked her scholastic colleagues to please look through any book that they might have inadvertently carried away ('Me? Take some of poor Wright's books?') . . .

I'll see you in my dreams / Hold you in my dreams . . .

(*Burt says he has no idea who brought him the liquor Tuesday . . . Dear God, look after them. Look after them both . . .*)

* * *

'Ha! No man spurns the Lady of the Crimson Desert and lives!'

'Duchess?'

Emma startled as Frank Pugh dragged up another of the canvas folding chairs from in front of Kitty's make-up table and settled into it (with an ominous creak) close at her side.

He, too, she noticed with dismay, had a file folder under his arm.

She laid two pages of tomb layouts face down over *Toot-Toot-Tootsie*. 'Miss Burdon already spoke to me about Miss Violet's mother wanting changes.'

His big, startlingly heavy-muscled hand covered hers. 'That's great, Mrs Blackstone, that's great. Everybody here says what a great job you do.' He leaned closer, his breath a murk of coffee and cigars. Even in the intermittent kaleidoscope of lighting of the sets at either end of the shooting stage, the studio head looked exhausted. The flesh around his eyes, always puffy, was discolored with lack of sleep, and sweat glistened in the chubby bulge of his forehead as the bluish-white Kliegs heated even the vast barn of the stage.

'Can I speak to you in confidence?' He leaned close. 'In this business, you never know who's gonna go blab to the film magazines.'

'Of course.' She spoke her first thought. 'Have you received a ransom note?'

His long silence was almost answer in itself. If it hadn't been, his next words – 'Why do you ask?' – certainly were.

Without waiting for her to answer – and she wasn't entirely sure what to say or why he was speaking to her of this in the first place – he went on, 'In fact, we have. They want a hundred thousand.'

Even after nine months, it took her a moment to translate that into money that meant something to her. Twenty thousand pounds. 'Did they set a time? Or conditions?'

'They said they'd be in touch. Thing is' – those cold, jade-green eyes ducked momentarily away from hers, then returned – 'something may go wrong. These are desperate men we're dealing with, Duchess. She may have seen them – Selina may have seen them. Or seen something – maybe these are guys who can't afford any slip-ups. You understand?'

('Chip!' bellowed Laird Mullen at his cameraman. 'Let's try this one from outside her window!')

'This is the movie business, Duchess. My heart breaks for the poor kid, but I don't trust these jaspers, you know? We – the studio's backers, I mean: the money men behind the studio and the guys who run the distribution chain – we got to make sure every contingency is covered.'

He was gazing into her eyes with great sincerity and had put a second hand over hers.

('Ha! No man spurns the Lady of the Crimson Desert and lives!')

Madge Burdon, ordinarily a kind woman, plunging straight from a perfunctory query about a child in peril to the subject of script changes and schedules . . .

Hollywood . . .

'What are you asking, sir?'

'I'm asking you to rewrite the ending of *Tiny Miracle*,' said Pugh quietly. 'We may not need it – and I pray we don't. But if something goes wrong, we need to rewrite the last third of the picture with the kid just seen a couple of times in long shots. We can use her stand-in.'

Emma felt as if she didn't even possess the vocabulary to speak to the man. That words like *How DARE you?* were nowhere within his comprehension, and she couldn't imagine what words – what concepts – he *would* understand.

She was astonished at how calm her voice was. 'You mean you're going to finish the picture – *and release it* – if Susy and her mother are killed by the kidnappers?'

'We got a hundred thousand sunk in this picture, and close to forty thousand feet of film already shot. We can't not finish.' The meaty paws gripped tight. 'Can you do that, Duchess?'

The Klieg lights to her left went down. Innocent Rosebud Mary declared, 'About fucken time!' and Doc Larousse and his gaffer army swarmed down on the set. Zal's voice cut through Emma's thoughts, 'Don't go too far, Darlene. We'll reset—'

'Fuck you, Zal. Somebody gimme a cigarette.'

Emma felt Pugh's glance flick past her to the cameraman, like a reminder. *I may not be able to fire Kitty, and you may not care if I fire you, but you'll care if I make trouble for* him . . .

She took a deep breath. Το τα αδύνατα διώκειν μανικόν – *and there's nothing I can do about the situation as it stands* . . . 'I can certainly try.' She added, 'I don't know much about the technical side of picture-making, but I should think—'

'Just as a backup,' Pugh coaxed. 'We may not need it. I've already got you your own suite in Seven Palms for you to work in, or you and Kitty's little mutts can stay back here if you want, instead of going out to the desert tomorrow. And of course you'll get a bonus from payroll. But just in case . . .'

She met his eyes. *And you really think every movie-goer in the country isn't going to be disgusted when adverts for* Our Tiny Miracle *come out only weeks on the heels of headlines* Child Star's Body Found?

Again his eyes ducked away from hers, then returned. 'Just in case.'

This is America, Emma reminded herself. *People are different . . .* She recalled some of her employer's friends back in Manchester. *Not that different . . .* 'I know I've agreed this is in confidence,' she said stiffly. 'I would like your permission to speak to Mr Rokatansky about this, for advice on what's possible in using a double, or in using previously shot footage.'

The piggy glance went to Zal again, as if gauging how much of a grip he had on the man. If he'd need threats to make him keep his mouth shut, and if so, what kind and how strong? After a moment, he said, 'Sure. Sure. I'll talk to him, make sure he knows this is just a contingency plan. He understands the business.'

He patted her hand again, dropped the scenario of *Our Tiny Miracle* on top of Professor Wright's curiously incomprehensible notes and strode off in the direction of poor little Rosebud's wretched attic room, where Zal was adjusting the focal length on his Bell & Howell while Darlene's stand-in sweated under the lights. Emma's mind went back to the terrified child. Locked in a room somewhere? Maybe without even her mother to talk to? Maybe having already seen . . . what?

While her aunt and her grandfather sued one another over who was going to get custody of her (and all of her earnings), if she came out of this alive. And while her studio made contingency plans about how they'd finish her picture if she didn't.

In the blinding glare of the Kliegs, Pugh laid a hand on Zal's shoulder, as if to remind him of the firmer financial grip he had. Explained something quietly, with gestures of his free hand.

Zal's glance went immediately to Emma: *You OK with this?*
She nodded.
Hollywood.

* * *

'At least that disposes of the possibility that Mr Pugh and Mr Fishbein – with or without the assistance of Miss Sutton – cooked this up between them.' Emma loaded Kitty's make-up box – *one* of Kitty's make-up boxes – into the small rear seat of the Packard and went to untie the leashes of the three Pekinese from the stout stem of the wisteria that shaded this portion of the arcade. Zal – who had driven the big car over from the lot behind the film-processing building – closed Kitty's dressing-room door and set down the three wicker carry-boxes in which the celestial cream cakes rode back and forth from Ivarene Street to the studio.

It was past midnight, and a magical dry desert heat brought the smells of sagebrush and dust from the hills to the north. In eleven hours, they'd be loading on to the train for Seven Palms, in the heart of the Mojave Desert, nearly a month deeper into summer than intended.

Kitty herself was not in her dressing room. With the conclusion of the whole murder-at-the-hunt-meet sequence (which now included not a frame of anybody on a horse), she had effusively thanked the crew and assured Emma, 'I'll meet you back at my dressing room in a few minutes, darling. I just need to go for a little walk . . . No, just have my things ready . . .'

Enough time to get some sleep, Emma reflected, provided Professor Halford Partington didn't ring her up yet again offering to edit his colleague's papers. *The man's specialty is the Renaissance*, Julia Denham had said indignantly, when Emma had told her of his several telephone calls. *He couldn't tell an Etruscan from an Episcopalian. More than that, he was ready to scratch Professor Wright's eyes out about trade routes in the ancient world, and I wouldn't put it past him to ink out some of Wright's findings and put in his own.*

Zal was right, she thought wearily. Hollywood wasn't the only place in the world that resembled the Looking-Glass Land.

'I'm honestly sorry that it isn't Mr Pugh behind it,' she sighed. 'Words I never thought I'd speak. But Mr Pugh at least wouldn't let actual harm come to Susy and Miss Sutton. As it is, I can only hope Miss Sutton keeps her head and doesn't do anything foolish. A hundred thousand dollars is nearly the cost of the picture, isn't it?'

'It's pretty much exactly the cost of the picture,' agreed Zal in a dry voice. The lights of Laird Mullen's roadster and of Larry

Palmer's serviceable old Ford flashed across his glasses as the two cars turned to go out the studio gates on to Sunset. The shadows of grips and gaffers, the men and women of wardrobe and make-up, faded back to let the vehicles pass, before setting forth down the boulevard to catch the last streetcars for home. 'And it's pretty much exactly what *Susy and the Bad Men* made in its first six months – down nearly seventy thousand from *Susy Goes to Town* last year.'

Emma heard the glint of anger in his voice. Weirdly, she felt no shock. As if she'd known this all along. 'You think they're not going to pay.'

'What do you think?' He leaned against the side of the car. 'You think Frank got that note today?'

She opened her mouth to answer, then closed it. 'They've been trying to figure out what to do.'

'Frank's been on the phone – or out of the studio – pretty much all day,' said Zal quietly. 'Where do you think he was all yesterday? Who do you think he's been talking to? I don't know for sure,' he added. 'But I was in Minnesota in '17 during the lumber-workers' strikes, and I saw how bosses think when they think somebody's gonna ask them for money. So I can take a guess.'

And Kitty sleeps with that man . . .

'We can't prove a thing,' he went on after a moment. 'And it's no weirder than some of the stories you're already seeing in the fan magazines. Did you read the one today about Susy's mother being a Communist and getting her to go make pictures in Russia? Or about Susy being snatched by Mexican rebels to raise money to fund de la Huerta's revolt against Obregón?' He knelt to open the doors of the little wicker crates and gently scootched Buttercreme, Black Jasmine and Chang Ming inside.

'But the fact is, Susy's going to be eight at her next birthday.' He straightened up, his eyes somber. 'You can already see how they're dressing her down, with those little-girl dresses, to make her look like she did when she was five. Alvy Turner was telling me he's got orders never to shoot her in a medium shot standing next to an adult, so nobody can see how much she's grown.'

'She's tiny!' protested Emma.

'Not as tiny as she was. Yeah, she's small for her age, but they've already got Volmort making her up younger. You know they shoot Nellie Boardman standing on lifts in scenes with her? Or sitting down? You know Kitty's been claiming twenty for about four years, and Mary Pickford's still got those Pollyanna ringlets and she's thirty-two – and I'll bet she'll still have them when she's forty-two. The men who represent the theater chains may not think Susy's gonna be worth it, at a hundred thou.'

The last of the crew cars – Mary Blanque's modest Oldsmobile – trundled through the gate. Sunset Boulevard had grown quiet. Arnie the night guard stepped out of his kiosk, looked across the dusty quadrangle to the big yellow Packard in front of the dressing-room wing, then retreated again.

After a long moment, Emma whispered, 'They can't.'

Zal raised his eyebrows. 'Hide and watch 'em.'

Kitty appeared shortly after that, tousled and giggly and smelling of gin and cigarette smoke mingled with the sweetish, smoky pungence of raw film stock in her hair. She chattered gaily all the way up Vine Street and into the velvet blackness of the Hollywood Hills, stopping now and then in her encomia of Jack Lee's good looks and Herculean stamina to remind Emma of things indispensable to her own comfort, or Emma's, or that of the dogs: 'Don't let's forget extra stockings! Goodness knows where we'll be able to buy them out there!' or 'Oh, remember to pack Buttercreme's sock!' (A cotton sock once worn by old Mr Shang, the gardener, and now, tied in a knot, serving the shy little dog as a pull-toy.) Occasionally, she strayed into animadversions on Marsh Sloane's shortcomings as an actor ('Honestly, it's like trying to do a scene with an Indian from outside a cigar store!') or her disappointment with that afternoon's fare in the studio commissary ('I swear that's *exactly* the same lettuce they were trying to serve up yesterday! I recognized the spots on the leaves!').

When you wake up in the morning, the philosopher-Emperor Marcus Aurelius had once written, *tell yourself: the people I deal with today will be meddling, ungrateful, arrogant, dishonest, jealous and surly* . . . This will keep you from anger and disappointment, he had said. If you go to the baths, you're going to get splashed. Only crazy people expect differently.

And if you live in Hollywood, and work at Foremost Productions, you're going to . . .

Emma sighed.

You're going to encounter the Frank Pughs of the world.

And the Kitty Flints, who drink life one brimming cup at a time.

His Imperial Majesty, she reflected tiredly, had undoubtedly seen much worse.

It had been dark when they'd left the ersatz pink palace on Ivarene Street that morning; the light on the high, tiled porch was still on. Supervised by Black Jasmine, Emma did the final packing ('Darling, have you seen my brocade heels?') (*Where are you going to wear red-and-gold brocade shoes in the desert?*). Yesterday's mail had brought six letters forwarded from the university, plus a seventh envelope of heavy cream stationery, business size and shape, her address typed, the return address embossed letterhead. She recognized the name – Doyle Dravitt. Wilson Dravitt had been one of Professor Wright's students. The other six correspondents were also students in Classics 102. After opening the first two and finding letters obliquely hinting at financial remuneration should the research papers be unfortunately unobtainable, Emma simply packed the rest into the box with Wright's notes.

If I'm to have my own suite at the Araby Hotel, I can certainly read them there when I'm awake after the journey rather than . . .

The distant clank of the door knocker downstairs and a soprano salvo of barks. Canine toenails clattered on the dark oak of the upstairs hall outside Emma's door, as Chang Ming, Black Jasmine and Buttercreme pelted out of Kitty's room. The two smaller Pekes halted at the top of the stairs – being too small to negotiate the risers themselves – while Chang Ming barreled down to the lighted well of the living room, barking all the way.

Emma looked at the clock. A quarter to three.

Her solar plexus seemed to tighten. *If the news was good, we'd get a telephone call in the morning* . . .

'All right, all right, my tiny angel muffins . . .' Kitty rattled downstairs in slip, heeled slippers and kimono, pausing only long enough to gather Black Jasmine and Buttercreme in her arms.

Emma followed. *No. Please, no* . . .

Burt Sutton stood on the front porch, wearing the same ruinous checkered shirt, stained undershirt and rumpled dungarees he'd had on Friday – and presumably most of the previous week. His eyes had a hectic glitter, and his breath – and clothing – reeked of liquor both old and fresh.

'It was Selina,' he said, looking from Kitty to Emma and back. 'Selina took her. And I know where they gotta be.'

EIGHT

'It was the cat.' Burt Sutton slumped into the wooden chair at the kitchen table, groped for the coffee Emma had poured out for him and emptied the cup down his throat as if pouring it into a funnel. 'Mr Gray. Susy's cat. They took him.'

Looking back, Emma realized she hadn't seen the animal on Friday. A dog might have lingered in the nursery or the downstairs. Even the most loyal cat – and a cat accustomed to the constant noise and movement of a film studio – would have taken to the shrubbery with the arrival of thirty cars full of sightseers and their running, screaming children. Emma still wondered if any of those over-excited youngsters had ended up in the swimming pool, and if so, whether any adult had been on hand to pull them out.

Emma refilled Burt's cup. Kitty climbed the three steps to the little foyer between the kitchen and living room and returned with a bottle from the carved Chinese liquor cabinet. Burt's fist clenched momentarily and he looked aside; without turning his head, he waved the offered drink away. Kitty dosed her own cup, then went up and replaced the bottle, coming back with two cigarettes in her mouth, both of which she lit. She inhaled to get them both going, then put one in Burt's hand.

He drank the smoke as if it were the first oxygen he'd had all day.

'Thanks,' he said. 'Thanks, Kitty.' And coughed like a dying horse. Chang Ming stood on his hind legs, worriedly put silky paws on the man's knee and licked his own flat nose. *You OK, Mister?*

Emma almost had the sensation of watching Burt Sutton's true consciousness – his soul – resolidify out of the air and stick itself again to his bones and flesh and smelly old clothes.

He cleared his throat, nodded towards the three wicker carry-boxes visible through the door into the foyer, lined up ready to have the dogs loaded for the trip to Seven Palms in the morning. 'Mr Gray's carry-box is gone,' he said. 'Regular kidnappers wouldn't have taken the cat, y'see. But Selina would.

'Selina used to tell Susy, if she didn't learn her scenes, or didn't do exactly what the director said, she'd take Mr Gray and drown him in the swimming pool. She did it once, too, when Susy tried to run away from home. Susy had Mr Gray in his carry-box – taking him with her – an' Selina took an' sunk it in the water, an' only pulled him out when Susy swore she'd never be bad again.'

Emma bit her lip in her effort not to ask, *And where were you while this was going on?* No more than his daughter, she guessed, could Burt Sutton imagine where he could go, how he could survive, without the shelter Selina Sutton gave him, the food she had the housekeeper leave on his doorstep and the garments she bought for him with the money Susy made. At least Susy – *How old had she been then? Six? Five?* – had tried.

Tried to go where? To Ardiss Tinch? Grandpa Snoach?

She remembered Zal saying, *She could have saved Magnum if Burt hadn't drunk half the profits and Selina hadn't blown the rest . . . Frank bought her the house . . . about two years ago she damn near lost that over some cockamamie investment scheme . . .*

Remembered the other rampant misdemeanors, financial and sexual, that had been released for all the world to read in that morning's *Times* by Mrs Tinch's own father – not to speak of the man's denunciation of the 'filthy cat.' Emma winced at the thought of Susy seeking refuge with either of them. She wondered if the little girl had pilfered the household money to take a cab, or if she'd planned to walk.

After long silence, Burt coughed again and went on. 'She'd take her out to that house she bought in Palm Springs. Fifty thousand, it cost, without even the furniture – the lamps an' door handles alone cost six thou. Fifty-six grand, of Susy's money, an' she'd go out there with some man or other . . .'

His face worked with pain at the memories. 'Selina told me it got sold, when that make-up business she was tryin' to start went to smash – or was it toothpaste? It was the toothpaste.' He took another drag on his cigarette. 'But Selina lies like the parlor carpet. Pugh made her sell it so what she owed wouldn't get in the papers, but I don't think she did. I swear there was more money in the account even after the toothpaste thing took a dive, an' all of a sudden there wasn't nothing. She swore up and down she'd sold her diamonds, but – last month? Back in April? Anyway . . . I found an invoice in Sandow's office at our place for a bank box – I had no idea where it was or what was in it. It wasn't the one she an' I had together at Farmers 'n' Merchants . . . an' I swear I never took out the cash we had in that bank box, either. She swears I did.'

He swallowed another gulp of coffee. 'I ain't been the best daddy in the world,' he added softly, tears filling his eyes. 'I know it. I just . . .' He shook his head. 'Anyway, Selina said more'n once that Susy's contract's got two more years on it. She'll be ten, then – *An' who wants to pay money to see a ten-year-old*, she says. Lately she's always been raggin' on poor Susy not to be a tomboy, an' sold her pony that she had, sayin' it made her look coarse. Susy's good.' His voice turned pleading. 'She's a good little actress. That last picture of hers scratched 'cause it just wasn't any good, not 'cause of anything she did. I can see Selina kidnappin' Susy herself – takin' the cat along to make sure she keeps quiet. Even settin' that ladder up under the window, an' takin' it down again – make it look like that's how they got in. She bought another house, a lodge up in Big Bear – twenty thousand – but people up there know her. She'd take her to Palm Springs.'

He dropped his head to his hands, and a shudder went through the whole of his body.

'She'd take her there.'

Then he glanced sidelong up at Kitty, asked softly, 'You know, I will take a little of that gin you offered me just now. Just to set me up. I won't have more'n one.'

Emma called a cab when Burt passed out, and Kitty gave the driver an extra twenty dollars to make sure Burt got into his cottage at the end of his ride. Before the cab left, Kitty found a piece of notepaper by the telephone and wrote, *Your car is at my house, Kitty*, and tucked it into Burt's pocket. To it, after a moment's thought, she added a ten-dollar bill.

'He'll just spend it on liquor,' said Emma sadly, as the lights of the taxi swung their way up the steep slope of the drive, and away down Ivarene. The two women – and the three dogs – stood beside Burt's spavined Model-T in the hot dark in front of the house as the dust settled slowly and the stillness returned. Above the hills of Griffith Park, the stars dimmed against graying sky.

Kitty sighed. Without her usual flippancy, she opined, 'It won't make it that far. If he throws up in the cab, the driver'll search him and find it, and I don't blame him. You can only do what you can do.'

That that is, is, the wise Fool says in *Twelfth Night*, to the scheming inhabitants of Illyria. And Burt, reflected Emma, was what he was.

'Do you believe him?' She bent to pick up Black Jasmine, who had bustled out to the porch to make sure Burt was properly carried down the steep, tiled steps and then had quacked to be borne down himself to supervise the loading. 'About Miss Sutton?'

'I wouldn't put it past her, dear.' Cradling Buttercreme in her arms, Kitty mounted the steps, Emma at her heels. This far up Ivarene, there were few houses; across the street, the dark shape of the hills rose, blanketed in sage and manzanita. Somewhere Emma heard the crying of coyotes and a nightbird's eerie scream. 'She's sure not going to get fifteen grand a week out of Frank on Susy's next contract, if Frank offers a contract at all. One of the smaller studios like Monarch or Blue Star *might* take a ten-year-old featured player on a one-year contract. Or she could go into vaudeville.'

She closed and latched the screen door behind her. To Emma, the living room – or the kitchen, where Kitty again led the way to make more coffee – had the flat, queer look of electrical illumination in the small hours: *Or maybe anyplace looks queer if you've been up for almost twenty-four hours . . .*

'A hundred thousand dollars could set Selina up in business,' pointed out Kitty, as she fished another cigarette from the drawer that held them. 'Buy her a couple of rentals. Or pay rent herself, for God knows how long, if she doesn't turn around and do something stupid with it.'

She scratched a match on the side of the stove, then stooped, graceful as a child, to pick up Black Jasmine in her arms. 'Mitch Sandow got her to sell three or four of the cars she bought with Susy's salary – I think he was the one Frank put in charge of selling the Palm Springs house. I know she didn't make back more than a couple of thousand on the cars – she's spent that much on a dress. I've only got a couple more things to pack, honey, so maybe you could wake me up at ten and make us some breakfast while I get cleaned up – oh, and be sure to brush the little sweetnesses before—'

Knowing it would take Kitty at least two hours to 'get cleaned up' (bath, skin cream, make-up, selection of the proper attire for crossing the concourse of Central Station – not to speak of a four-hour journey by train), Emma set her alarm for six thirty, two hours (if that) being better than nothing. As it was, making breakfast *very* shortly thereafter in the clear light of early summer morn, she had time to glance over the remaining letters from Professor Wright's students (or, presumably, their fathers).

As she'd suspected, there was another outright offer of a bribe to waive the summer term research paper of the student in question ('It is surely unreasonable to expect one instructor to hold a student to the same standards established by his predecessor . . .') and three tear-stained pleas to give the students more time ('This is my last class before graduation . . .' 'I simply must pass this course, I have already been accepted to law school contingent on this term's grades . . .' 'If I don't pass this class I'll lose my place on the football team . . .') or to disregard the requirement entirely.

The letter from Doyle Dravitt requested an appointment to speak with 'Mrs Blackstone' on Tuesday, July fifteenth, at three p.m. at Mr Dravitt's downtown office in the Dravitt Building on Wall Street. 'Regarding arrangements for the completion of Mr Wilson Dravitt's Classics 102 class.'

Presumably, reflected Emma – making a neat packet of all offers and replacing them in the box of Etruscan materials – that attempt upon academic integrity would be made in person.

Emma's prior experience precluded the delusion that further sleep would be possible on the train to Seven Palms. Kitty invited Mary Blanque, Harry Garfield (the extremely handsome gentleman slated to play her love-slave in the desert) and Harry's friend Roger Clint (a member of the Evil Zahar's camel corps, despite his broken arm) to join her in her first-class compartment for cocktails, gossip and mah-jongg. ('Of course Zallie can come! He knows *all* the dirt on *everybody*!')

The hours were further enlivened – in between discussions of how many doubles were given for Thirteen Unique Wonders if the holder of that hand was West for the round and also West for the game, and did that beat out Four Blessings Hovering Around the Door? – by the armload of newspapers Zal brought with him. Kitty's speculation about Burt's theory was immediately capped by Roger's suggestion that Selina had been bribed by MGM to take her daughter to China via a slow boat (evidently, no one had heard of the ransom demand yet), and the *Examiner*'s 'proof' (from a woman who claimed to be Elena Montoya's sister) that Little Susy had died from drinking rat poison and her body buried by the nursemaid, who had been drunk at the time. (*How long would it take a drunken woman to dig even a shallow grave? And did anyone examine the earth in the garden beds? Or the garden shovel?*) The *Times* had amplified this tale with the contention that, in fact, the lethal liquid had been illegal gin made from stolen commercial alcohol, which had been 'denatured' (by government decree) with strychnine, and moreover Miss Montoya had been engaged in illicit sex with the little girl's father at the time.

There were also further details about the purchase of the lot in Palm Springs, and the building of the eight-bedroom courtyard house with a music room, a screening room (electricity provided by a generator on the premises, as the little desert village had none), a formal dining room overlooking a rose garden and yet another in-ground swimming pool ('You *gotta* have a pool if you live in one of those desert towns, honey!').

According to Mr Frank Pugh, all the papers agreed, no ransom note had been received. Pugh and the financial backers of Foremost Productions joined in their pleas that the police undertake no investigation of the crime 'until we know what they want.'

In time, she did in fact sleep, her head on Zal's shoulder and Buttercreme, pink tongue protruding half an inch, drooling gently in her lap. She dreamed of the dark, book-lined office at the university, of a man's body sprawled spreadeagled on the floor in the center of the room, papers littered everywhere around him. The desk itself was clear, as if someone had swept its surface with a furious arm, and another man beside the desk bent and straightened, bent and straightened, scrabbling through those scattered papers and glancing, again and again, at the dead man on the floor. A noise made him startle – and from another world entirely, she heard Zal's voice . . . *Might have surprised them. Maybe even recognized some of them* . . .

The searcher stood listening for a long moment. Then he bent and seized the dead man's heels. Dragged and pushed him out of sight of the door, between the desk and the window . . .

'. . . left town before her body could be discovered,' argued Harry Garfield persuasively. 'She'd know everybody would say she had a hand in it . . .'

Half waking, Emma blinked at the glare of the window, the miles of orchards and the distant, dusty green of mountains beyond.

'Was the kid insured?' asked Roger Clint.

'Left town how?' Zal spoke softly, his chest vibrating under Emma's cheek. 'All her cars were still there – the Rolls and the Mercer are both on blocks, according to Lupe's husband. What's she gonna do, take a taxi?'

'And pay with what?' added Mary's creamy South Carolina alto. 'After that chinchilla she bought herself last November? And the place in Palm Springs? And that latest car? You know how much a Velox costs? Even without that leopard-skin upholstery? And that trip to Paris she took with what's-his-name? Dex? Del? Works in the office over at Triangle? Pushin' Mr Ince's papers around won't pay for those shoes he wears, honey, or the silk shirts.'

'Dex Maiden?' inquired Kitty, knowledgeably. 'Sweetheart, I know *exactly* how much he spends on shoes. And he's almost worth it . . .'

'Don't you ever feed these poor guys, Kit?' added Zal, reaching down to offer Chang Ming a scrap of pastrami from his sandwich. 'Oops – Hey, Chang, it's time for your beating . . .'

Emma drifted back towards sleep.

'Oooh, mah-jongg, darlings! *Nobody* spurns the Lady of the Crimson Desert and lives!'

The Foremost Productions camp had been set up the previous day, twenty-five miles to the east of Seven Palms and close enough to the tiny oasis of Twenty-Nine Palms that water could be trucked in for the animals. (And, as an afterthought, for the extras.) Following an early dinner, ten hours of sleep at the Araby Hotel and a good breakfast, Emma felt up to boarding one of the studio's rented buses in the hot twilight of desert dawn with every insect in the barren landscape humming and buzzing and clicking. 'This's when they all come out,' Rog Clint informed her, picking up Chang Ming's carry-box in his good hand. 'Once the sun's been up an hour, heat'll kill 'em.'

Camp Turpitude – as the crew referred to it – covered half an acre in the midst of the so-called Colorado Desert, including the animal pens. A rancher from Seven Palms had contributed ten camels and a ranch hand named Dave to look after them; a date farmer from Indio who called himself Omar al-Salem but was in fact a full-blooded Cahuilla named Marty Morongo rented Foremost another twenty-five. To these, Grenville Torley had added a train of a hundred and fifty – which he and Morongo petted like children

– as well as three lions, two jackals and a capuchin monkey named Mrs Bennett. Tents and tent-canvas shelters stretched everywhere, and a gasoline generator pumped electricity to a hundred fans in make-up tents, the film storage shelter, the mess tent, changing tents of the principal stars and the lions' tent. The lions got three fans. The extras got one. Doc Larousse, who, in addition to setting up the lights, was in charge of the generator, pontificated to anyone who'd stand still and listen that he'd *told* Pugh they'd need such an arrangement if the shooting schedule slipped from June to July . . .

'Pugh'll need to rent Gren Torley's lions again,' Zal observed, when Emma remarked on the oven-hot quarters of the extras. 'There's *lots* of extras in LA.'

Caravans swayed across the dunes. Young Lord Harlan Fairfax staggered, sweating with extreme realism, over the same dunes just out of camera range of the camel tracks, and fell gasping on the sand, for ten takes. Plus close-ups. Poor Rosebud Mary performed the same activity on a nearby dune, clothed – for purposes of the plot – in the rags of what had once been pre-War 'combinations' (well did Emma recall such voluminous ensembles from her school-days), as well as copious applications of olive oil and the juice of aloes. ('It could be worse,' Emma comforted her. 'In ancient times, they used mud.' 'Fuck you, Duchess.') Zal, Chip and director Larry Palmer placed the cameras carefully so that shadows wouldn't make it obvious that these shots were taken early in the day – they'd be intercut (according to the scenario) with shots of the noon sun glaring like the Wrath of God overhead. Larry Palmer, (*Thank goodness*, reflected Emma) was not a man to insist on realism to the extent of putting a third of his crew in hospital with heatstroke – unlike some directors she'd encountered.

As the coming evening moderated the heat – with the temperature still hovering at ninety degrees – Kitty, resplendent in black silk with her jeweled dagger glittering evilly at her belt, sneered at Darlene crumpled on the sand before her in her underwear (Emma searched through the script to discover how poor Rosebud Mary had managed to lose her clothing so soon after leaving Port Said) and turned away. She was immediately helped down from Ariadne the Camel's back and replaced by a young extra named Bobbie Wiegand who actually could ride a camel.

'Which is an insult to poor Ariadne,' grumbled Gren Torley, as Bobbie – clothed in black silk and a splendid black wig (evidently, no woman in the Crimson Desert had ever heard of veils) – rode to join 'her' band of warriors on a distant dune. Rosebud, in the foreground, stretched a despairing hand after her, pleading not to be left alone to die. (*Did she actually walk all this way across the Empty Quarter wearing those high-heeled shoes?*) 'Ariadne knows this business and wouldn't let Miss de la Rose fall off her if you gave her a cup of sugar.'

The shot was wrapped in three takes, to everyone's intense relief, and they all went back to the camp. (Close-ups to be done first thing tomorrow, when Darlene's make-up was fresh.)

At intervals in this activity, with a certain grimness, Emma retreated to the fan-cooled mess tent and devoted herself to the question of how to remove Little Susy from *Our Tiny Miracle* three-quarters of the way through – before she managed to prevent the wicked Jed Blankenship from blowing up her parents' gold mine – without making the story an irredeemable tragedy. But she found her mind returning to speculations on the accuracy of her half-recalled dream, and wishing she could go back to the university offices and have another look at the floor.

Which they mopped, so it wouldn't tell me anything . . .

But how else could he have hit the back *of his head on the edge of the desk, and still ended up where he was found?*

She unpacked and reread all seven letters from students (or their parents).

She counted thirteen different varieties of handwriting or typescript on the random pages that had been mingled with Wright's notes. One of these student papers had the pages numbered and the name *Nuddle* typed at the top. Pages five, eight, nine, ten and sixteen were missing, as well as anything that might have come after sixteen – page fifteen ended in mid-sentence. Well aware that she should be concentrating on who was actually going to go down that mineshaft and dispose of the dynamite, instead she compared the handwriting of Messrs Ort, Rampick and Paine – and the typeface on the letters of Messrs Farrell and Dravitt, and Miss Barger – with the pleading (or bribing) letters. The letter from Mr Wilson Dravitt that begged for exemption from turning in the research paper altogether ('This is my last class before graduation . . .') had not been typed on the same machine that had produced the letter from his . . . father, presumably. Nor was the paper the same. It was, however, exactly the same paper as that of the letters from Messrs Ort and

Paine, and Miss Barger – presumably, whatever was cheapest at the stationery store near the campus.

So what does that tell me, if anything?

She checked the Pekes' water bowl, dipped from the drip tray of the icebox that had been lugged out to the encampment with the gasoline generator, then turned back to study Mr Doyle Dravitt's summons to an appointment. She had phoned the number given on the letter in the ten minutes in which she had been awake, between her arrival yesterday evening at the Araby Hotel and collapsing into dreamless slumber in front of an electric fan in her large private suite. Mr Dravitt's secretary, sounding nervous to the point of terror, had done everything in his power to coax or bully her into returning the following day to meet with Mr Dravitt ('There's a train at three twenty-eight from Seven Palms that gets into Central Station at seven thirty. It's only ten minutes by taxi to the office and I would be happy to schedule the appointment . . .').

Only two pages – unnumbered and without superscription – of repetitive and circumlocutory plagiarism from Livy were typed on what looked like Wilson Dravitt's machine – which admittedly looked very like that of Henry Ort (same manufacturer, presumably), only Ort used different margins and knew how to spell 'predecessors.'

Why are there pages missing?

Why the duplicated pages from Wright's work? And why was the typeface on two of them the same?

What was in that account of painted tombs and Egyptian grave goods that was so important?

Important enough to kill *over?*

That's ridiculous. Zal's joking aside, this is archaeology we're talking about, not buried treasure . . .

Two fragments of a Twenty-Fifth Dynasty Egyptian votive did *not* constitute 'buried treasure' to anyone but her father.

She realized that beyond the pool of lantern light on the table, the last of the voices in the mess tent had disappeared. Frenchie the Cook went out, bearing a box of tin dishes in his arms. When he came back in, Zal was with him – Zal thick with dust save for his face and hands where he'd dunked them in one of the water troughs. 'Gotta pack it up, Em,' the cameraman informed her, as Frenchie switched off the big electric fan. 'Bus is loading.'

It was dark outside. It was still ninety degrees under the tent canvas, and without the fan, it felt like a hundred and fifty. But the Pekes snuffed the intoxication of the night air and, when the distant coyotes raised their voices across the desert wastes, lifted their flat little noses to the moon and joined in.

They drove back to Seven Palms by moonlight, every window in the bus open and bottles of tepid beer passed around as if Prohibition had never existed. Black Jasmine and Chang Ming panted happily on Emma's lap, and Zal's, still ecstatically sniffing the night. Buttercreme dozed in the safety of Kitty's arms, while Kitty, Darlene and Harry Garfield compared notes about the comeliest of the camel drivers. Beyond the open windows, the desert was a world of indigo and crystal, a different planet, thought Emma, from the timeless towers of Oxford, the misty softness of those familiar streets through which she still walked in dreams, trying to find her way home.

'We better not get another damn flat,' groused somebody in the darkness of the bus. (They'd had one on the way out. The road to the camp was unpaved.)

Someone in the rear of the bus began to sing, 'There's a Long, Long Trail a-Windin'.'

Against the shoulder of Mount San Jacinto, widely scattered pinpricks of dull gold kerosene light speckled the darkness.

'Palm Springs,' identified Zal softly. 'How you feel about getting enough sleep tonight, Em?'

'How did Romeo feel about getting Juliet's telephone number?' returned Emma, leaning back so that their shoulders touched in the darkness. 'Why do you ask?'

'Well, depending on how you feel about waking up at four a.m. to head back out to Camp Turpitude, I thought maybe after dinner, instead of making love like crazed weasels, you and I could drive out to Selina's house there and have a look at the place.'

'Only if we can make love like crazed weasels afterwards.'

Hollywood, Emma reflected, was definitely having the effect on her morals that her aunts would have warned her about, had they ever in their wildest dreams have thought she would end up here.

'You have my promise.'

NINE

They got the address from Harry Garfield, who had attended enough of Selina Sutton's desert fêtes to remember it without reference to his (coded) pocket address book ('You never know who's gonna pay somebody to steal things . . .'). The house, nestled under the shoulder of the San Jacinto mountains, was a sprawling ersatz-Spanish palazzo with a Palladian pillared porch and a couple of out-of-scale Baroque window surrounds on the upper floor. Emma could easily believe it had cost Mrs Sutton (actually poor Susy) fifty thousand dollars (not counting the door handles), but why anyone would deliberately pay for architectural ugliness had always been beyond her.

(*Did conservative Athenians make rude comments about Corinthian pillars when they first appeared on temples?*)

A full moon sailed galleon-like in the black crystal sky. No light broke the dim shape of the house. The 'village' of Palm Springs was innocent of both electricity and telephone service (and apparently proud of the fact). Through the iron scrollwork of the padlocked gate, Emma saw a coyote trot unconcernedly across the gravel drive. The lawn did not look as if it had been watered or trimmed since Easter.

'Palm Springs isn't a place you want to come in summer if you can help it,' remarked Zal, returning with a ladder from the small truck he'd borrowed from the lighting crew. The flashlight in his free hand was unlit. 'Selina would throw parties out here, then drive all night to get back to Hollywood in time to have Susy in front of the cameras in the morning; no wonder the woman sniffs cocaine like King George snorting snuff. If you ask me, that's where most of her money went, never mind buying this house and taking her snugglepup to Paris to shop for shoes.'

He handed Emma the flashlight and set the ladder against the wall. Emma followed him up it dubiously. In between Lord Harlan's attempted flight from the Bedouin portion of Camp Turpitude (twelve takes of him being stopped by the Evil Zahar's guards, plus close-ups) and the desert confrontation between Zahar (mounted on

Ariadne the Camel) and the under-clad Rosebud (*Why is she not sunburnt*?), a telegram had reached the camp HQ tent heralding the arrival – the following day – of Frank Pugh, with two of Foremost's principal stockholders and a representative of the company's chain of affiliated independent theaters. All they would need, reflected Emma, to add to their concerns about a missing child star and an exorbitant ransom would be a lead cameraman and a part-time scenarist jailed for burglary.

Particularly if it turned out that the house had in fact been sold and was now inhabited by a wealthy middle-aged couple from Delaware.

'Don't tell me you know how to pick locks,' she whispered as they circled the house.

'Nah.' Zal's decrepit sneakers crunched on the gravel of the path. The shrubbery along the wall – rose bushes and jasmine – was intermixed with a forest of hardier weeds, but it was all parched and brittle. *Surely if she'd sold the place, the new owners would have kept it up?* 'But here below the hills, the wind can get up pretty strong.' He pulled a couple of clean handkerchiefs from his pocket – he seldom carried less than a dozen, to keep his camera lenses spotless – and wrapped them around his hand, to pick up a stout frond of palm from among the weeds. Palms surrounded the house: spikey, fan-shaped palmettos, or twelve- and fifteen-foot feather dusters, like college students in raccoon-skin coats of dead foliage, against the starry sky. 'Broken windows aren't uncommon.'

'Such a thing would certainly be convenient,' agreed Emma.

'Sure would.' Zal waded through the wasted brown foliage overgrowing the steps from a French door to the dry swimming pool. 'Get back, Em,' he warned, and gripping the spiny stem of the frond like a spear, he drove it into the glass pane nearest the handle of the door. Then he sprang back, caught Emma's arm and dragged her into the shadows behind a desiccated screen of lantana bushes.

Nothing stirred within the house. Close by, something scuttled in the shrubbery, and a bat flitted crazily against the moonlight.

Zal glanced at his wristwatch and didn't move.

When five minutes had passed, he stepped cautiously out and crossed to the broken French door. For another minute, he stood listening. Emma had 'doctored' enough scenarios to fully expect masked bravos – led by the Evil Miss Sutton – to burst through the door the moment he reached inside for the latch ('Ha! No man spurns the Evil Miss Sutton and lives . . .').

But Zal motioned her to stay where she was, reached through the broken pane without incident and, a moment later, slipped inside. The flashlight's beam – muted by a handkerchief or his hand – flickered dully against the closed curtains, then retreated further in. It brightened as he reappeared and signed her to approach.

Zal had already checked the mailbox outside the gate. It had been crammed with bills, bank notices and advertising circulars, more of which piled the gilt-and-enamel telephone table in the hall. 'All for Selina.' Zal directed the flashlight beam on a handful as he sorted them. 'Postmarks in March and April. She probably stopped the mail in April, since that's when it gets hot out here. No other owner.'

'When did you say she'd gotten into trouble over – what was it, radium toothpaste?'

'Almost two years.' Zal shuffled another handful of envelopes. 'That's when she supposedly sold the place. A couple here from Frank. One from Goldwyn at Metro. Whew,' he added, holding up a small, expensive-looking envelope to the light. 'Maya Pearl. Hot stuff.'

'Maya Pearl?'

'Woman who's got a big place out past Indio. Iron Joe Ardizzone runs a distillery on her property. She brings in coke from Mexico and holds the *really* hot parties, the ones you go to if you want things you can't get away with even in Hollywood.'

'I was not aware,' remarked Emma drily, 'that there *was* anything you couldn't get away with in Hollywood.'

Behind the thick spectacles, Zal's eyes glinted suddenly somber and angry. 'Oh, yeah,' he said. 'There is.'

'I don't think I want to know.'

'Sure wish I didn't. Doesn't look like anybody's home.' He dropped the letters back on to the table and led the way into the dark of the house. The rooms were stifling with the trapped heat of many days, and black as a cave, cut by stilettos of moonlight. The kitchen sink was bone-dry. Emma had glimpsed a water tank behind the house, but when she turned the taps, nothing came out but the groan of the empty pipes. Despite this evidence of neglect, they checked every room and found nothing but an assortment of Patou, Poiret, and Lanvin in the closets, and in one bedroom, three drawers of gentlemen's shirts and underthings. 'Makes me wish I *was* a burglar.' Zal held a very fine blue Van Heusen up against his chest. 'Fifteen-inch collar, it looks like – Burt's heavier than that.'

There was also a filing cabinet crammed with some of the most repulsive pornography Emma had ever seen – not that she had seen anything worse than a few of Beardsley's steamier efforts from the '90s.

'I suppose one could get into serious trouble for interfering with United States mail?' she asked, when they returned to the front hall.

'Oh, yeah.'

'Then if you would hold this torch for a minute . . .' Emma dug in her pocket and produced the notebook in which it was her duty to count the number of close-ups Kitty got per scene. (Darlene Golden employed one of the ladies in wardrobe to keep a similar count of *her* close-ups, lest her rival be unfairly advantaged.)

'Some of those envelopes from department stores and banks have a distinctly *businesslike* appearance. If we ever found ourselves in need of evidence for anything, someone could probably go back to' – she held up one of the envelopes to the light – 'Bullock's, or Cartier's, or the Chase National Bank, and find the originals of these communications . . .'

'. . . and see how much they were dunning her for.' Zal cocked his head to one side, watching as Emma wrote down the list of senders and postmarks. 'You're pretty sure Selina's behind it.'

'I don't know.' Emma drew back in disgust at the idea that she'd believe a drunkard's ramblings about a woman who might very well be a captive somewhere, in fear for her life and quite possibly worse . . . Against her will, she saw again the fleeting glimpse of some of the more brutal photographs in that filing cabinet in Miss Sutton's bedroom. *Surely they wouldn't* . . .

The pictures had not looked staged. Nor had all of the women being so used been adults.

How much of what Burt said was the truth?

Over against that slurred, rambling voice, she seemed to see Miss Sutton's casual glance at Susy, while her attention had remained focused on the columnist. *Nothing really happened, did it, dear?*

She took a deep breath. 'In a way, I hope she is behind it. Because Susy is her meal ticket. Whatever she threatens, she won't actually harm her daughter.'

Zal was silent as they stepped back out into the drench of desert moonlight, and Emma held the flashlight as he relatched the door and arranged the palm-frond convincingly stuck through the broken glass. As they returned to the truck, she asked, 'Is there any other place Miss Sutton could have taken her? If it *was* Miss Sutton . . . Burt said she had a place in Big Bear.'

'That's a three-hour drive,' said Zal. 'Not counting the time it'll take creeping around all those little mountain roads trying to find the place once we get there. And Frank may have gotten instructions about the ransom.'

The lighting crew had rented the truck in Seven Palms, a pre-War Ford. Privately, Emma would not have been surprised if it had antedated the Spanish–American War. She had been trained by her father – and later in the Volunteer Ambulance Drivers – to catch the precise timing of when, during Zal's cranking, to throw over the spark lever and adjust the throttle. Working as a team, they managed to get the superannuated vehicle into a shuddering idle with only four tries. 'Whether he's told those backers of his or not – that's another story.'

'Which I suppose we'll find out tomorrow.'

Zal mimed astonishment as he clambered into the cab. 'Such trust is a shining inspiration to us all. Damn it,' he added, as the engine died again.

Owing to the fact that Zal duly kept his earlier promise to her, Emma dozed on the bus to Camp Turpitude in the pre-dawn dark of the following morning, Buttercreme's wicker carry-box on her lap. Even a tire puncture on the stony, unpaved road failed to wake her. Harry Garfield was scheduled to be devoured by lions that morning, while it was still relatively cool (although Emma considered eighty-five degrees a questionable definition of *relatively*). 'Heat like this ain't good for them,' worried Gren Torley, who had spent the night at the camp, as he refilled the huge water pans in the great cats' shaded enclosure. Emma debated whether to ask the animal wrangler about his sister-in-law's real-estate holdings, but decided against it. The wiry little man was, she knew, due in the wardrobe tent, to be fitted out in a copy of Harry's gallabiyah.

As far as she knew, no explanation was to be offered the audience as to why Harry, who had been fairly unclothed throughout most of the film, would suddenly cover up (after being flogged) to be thrown to the lions. Torley – who did not resemble the six-foot-two, dazzlingly handsome Harry in the slightest – was doubling for the actor simply because Torley regularly wrestled in play with his pets and had no qualms about doing so before the camera, qualms that the rest of the company experienced wholeheartedly. An hour and a half later, standing beside the wooden enclosure in which the – *does one call such an event a lionization?* – would take place, while Zal and Chip Thaw set up their cameras, Emma considered the two men in their identical robes, the bald-pated Torley further embellished in a dark wig and a fake mustache that wouldn't have fooled a child at thirty feet . . .

But, of course, he *was* going to be shot from thirty feet away, and from behind. It would be Harry in the close-ups, screaming as he was devoured by a lion-skin rug from the prop department. And it would be Harry's body – in a strategically placed rag, a lot of blood and not much else – that would occupy the final close-up, while poor Lord Harlan and the Evil Zahar watched from a dais high on the side of the enclosure.

And *that*, realized Emma suddenly, was how she was going to write herself out of killing off the Tiny Miracle and turning in a scenario that nobody would pay money to see.

Reasonably confident that the lionization would take at least five hours (if one included close-ups of all parties involved, including the lions), Emma wove her way back through the Bedouin tents of Zahar's followers, to the section of Camp Turpitude where the tents – though outwardly Bedouin-ish – faced away from any possible camera angle. These contained things like racks of cloaks, gallabiyahs, turbans and armor, or long tables where extras from the Sonoratown section of Los Angeles were applying make-up or drinking warm Coca-Cola. In this quarter of the camp, generator cables snaked back and forth over the ground and moving fan blades glittered in the shadows of the tents.

And an incongruous form ducked around the tent nearest Emma and nearly ran into her.

'Mrs Turnbit!' Emma exclaimed.

The columnist made one instinctive feint in the direction from which she'd come, thought better of it and turned back with a beaming smile. 'Mrs Blackstone—'

'Emma,' corrected Emma, returning the smile. 'What on earth are you doing here?'

'*Can* you ask?' Thelma Turnbit wagged her plump hand in a flirtatious gesture twenty-five years too young for her. 'I heard that the most amazing sequences were being filmed out here, so I thought I'd risk it and nip out to have a look. Surely Mr Pugh could have no objections.'

'I wouldn't go so far as to say that,' Emma temporized. (*And 'nip' is a generous construction to put on a drive of over a hundred miles . . . with or without punctures.*) 'And you may want to be a little careful who sees you. He's going to be here later today.'

'*Really?*'

The line was perfectly spoken – Thelma Turnbit had spent ten years around film actors and had learned every gesture and head tilt and movement of the eyes.

She's lying.

Two figures emerged from the dressing tent across the way: Darlene Golden (still in an ever-more-bedraggled-and-torn set of combinations and high-heeled shoes) . . . and a young gentleman whom Emma recognized as Rex Niddy, a 'Hollywood News' writer from *Photoplay*.

She knew Mr Pugh would be here today.

Young Mr Niddy checked in his tracks. Darlene tightened her grip on his elbow and kept walking: 'Everyone is just devastated,' Darlene continued. 'And poor Mr Pugh is beside himself! I think that's why he's coming out here today, because he's so concerned that this . . . this cloud of anxiousness' – she recited the words carefully – 'that's darkened everyone's days doesn't affect other productions . . .'

No, reflected Emma, as Mrs Turnbit scraped her off with a polite excuse and headed for the wardrobe tent. *He's coming out here today to show the studio backers that Foremost still has a viable property in the works.* And to check on whether *Our Tiny Miracle* could be salvaged with a little fancy footwork.

Would a writer from Photoplay *share a tip about Pugh's visit with a columnist from* Screen World? She doubted it.

Pugh would be livid.

When, a little later as she walked the dogs (who seemed perfectly happy for another chance to claim every tent pole and crate in the camp as their own, the heat notwithstanding), she caught a glimpse of another man, in a city suit, city shoes, notebook in hand, emerging from the make-up tent, she was sure of it. 'Someone tipped reporters off,' she said to Herr Volmort, as she stepped into the gloom of the tent. The dogs made a beeline for the path of the nearest electric fan.

'He's the fourth one this morning.' The little man's pale eyes narrowed. Kind and scholarly, the make-up chief looked and sounded like the direst villain of melodrama – Emma half expected him to produce a dagger from his trouser pocket and hurl it at the reporter's retreating back. 'One of them asked if I'd heard the rumor that a ransom note was received Friday.'

'Good Heavens.' She hoped she sounded surprised. 'And was one?'

By his enigmatic look, she guessed her expression of innocence was less convincing even than some of Kitty's cinematic efforts.

'I hope they paid their informant well.' He turned back to his mirror, setting out brushes, wax, pots of dark stage blood, for all the world like a scientific Mephistopheles preparing some experiment of nameless horror. He then spoiled the illusion by adding, 'I have some ice chips here – in that chest – if you'd like some for *die kleinen Wächter*.' His name for the Pekes: *the little guardians*. 'Whoever informed the press, Mr Pugh has his bankers with him today, and he will not want an audience.'

Unless Mr Pugh called them himself, reflected Emma, returning to Kitty's tent with a small sack of ice chips to put in the dogs' water (and a few for her own tepid lemonade). Like the lions Big Joe, Sheba and Randall, the Pekes didn't do well in the heat. *To manipulate a situation?* Nudge the financial powers that were behind Foremost into stumping up a hundred thousand dollars – nearly the cost of the entire film! – to retrieve a little girl?

Was somebody saying, *It's too much risk. How do we know they'll deliver, and then we're out a hundred grand plus the cost of the funeral?*

Was somebody saying, *This is comin' out of your salary, Pugh?*

And do I seriously think Mr Pugh would then go against the money men?

Who, then?

It was extremely difficult to sit down in Kitty's tent and rough out where a double could be used to show Susy buried in a landslide (*And will Mr Pugh insist on a genuine landslide*?), to be rescued in long shot by a grizzled prospector (Gully Ackroyd – the elderly actor specialized in grizzled something-or-others) . . .

Long shot of Grizzled Prospector lifting a limp double from a pile of dirt and stones . . .

Scene 500 – Nell and Fred weeping when the news of their daughter's death is brought to them.

Intertitle – Ten Years Pass

Scene 501 – Repeat of landslide sequence, gel iris clouding edges of shots to indicate that it's a dream.

Scene 502 – Older Susy [now 16] awakens in a beautiful four-poster bed in a handsome Boston mansion, shocked and terrified at her dream

Scene 503 – Older Susy runs to clutch the Grizzled Prospector and his wife (both a little more grizzled than in previous sequence, but now obviously wealthy citizens)

Intertitle – 'I remember! I remember! Oh, horrible, I remember!'

Scene 504 – Prospector and his wife exclaiming in amazement and joy.

Intertitle – 'After all these years! When we found you, you didn't even remember your own name, darling.'

Intertitle – 'It's Susy! Susy Martin! Oh, Mama! Oh, Papa! They must be so worried about me!'

Scene 505 – Older Susy embraces Prospector's wife, who begins to weep with both joy and grief

Intertitle – 'You remember them! Oh, but that means you won't be OUR Little Susy anymore!'

Scene 506 – Train station in Western town. Older Susy, dressed as a fashionable young lady, leaning out of train window as the train pulls in, scanning the platform

Scene 507 – Nell and Fred clutching the telegram they received

Close on telegram – Mama! Papa! I am alive! I am coming home!

(Will Mr Pugh give me trouble if I point out to him that exclamation points are never used in telegrams?)

Scene 508 – Older Susy springs down from train into her parents' arms. Prospector and wife, also prosperously dressed, debark behind her, stand happily close while Older Susy is reunited with her weeping parents . . .

And don't you dare, don't you DARE, show this to your bankers and tell them you can still release that film even if they don't pay the ransom . . .

For a moment, she sat in the stuffy heat of the tent, wondering if she should tear up her notes and tell Mr Pugh that she couldn't, after all, come up with a way to finish what would be billed as Susy Sweetchild's last film.

She closed her eyes. *If I do that, he'll only find someone else.*

And if I quit Foremost, where can I go? Work for Harry Cohn at Columbia ('The only man in Hollywood even Darlene Golden won't sleep with!' Kitty had described that executive). O*r the Warner Brothers? Or stay on as Kitty's lady-in-waiting and dog-brusher?* That seventy-five dollars from sorting illegible Etruscan notes wouldn't remain in her bank account long. (*And who would have clubbed poor Professor Wright over a class paper?*)

Were those strange, duplicated pages evidence of plagiarism?

But several of the suspect pages had been typed on Wright's own machine.

Her father had always told her, *Find out what you're actually talking about before you make any decisions. Sometimes by the time you get to a crossroad, you'll find the map pinned to the nearest tree.*

It was just possible that Mr Pugh had hinted to all those reporters to be on the set this afternoon to somehow pressure his backers into approving the ransom money. Nobody – not even men who financed a Hollywood studio – wanted to get their names plastered in every film magazine in the country for not paying to save Little Susy's life.

Such trust is a shining inspiration to us all.

Damn you, Zal.

Frank Pugh and the three Foremost backers who lived in Los Angeles arrived in Camp Turpitude just after lunch that day – Wednesday, July sixteenth – in Pugh's gleaming black Pierce-Arrow. The Evil Zahar had just discovered Rosebud's hiding place in her camp and had ordered Harry to be dragged away by the guards (to be devoured by Big Joe, Sheba and Randall a few hundred feet later). She was confronting poor Lord Harlan – struggling manfully in the grip of yet more guards – when Pugh's gritty voice boomed, 'Cut!'

Larry Palmer took one look at the three nondescript, hard-faced men sweating in business suits beside Pugh and yelled 'CUT!' into the middle of what everybody had hoped (after seven previous tries) would be the final take of the scene (not counting close-ups).

Palmer may have been an uninspired director, but he was an authority on which side of the bread had butter on it. 'Mr Pugh.' He didn't bow, pull his forelock or prostrate himself to kiss his boss's shoes, but a youth spent on the theater stage had transformed his voice into a symphonic interpretation of all three actions.

'I'd like to introduce Mr Bandog, Mr Goldman, and Mr Lutz,' announced Pugh – to the assembly at large, but only the featured players, and the director, were invited to come up and shake hands. 'They're here to see with their own eyes that although Foremost Productions is, of course, devastated by the heinous abduction of our Little Susy, it goes without saying that all cast members and all crew members are dedicated professionals – as dedicated as Susy herself! – whose work adheres to its usual high standards despite any and all adversity.'

No mention, Emma observed, of Selina Sutton.

'All of you – please do answer all and any questions that our guests may put to you. We wish to show them that shaken though we are by these horrible events, Foremost Productions is bigger than any single star, any single production, any single element of this community.'

Emma wondered whether Conrad Fishbein had written this stirring peroration. And as the afternoon progressed, she observed that the studio chief was careful to keep his guests under his eye, and to make note of which crew members they spoke to.

She observed also that Pugh tended to suggest that Messrs Bandog, Goldman and Lutz speak to Darlene, or Kitty, or the most lovely of the extras, a young lady named Dove Singleton. This the oleaginous Mr Lutz and the trimly mustachioed Mr Bandog seemed delighted to do. Mr Goldman – tall, elderly and strongly resembling Cato the Censor in a Brooks Brothers suit – merely regarded his colleagues and everything else around him with calculating distrust.

Iced tea – the ice was imported from Los Angeles in an insulated box – was procured from the mess tent. The actresses retreated into the stuffy shade of the nearest pavilions with the two more susceptible financiers following like Mary's Little Lamb. During these interludes, Mr Pugh made repeated attempts to speak to the hovering journalists, but these interlopers fleeted away like guppies before him, and, Emma noted, Pugh did not follow. He was not about to leave his 'guests' unattended.

When Zal, Chip and Doc Larousse's myrmidons (all pouring sweat like racehorses) began to reset cameras and reflectors for the close-ups – the lighting among the tents was tricky, because the whole sequence was supposedly taking place at night – Emma again retired to Kitty's tent with another bag of ice chips for the dogs. (Three extras had already succumbed to heat exhaustion.) The heat, and lack of sleep, made her feel drowsy and stupid, but she knew Pugh would eventually turn up asking about the changes to the scenario. She could follow the progress of the young hero's reiterated pleas for his beloved's life by the occasional 'Cut!' that drifted, like a stray church bell, through the hot afternoon air.

When you reach the crossroad, the instructions will be pinned to a tree . . .

Doubtless, she reflected, *with the Evil Zahar's ruby-hilted dagger. I can't do it. I won't do it.*

She tucked her notes on *Tiny Miracle* out of the way, brought out the seven incomplete student papers and moved aside a make-up kit the size of a Mark IV tank to make room for them on the folding table. In another stack, she assembled her tentative ordering of Professor Wright's monograph, book and article. Then she began to work through them, sheet by sheet, comparing them as if they were pottery shards: handwriting, typewriter lettering (the ribbon on the machine apparently shared by Alonzo Paine and Wilson Dravitt was so old as to be nearly illegible) and, in two inconclusive cases, characteristic mis-spellings. *I'll have to ask Julia Denham about these students . . . and about Doyle Dravitt.*

Were Paine and young Wilson flatmates? Two of those anomalous, duplicated pages were in that same faded-out ribbon . . .

She would also, she reflected, have to ask Julia about the potsherds and fragments. Thirty-four were listed in Wright's notes; by her count Friday night, the box had contained only twenty-six, some carefully wrapped in tissue, others simply dumped in on top. A count that was off by one or even two, she reflected, might be attributed to carelessness or too many nights with too little sleep . . .

But not eight.

The same people who helped themselves to Professor Wright's bookshelf . . . ?

Black Jasmine leaped to his feet from in front of the electric fan and barked a shrill challenge. Buttercreme scuttled for cover. Shadow darkened the tent door.

'Mrs Blackstone?'

It was Pugh.

'I was wondering if you'd made progress on – well, on the rewrites we discussed back in town.' He came over to her table, picked up the top sheet of her notes (uninvited), then looked down at her with a puzzled frown.

'I have not,' replied Emma, 'made the progress you had hoped, Mr Pugh. This is mostly because I'm still grappling with the problem of how to remove poor Susy from the story without turning it into an unmitigated tragedy. Given the humor in the first two acts of the story' – she knew the first five reels had already been shot – 'simply changing the tone that sharply would be jarring, to say the least. And because if we *do* need to film an alternate ending – God forbid! – everyone in the audience will know why.'

Pugh opened his mouth to object to this view of the matter, and Emma went on quietly, 'The critics will tear it apart, Mr Pugh. I haven't found a way around that yet. This' – she gestured to the neat stacks of academic (and sophomoric) prose – 'has been my way of clearing my mind, so that I can approach the project again this afternoon with new perspective.'

The studio head rumbled deep in his chest, like a dragon with indigestion. But whatever else could be said of him, Pugh wasn't stupid. He understood the problem. 'Do what you can, Duchess,' he said at last, and looked vaguely around as if wondering why there was no plate of cookies handy. 'Maybe we can have an ending scene with her mom and pop standing by her grave in front of the mine, and we see her face appear in the clouds over the mountains? Kind of giving them her blessing? They can do that in processing, and we've still got some of the cut footage from *Susy and the Bad Men* . . . But we gotta have something.'

Not with Susy's face floating in the clouds over her grave, we don't!

She hoped her expression of calm inquiry was better than her earlier attempt to look innocent for Herr Volmort.

'Thing is, yesterday we got a second ransom note. It was handed in at the front gate – Floyd didn't see the person who delivered it. They've upped the ante to two hundred thou. The hand-off is for Sunday night, at the Tar Pits, out near the oil fields on Wilshire west of town.'

'Is that why you've brought your – guests – here today?' asked Emma softly. 'To show them that the studio can afford to lose that much?' And, when Pugh hesitated: 'Do they know about the second note?'

What Pugh would have responded to this, Emma never knew.

Because the muted hum of the camp was suddenly swamped by shouting. Zal's assistant Herbie Carboy was yelling, 'Mr Pugh! Mr Pugh!' and two wardrobe assistants dashed past the bright triangle of the tent's entrance.

'Mr Pugh!'

Pugh strode from the tent – Emma had sensed that he was keyed up for nearly anything – Emma herself hurrying at his heels. The set among the tents had been deserted, the lines of string that demarcated the shot trampled into the dust. The cameras were missing, carried off bodily – tripods and all – by Zal and Chip the moment people started running towards the edge of the camp.

These – and the viol played by the middle Rothstein Boy – stood beside the last of the tents, guarded by Chip Thaw, while everyone else in the camp, it seemed (except Darlene, Miss Singleton and Messrs Bandog and Lutz, who apparently were otherwise occupied), streamed out into the desert beyond. Emma stopped beside them, shaded her eyes . . .

And saw, coming down the dune that backed the camp, director Larry Palmer – surrounded by Zal, Harry, Ken Elmore and assorted members of the Evil Zahar's guard – carrying the unconscious form of Selina Sutton in his arms.

TEN

'I don't know.' Selina threshed her head back and forth on the flat infirmary pillow and brought her knuckles to her forehead. Tears trickled from those doe-like dark eyes. 'I was blindfolded – they made me drink something. Walked me in darkness down the hall, I think. I can't remember.'

She looked up then, clutched desperately at Pugh's wrist. 'Please! Please, do whatever they ask! Anything to save my poor little girl . . .'

Kitty murmured, 'I'll take that,' to the mess-tent boy who'd just rushed into the Camp Turpitude infirmary tent with a glass of water. She looked around, possibly for a clean facecloth but coincidentally to make sure that at least half of the journalists crowding the open tent flaps had cameras. She poured just enough water on the facecloth to wet it through (not spilling so much as a drop on to her silken pantaloons or her diaphanous cloak). Wringing it out, she laid it tenderly over the prostrate woman's forehead and looked up into Pugh's face. 'Is there anything we can do, Frank?'

Florence Nightingale could not have spoken more kindly. Cameras blazed and rattled like an artillery barrage. Pugh appeared to be on the verge of apoplexy.

'Please!' Again, Selina seized Pugh's hand. 'Please, no police! They said they'd kill her – they'd kill us both – if you brought the police in. Oh, Frank, pay them what they ask!' She clung tighter, and the tent walls bulged inward from the press of journalists who couldn't see over the crowd in the entryway.

'Did you see them?' asked Zal.

Selina shook her head. 'Sometimes I was blindfolded, or the room they kept me in was shuttered, dark. I begged them to let me see my darling Susy, see with my own eyes that she was well. They just laughed at me.' Her voice caught on a sob. 'But sometimes I would hear her crying in the night. I don't know how many nights I was there. Whatever it was they gave me to drink – it was hard to keep track of the time.'

She began to weep again, and Dr Plaister – whose job at Foremost seemed, to Emma, to consist of writing prescriptions for cocaine and performing the occasional abortion – reached down to stroke her wrist. 'She must rest,' he said to Pugh. 'I'll take her back to the hotel, but she must have quiet. We're not within thirty miles of a house, in the direction of the desert. She must be exhausted, and suffering from heatstroke. She needs rest.' He turned to the men and women gathered both in the tent and outside its entrance. 'All of you. Please. She must have rest.'

'Please,' whispered Selina, as she sank back on to the pillows and Kitty gently adjusted the infirmary's fan so that the cool air would waft across her (stinting a horse-wrangler and the extras who had been brought in with heat exhaustion earlier in the day). Selina's dark eyes gazed pleadingly up into Pugh's, even as they began to slip closed. 'I beg of you, Frank, save my child!'

'Look,' said Kitty, as she, Emma and Zal retreated in the direction of the set, leaving the three financiers and Pugh to glance worriedly at one another and at the phalanx of journalists clustered thick outside the infirmary tent.

She held up the damp facecloth which she'd retrieved, and opened it to display swatches of powder and rouge. 'The rouge is Persian Bloom – the shade she usually wears – and it was put on today. So was the powder: Pompeïa, also her usual brand. If she was kidnapped, then I'm Grover Cleveland's long-lost love-child. Did you see her dress?'

'It was clean,' said Emma quietly. 'It didn't look – or smell – like a garment that's been worn constantly for . . . What has it been? A week? And her hair was clean.'

'Not to mention her drawers. I bet if one of us went back to town with Torley when he takes the lions back on Thursday, and talked to Lupe Santini, she'd tell us that *somebody* packed things like underwear and a toothbrush and make-up and clean clothes. Who does that during a snatch?'

'It has been,' repeated Emma, 'eight days. They've been *somewhere* – somewhere that has cooking and washing facilities, probably, and is far enough away from neighbors that nobody's asking questions.'

She took the cloth, examined the smudges on it for a moment. 'And barely a smudge of dust. She isn't sunburned, either. So she hasn't walked far.'

'In those shoes, she couldn't, darling.' Kitty dragged on the cigarette she'd cadged from an extra.

'Do you suppose this Mr Sandow would give us access to Miss Sutton's financial records, to see if she did, in fact, sell her cottage in Big Bear?'

'Wouldn't tell us anything,' objected Zal. 'Sandow thought she sold the Palm Springs place, so it sounds like she's been working with somebody else and cooking the books. And if it was Selina behind it, she'd be in a position to slip poor Nurse Elena a Mickey Finn last Tuesday night. Not to mention handing poor Burt a bottle. And she'd have known to call all those reporters yesterday, to make damn sure Pugh coughed up. Burt might know something,' he added. 'If we can catch him sober.'

There was genuine sadness in Kitty's voice. 'How likely is that? Gren might.'

Gren Torley was with Marty Morongo and David the handsome camel-wrangler, working his way through the camel pens, checking knees, feet and backs for sores, and occasionally scratching noses and foreheads as the big, dusty animals jostled up for treats of carrots or salt. The trucks from Twenty-Nine Palms had just brought water, and more camels clustered around the barrels, moaning and spitting and cursing like coal miners in a saloon.

Torley listened without comment to Kitty's account of Burt's theory, his dark eyes sad. 'Doesn't surprise me Burt'd believe it of her,' he said at length. 'He loved her somethin' frantic. Still does, I think – and keeps hopin' she'll go back to bein' the woman he married. Not seein' that she *is* the woman he married – and that woman was and is a liar who knew exactly what he'd been lookin' for all his life. I don't think she ever forgave him for losin' the studio.'

He sighed and shook his head. Ariadne – who seemed to be the matriarch of the herd – bent her head down to rest her chin on his shoulder; he stroked her broad, flat cheek while she nibbled the collar of his shirt.

'And, yeah, Dad had what used to be a date ranch out at Cleghorn Lakes, about twenty miles from here. Feller who sold it to him didn't mention that those lakes hadn't had water in 'em since dinosaurs walked the Earth. I think Dad traded three lots in Florida for the place and I wouldn't swear those Florida lots were on dry land, so I don't know who saw who comin' on that deal. Desert Light, the place was called.'

'Would Miss Sutton have access to the place?' Emma asked.

'She might. Burt might have filmed out there, for all I know, when he had the studio. Most of Dad's land holdings got sold up when he passed, and the money split between us. But we couldn't get a taker for Desert Light. And once Selina got Burt convinced I'd cheated him out of part of his inheritance – that's another long story – neither of us could sell it because we'd both have to sign off on it, and he wouldn't speak to me, not for years. You want me to go out there with you this evenin'?' He ran a callused hand over Ariadne's shoulder, scuffing the dust from her fur.

Emma said, 'If you would.'

Between the tents, they could see the newest of the trucks draw up to the infirmary tent, cast, crew, financiers and journalists all clustering around as Selina Sutton was gently put aboard. Cameras blazed.

Minutes later, as Messrs Bandog, Goldman and Lutz were coaxed into the mess tent, Pugh summoned Larry Palmer for a hasty conference. Zal squinted up at the sun – it was three in the afternoon and the hottest part of the day yet to come. 'Bet me we pick up Scene four hundred eighty-eight while the money boys are still here.' He'd dipped a bandana into the camels' water trough, wrung it out and tied it around his head under his cap, tiny rivulets streaking the dust that covered his face. His glasses, as usual, were spotless, and through them his eyes blinked tired and red. But he only sighed a little, when Palmer barged out of his mess-tent conference waving for Kitty and Darlene, Ken and Marsh, Zal and Chip to rejoin the fray.

Through the heat of late afternoon, Lord Harlan struggled – repeatedly – to rescue his Rosebud from the Evil Zahar's guards, among the tents where shade and water were readily available, while Bandog, Goldman and Lutz sipped iced tea in the mess tent and came out occasionally with Pugh to watch. In her own corner of the mess tent, Emma worked at sorting out which pages in Professor Wright's handwriting or typewriter-face belonged to *Etruscan States of Umbria vol. 1*, which to 'Four Painted Tombs: A Comparison' and which to 'A Lost Etruscan Trade Hub?', increasingly puzzled over the duplicated – sometimes triplicated – blocks of text.

Thrice during the course of the afternoon, the low-voiced conversation of the men rose to audible levels: '. . . and where the hell is that two hundred thou gonna come out of?'

'You think anybody's gonna cross the street to see a Foremost Picture if we *don't* . . .'

Four heads turned, briefly, to note Emma's presence in the shadows. The voices sank again. Emma felt a momentary pang of pity for the columnists from *Photoplay, Screen World* et al., sweltering along both sides of the tent outside trying to listen in – she could see the bulges in the canvas – and then forced her mind back to the conundrum of where most of Mr Paine's research paper (if 'research' was the proper term for the labored plagiarism of the few surviving pages) would have gotten to . . .

She could understand pilfering information about aristocratic Etruscan tombs if they contained valuable grave goods. But the outpourings of a young man whose only goal, apparently, was to pass the class so that he could remain on the football team?

She caught the words ' . . . so do you have a script yet to finish without her?' and the voices shushed again.

Pugh said, 'Relax, she can't hear us over the fans.'

Outside, Larry yelled, 'Cut!'

When they returned to the Araby that evening, Dr Plaister reported that Miss Sutton was asleep under sedation. But she had told him, he reported, that she had no idea where she had been and had never seen her captors' faces. There were three of them, she had said, and she thought a fourth – a woman – at the shack to which she had been taken. But she had wept herself into convulsions, for fear that her poor child would come to harm.

It was nearly four hours' drive, after a hasty supper, from the dusty lot behind the Araby Hotel to the boarded-up frame house that had once been called Desert Light. Once, Emma woke, to the gunshot explosion of a blowout, and clambered stiffly from the cab of Gren Torley's truck to see deep desert all around them. Colorless moonlight blanched endless sand, made nightmare shadows of the few parched clumps of brush, the upthrust promontories of bare rock and some of the most bizarre plants – *trees? Cacti? Barsoomian hollyhocks?* – that she had ever encountered. Not a light pierced the endless miles.

The men mended the puncture, cranked the engine, drove on.

Kitty, apparently, had no problems sleeping next to Zal on a couple of Mexican blankets in the back of the truck, which, despite Torley's scrupulous cleaning, held a musky reminiscence of lions. To this had been added the stink of the two five-gallon cans of gasoline, for the return trip. She and Zal traded off driving with

Torley and in between shifts fell asleep again with the instant unconcern of soldiers who know they'll be back on duty soon.

Kitty, Emma noticed, had renewed her make-up before leaving the set and wore her usual stylish Patou frock, along with the brocaded red-and-gold pumps. *No wonder it took her only seconds to spot Selina's masquerade – if it is a masquerade . . .*

The house itself had been built in the 1880s. By the look of the truncated remains of hundreds of date palms around it, if there had once been water on the property, it was played out now. What was left of an older building – adobe, like the original hacienda on the Foremost lot – had apparently enjoyed a brief after-life as storage for the crop before being left to crumble to the elements. The house itself, under the glory of that brilliant moon, seemed in good shape.

They drove without lights for the last three miles, and left the truck where the ruined palms grew thickest, to walk up to the building itself. It was just before midnight. No lights shone in its windows, but even by moonlight – a day or two past full – Emma could see tire tracks in the parched dirt near the door.

Zal breathed, 'No cars.'

'Don't mean there's nobody here,' Torley replied.

The two men circled the house, leaving Emma and Kitty by the truck. Emma could see the windows were still boarded up, but Kitty whispered, 'Look at the brush around the water tank. It's been cleared.'

And something else, thought Emma. *A smell . . .* She angled her wrist watch to the moonlight spearing through the palm shafts. Ten minutes.

Through the boards of the windows, dim needles of yellow light flared. A moment later, the front door opened, and Zal – glasses like insect eyes – signaled them to come.

'They were here.'

Emma halted on the plank step. Closer to the house, it was unmistakable. 'The incinerator.' She nodded toward the stumpy brick chimney behind the adobe outbuilding. 'Can you smell it?'

Fresh ashes, charred wood. Faint but noticeable in the bone-dry air.

Zal led the way around the house and across the yard, flashlight beam bobbing on the sand before them. Ashes had been raked out of the little firebox, scattered carelessly on the ground all around. Wind had dispersed some of them, but clumps remained closer. A rake and a fire shovel were propped carelessly against the brick. Somebody had been burning trash, bits of paper plates and cups. It was difficult to tell by moonlight and flashlight, but they looked fresh.

When the little furnace's rusty iron door was opened, Zal raked out half-burned tangles of cloth, recognizable still. A woman's silk frocks and blouses, underclothing and stockings. Too many, and piled in too thickly, to burn effectively.

Beneath those, rags of toweling, barely scorched but caked with blood.

Emma's breath caught with horror, and Zal said, with deliberate calm, 'None of the clothes have blood on them. And you notice, none of the clothes are Susy's.'

'I don't think they took any of her clothes.' Emma forced her eyes back to the worn cotton rags. 'And whose blood—?'

Zal shook his head, burrowed a hand into the ashes. 'Still warm. I didn't see blood in the house, but you'd need real daylight if the towels were used for clean-up.'

'There's a lot of it,' said Emma softly, 'for just an . . . accident.'

There was silence for a time. Then Kitty whispered, 'Are there boxes in the house?' as if the kidnappers were still on the premises and might overhear. 'From food?'

'They probably burned those too,' said Zal. 'The place looked pretty well cleared out.'

'Balls.' Kitty's beautiful lips pouted. 'You have a knife, Zallie?'

He produced one – a French Army trench knife. She took it, and Emma's flashlight, and retreated to the ruins of the adobe, returning a few moments later carrying what Emma realized was her silk slip. She had cut it up the back to produce a rectangle of clean cloth some forty inches by forty, on to which she carefully shoveled the half-burned garments and bloodstained towels. Kitty, reflected Emma, for all her air of empty-headed silliness, had acquired a quite startling knowledge of the world in her twenty-eight years (she claimed twenty-two) of life.

As Zal had said, they found no visible signs of struggle inside the house, though with only the flashlight's glow it was difficult to tell. The kitchen counter was without dust but liberally scattered with breadcrumbs. A little water dribbled from the single tap when Emma tried it, connected to the water tank outside. The old-fashioned pump at one side of the sink was rusted almost solid. Beds had been made up in one downstairs bedroom, and two upstairs – 'The sheets is from here,' Torley murmured. 'Same as those towels. Mama always went on about what a nuisance linen sheets were to iron. Kept in the hall cupboard. Blankets from here, too.'

Her heart still pounding with dread, Emma recalled the hard chill of the desert nights, even in blistering summer. The blankets were much like those Torley himself had in the back of his truck: purchased cheap in Mexico, wool striped white, gray and red. She glimpsed others – sheets and towels as well – as they passed the cupboard in the hall.

In the smaller of the upstairs bedrooms, the window had padlocks on it, and a chamber pot in the corner, used a few days before and not emptied. By the look of it, it had never been properly cleaned. Thanks to Mrs Pendergast, Emma knew all about proper chamber-pot hygiene.

Though she knew that if the kidnappers had killed their victims, they wouldn't necessarily have done so in the house, still she insisted on examining every square inch of the room: walls, floor, bed. But all they found was a thin line of crumbled sand, mixed with ashes and a few fragments of shredded newspaper, stretched for about two feet, parallel to the wall and some two feet from it. The smell was unmistakable. Mrs Pendergast's cousin, Mrs Jussive, had kept a cat, and had insisted that cats could be trained to use a box of sand, ash and torn newspaper indoors at night rather than being let out. Mrs Jussive had had servants and kept them at their work. But the faint ammoniac smell had pervaded every corner of the house.

Torley knelt beside the line, brought the flashlight close and touched a hard little chunk of something in the ash, then sniffed his fingers. 'Sardine,' he said. Again he stirred the line of debris. 'I think this here's deviled ham. She was feedin' him through the cage bars, probably bits of what they were givin' her. They make chicken cages this size.'

He picked up the deviled ham, mushed it between callused fingers. 'This ain't more than two days old.'

Emma turned her face away, uncontrollable tears constricting her throat. In a perfectly conversational tone, Kitty said a word that Emma had only heard from Army mule drivers when they were badly wounded. Zal was silent.

They found kerosene lamps downstairs, still with a little fuel in them. The flashlights were brighter. They searched the house, but found nothing further than a couple of cans of sardines and some of tomato soup. Nothing that hinted whether Selina Sutton had been a prisoner in that other upstairs room as well, or whether she'd had the freedom of the house. The chamber pot in that room had been recently used, then wiped in a perfunctory way – but not properly scrubbed with kerosene – and stowed under the bed. 'Which doesn't tell us anything,' said Emma. 'Many people still use thunder mugs at night, rather than going out to the outhouse, especially if stairs are involved.'

'Yeah,' said Zal drily. 'That's what servants are for.'

Darkness prevented them from seeing where blood might have been wiped up.

A window from the cab of the dark-red Sixth Morning truck opened directly into the barred, feral-smelling rear compartment. Kneeling beside it, Zal could participate in the discussion in the cab, everybody half shouting over the rattle of the truck's engine, the juddering of the chassis on the unpaved roads.

'If they didn't have Susy alive,' Zal said, 'they wouldn't have kept the cat. Even if they got rid of its body – or turned it loose for the coyotes to get – we'd have found the empty cage.'

Emma shut her eyes, praying he was right.

'So either the kidnappers took the kid and her cat, burned Selina's duds, and cleared out the minute they discovered Selina had escaped,' Zal went on, 'or else moving Susy – and Selina "escaping"' – his voice supplied invisible quote marks – 'were part of the plan, whatever the plan is. You have any idea where the nearest telephone is, Gren?'

'Prob'ly Twenty-Nine Palms.'

'Twenty-nine palms and twenty-eight people,' sniffed Kitty. 'If there's three phones in the whole town, I'll eat your hat, Gren. So we might be able to get a description of one of the kidnappers there, unless they snuck into Doc Larousse's wireless tent at the camp . . .'

'If one of the kidnappers is driving into Twenty-Nine Palms anyway' – Emma opened her eyes, turned to those dark shapes of her friends in the crowded cab – 'they could just as easily slip into the camp and listen to the radio in the mess tent for news. With a hundred and fifty extras, plus camera crew, and the local horse handlers . . .'

'Somebody'd notice someone coming into town and asking to

use the phone to call eleven movie magazines long distance,' pointed out Kitty. 'They could have been bribed. Or whoever it was just said, "Hey, I'm from the movie company." But if you get the San Bernardino County sheriff in there asking questions about a kidnapping—'

'They wouldn't need to phone eleven movie magazines.' The truck jolted on yet another pothole, and Zal caught the crossed bars that defended the window from whatever it was that Grenville Torley customarily drove around with in the back of his truck. 'All they'd need to do is phone a stooge back in LA – or send him or her a telegram the minute Doc leaves that wireless tent – and have *them* phone everybody from the corner drugstore. The question is, do we call the sheriff?'

The two women simply looked at him.

'What if what we've been told is the exact truth?' he went on, more quietly. 'We're all pretty sure Selina is behind the whole thing, but what if we're wrong? What if there *is* no fake, no smoke and mirrors? What if they're really going to kill her if the cops get called in?'

Kitty was silent. It was a thought that had been going through Emma's mind since she'd smelled the smoke of charred cloth from the incinerator.

'It's clear there's an inside job going on someplace,' Zal went on. 'But you put me up against a wall, and there's really no way I can *prove* Selina's behind it. I don't like the woman and I know she's a liar about other things . . . but there's other ways these guys could be getting their information. And they may be ready to do exactly that: cut their losses and run.'

'Or they could have done it already,' said Kitty after a moment.

The headlamps glared across his glasses as he shook his head. 'Even if they'd buried bodies, we'd have found the cat cage,' he reasoned. 'But once we get the Berdoo County sheriffs on their trail . . . Yeah, they'll start checking grocery stores and gas pumps and whoever they bought their water from. But if you think the LA cops are Keystone clowns, you think about the manpower they've got to choose from out here. Especially,' he concluded grimly, 'if our kidnappers are actually working with some of the bootleggers. Or have somebody on the inside.'

'Other than Selina, you mean?' Kitty dug in her beaded handbag for a cigarette, looked guiltily at Emma – who sat between her and the window – and replaced the packet. 'Was I the only one who noticed that there was no broken window or rope made out of bedsheets or smashed wine bottle that a woman could have clonked her captor with? And I looked around that adobe out back when I was there.' She nudged the pale bundle of knotted silk at her feet. 'If that's the "shack" they were keeping her in, she'd have gotten away the first night.'

'There's deserted ranch houses all over these hills.' Zal gestured to the window just beyond Emma's shoulder, to the far-off outline of what could have been a ruined house, set among cactus at the foot of a monstrous formation of rock. 'And about thirty little wildcat goldmines that I know about. Most of the mines turned out not to be worth the cost of dragging in supplies to dig them, but the mine shacks are still standing. That's not even taking into account the stills being run by the LA bootleggers, in people's barns or on those empty ranches, wherever they can get water.'

'She said she was kept drugged,' Emma reminded her. 'So . . . do we call the sheriff? Someone was wounded – badly, it looks like. Do we risk the hue and cry? Or do we simply tell Mr Pugh and let him make the decision?'

'Him and the Three Wise Men he's got with him?' Emma could hear Zal's cocked eyebrow in his voice.

'Whatever actually happened,' said Kitty thoughtfully, 'bet me Selina's going to be as surprised as everybody else to hear where she was. And she won't remember a thing about how she got away, or how she got from there to the set. What is it – ten miles? It was just an *amazing* coincidence that someone *happened* to phone all those journalists on the very day she turned up, so nobody can say, *Oops, poor Susy got killed accidentally.*'

'And I'll be even more curious,' said Zal, 'to hear what details she *does* remember, if nobody tells her what we found.'

ELEVEN

However, a telegram arrived just as pre-dawn breakfast was concluding in the Araby's exotically decorated dining room (fake palm trees not nearly as convincing as those that decorated the Coconut Grove, murals more reminiscent of *The Sheik* than of anything actually seen in Algeria, and a menu consisting chiefly of pancakes, shredded wheat and fried eggs).

Upon entering the long room, Kitty made straight for Frank Pugh, who was sharing a table with Neil Bandog and the smilingly attentive Darlene Golden, Mel Lutz and the smilingly attentive Dove Singleton, and a grim-faced Irving Goldman. Pugh beamed a greeting – secure in his own virtue (Miss Golden having been otherwise occupied last night) – and was rewarded with a smile that could indeed have launched a thousand ships and burned the topless towers of Ilium. Kitty had told him last night she was going with Gren Torley (no romantic or financial competition in anyone's books) to observe the night fauna of the desert. ('I want to understand what this place *is*, Frank! I want to *understand* the desert at night!' She had clasped her hands passionately to her bosom. 'And besides, Emma is coming with me.') Seeing her re-enter with her chaperone still in tow, his faith in her devotion was renewed. Moreover, she had completely reapplied her make-up by flashlight in the cab of the truck during the last hour and a half of the journey, so it had taken her but a moment to cache her bundle of charred evidence in her room on the way to the dining room. (And she looked, Emma had to admit, radiant.)

It was just as well that she had. Entering the long room, they had found every table around Pugh occupied by journalists, and every journalist – while ostensibly slurping up cereal – focused on the studio chief and his financial backers. 'I don't even want to think about how much they had to pay the waiters to arrange that,' Emma murmured in Zal's ear, as they joined Harry Garfield, Roger Clint and Ruby Saks at a table in the corner, and Harry poured them all coffee. Torley, as always more concerned about his animals than breakfast, had taken the truck and gone on ahead to Camp Turpitude to feed the carnivores and prepare them for the long drive back to the San Fernando Valley. ('Sheba gets car-sick,' he had confided worriedly as he cranked the engine once more.)

At a table near that of Garfield's little party – and hemmed in protectively by Dr Plaister, Mary Blanque and two of the studio guards – Selina Sutton dipped toast into her tea and winced theatrically at every sound. Looking across at her in the electrical glare of the dining room's lights, Emma observed that even in her hour of travail, the bereft mother was again completely made-up (*whose cosmetics did she borrow for that?*). Despite her apprehensions, she could not but wonder how much those hollow eyes and pale lips owed to rice powder and kohl. Even during his ponderous romantic badinage with Kitty, Pugh's eye kept sliding over to that tragic Delilah. Not with concupiscence, Emma judged, but with concern lest any journalist attempt to speak to her. The glare he directed towards the columnists themselves would have stripped the hide off any elephant in Gren Torley's herd.

Kitty devoted herself to distracting his attention from these objects, since any information about last night's discoveries would become immediate public knowledge: caressingly admired the closeness of his morning shave and fed him fragments of bacon from his plate.

To this fraught scenario entered fair, bespectacled Eando Willers – who had come out with the financial brigade yesterday to fix flats en route – bearing the pale-yellow sheet of telegraph paper and wearing an expression of shock and distress. Eleven reportorial utensils suspended Quaker's Muffets or pancake mid-air, and eleven journalistic heads turned.

Pugh read the telegraph, did what Zal or Kitty would have described as a double take and threw an immediate glance towards Selina Sutton. Kitty, at Pugh's side (in his lap, in fact, nibbling delicately on a scrap of bacon), plucked the paper from his fingers, and even in a corner of the dining room, Emma could hear her gasp, 'Holy *shit!*'

Pugh snatched the message back. Miss Sutton was already slipping and dodging between the tables and reached his side in time to grab it. With journalists surrounding his table, Emma reflected, he couldn't very well swat her aside, which was what he clearly looked as though he wanted to do. Miss Sutton tore it from his hand, read it before he yanked it back.

'No!' Her word was a scream.

'Selina—'

'*No!*' She flung herself at him, as if to grab his shirt, and, fatally, he put the telegram down to fend off her hands.

Neil Bandog snatched it up, read it and did a double take that would have embarrassed Stan Laurel. The banker stared wildly at Pugh, who had Selina by the wrists now and was holding her at arm's length. Emma didn't hear what Bandog shouted at Pugh, for by that time they were only intermittently visible in the mob of journalists closing around them like bees in swarming time.

Dr Plaister and the studio guards, however, had made it to them a split second before the journalists did. Only moments later, it seemed, Miss Sutton – weaving on her feet like a woman overcome with horror (or a woman who had just received a quick injection of intramuscular phenobarbital in the confusion) – was being led by Plaister and the guards through the crowd, out of the dining room and, presumably, back to her room. Pugh followed solicitously, stuffing the telegram into his pocket and shepherding Messrs Bandog, Goldman and Lutz before him, talking in a low voice all the while.

Emma would have given a great deal to hear what he said.

'What the Sam Hill—?' Harry Garfield turned as Kitty elbowed her way through the press to their table.

'The telegram,' gasped Kitty, 'was from Fishy. Marked *Urgent* in great big letters. They just got another ransom note, with a lock of Susy's hair. It said, *Earlier notes fake. Genuine instructions to come.*'

'Terrific,' said Zal.

'Correct me if I'm wrong,' said Zal, as they crossed the hotel courtyard in the dim blue light of dawn. 'Did it look to you like Selina was expecting that telegram?'

Emma shook her head. Behind them, light streamed from the open doors of the lobby, along with a cacophony of voices shouting, questioning – cursing, too, Emma guessed. 'Goodness knows how long it will take Kitty to get Frank alone to give him those burned clothes . . .'

'Even then, God knows what he'll decide to do about them. You can bet it's gonna be noon or later before we get out to the set, and all Frank's gonna be thinking about is paying those extra extras for yet another day . . .'

But when they reached the door of Kitty's suite – which opened, hacienda-style, straight into the tiled courtyard – they found their friend in no state to even remember bloodstained towels or abandoned desert hideouts.

'I should never have brought them!' Kneeling on the floor beside three little dishes of untouched dog cakes, gravy and lightly grilled chicken livers, Kitty raised tragic eyes to her friends. 'My poor little angel muffins! It's all my fault!' She turned as Chang Ming, Buttercreme and Black Jasmine crowded around her, nudging and nestling and licking their flat noses with distress at her remorse. 'Mama is so sorry, darlings! Can you ever forgive her?'

The Pekes seemed perfectly willing to do so. Standing just inside the doorway, the motherly Ruby Saks – her ample flesh crammed into a copy of the Evil Zahar's silken salwars and jeweled brassiere – said, 'They'll be all right, Miss de la Rose. It's just the heat.' The stand-in had been, Emma recalled, put in charge of the celestial creamcakes while Kitty was away chasing kidnappers in the night. 'They'll feel better once they're back in town.'

It took, Emma was well aware, severe fatigue to keep Chang Ming from gobbling up every morsel in sight.

'But I should have known!' Kitty turned toward Emma again, dark eyes flooded with unscripted tears of distress. 'Darling,' she whispered, 'could you – do you think you could – take them back to town? Gren's going back with the lions – they're all off their food as well, poor guys, he says . . . Or maybe you could hitch a ride with Thelma Turnbit or Mrs Parsons or one of the other journalists . . .'

'Frank's hired cops from Seven Palms and Twenty-Nine Palms and the county sheriffs too, I think,' explained Ruby, 'to keep journalists away from the set, so a lot of them are going back.'

'I just can't forgive myself' – Kitty wiped her eyes, heedless, for almost the first time since Emma had known her, of her mascara – 'for bringing my poor celestial cream cakes out here.'

'It's all right.' Touched by her love for creatures other than herself, Emma knelt at her side and put an arm around her shoulders. 'Of course I'll take them back, dearest. But you must promise me to wire or telephone every evening,' she added briskly, 'and let me know what's going on—'

She got no further. Kitty threw her arms around her, kissed her, then reached down to kiss each celestial angel muffin in turn. 'I promise! And I'll keep an eye on Zallie for you – and if you ride back with Thelma Turnbit, you can find out how much she knows. She's taking Mrs Parsons, and Sheila Fielding from *Picture Play*, and—'

But nothing in the world would have induced Emma to spend four hours in a car full of journalists, particularly since word seemed to have gotten around that the scenario of *Our Tiny Miracle* was being rewritten. She also knew that Sheila Fielding smoked like a Model-T in need of a tune-up. Thus she returned to Hollywood in Gren Torley's truck, with Big Joe, Sheba and Randall snoring in the back and Chang Ming, Buttercreme and Black Jasmine snoring in their wicker boxes around her feet. On the drive, among many other things, she was able to learn a little more about the marriage of Selina (née Snoach) and Burt (né Torley) Sutton.

'Burt always drank,' sighed the older brother, his gaze on the narrow track that led (eventually) to the highway through Cabazon and Riverside and thus to Los Angeles and the studio. 'We both did – our dad, too. He had a fleet of trucks back in Shreveport. Why it hit Burt so bad when our folks died, I can't say, and I guess nobody ever knows somethin' like that. We were both out on long-distance hauls when that train smashed into Dad's car, and there was nothin' either of us could have done if we'd been home. But afterwards, Burt never could let go of it – or it never could let go of him. How they lookin' back there?'

Emma glanced through the little barred window at the three huge ocher cats crowded up together, for all the world like her aunt Phyllis's overweight tabbies asleep on the window seat of that Queen Anne house on the Botley Road. She had never been this close to lions, and to her they looked incomparably beautiful, the fur on their noses like velvet, their big, soft paws flexing with dreams of pursuit.

'They're doing what cats do,' she reported, and glanced into the wicker box on her lap. 'Dogs, too,' she added with a smile.

It was already hot in the truck.

'Good,' said Torley. 'That's good. Burt and I both came back out to California after the accident – Dad always talked about goin' back to the date farm, but he never did. When we got the money from Dad's will, Burt bought Magnum Studios down in Culver City – little more than an open stage and a couple of bungalows. I knew already that one thing every studio needed was animals. Some studios still got their own zoos, but more and more, the smaller ones just rent by the day. Not that I'd rent so much as a horn toad to DeMille 'cause of the way he treats 'em. But I bought the cats and the elephants from a circus that went bust in Fresno, and the camels and three goats from Monarch when they sold up their zoo. Ronnie and I have been adding to 'em ever since: Ronnie's Mrs Torley. She worked the vaudeville circuit for fifteen years as Rondara the Jungle Princess. But Burt . . .'

He shook his head. 'It's like part of Burt never really healed, after our folks went. I was already married to Ronnie and livin' in our own place, but Burt was still at home. He was Mom's boy. And Selina knew it, like a shark smellin' blood in the water. He never would see that the whole time she was tellin' him that he was a drunken bum and couldn't be trusted to run the studio, she was eggin' him on to drink, puttin' drink in his way. Every evening or so, it was "Oh, Burt, I need a drink, you just have one to keep me company." And meantime, *she* was the one runnin' the studio, and keepin' the books, and that was just the way she wanted it.'

Emma recalled that strong-boned, unshaven face looking at her from the dark of the cottage parlor, the desperate grief in the blue-green eyes. The cheery way Susy had chirped, 'No, ma'am,' after she'd nearly been killed under the hooves of a furious horse, and that one moment of terror in her eyes. 'Do you think she's behind it?'

Had that passionate scream *No!* in the dining room that morning been acting? A means to force Pugh's hand in the presence of a dozen journalists?

For a time, Torley said nothing, his gaze on the empty thread of asphalt stretching before them into sandy eternity.

'Colt Madison – the detective Mr Pugh hired – says the organized criminals in Los Angeles don't know anything about it.'

'The organized criminals in Los Angeles – the *best* organized criminals – are the ones running City Hall,' the little man reminded her grimly. 'And payin' off the police. And Colt Madison couldn't detect a murder if he tripped over a corpse in his living room.'

'I gather Miss Sutton knew a number of those people,' continued Emma worriedly. 'At least, Zal tells me she got invitations to Maya Pearl's parties, where she could have met practically anyone. And Miss Sutton's house up in Benedict Canyon is sufficiently isolated that anyone could come and go, on the days when Mr Sandow was working elsewhere and Burt was away. And who would be the wiser?'

The animal trainer sighed. 'I don't know.' He took a pull on the bottle of tepid Coca-Cola he had wedged between his seat and the door, squinted against the road glare and the dry wind whipping through the open window. 'But it's a damn long way for her to have walked, if Desert Light was where they was keepin' them. And I can't think of another building out in the desert between it and the film camp. Not even an empty ranch house. If you was to ask me, I'd say she got a ride from somebody out to Twenty-Nine Palms, and then walked in from the road.'

Back at last at Kitty's Moorish love nest on Ivarene Street, Emma washed her face, brushed the dust from the fur of the Pekes and spread Professor Wright's papers out on her bed: fragmentary student efforts, what appeared to be chapters from *Etruscan States*, the core of the article about his discovery of tombs in (*Corzo? Corso?*) and the monograph about trading patterns, which seemed to be mostly complete. At least, she reflected, Burt's rattletrap brown Ford was no longer in front of the house. She also took out the notes she had made about the artifacts listed as discovered in (*wherever it was*), preparatory to going through the box of potsherds again to compare them . . .

She sat back in the white-painted bent-willow chair she'd drawn from her dressing table, thinking again of that long night drive into the desert, of the dark ranch house glimpsed in the shadow of towering rocks. *There's deserted ranch houses all over these hills*, Zal had said.

It was just past noon.

A warm day, but nothing like the desert.

She gave the dogs – who seemed to have made a complete recovery – a valedictory pat, descended the stairs to the hall and took the keys to the Packard from their accustomed drawer in the telephone niche.

'He's gone.' The housekeeper Lupe Santini shook her head as she stepped back to let Emma pass before her into Selina Sutton's Benedict Canyon palace. None of the small gaggle of sightseers at the gate had attempted to push past Rico Santini – Selina Sutton's chauffeur – when he'd undone the padlock and chain to let Emma's car through. A few of these had been children – mostly school-aged boys – and

Emma had wondered whether any of last Friday's young intruders had managed to fall into the swimming pool, and if so, whether any of the adults had been paying enough attention to fish them out.

She wondered, too, at what point the Santinis had gotten permission to lock the gate, and from whom.

'Gone? You mean, left town?'

'His car is gone,' said Lupe. Her husband – the chauffeur – had gone up to the house before opening the gate. By the housekeeper's forthcoming mood, Emma guessed he'd mentioned the amount of the bribe she'd handed him. 'I thought maybe it was 'cause he found out somehow the cops was coming. The car was gone Monday morning, and the cops showed up that afternoon.'

'The police? But . . .'

'Yeah.' The older woman's voice twisted the word: a lifetime of living with one eye always cocked for the minions of authority. 'Just routine, they said. No report had been filed. Me, I think the police chief, he just wants to cover his ass from the newspapers. You want a drink, ma'am? Or ginger ale, maybe?'

Definitely goodwill from the bribe.

When Emma denied any need for refreshment, the woman asked more quietly, 'It true she got away? Miss Sutton?' She gestured at the morning's papers, laid neatly on an extravagantly inlaid sideboard next to the door.

> ESCAPE FROM DEATH
> SUTTON RETURNS!
> 'I REMEMBER NOTHING . . .'
> SUSY STILL A PRISONER
> KERN COUNTY SHERIFFS REPORT
> WITNESS IN SWEETCHILD CASE
> SUSY SEEN IN MEXICO

'It's true.' *How much am I supposed to know about any of this? How much were these poor people told by the studio?* 'I've just come from Seven Palms this morning.' *Has Kitty even had a chance to talk to Mr Pugh alone yet?* 'I understand Miss Sutton is being kept under sedation by the doctors – at least, she was this morning – but remembers nothing clearly of where she was.'

'And *la niña*?' Lupe's eyes clouded with anxiety. 'They say Miss Sutton escaped somehow, but not the poor little one?'

Again, Emma shook her head, and Lupe crossed herself: '*Madre de Dios*, keep her safe. Cops.' She almost spit the word. 'I hope nothing bad comes of it. Took me all day and half the next to clean up, with the mess they made. They go through the cottage like they think he's hiding there. It take me all day yesterday to clean up. That place was a pig sty even before they go through it. Except even pigs would not live in such a way.' Compassion mingled with the anger, the exasperation, the disgust in her eyes.

'Me,' she went on, 'I think poor Mr Sutton went out someplace to get drunk and forgot the way home, you know? I think he's with one of those women he runs around with, those *putas* who used to hang around his studio, or the ones now he meets in the bar rooms.' She shook her head. 'Poor man gotta get some lovin' someplace, I guess.'

'Did the police ask about any of these . . . these other ladies that he visits?' Emma looked past the housekeeper to the French doors at the end of the house's central hall, the manicured plots of grass and the blood-bright roses beyond. 'Is there any one of them more than another that he might be with?' On the drive back from Seven Palms, Gren Torley had mentioned in passing that his wife had telephoned him every night at the Araby, to let him know that all was well at Sixth Morning Ranch. Had Burt been there, Emma suspected the older brother would have spoken of it.

Does Burt even know yet that Selina escaped?

Lupe made a vulgar gesture. 'They don't care. *La chota.*'

'Do you know? Or know if he has any friends who might know where he is?'

'They go through his desk. You can look, too. I put all those telephone numbers, those scraps of paper, in one drawer, but I don't know who they are. A man doesn't care enough to stay sober and protect his child, why should I care?'

And why should I? Emma wondered, as she walked, key in hand, down the gravel path of the now-silent garden and let herself into Burt's dim, hot, smelly little cottage. Recalling what it had been like a week previously, she could only salute the housekeeper's sense of duty and cast-iron stomach. Every dish had been washed (and sterilized, she hoped). The kitchen was clean, the old newspapers folded and stacked, and the rooms reeked of bleach rather than the ghosts of stale booze and old vomit. From the drawer of the battered desk, Emma collected every scrap of paper that bore a telephone number with a name appended.

Burt may know something. He may know something that he isn't aware that he knows.

Or he may know something that he is *aware that he knows . . . that someone else may know that he knows.*

The silence seemed to settle around her. She almost missed the shrieks of the ill-tended children, the hollers of the gentleman in the striped blazer as he tried to jimmy the windows open. For a place so close to downtown Los Angeles, Benedict Canyon's silence was eerie. *Anyone could come and go*, she had said, *and who would be wiser?*

Her fingers turned a grubby half-sheet of torn-out notebook paper: ARDISS TINCH. 7029 Cedar LB HE-6325. There was a business card from Foy Snoach, Stockbroker, with an office on Figueroa Street downtown and, scribbled on the back in pencil, 1203 Bagley CC SE-0064 – presumably the home telephone number, since it was different from the one printed below the office address.

Another scrap of paper – one of many – contained, Emma was interested to note, the name and telephone number of Maya Pearl, that purveyor of things one couldn't get or do even in Los Angeles. Another business card proved to be that of Thelma Turnbit, listed as 'journalist.'

Did she come here to interview him for *Screen World*? Emma looked around the cramped room, stifling in the early-evening heat. What had she made of him? Of this place?

Or had that been before he had moved out of Selina Sutton's demi-Versailles at the other end of the garden? Perhaps Mr Pugh had ordered his baby star's mother to bring her poor husband out of his cell here and pretend that he still shared her bed and board? Pretend that Susy Sweetchild had two loving parents, like every other child in America was supposed to?

And what, she wondered, *did Susy make of all this?*

Another thought crossed her mind. After a moment's consideration, she tucked all the addresses into her handbag.

'Missus Brackston . . .'

Kitty's gardener, old Mr Shang, emerged from the potting shed to open the doors of the garage as Emma guided the Packard around the corner of the house and into the graveled rear yard. The small promontory on which perched the house itself rose almost to the level of Ivarene Street in front of it, but separated from the street itself by a narrow vale perhaps seven feet deep and thirty across, tapering to the south where the promontory joined the main mass of the hill beside it. The land continued to fall behind the house, which made negotiating the driveway around to the garage a challenge to a woman who had learned to drive – and had driven since the age of eighteen – on the left, rather than the right, side of the road. Emma was rather proud of herself for having piloted Kitty's showy yellow ocean liner out of the hills, along Sunset Boulevard to Benedict Canyon Drive and up through more hills to Shadygrove Terrace without mishap. After nine months, she was becoming adept at judging distances from what she still felt was the wrong side of the front seat, but was glad of a spotter to help her back into the garage itself.

The old man guided her with signals into the building's shade, opened the car door for her with crooked-fingered hands. 'Gentleman comes look for you,' he said.

'Mr Denham?' Had Julia located the rest of Professor Wright's artifacts? The old Chinese gardener had helped Oscar Denham carry the original boxes in and would know him.

'This gentleman not here before,' Shang said. 'So tall' – he sketched an indication of nearly his own six-foot height – 'not thin gentleman, not fat gentleman. Hair was black' – another gesture established further that the visitor's hairline had been in full retreat up both sides of his forehead, as was Mr Shang's – 'little white.' The bent fingers brushed his temples. 'Dark-blue eyes.' A tap on his own blue sleeve identified the color. 'Costly suit, silk tie, very nice. Sandalwood.' His expressive inhalation identified the stranger as a user of eau de Cologne.

'He said he want you,' the gardener went on. 'Missus Emma Brackston, he say. When this insignificant servant tell him you are not here, he ask where you have gone. He get in his car and drive away – big car, Delage, brown and yellow, shiny, license one-four-seven two-five-eight. Someone polish it every day, and not this man, I think. But later, I see this man again, walking around the front of the house, looking up at it. I was here' – he gestured to the tangles of jasmine and bougainvillea that mingled with the wild sage on the hillsides that embraced the property – 'I see his car, up on the street. I go around to see the front of the house, and I see him on the porch. His clothes are different, but the car is the same. He tries the door, then he tries the windows.'

'The *windows*?' Visions of the gentleman in the striped blazer flashed through her mind.

'Even so, Madame. When I come down the hillside, he runs down the steps and up to his car. He is gone before I can come close, to ask him, can this insignificant servant be of help.'

'He tried to get in the *windows*?'

'So it seem to this insignificant servant. It was many yards away, and it may be that I am wrong, and have mistaken what I believe that I saw.' He made another bow, in no way subservient, but like a king acknowledging his brotherhood with the humanity of the world.

Emma climbed the long rear steps to the kitchen, let herself in with her key.

Had someone been at one of those houses, after all? The neo-Spanish extravaganza in Palm Springs? The desiccated farmhouse called Desert Light? Both had been pitch-dark, defying the dim gleam of Zal's torch. Her memory went back to all those coal-sack doors, the distant creaks of floors and beams. The brilliance of the moonlight outside. Any of those men prowling around Camp Turpitude yesterday could have been Selina Sutton's partner in crime and not a journalist at all – if she *had* a partner, if she *was* behind the kidnapping . . .

But if she were not, the same applied. Anyone could say they were writing for *Photoplay* or *Film Fun* or *Screenland*, and even have something that looked like credentials to prove it. *They can't all know each other* . . .

The lock clicked and for a moment fear caught at her throat, the fear that she'd open the door and there he would be, a tall man with dark hair . . .

But the only thing that greeted her was a trio of small, fluffy lion-dogs, fully recovered from the desert's heat and insisting that they had not been fed in many years. Emma shook her head at her own over-active imagination. *This is what comes of making up stories about frightful things happening to people* . . .

> . . . as imagination bodies forth
> the forms of things unknown, the poet's pen
> turns them to shapes . . .

Which made her wonder what sort of bad dreams Mr Shakespeare must have had.

'All right, children, I am a bad mother for coming home this late,' though it was in fact just before four o'clock and nowhere near their dinner time. She fetched their leashes – she was in no mood to go hunting one of the two bold males should they catch sight of a rabbit on the hillside – and took them down the steps again. Afterwards, all three celestial cream cakes followed her interestedly around the house as she looked into every room, checked every window latch and door handle, and found nothing out of the ordinary. No sign that ingress had been forced or even attempted.

A telephone call to Julia Denham's office confirmed that Professor Halford Partington – authority on Renaissance and Reformation at the university – stood nearly six feet tall and had black hair thinning away from his temples, and that his eyes were dark blue. 'Yes, always very well dressed,' affirmed Julia. 'I don't think the man owns a sweatshirt. Why do you ask?'

Why indeed? Emma settled the receiver back into its hook. The description would fit Burt Sutton (if one cleaned him up) or three of Emma's former instructors at Sommerville College.

A 'nice' suit and silk tie could be purchased, borrowed or stolen. The big, sleek car said, *Money.* That could have been borrowed or stolen as well. Her mind went back to the detective Colt Madison, still presumably hot on the kidnappers' trail and quizzing every gangster and bootlegger in Los Angeles about what they might have heard. *Colt Madison couldn't detect a murder if he tripped over a corpse in his living room . . .*

And if they were genuine bootleggers they'd have false plates, of course. In any case, what police force in this country would believe the word of a Chinese gardener against a white man (and a professor at the university at that) even if they did trace the car to him.

She descended to the kitchen, with the dogs trailing hopefully behind her, to make tea.

. . . *in the night, imagining some fear*
How easy is a bush supposed a bear?

The chances of armed Bedouins breaking into the house and carrying her off to the desert were, she reminded herself, slim.

She glanced at the bright windows, the hillsides blanketed with acacia and chaparral, the haunt of coyotes and wild quail and, some people said, cougars and bears. The traffic, drugstores and streetcars of Hollywood might have been on another planet.

The same could be said of this place that she had said of Shadygrove Terrace. *Anyone could come and go . . . no one would be the wiser.*

And here, as there, the stillness was almost absolute.

Curious, all the same.

She went to the telephone, dug a scrap of paper from the collection in her pocket and dialed.

TWELVE

'Mrs Turnbit?' Emma breathed a sigh of relief that the journalist was still in her office at half past six on a hot day after a four-hour drive from the desert. At least the woman had had Rex Niddy along to fix flats. 'You may not remember me; my name is Emma Blackstone.'

'Of course! Miss de la Rose's lovely sister-in-law. And one who writes, I am reliably informed, scenarios these days for Foremost...'

'Only one,' responded Emma, laughing. 'And I scarcely dare claim credit for any epic that shall appear under the title *Hot Potato*.'

'Nonsense, dear! Everyone has to start somewhere. I daresay Shakespeare fed his family for two years writing advertising copy for *Ye Bear Baiters' Weekly* before he got his first hit.'

Emma laughed out loud at that, her trepidation at calling the journalist dissolving, and Mrs Turnbit asked with a kind of cheerful gentleness, 'And what can I help you with today, Mrs Blackstone?'

'Emma. I meant what I said about calling me Emma. And yes, I do need . . . I'm not sure it can be called a favor. It's an imposition, and please don't hesitate to tell me that it's not the sort of thing you feel comfortable doing.'

Which was, Emma was fairly certain, a complete lie. From nine months of observation of Mrs Thelma Turnbit and her spiritual sisters and brethren, she guessed that the woman would leap on her suggestion with squeals of delight.

And she was right.

Mrs Ardiss Tinch lived in Long Beach, a seaside community some twenty-five miles south of Los Angeles. With the discovery of oil under Signal Hill, that peaceful town – and it had been a peaceful little town, away from the harbor and the breakwater – had been transformed almost overnight into a wasteland of oil derricks that sprouted like unwholesome trees in back yards, in vacant lots, on street corners and on the city's beaches barely above the tideline. Even in the few neighborhoods that had been spared the invasion, the air reeked with the dark stink of oil.

Mr Stanley Tinch was listed in the city directory as a salesman of real estate. His neat white frame house lay just far enough south, on Seventh Street, to avoid having an oil well in his back yard, but the garden in front did not look healthy. Ardiss Tinch met them at the door, beautifully made-up and dressed with the same tailored care that she'd displayed at the studio on the previous Wednesday morning (and in the half-dozen newspaper photographs since then). Mrs Turnbit had telephoned her to make the arrangements, and introduced Emma as a social worker with particular experience in the education of children. Mrs Tinch practically kissed her hand.

Over freshly made checkerboard cake and freshly brewed coffee – brought in by a black maid – Ardiss Tinch elaborated on her love for, and lifelong concern for 'poor Little Susy.' 'Of course my sister is a kind and well-meaning woman' – she assumed an expression of affection mingled with worry – 'and as you know, Mrs Turnbit, she loves poor Susy dearly. But as I'm sure you also know, Selina is dedicated to her profession, and that profession is a demanding one.' (Emma had wondered how the older sister was going to express her concern for Miss Sutton and in the same breath repeat the accusations she'd been making to the courts – and to every newspaper in town – all week.)

'In many ways, I know she is torn between her calling as an actress and the needs of motherhood. And – please don't take this the wrong way, ma'am; it is not meant to be critical or judgmental in the least, for I love my sister dearly' – *Oh, do you, indeed?* – 'sometimes I wonder if her desire for her own art, as well as her drive to create in Susy the perfection for which she herself has always striven, might cause her to . . . well . . . to forget that Susy is a child.'

That said, she proceeded to vivisect her sister's reputation and qualifications as a mother in the sweetest possible terms.

Emma had suggested, in the previous afternoon's telephone conversation with Mrs Turnbit, that the interview be cast as a background piece on the imperiled child's loving family. 'But in fact . . . well' – she'd thrown all the guilt and hesitation of which she was capable into her voice and had felt almost sick with guilt about the comprehensiveness of the lie she was telling – 'in fact, I've been asked by a lawyer – and I can't give further details than that, I'm afraid – to have a look at the homes of both Mrs Tinch and Mr Snoach.' This was after she had promulgated the myth of her own experience with social work and the education of children. She still wasn't certain that Mrs Turnbit had swallowed that one or only accepted it as a useful excuse to do some snooping of her own. And despite Mrs Turnbit's concern over the near-catastrophe with Vic Duffy, she had practically heard the sparkle in the columnist's eyes over the telephone wires.

'Of course I won't use a thing until you clear it with your lawyer friend,' Mrs Turnbit had sworn, on the drive through the orchards and barley fields down to Long Beach that forenoon. 'But Ardiss Tinch will tell me anything I ask, if she thinks it will help her get her hands on that poor child. And I can always use it later. You wouldn't happen to know if follow-up instructions have come to the studio yet, about that new ransom demand? Oh, dear,' she whispered, in what appeared to be genuine distress, when Emma had shaken her head. 'Oh, the poor child.'

(Much later that night, Emma would fight a losing struggle not to imagine lead lines for Mrs Turnbit's column on the subject: COULD HER MOTHER HAVE STOPPED THEM? – SUSY STILL IN PERIL – AN ARTIST'S PERFECTION OR A MOTHER'S LOVE?)

After forty-five minutes of character assassination which included not only her sister ('I'm afraid that poor Burt's drinking habits have rubbed off, to a shocking degree, on Selina herself . . .') but their father as well ('Well, as the older girl, I suppose I came in for the worst of the beatings, but after I left home, I know he took out those uncontrollable rages on poor Selina. Maybe that's why *she* . . .'), Emma suggested a tour of 'your beautiful home.' Mrs Tinch leaped on this idea like a cat on a crippled lizard.

Emma had already concluded that there was no cat being kept caged anywhere in the house. The smell, though faint, would have been ineradicable. But the house, moderately large, didn't appear big enough to conceal an imprisoned child, and the presence of the maid would have further complicated the effort to do so. (Depending, as Zal had observed, on how one felt about being blackmailed . . .)

On the other hand, a grave-faced question about Mr Tinch's real-estate business confirmed that the Tinches had access to half a dozen vacant properties between Los Angeles and Long Beach, some of them not only uninhabited but fairly isolated in the agricultural wilds of Orange County. And when Emma casually mentioned that she had heard that at one time Mrs Tinch's husband had been in business partnership with Miss Sutton, Ardiss returned, 'Oh, that wasn't Mr Tinch; that was my – well, I married, very foolishly, a man named Bovard – I was practically entrapped into it, you know.' Her tone implied that Mr Bovard had been her first union, something Kitty had told her was not the case.

'And it was, in fact, a very good opportunity to invest Susy's earnings in such a way as to have that money work for her benefit later in life. But Selina . . . well, she demanded more control over Susy's money than she had experience – or judgment – to cope with. And of course poor Burt was in no shape to stop her. She made some *very* poor decisions. I love Selina dearly' – this was her eighth or tenth repetition of this assertion – 'but between her drinking and her . . . well, her *men friends*, the poor girl is better off if she isn't given charge of her *own* funds, let alone poor darling Susy's.'

For the rest, the house was lavishly furnished in the newest and most polished of furnishings. Angular mirrors, elaborate pieces of modern lacquered cabinetry, elegant woodwork and what was clearly a liquor cabinet that had been hastily transformed by filling it with flowers . . . Emma wondered where the liquor had been stashed. The cupboards in the kitchen were suspiciously overcrowded with highball and champagne glasses, and assorted bottles of bitters and sweet fruit syrups, and cocktail shakers lined the kitchen counter as if casually left there during the cooking of dinner. When Mr Tinch strode in towards the end of the interview and headed straight for the cabinet, he stopped short, cursed and changed course for the kitchen. 'Excuse me,' said his wife, and followed him in for a low-voiced colloquy that ended with his angry exclamation, 'I'll drink what I fucken want to in my own house!'

'Shut up, you stupid—' Ardiss's non-company vocabulary would have shamed a truck driver. She immediately dropped her voice for the follow-up lecture.

Mrs Turnbit glanced sidelong at Emma and raised an eyebrow. From the kitchen came the sharp report of a slap, followed immediately by a second. Then after a long few minutes the couple emerged, sleek and smiling and filled with concern. 'Was there anything further you wanted to see?'

Emma had the feeling that she'd learned enough. Kitty, she suspected – or possibly Oscar Denham, who worked at City Hall – would know if there was a way to check which properties were being handled by the widely grinning Stan Tinch, and where they were.

Mr Tinch, she observed, impeccably suited in medium brown, was about six feet tall, his dark brilliantined hair retreating from his temples and faintly flecked with gray. When she and Mrs Turnbit took their leave, she saw also that the doors of the garage at the back of the property, which had stood open – the shelter empty – when they had arrived, were now shut.

Mrs Turnbit treated Emma to lunch at Lexie's Seaside Cottage on Ocean Boulevard, close to the so-called 'Pike' of seaside nickelodeons, chow-mein parlors, penny pitches and the Majestic Ballroom – mostly because the cool offshore winds made it one of the few places in the little town that didn't stink of raw petroleum. The journalist proved to be good and friendly company, refraining from 'pumping' Emma on the subject of her beautiful sister-in-law and instead asking her about Oxford, about archaeology, about her impressions of Hollywood and of American food. Never, Emma noticed, about her purported background in childhood education.

Tact, or simple technique to put a potential source off guard?

Mrs Turnbit, for her part, seemed to know everybody in Hollywood and Los Angeles (and on Broadway in New York), and was an endless source of anecdote and information.

It transpired that she already knew a great deal about Foy Snoach, and about the history and downfall of Magnum Films under poor Burt. She was a goldmine of gossip about such widely differing local personalities as Mayor Cryer and his 'City Hall Gang' (and its connection with prostitution and the smuggling of liquor and drugs), Mr W.F. Creller who was in charge of the Pasadena Tournament of Roses this year (and his legal troubles with the contractors in charge of building a new football stadium in Pasadena), and Tina Mesmer Griffith – no relation to the film director – whose wealthy husband had shot her and thrown her out a window, and later donated the land for Griffith Park to the city. ('She survived,' Mrs Turnbit assured Emma. 'Fastest divorce decree in history – the jury was out four and a half minutes.')

Inspired by this encyclopedic compendium of information, Emma inquired – halfway through crab-claws, coleslaw and French-fried potatoes – had Thelma ('Please do call me Thelma, dear . . .') ever heard of Mr Doyle Dravitt? The carefully penciled eyebrows peaked up, then dropped sharply. 'What dealings have you had with Mr Dravitt, dear?'

'None as yet,' Emma replied. *How do I ask this without causing the poor man trouble if my suspicions are wrong?* 'I have the impression – but I could be absolutely mistaken about this – that he's attempting to bribe me.'

The eyebrows went up again. 'Oh, please don't feel that you were singled out. The man has bribed just about everyone in the city government and a fair percentage of our representatives in Sacramento. He's an architect – well, I suppose one could call him a developer, really. He owns a great deal of land in Orange and San Diego Counties, and is good friends with the likes of Mayor Cryer and Charlie Crawford – the Mayor's *eminence grise*, you know. And well in with gamblers like Farmer Page . . . In fact, he's the brother of your Mr Pugh's second wife. I believe they still play tennis together at the Los Angeles Athletic Club . . . Good Heavens, Foremost wasn't connected with that scandal at the university last month, was it? When Dravitt tried to bribe one of his son's professors?'

She must have read the answer in Emma's startled expression.

'It seems he stormed the poor man's office when he received the bribe money back in the mail,' she explained after a moment. 'He'd already made arrangements to have the boy admitted to law school. Rather expensive arrangements, I gather, and there was a shouting match that could be heard all over the building. I understand Dravitt has an unfortunate habit of throwing objects and sweeping things on to the floor when vexed. Then sometime that night, the poor professor had a stroke and cracked his head on the corner of the desk, and died of it. And it's my understanding' – Mrs Turnbit lowered her forkful of buttered crustacean and leaned close – 'that although Mr Dravitt has three employees who swear they were with him at his offices on Wall Street until four o'clock the following morning, the police have their suspicions.'

'I can see that they might,' Emma agreed, a little hollowly. 'On the subject of police suspicions – and purely for my own information – how did you know to come out to Twenty-Nine Palms Wednesday? If it was a flash of sheer journalistic intuition, it seems to have been awfully widespread.'

Mrs Turnbit laughed. 'A "tip," I believe the police call such things. A woman telephoned me at my office – and, evidently, Rex and Sheila and Louella and I don't know who-all else – Tuesday morning, and said that a ransom note had been received and that a secret meeting was to take place somewhere near the set on Wednesday for the hand-off to be arranged. All tosh, as it turned out. I wouldn't be surprised if it was someone who hated Pugh – like Lou Jesperson at Enterprise, or that dreadful Harry Cohn at Columbia – who arranged it, though it did all work out in the end, didn't it? It's almost as if *someone* knew that poor Miss Sutton would escape and find her way to the set.'

Foy Snoach owned a medium-sized house of the sort described as 'Spanish colonial' – meaning it was stuccoed and had interior arches from living room to dining room and a flat, tile-trimmed roof – in Culver City, not far from Triangle Studios. The garden of roses, lilies, exquisitely trimmed hedges and magnolia trees surrounded it. More checkerboard cake (stale) was presented by a gray-faced, crushed-looking woman who immediately retreated to the kitchen, propelled by a glance from Snoach.

Mrs Turnbit had taken care to invent a reason to hold the interview at the Snoach house rather than his office downtown, and Emma suspected Snoach had concurred in this so as not to leave Mrs Snoach alone with journalists. On the few occasions on which the woman appeared, it was to say, 'Of course, dear,' and 'Yes, exactly,' and retreat to the kitchen again at once. Emma heard the sound of cleaning. The house smelled of carbolic soap. The coffee was weak and, by the taste of it, had been reheated several times over the past two days.

'There's no reason the girl can't be another Bernhardt,' declared Snoach in his customary roar. 'No reason at all – except for that slack, lazy, selfish mother of hers. She's my daughter and I still say it of her: useless, the whole damn family. Beauty's the only thing any of that tribe has going for 'em. You should have seen Opal' – he jerked his head towards the closed kitchen door – 'when I married her, before she let herself go. If brains was gunpowder, not one of 'em could blow her own nose, and you can't trust either of those girls, or their mother, with twenty-five cents.'

He turned his ferocious amber-brown glare on Emma. 'You can bet when I get custody of my girl, *I'll* be the one raising her.'

'Does it look likely that the courts will find in your favor, Mr Snoach?' Mrs Turnbit leaned forward with an expression that conveyed that anxious hope for this outcome would keep her wakeful for many nights to come.

'Of course they will! If they're not nincompoops – or on the take,' he added grimly. 'Which, in that Godforsaken town, you can pretty well count on. My lawyers are trying to have the trial venue changed from Los Angeles to Anaheim, where there's a chance of a fair hearing of the facts.'

'Would you keep Susy in the film industry?' asked Emma, curious, earning a suspicious glare from the big man.

'What kind of a question is that? Of course she'll continue to star in films! More so than ever, with proper management and proper discipline to develop her talents. Slipshod, that's what Selina is – and I say it even though I'm her father! And that scheming slut Ardiss is worse. Just set it down,' he barked at his wife, who had entered again from the kitchen, her small face suddenly wooden at hearing this description of her daughters.

As the woman put down the gleaming silver tray with its matched vessels of sugar and milk, he went on, 'There's no reason Susy can't get two grand a week on her next contract. Selina let Foremost jew her down to a thousand because she let Pugh bully her. Dumb coosie got screwed into robbing her own daughter, in more ways than one.' He shook his leonine head angrily. 'That's something you won't see once *I'm* in the saddle.'

He returned to this theme several times during the tour he gave the women of the house – which included, Emma observed, a small bed already made up in a corner of the parental chamber ('It's a mistake to give a child her own room. Who knows what kind of monkeyshines they get up to when the lights are out?').

'And you won't see me wasting good money on servants. The girl'll make her own bed and do her share of the housework, the way a woman should. No reason she can't do her chores in the morning before she goes to the studio, or after her dance lessons. Every girl should know how to wash a floor properly, and do laundry. It's all of a piece with Selina's wasting every dime that child makes; I'll make sure that money's put to proper use. And no slick "financial manager" hanging around with his hand in the till every week. Living at her place, too, by what I hear these days. If her own Grandpa doesn't know how to use that money for her own good, who does?'

Despite Snoach's views on childhood discipline and being watched over day and night, Emma noted that there was a second room in the house that had probably once been a bedroom, now in use as Snoach's office. She wondered if Snoach's two daughters had shared it at any point. Or did purchase of the house post-date the girls' marriage and Selina's stardom?

'It's all a matter of training a child. Teach her to follow instructions – and you can bet I'll be the one on the set giving those instructions, not some nancy kraut director who couldn't tell a story if you wrote it out for him on a billboard. With the money she'll be making, we can start up our own studio . . .'

Every floor in the little bungalow had been scrubbed and waxed, recently and often. The place smelled of soap, iodoform and bleach, with no trace of a cat's presence. *Which doesn't mean he didn't drown poor Mr Gray the minute he snatched Susy from Desert Light*, if *he snatched her* . . . Lagging slightly behind Snoach and Mrs Turnbit, she had the chance to look over the house and could find no indication of a space where a child was or could be hidden.

But she shuddered at the thought of a seven-year-old girl suddenly put under this man's exclusive control.

And she felt like a prostitute, when, at the end of the afternoon, Mrs Turnbit whispered to her, 'Not a word to anyone else, mind,' and slipped a ten-dollar bill into her hand.

'Oh, hell, no,' Zal comforted her, when she told him about it a few days later. 'That's five times what the average hooker in this town gets. And you got lunch besides.'

'Beast,' said Emma.

THIRTEEN

Letters from Hal Partington – this time threatening to complain to the regents of the university – and from Mr Doyle Dravitt waited for Emma when she returned to Ivarene Street late that afternoon. Partington's was simply annoying – she had already invited him to take the matter up with Professor Denham, not herself. But Dravitt's peremptorily informed her that an appointment had been made for her to meet with Mr Dravitt at his offices at four o'clock the following afternoon, Saturday, July nineteenth, 1924. She glanced at the clock – it was just after five – and wondered if Oscar Denham, who had impressed her as a man of considerable strength under that quiet exterior, would or could accompany her to the meeting.

Zal, Harry Garfield and Roger Clint were all still out in the desert. Probably, Gren Torley had driven back to Camp Turpitude today as well, to look after the camels, having left the lions to be coddled by Mrs Torley. Something about Mr Shang's tale of an attempted break-in put chills up her spine. *He'd already made arrangements to have the boy admitted to law school*, Thelma Turnbit had said. *There was a shouting match that could be heard all over the building . . . . sometime that night the poor professor had a stroke . . . cracked his head . . . the police have their suspicions.*

Papers all over the floor and blood everywhere, Julia Denham had said.

Including places where it would not have been, had the injury and death been an accident. *I didn't know archaeology could be so exciting.* Zal's jest no longer sounded like a joke.

And Mrs Turnbit's words returned to her also: *Good friends with the likes of . . . Charlie Crawford . . .* After nine months in Hollywood, Emma was well acquainted with the name of the man behind a significant portion of the Los Angeles underworld.

Was it fair to entangle her new friend and her husband in affairs that might get poor Oscar . . . ? Her mind hesitated from even framing the words. *Not* shot, *surely . . . Not over the grade in a history class.*

Her hand shaking, just slightly, she reached for the telephone – and she nearly jumped out of her skin when it rang at her touch.

'Mrs Blackstone?' Conrad Fishbein's light, silky tenor was unmistakable. 'Thank Heavens I've caught you. I've been trying all afternoon. Can you come to the studio? Now, tonight. We've got the newest ransom note.'

On Monday night, leave $200,000 in small, unmarked bills in the back seat of Miss Sutton's green Vauxhall in Daisy Dell, at the mouth of the dell where the road runs down to Cahuenga Avenue. I will be watching, so do not put men in the dell. If you obey these instructions, Susy will be returned to you safely the following morning. If I see anyone near the car, I will not touch the money and you will find Susy's body sometime the following week. I mean it.

A second note, like the first on brownish newsprint in an illiterate child's painful scrawl: *I havnt see them they wont hurt me pleas do what they say*

At the bottom of that paper, tiny fingers had been lightly smudged with ink and pressed below the words. Enclosed in the note's tight folds was a curl of light-brown, baby-fine hair.

Emma looked aside. Rage, hatred and terror turned her almost sick.

Burt waking up hungover to find his daughter gone. Selina staggering into camp Wednesday afternoon . . .

Half-burned towels caked with blood . . .

'We can't call the cops on this.' Fishbein refolded the two notes, slipped them into a larger yellow envelope on which CONRAD FISHBEIN had been typed. 'Not after that circus act of calling in the fan-magazine gang. We've got to keep this tied up tight.'

Emma wondered if Kitty had managed even yet to get Mr Pugh alone, to give him the charred contents of the Desert Light incinerator. Or if Mr Pugh had informed the publicity chief of this new development, let alone the San Bernardino County sheriffs. 'Is the studio going to pay?' she asked.

Fishbein's reaction of shock and horror at the mere thought of such a question would have done credit to any actor on the lot. 'Mrs Blackstone, I completely understand your suspicions. Producers and studios have a terrible, and not always unmerited, reputation. But I swear to you' – he actually raised his right hand as if taking an oath – 'neither Mr Pugh nor any of the men connected with Foremost Studio would go so far as to endanger a child's life in these circumstances! Please believe me when I say that there has never been a question of not paying.'

'I'm glad to hear it.' Emma made her shoulders relax and remembered to take a breath. Her eyes still held his. 'Then I can stop worrying about this alternate ending for *Tiny Miracle*?'

For one split second, in the hard electric glare that illuminated his office, Fishy looked nonplussed. But he had the recovery time of a trained athlete. 'Put it right out of your mind.' The round, pasty face, the wide blue eyes behind the lenses of his glasses transformed, within an instant, to those of a mother concerned with nothing but the life of her beloved child (for instance, those of Lillian Gish in *Way Down East*). 'Whatever happens, it's something that can be dealt with later.'

'Tomorrow,' he went on, turning to the envelope once again, 'I need you to take this out to Mr Pugh in Seven Palms. Colt Madison swears that none of the racketeers in this town have anything to do with the kidnapping – and he's a man who should know. But . . . I wouldn't want any word of this slipping out before Mr Pugh and, more importantly, our studio backers have had a chance to talk about it. That rules the police right out. I know I can trust you, Mrs Blackstone.' His eyes met hers once again. 'And there's precious few people in this studio – in this whole town – that I can say that about.'

He pressed the envelope into her hands.

Emma removed the ransom note, reread the typed lines and automatically compared the typeface with the *CONRAD FISHBEIN* on the envelope. Same machine. New black-and-red ribbon, slightly ill-fitting, so that the Ps, Gs and Ys all looked as if they'd dipped their toes in red paint. 'How do they know what car to ask for?'

'Good question.' The publicity chief's voice was grim. 'Once we get Susy back, and turn all this over to the police, and they nab that chauffeur Santini and ask him that same question, I'm pretty sure his lawyer's going to say that every magazine reader in America knows all about that Vauxhall. Every columnist in the country wrote it up. It cost over ten grand, with custom paint and engraved door handles and the leopard-skin seats. That's if Santini's still in town when the cops go to call on him.'

He tapped the envelope with a stubby forefinger. 'They ask for the Vauxhall because it's a touring model. There's no trunk for the cops to plant a man in. That's another reason we need to keep this absolutely quiet. If the police knew this now, all they'd think about is catching their man – or men. And you know, the cops have been saying all along that it was an inside job.'

Perhaps not as 'inside' as Burt thinks it is . . .

She tried to sound as if Selina Sutton were her sister, who truly had been snatched from her home by strangers (*or maybe not strangers . . .*). Abused, locked in a shed, terrified for her child . . . *How can I doubt like this?* She felt sick at her own willingness to accept Burt's view of his wife . . . *And Kitty's. And the clean hair and the make-up and the shoes* . . . (She could just hear her mother saying, 'In a piggie's little eye . . .')

'And have you heard how Miss Sutton is? Does she remember anything further, do you know?'

Mr Fishbein's brow furrowed with concern as genuine as her own. 'Doctor Plaister brought her back to town yesterday. He has a small private hospital in Glendale' – *A Vacation in Europe* was what the studio crew called it, that being the excuse Pugh would give when anyone was under Plaister's care for drying out or ridding themselves of an unwanted pregnancy – 'and she's there under twenty-four-hour care.'

Emma wondered whether Miss Sutton's father, or her sister, had charge of making decisions about the amount of narcotic involved in that care. Or had Mr Pugh given the instructions about that? Certainly nobody was going to ask Burt . . . always supposing anyone could *find* Burt.

'There's a train out to Seven Palms at noon tomorrow,' Fishbein went on. 'Or if you prefer, the studio will pay travel expenses for you to drive out there in Kitty's car. You can leave earlier and get out to the set before the day heats up. Either way, I'll wire Mr Pugh—'

'I'll take the car, thank you,' said Emma. Upon her arrival at the house yesterday, and upon her return there that afternoon, in addition to the hectoring letters from Partington and Dravitt, she had found telegrams from Kitty, anxiously inquiring whether Buttercreme had regained her capricious appetite and begging her to hug all three Pekes 'extra for me.' (Emma had duly telephoned Western Union and dispatched reassuring messages both days.) Given her sister-in-law's expressions of desolation and grief (the presence of Mr Pugh, any number of riding extras and Dave the handsome camel-driver notwithstanding), it almost went without saying that Emma would bring the Pekes with her tomorrow. As she navigated yet again the dodgem-car extravaganza along Sunset Boulevard, in spite of her fears, she smiled.

Many people – including her surviving Aunt Estelle, and millions of churchgoers in America – would unhesitatingly describe Camille de la Rose as heartless. Yet it was only her numerous lovers, Emma reflected, whom Kitty did not love.

Reuniting Kitty with those she *did* love, thought Emma resignedly, would take the usual planning and care – stopping on the way to walk them and make sure they had water, to say nothing of flat tires en route. *And I suppose it will mean staying the night in Seven Palms* . . .

And that, too, brought a smile – and a curious sense of homecoming – to her heart.

I shall have to telegraph both Kitty and Zal . . .

But the smile was short-lived. It faded at the thought of Susy, wherever she was, trying gamely to feed the only one who truly loved *her* through the bars of his cage and trying not to give in to terror. Two hundred thousand dollars. Nearly twice the cost of a film, and almost three times what Susy's last film had earned the studio.

At least, she thought, Monday's 'unofficial' and 'routine' reconnaissance by the police hadn't resulted in Susy's murder, if the kidnappers had sent a new demand.

Not yet, anyway. (*The Police Chief . . . just wants to cover his ass from the newspapers . . .*)

Or had that 'routine' visit been authorized – or paid for – by someone who wanted the excuse to say, *Oh, too bad! What horrible people did this, what a terrible tragedy . . .*

The Chief of Police might not even have known about the visit.

Stop it! she told herself, as she turned the Packard (*finally!*) up Vine Street, and the warm, dusty darkness of the hills enfolded her. *Everything will be all right. Mr Pugh will come to some kind of negotiation . . .*

She didn't believe this for one second. *Monday*. And, *Who wants to pay to see a ten-year-old?* The horrible suspicion whispered to her, that with or without *Tiny Miracle* (with or without a ghastly vision of Susy's face smiling down upon her grieving parents and

the Miracle Gold Mine), upon Susy's death all those one- and two-reelers, and her five features for Foremost – including the disappointing *Susy and the Bad Men* – would rake in millions.
Hollywood.
The name clanged in her brain like a hammer on a tin washtub.
What am I doing in this place?
The silly turrets and extravagantly arched windows of Kitty's Ivarene love nest rose on their miniature knee of the hillside, blanched silver by the watery moonlight. Emma negotiated the steep drive but parked the car in front of the house, rather than wake the Shangs by taking it around to the garage. She had left the porch light burning for herself and stood for a moment beside the car, scanning the porch above her. Conscious, again, of the empty hillsides on the other side of Ivarene Street, of the weird cry of a killdeer swooping over the scrub. Of her heart beating hard.

Then she climbed the steep, tiled steps, door keys in hand.

Just as she reached the top, feet crunched on gravel below her, and the dogs – crowded as usual next to the door within – began to bark. Angry barking. Watchdog barking. *Die kleinen Wächter*: furious little lion-dogs warning of peril . . .

Emma flung herself across the porch as feet pounded the steps behind her, shoved the key in the lock. A man's hard hand grabbed her elbow, jerked her around. She had a glimpse of dark clothing, a dark kerchief bound over the lower part of a face – like a bad man in a bad Western film – and a black vizard mask. In his free hand, he held a gun.

'Don't make a—' he began, and Emma kicked him as hard as she could in the shin and, when his hold broke, twisted the key in the lock.

She had meant to slip through the door and lock it behind her, but the dogs – even shy little Buttercreme – streamed out through the aperture like the hounds of hell and hurled themselves on the attacker's ankles. The masked man sprang back, tried to kick Black Jasmine, lost his balance, tripped over Chang Ming and went backwards off the porch and down, flat as a falling tree, on his back on the seven-foot flight of steps. Emma heard the crack of his skull on the ornamental tile.

The Pekes scurried to the edge of the steps, stood in a line and barked scorn at their fallen foe.

Horrified, Emma ran down the flight. Her erstwhile attacker lay, arms outflung, legs sprawled untidily up the stair; she could see him breathing in the reflected glow of the porch light. Even as she yanked the gun out of his hand, she thought, *He might not have been alone . . .* and screamed, 'Help! Mr Shang!' *I need to make it sound like there's an army . . .* 'Jose! Jack! Harry!'

Nobody emerged from the darkness. Nor did anyone flee towards the road. She retreated halfway up the steps, gun pointed. 'Help! Mr Shang!'

After a long minute, the gardener emerged, silent as cold murder, from around the big eucalyptus that shadowed the turn of the driveway. *He must have checked to make sure there was no one hiding . . .*

She guessed the old man was somewhere in his eighties, but he could easily have passed for a hundred and fifty. His long white hair shimmered in the thin starlight, and he held the six-foot staff he sometimes walked with like what it actually was – a weapon. Emma came down the steps and knelt again beside her fallen assailant.

Blood was pooling on the bottom step under his head. During the War, she'd driven ambulance-loads of young men from the station to Bicester Hospital, but the medical staff – both in the hospital trains and at Bicester itself – had made sure that the VAD drivers were well schooled in first aid: *Just in case we need a helping hand sometime . . .*

With delicate care, she slipped her fingers under the sticky, warm mat of his hair. It didn't feel as if his skull were fractured, and his cervical vertebrae seemed to be in alignment. His breathing was steady. His pulse, though fast, was strong.

She pulled the vizard up, the bandana down, and saw a young, firm-jawed face, like the boys she'd taken to hospital.

The eyelids fluttered.

She handed Mr Shang the gun. 'I'm going to call the police.' Systematically, she went through the pockets of the young man's sports jacket and trousers. No other weapons; a wallet, an empty envelope, three folded bits of notepaper and a ring of four keys. His inner jacket pocket contained a thick wad of papers folded lengthwise. 'I'll be back down in a moment. Shout if you even *think* you see anyone . . .'

Mrs Shang emerged from the shadows at the far corner of the yard, swaying on her tiny, mutilated 'lily' feet and carrying not only a staff but what looked like a cut-down rice-flail that had been modified into a truly murderous bludgeon. 'No one here,' she reported cheerfully. 'Car down road. Big car, brown and yellow, license one-four-seven two-five-eight.' Tucking her rice-flail under one arm, she groped in the pocket of her baggy blue *chang'ao* and produced a small brass key – the sort Emma recognized as being used to switch on the electrical system of more modern automobiles.

As Emma turned to mount the steps, the young man at her feet whispered, 'Please . . .'

At the same time, Mr Shang snapped the gun's cylinder closed and reported, 'Gun not loaded, Madame.'

Emma knelt again. 'And did you intend to frighten me to death?'

The young man turned his head, and his breath hissed with pain.

In a kinder voice, Emma asked, 'Can you move your feet? Your hands?' She flipped the wallet open, held the driver's license up to the glow of the porch light.

Wilson George Dravitt.

FOURTEEN

'It was a stupid idea.' Wilson George Dravitt flinched in agony from the touch of the ice-bag on his head, then settled gingerly on Kitty's chrome-and-velvet living-room couch. Mrs Shang brought in a cup of some herbal infusion from the kitchen; Mr Shang remained on the porch, watching for the ambulance. 'Al needed the money something desperate – Alonzo Paine.' Emma recognized the name of another of Professor Wright's students. Recalled that his paper and Dravitt's had been typed on the same machine, with the faded ribbon. 'He and I share this apartment across in Boyle Heights, and he's like a brother to me. More than a brother. His family . . .'

The young man flinched again, and Emma recalled those peremptory notes from Doyle Dravitt, expecting her to come at call. *Bribed just about everyone in the city government*, Thelma Turnbit had said. *Well in with gamblers like Farmer Page* . . .

At length, Dravitt whispered, 'He's my dad and I love him, but I . . .' He then turned his face away. 'Anyhow,' he went on after a moment, 'Al's family sort of took me in when we were in catechism class together at St Basil's. It meant everything to have a real mom and a real brother, who'd talk about something other than real estate and stock prices. His sisters are like sisters to me. I don't know if I can make you understand.'

'Since I had a real mother,' said Emma quietly, 'and a real father, and a real brother' – she paused, to keep her voice from shaking – 'I can't really picture what it would be like not to have had them . . . ever. But I understand.'

His breath whispered in a sigh. In the better light of the living room, Emma could see the difference in the pupil size of those dark-blue eyes, and he'd been unable to tell how many fingers she was holding up ('Uh . . . you want the number from all three hands?'), but his movements, though they spoke of serious bruising and pain, told her that he hadn't broken his neck or his back. *Please God, I hope he isn't bleeding into his brain* . . .

'So Anna – Al's middle sister – is going to have a baby. It's a long story, and her boyfriend Izzy's on a construction job in Oklahoma, and his parents don't want anything to do with Anna because they're Jewish and Anna's not. It's a long story,' he repeated, closing his eyes and turning his head a little. 'She's going to go stay with friends in Oregon, to have the baby and sort of hide out until Izzy gets back, which'll be around Christmas, but she needs money. Dad hates them – all through high school, I had to sneak out to hang around with Al. But I went to Dad's business manager. And he said he'd loan Al five hundred dollars, if . . .'

His voice stammered to a halt. Mrs Shang touched his hand, held the cup of tisane so that he could drink from it. Outside, through the open door, the night wind stirred the smells of dust and sage from the dry hills on the other side of the street. Hollywood seemed a thousand miles away.

Dravitt sighed again. 'So he asks Al to throw the exhibition football game between us and USC at the end of the term. Al's the star quarterback and the best player on the Grizzlies. The other guys are good, but the Trojans pretty much kicked everybody's butt the last couple of years. If Al works against our guys in the game, they're gonna get whipped.'

'And I assume' – Emma gently took the cup from her erstwhile attacker's hand – 'Mr Business Manager has money on the Trojans.'

'A lot.' The young face twisted for a moment, with pain and regret. 'Not just on win or lose, but on point spread under about six different names. I didn't know it then, but I found out a couple days ago that he really needs that money, too. Dad caught him cooking the books to the tune of about a hundred grand. He gave him thirty days to make that money good, because he's my cousin, and part of the family, and I guess he borrowed the money, to cover what he took, from a lot of his gambler pals, Charlie Crawford and Farmer Page and Iron Joe Ardizzone – people you really, *really* don't want to stiff.'

'And then it became obvious that you – and Mr Paine – were going to fail Classics 102.'

If I don't pass this class, I'll lose my place on the football team, Alonzo Paine's letter had pleaded.

Dravitt murmured, 'Yeah.' He shifted uncomfortably, his eyes sliding closed.

Emma held up the sheaf of folded pages, typed in the faded ribbon with the worn-down 'g.' Even a brief glance had shown her that some paragraphs were identical to those of the unknown papers which had plagiarized Professor Wright's work; others were hopelessly clumsy in their wording. ('Necropolis,' 'cremation,' 'deceased' and 'gladiatorial' – words used in Professor Wright's analysis of the tombs he had discovered – were all consistently misspelled in these latter paragraphs, as was 'Etruscan.') 'Who actually wrote those papers you – and I presume your friend Mr Paine – turned in? I mean, who wrote the portions of them that weren't taken straight from Professor Wright's unpublished articles?'

Dravitt sighed, like a beaten man. 'Frankie Styles,' he said. 'She was Professor Wright's star pupil . . . couple of years ago. She works for him now, office stuff, but she types his articles for him . . .' ('Thank you, Frankie,' Emma could hear Julia saying to the typist who'd handed her the office keys.) 'Al and I lived on canned beans and oatmeal for two weeks, to pay her to write our papers. I never could make head or tails of those Etruksuns, and between working at the Vermont Café and football practice, Al just didn't have time. She didn't get the papers to us till the day they were due, and it wasn't until after we turned them in – I guess this was Wednesday a week ago – that I read the carbon copy she gave me.'

'And realized she'd copied whole paragraphs out of Professor Wright's unpublished article on Etruscan tombs?'

His eyes opened and he flinched, even at the shaded glow of the living-room lamps. 'Oh, shit – shoot, I mean, ma'am, I'm sorry . . . Damn it! Darn it . . .' He shook his head. 'I didn't know that. But right smack in the middle of about three different pages, she talked about these tombs or temples or whatever they were – he'd lectured about them in class, but he didn't say where they were. But she gave the names of the places – Corciano, in Perugia . . . and some other place . . .'

'Pietralungia?' Emma recalled that one from both Wright's paper and one of the questionable pages.

'Something like that. Names she could only have got from typing his article . . .'

Emma recalled her father's comments about students who had taken what had appeared to them to be the easier way out. 'Oh, dear.'

'I had to get them back.' He shook his head feverishly, and Emma felt his wrist again, the beat of the pulse still strong.

'You should rest.'

'No!' His face twisted with pain. 'That's what I'm trying to tell you, ma'am. She'd mentioned that stuff in both Al's paper and mine, and I figured Wright was going to read them over the holiday weekend. He'd spot it in a minute, that we'd got somebody else to write our papers. I knew our only chance was for me to steal those pages back out of both our papers, and substitute pages with stuff he wouldn't recognize from his own work. Al was at work by the time I read the stuff, so I typed up about five new pages with all this stuff I looked up in the encyclopedia and the textbook to make it sound good, and it was about six o'clock before I finished. I phoned Frankie to ask if I could come in and sneak into Wright's office and swap the papers, and she said my dad had been there and had a fight with Professor Wright that you coulda heard on Catalina. Yelling and threatening like he does, and throwing things, like *that's* gonna give him a better opinion of me.'

'But my dad didn't do it.' His voice sank, and his eyes slid closed again. 'I swear to God, no matter what he said when he was mad, my dad wouldn't have laid a finger on him. He just gets that way. I got there at midnight. Even Wright shoulda been gone by that time. But he was lying on the floor in the middle of the room with blood all over the corner of the desk. He was . . . He was breathing, but he sounded really bad. There was stuff from the desk all over the floor,' he added shakily. 'Not just papers, but those little statues and pieces of pottery. I had to . . . to push Professor Wright out of the way, to look at them all, and I nearly broke my neck on something like – I don't know, like a pill bottle or a piece of pipe . . .'

'It was a neo-Babylonian cylinder seal.'

'That round thing he kept on his desk? I coulda killed myself, stepping on it . . . Anyway, I had to hunt through all those papers just in the light that came in through the windows from the streetlights outside. The pages were all mixed up from where my dad threw everything off the desk, and I kept dropping them and trying to put them in order. I couldn't just leave the new pages – I had to find the old ones, because whoever took over the class – and I knew it'd probably be Partington, and he hates Al – would flunk the both of us for sure. Then Professor Wright kind of moaned and thrashed, and I nearly jumped out of my skin and dropped everything—' His voice cracked, and he looked away, sobbing.

'Rest now,' said Emma, and brushed aside the dark hair from his brow.

She tried to force her mind away from those other young men she'd sat beside, the stretchers lined up in the hallway at Bicester, or waiting at the stations for the trucks to come. Young men no older than this boy, whispering the memories of going over the top with their brothers-in-arms. *The officer kept yelling at us, 'One more time,' and blowing his whistle . . .* Or talking to her about cricket games they thought would be the following afternoon – those warm green afternoons of the summers long gone. *Is Gus all right, Lizzie? Don't let him pine – you know how he pines when I go up –* 'Up' being, 'up to Oxford.' And she'd whispered back, *Of course Gus misses you but he's not pining. He's eating well, and plays with the other dogs . . .* And the boy's hand had tightened on hers.

She sometimes wondered if, six years on, Gus was still pining for the friend who was never going to come back at term's end. Or had they joined one another again already, in the place where it would always be summer afternoon?

'My dad didn't have anything to do with it,' Dravitt insisted. 'Yeah, he tried to bribe Wright – he told me that the next day . . . He was mad. He'd never have touched him. Then by the time I found everything – or thought I found everything – I turned around back, and he . . .' His voice thinned to a stammer again. 'He'd . . . His eyes were open, but he . . .'

'It's all right.'

He shut his eyes, the words dribbling from his lips now in spurts. 'Dad didn't do it. I knew the cops would blame my dad, or blame me if somebody came and found me there. I couldn't hardly breathe, and I couldn't think . . . I dragged him back behind the desk and I nearly broke my neck again, slipping on that damn cylinder or whatever it was under the papers. Dad wouldn't have done it,' he sobbed, trembling all over now and clutching at her hand. 'He wouldn't have.'

She couldn't keep herself from asking, 'Was that your father who came here yesterday?'

'He wanted to get all the pages of my paper back from you. Pretend Wright had lost it. I told him – Sunday . . . Got home that Wednesday night and hid all the papers in my room, then I had to go to Dad's for the whole Fourth of July . . . family picnic . . . didn't get back to look at them till Saturday night and I saw I hadn't got everything, and still had some of the new stuff. His death was in the papers, and I got a letter from the school saying Denham would be taking over. Dad said he'd take care of it.'

His fingers groped for the teacup, but when Emma helped him to drink, the tepid liquid dribbled from a corner of his lips. 'All he thought about was me getting into Yale. Al . . . I didn't tell him about Al, but he told me where you were, and I got his car Thursday afternoon and tried to break in when I figured everybody'd be gone. Find Al's paper. Put the new pages in. Al has to be in that game . . .'

Headlights gleamed in the darkness beyond the porch, made the turn from Ivarene Street to the steep drive. *They probably got lost . . .*

'Dad didn't do it,' the young man whispered. 'He didn't.'

He was unconscious by the time the orderlies came up the steps.

Emma rode to Clara Barton Hospital with him in the ambulance, still holding his hand. In the waiting room, she took young Mr Dravitt's wallet from her pocket and searched through the cards for his father's home telephone number; finding nothing, she thumbed the collection of miscellaneous notes and the empty envelope she'd found along with it. Nothing. It was nearly ten o'clock, and she knew calling Doyle Dravitt's office would get her nowhere.

In the end, she telephoned the Shangs, in their cottage behind Kitty's house, and Mr Shang obligingly hiked up Ivarene Street a little distance to where Wilson Dravitt had left his father's handsome brown-and-yellow Delage (license number 147-258). In twenty minutes, he called the hospital back with the information from the vehicle's registration. Emma hoped that while he was there, he had replaced the electrical system key.

'Mr Dravitt?' she said to the gruff, angry voice that answered. 'My name is Mrs Blackstone – I understand that you've been trying to reach me. I'm very sorry to say this, but your son attempted to retrieve the papers that you've wanted to speak to me about – by threat of violence, I'm afraid – and in the process, he suffered a fall down the front steps of the house. He's at Clara Barton Hospital on Vermont Avenue, with a concussion. I don't know yet how bad it is.'

Over the wire, she could hear the hiss of his breath.

She went on, 'I repeat, the fall was completely an accident, and because the gun he threatened me with was not loaded, I have not contacted the police . . .'

'Will he be all right?'

'I don't know yet. He did speak to me after the accident, and he didn't seem disoriented; he was able to move his hands and feet, and there doesn't appear to be any numbness. But—'

'Are you there with him?'

'I'm in the lobby.'

'I'll be there.'

Wealthy as the man was, she assumed that he owned more than one car.

Doyle Dravitt looked pretty much exactly as old Mr Shang had described him: tall, formerly rangy and now running to paunchiness and a trace of a double chin, the edges of his dark, retreating hairline feathered with gray. He strode across the lobby's tiled floor to the receptionist's desk without so much as a glance at Emma, demanded the attendance of his son's physician and waited by the desk until a surgeon appeared. A glance at her watch made Emma groan inwardly – it was now eleven o'clock, and rosy-fingered Dawn was scheduled to leave the gates of Apollo's palace just as soon as she finished her tea. It would be a long drive through the rising desert heat.

But she'd seen too many men and women, gray-faced and shaken, hurry through the lobby of Bicester Hospital, desperately questioning overworked surgeons, to even think of leaving – even though she was fairly certain this man was what Kitty would call a *putz*. He yelled at three surgeons and, to judge by the hand he slipped into the front of his jacket, attempted to bribe the hospital administrator, before he gave up and came over to her.

'Mrs Blackstone?'

She saw that his eyes were reddened and swollen. Had he let his chauffeur see this, she wondered, in the dark of the car? Gently, she said, 'I don't think they can possibly know anything yet, sir. I drove for the Volunteer Ambulance Corps; with concussions, it's very hard to tell.'

He said, 'Thank you,' as if the words hurt his mouth.

She handed him the sheaf of folded papers – the replacement pages that young Mr Dravitt had inadvertently returned to his pockets along with some – but not all – of Miss Styles's more expert work. 'He was trying to help a friend,' she said. 'And to shield you. I assume if you lost your temper and swept the contents of Professor Wright's desk on to the office floor, your fingerprints would be all over the office. Your son guessed it, too.'

The harsh, pouchy face turned beet-red, but Dravitt said nothing.

'And I assume that if you found it necessary to browbeat your employees into swearing you were with them until four o'clock in the morning, you haven't any real alibi. Although the official cause of the accident is a stroke, I am fairly certain that what happened was that Professor Wright stepped on a Babylonian cylinder seal that was half hidden under the papers on the floor. It's about the size – and the shape – of a spool of thread. He was dying when your son came into the room and found him, hours later. Wilson had already heard about the quarrel. Of course, he was afraid of what the police might think.'

'The boy had no goddam business running errands for a cheating good-for-nothing.' The words weren't shouted. Flat, like the ruins of what had once been a wall.

'Everyone can make a mistake, trying to help a friend.'

'I don't mean the Paine boy, though how he got into the university is more than I can figure out. He doesn't even have the brains to cheat. But when you pay a man to look after your interests, set him up with clients in City Hall and the studios, with your friends . . .' He shook his head disgustedly, waved a flat, pale hand before his face, like a man tormented by gnats. 'It sounds like Will told you about that worthless cousin of his, borrowing money to cover what he stole . . . I didn't prosecute, but I sure fired his thieving ass. He can get himself shot by Farmer Page for all I care.'

The dark-blue eyes sharpened on her, calculating. 'Will said there were about three pages from the original paper that he didn't get back. I'll give you fifty dollars a page.'

'I will mail the pages to you in the morning,' replied Emma. 'Free of charge, because I am afraid your son will have to retake Classics 102 before he'll be able to graduate. Please tell him for me that I'll deal with his friend Mr Paine's paper. I suspect,' she added quietly, 'that your son will not be able to start law school in September in any case.'

Dravitt regarded her in silence for a time, his face still. He opened his mouth to speak, but at that moment the receptionist's Cuban heels clicked on the tile, and Emma saw the woman, followed by a man in a white surgical gown, approaching. Dravitt turned, and for an instant before his face assumed the belligerent mask of the *putz* in charge, she saw – as she had on Little Susy's in the hot dust of that nameless Western town – terror and dread.

Then his jaw came forward, and he turned back to her, held out his hand. 'Thank you,' he said gruffly. And after another moment, 'Thank you for not leaving him.'

And he strode away to find out what they had to tell him.

Across the room, Emma lingered long enough to see the first words exchanged, and how the man's body both relaxed and straightened, as if weight had rolled from his shoulders and a lodged weapon had been harmlessly removed from his breast.

Kitty's motto was that it was generally easier to stay up than to get up.

Emma tipped her cab driver to remain in front of the house until she had gone inside and investigated every room, though the eager welcome by the dogs told her all was well. After she waved the driver farewell, she bolted every door, jammed wedges into the frames of her half-open, upper-story bedroom windows, firmly herded the Pekes out of her preferred area of the bed and tried to recall what it was she had to do in the morning before leaving. (*Oh, yes, mail the pages back to poor young Mr Dravitt's father – oh drat, and his wallet as well . . . and let him know what's become of his car . . .*) Only then did she collapse into dreamless sleep.

From which she was wakened five and a half hours later by the jangle of the telephone downstairs.

It was Lupe Santini.

'Ma'am,' she said, 'Miss Sutton's been here.'

FIFTEEN

'She must have come in a cab, ma'am.' It was barely seven thirty in the morning, and cool blue shadow still filled the woodlands of Benedict Canyon. Still, Lupe Santini glanced around the green lawns of Shadygrove as she opened the door for Emma, as if she expected the man in the striped blazer and all thirty carloads of his friends were hiding on the other side of the wall.

But her husband was the only figure in the landscape, padlocking the gate once again.

'So she had the key? To the lock on the gate, as well as the house?' How could genuine kidnappers possibly have neglected to take those from her?

'She did, ma'am.' The housekeeper nodded. 'Rico sleeps up here in the house, and doesn't go down to the gate till nine, unless someone phones.'

As they passed through the front hall, newspapers on the sleek ebony hall table caught her eye:

IS SUSY IN MEXICO?
SEARCH FOR KIDNAP CAR
SUSY SPOTTED IN NEW YORK
KIDNAPPERS SEEN IN FRESNO

Others were folded open to the inner pages: *Sweetchild Grandparent Testifies*, *Sweetchild Lawsuit Hearing Scheduled* and *Sutton Unfit Guardian?*

'I only saw her when she got one of the cars – the Lincoln Phaeton – and drove it out the gates,' Lupe went on. 'Rico ran down the drive after her, but she was way ahead of him already. I went through the house and saw she'd been up in her own room getting clothes and make-up, and in the garden room that Mr Sandow uses for his office. She took the household money from the desk drawer, but he must have taken his keys to his files – I think he still has an apartment someplace in town. It looks like she broke open two of the file drawers. I don't know what she could have been after.'

'Show me.'

They looked in Selina Sutton's palatial State Bedchamber first. Emma had seen something of the kind in any number of films, generally associated with the names of C.B. DeMille, Theda Bara, Marion Davies or Gloria Swanson (or Camille de la Rose, for that matter). She hadn't previously thought anyone would really sleep in such acres of ruffled silk, beneath canopies and testers that ascended like wedding cakes to fifteen-foot ceilings. It made Kitty's Oriental fantasia on Ivarene Street look like a Spartan's barracks.

Marquetry doors inlaid with ebony opened into a private bath, a make-up room and a wardrobe chamber reminiscent of *The Thousand and One Nights*. The faint rumpling of the linen dresser scarf on the make-up table indicated that bottles and jars had once stood there. No comb or brush was to be found in any of the drawers. In the wardrobe, only gaps in the line of hanging garments and in the shelves of shoes betrayed that anything had been taken.

'And she took these this morning?'

'Yes, ma'am. I made a list of what was gone that first morning.' She took a folded paper from her apron pocket and held it out. 'Then after those cops came through Monday, I tidied it all up again, here and in Mr Sandow's office. Nobody's been in either place since.'

'Not even Mr Sandow?'

'Well, Mr Sandow's got his own key, that opens the garden door, too. So does Mr Burt, for that matter. And if they came or went late at night, after Rico and I turned in . . .'

'Thank you.' Emma took the document, glanced over it and put it in her own pocket. 'Can you do me a favor, Mrs Santini? Have any of those reporters tried to speak to you? Or to Mr Santini, or Miss Montoya?'

'They tried.' The older woman sniffed. 'They let us alone for a couple days, but they was back yesterday, asking us all this and that. Worse than the cops. Rico, he kept the gates shut and locked.' She shook her head. 'The kidnappers – if they say, *No cops*, you can bet they don't want reporters either.'

'Did they offer you money?'

Mrs Santini turned her face aside, but Emma saw the sullen glitter in her eyes.

Reaching into her handbag, she produced two ten-dollar bills, which she pressed into the housekeeper's hand. 'Please,' she said softly. 'Nothing to the reporters. Don't get yourself into trouble with the police, but the reporters will twist everything you say.'

'Twist? Huh.' Contempt dripped from her words. 'I don't know why I bother, 'cause if we don't say anything, they make it up anyway.' She pocketed the bills. 'I tell Rico and Elena, not a word, but I know they been keeping their mouths shut.'

She led the way down the hall to a handsome chamber fitted out as an office, and let them in with a key. The desk was the size of Frank Pugh's, back at Foremost, and a great deal tidier. Two telephones stood on it, one bearing the adhesive-paper label '1000' (for the house address, 1000 Shadygrove Terrace, Emma assumed), the other, of another number, presumably Mitch Sandow's private line. Emma realized she had been expecting a cubbyhole, where the household man of business kept track of the checks and paid the bills. Looking around her at the gleaming, modern furnishings, the French doors that opened into the garden, she recalled Foy Snoach's jeer: *Living at her place*.

Thinking back on the quality of the man's necktie and shoes, and that shining green Bugatti, it appeared that Selina's father had known what he was talking about.

And what had poor Burt thought about *that*?

What had Susy thought?

'Have you called Mr Sandow about this?' The desk's top drawer was open slightly – presumably, where the household cash had been kept – but two drawers of the handsome oak file cabinet had been forced open, the drawer facings bearing the marks of a pry bar and the cheap tongues of the drawer locks snapped off short.

'No, ma'am. I phoned his apartment as soon as I came in and saw this, but he doesn't answer. That's when I called you.'

At the 'Vacation in Europe'? But no, Miss Sutton's left the place . . .

'And at this hour, he wouldn't be at his office . . .'

'If he's still got an office,' Mrs Santini remarked drily. 'The kitchen's clear on the other side of the house, so even if he let himself in by those French doors, I wouldn't have heard.'

Emma glanced doubtfully at the broken file drawers. 'Do you and your husband sleep in the house?'

'Our room's in the basement below the kitchen.' Mrs Santini's eye followed Emma's. 'I don't know if we could have heard this, if it was done early in the morning while we were still downstairs. We only saw Miss Sutton when she was most of the way down the drive, going like the Devil was after her.' She crossed herself. 'How long she'd been in the house, I don't know.'

One file drawer proved to contain the paperwork connected with the purported sale of the house in Palm Springs, and of other properties owned – or formerly owned – by Burt and Selina Torley, or Burt and Selina Sutton. Shuffling hastily through, Emma noted documents associated with the probate of the will of Henry Torley, of Shreveport, Louisiana, and of a 1917 court case between the brothers, connected with the property on Cleghorn Lake Road. The other drawer held paperwork from Sandow's other clients, which included Lou Jesperson – the owner of the rival Enterprise Studios – costume designer Natacha Rambova, Doyle Dravitt, Dr Plaister, the notorious Maya Pearl, former Los Angeles mayor Frederic Woodman and a number of others.

What was she looking for here?

Emma herself hadn't the familiarity with what should or shouldn't have been in these files, so couldn't tell if anything had been taken, but she did note that all of the more recent correspondence was received at Post Office Box 2142, Los Angeles, rather than at an office address.

And was someone – *who?* – with her? Miss Sutton, while certainly shapely, hadn't looked strong enough to break even the cheap locks on the drawers, though there was no telling what kind of pry bar she'd used. δῶς μοι πᾶ στῶ καὶ τὰν γᾶν κινάσω, Archimedes had said: *Give me a lever long enough, and a fulcrum on which to place it, and I will move the world.* She doubted that the actress was familiar with the words of the philosopher or the principles of leverage, but stranger things had happened . . .

The unlocked desk drawers contained duns from Bullock's, the Broadway, Tiffany's New York, Hellstern et Fils shoes, as well as a memorandum book with telephone numbers – including those of Frank Pugh, Foremost Productions and Kitty's bootlegger in a number of different hands.

Bother. Her hand slid over the leather of her bag, where the yellow envelope of instructions – the folded sheet containing that desperate plea from Susy, with her fingerprints and the cut lock of her hair – seemed to burn like slow-acting poison. Her eyes went to the chrome-and-enamel clock. Ten minutes after nine.

'Did you call Mr Pugh?'

'I tried, ma'am. But the man at that hotel in Seven Palms said they'd already left for the place where they're shooting today.'

Double bother. Of course they'd leave while it was still dark. But what could I tell him? That Miss Sutton has sneaked away? Would Mr Pugh think I should call the police? And say what? That the woman has driven off in her own car?

First things first. And the first thing that must be done is to deliver these instructions to Mr Pugh, so he can start making arrangements with Messrs Bandog, Goldman and Lutz. Maybe the sight of a child's handprint, the reality of those clipped hairs, will convince them . . .

Again, she heard Zal's voice: *Such trust is a shining inspiration to us all.*

As she thanked Mrs Santini, walked back down the driveway to her car, she found herself thinking, *He can't – they can't – really contemplate telling the kidnapper to run away and chase himself . . .*

If the kidnapper isn't really in league with Miss Sutton . . .

If the kidnapper hasn't decided to double-cross Miss Sutton . . .

The actress's scream of rage in the dining room of the Araby, the day before yesterday, had sounded genuine, shocked and furious . . .

But of course it's her job to sound genuine. The same way it's Little Susy's job to sound cheerful and chipper when she's just nearly been killed and her mother can't spare her a glance away from her interview . . .

Ill with dread, she returned to Kitty's miniature palace, and Mr Shang helped her load the Pekes in their boxes into the rear seat of the Packard. Mrs Shang presented her with a thermos flask of tea, and a cardboard carton containing two hard-boiled eggs and two thin Chinese pancakes stuffed with cooked vegetables.

It would be mid-afternoon before she reached Camp Turpitude. Later, depending on the state of the unpaved portion of the road.

The ransom money was due the day after tomorrow.

'Where the hell you been?' Frank Pugh broke away from the little group clustered under beach umbrellas at the bottom of a vale between two sand dunes, as Emma carefully piloted Kitty's yellow Packard along the gravel road to the staging camp chosen for the day's filming. (She'd fixed one flat on the paved highway just east of Banning and had no desire to risk another. *And thank God for electric self-starters!*)

A sandstorm had blown up the previous forenoon, strong enough to prevent filming of the battle between the Foreign Legion and the Evil Zahar's Bedouin armies. Riley in the wireless tent had informed her that two hundred extras had arrived yesterday afternoon and that Mr Pugh had been fit to succumb to apoplexy because they couldn't be used the same day . . . ('But you should see the footage Zal and Chip got of the storm!')

Today, the blow had decreased to a soft, steady, dust-smelling breeze which caused cloaks to billow spectacularly and Darlene Golden's hair to float halo-like around her angelic face. Thus, instead of the battle – which Larry Palmer swore would be started late that afternoon – the whole sequence of Zahar's discovery and abandonment of Rosebud in the desert was being reshot, to take advantage of these exquisite atmospheric conditions. Bets were being freely taken as to whether the battle would indeed begin before the light failed, or whether the two hundred additional extras would have to be put up at Camp Turpitude (and fed) for yet another night. Side bets included wagers on whether Pugh would cut his own throat or Larry Palmer's before the day was out.

Frenchie the camp cook, whom Emma had encountered outside the main camp's wireless tent before setting forth on another half-hour's drive to the dunes, had reported that Mr Pugh had received a telegram from Fishbein last night apprising him of Emma's arrival first thing in the morning. The cook then ordered one of his assistants to accompany Emma to the location in case of another flat, and had further informed her that the banker Neil Bandog – who seemed to have fallen desperately in love with Darlene Golden – and Irv Goldman – who wished to keep an eye not only on the progress of filming but also on Mr Bandog – were both at the location as well. (Mel Lutz had bidden a tearful and expensive farewell to Miss Singleton and gone home to his wife.)

'I'm very sorry, Mr Pugh,' said Emma firmly, producing the envelope from her handbag. 'But I was held up at gunpoint last night on Miss de la Rose's front porch—'

He snatched the envelope from her hands (without so much as a perfunctory 'What happened?'), cast a swift glance back at Messrs Bandog and Goldman standing near Zal's camera, then grabbed Emma by the arm and propelled her to the far side of the crew tent.

'Does anybody know about this?' He pulled out the notes, shook them open and scanned both while the whisps of Little Susy's light-brown hair whirled away on the cinematic breeze.

The green eyes flicked to her face.

'To the best of my knowledge, no. But early this morning, Miss Sutton's housekeeper saw Miss Sutton drive away from the Shadygrove Terrace house in one of her cars.'

'Damn it!' The studio head's cheeks turned an even more alarming hue. 'Plaister telegraphed she'd sneaked out.'

'She entered her own house through a side door, probably before dawn . . .'

He nodded, waving away further exoneration of the housekeeper.

'. . . and retrieved some clothing, and her make-up, from her bedroom. She also broke into her business manager's files in his office in her house. I don't know what she was after, or what she might have taken.'

'Bitch is behind this, isn't she?'

Emma hesitated, then said, 'I don't know, sir. Did Miss de la Rose tell you anything of what we found out at Cleghorn Lake on Wednesday night? We . . .'

'She showed me.' A grizzly bear surprised from a nap would have growled less threateningly. 'But they're not there now, so what good does it do?' His eyes narrowed and hardened. 'You didn't tell anybody else about that, did you? The last thing we need – the last thing this studio needs – is cops clambering all over the place and shooting off their mouths to every screen rag in the country.'

'No, Mr Pugh.' He was right, of course, reflected Emma, through another wave of anger. Given all Zal had said of the local constabulary, and the way rumors spread . . .

A hundred yards away – and carefully out of any possible camera angle of the camp itself – Kitty appeared on Ariadne the Camel, the rubies on her dagger glinting lethally and her black silk cloak (a new one, at least twice the acreage of the old) floating upon the wind like the shadow of death.

Darlene raised her face from the sand, stretched forth her arms. The wind fluttered the few ragged remains of her combinations, like the feathers of a dove's broken wings.

Emma understood that she had been in Hollywood too long when the thought flitted through her mind, *I hope the wind holds out for the close-ups* . . .

'Listen, Duchess.' Pugh crumpled both notes and shoved them into his pocket. His grasp on her arms might have been meant solely to emphasize the desperation of his anxiety for Susy's safety, but it felt to Emma like a captor's grip. 'God knows what that silly dame is going to do or who she's going to call into this. It's more important than ever, now, that you get me a finished script for *Miracle*. A good one, one that won't have the critics working themselves all into a lather over.'

Emma stared at him in shock. *He can't mean he isn't going to . . .*

He shook her. Not hard, but the grim clutch of his hands gave him away. 'We need to be able to finish the picture, come what may.'

Is he even going to tell *the backers that he got instructions for the ransom?*

'I need your promise,' he said quietly. 'I need your oath. What you told me goes to no one, understand? *No one.* Did you read what was in that envelope?'

Emma shook her head. 'Mr Fishbein only said that it was imperative that it be delivered to you as soon as possible, and that I speak to no one of it. I would have set out as soon as it was light – I don't believe I would have been safe driving, as bad as the roads are, had I left that night. But Mrs Santini telephoned me about seeing Miss Sutton shortly before six.'

'Had she told anybody else about seeing Selina?'

'I don't think so, no. I asked her not to speak of it to anyone – and gave her and her husband twenty dollars.' She could see by the set of his mouth that he was counting up all the other potential sources of rumor.

And that he was putting together his own version of what to say, when Susy's body was discovered.

'We're dealing with desperate men,' he announced finally. Emma, through growing fury, could almost see the words on a title card. 'And God knows how Selina's crazy ideas are going to set things off. We have to be ready.'

And before she could reply, he strode off to where the representatives of finance and distribution had retreated to the shelter of beach umbrellas and lukewarm drinks. Zal and Chip – faces red from sunburn and scored all over with the cuts of blown sand – reset cameras, and Doc Larousse's minions rearranged reflectors. Gren

Torley made Ariadne the Camel kneel, helped Kitty down from the saddle and told her something that made her squeak with joy and run – black cloak still floating behind her like the sinister wings of Death – to the Packard, where all three Pekes stood on their hind legs on the back seat, begging for attention and kisses.

Pugh turned his head to watch her, a fatuous smile momentarily wreathing his lips. It was like seeing Kaiser Wilhelm stop to smell a flower. Darlene, barely slipping a kimono over her shoulders, made straight for Mr Bandog with an expression of welcoming joy. Mr Goldman, drinking his glass of water ('You know what it costs, to have all that ice brought out here?'), glowered.

As far as Emma could see, Pugh made no reference to the wad of papers he'd shoved into his pocket.

Don't you dare, she thought, aghast. *Don't you dare . . .*

And within two hours, secrecy was out of the question.

SIXTEEN

It was the dogs who found the body.

A small tent had been set up for the exclusive use of the two stars. Emma wondered whether the icebox in it had been trucked out from Seven Palms for Kitty alone or as part of Darlene's reward for fascinating Mr Bandog. Kitty, however, remained beside the car, caressing and cooing to her tiny bodyguards while Larry Palmer and the assistant cameramen began to marshal the extras for battle. Red, green, blue and yellow signal flags fluttered in the dying wind. Sharpshooters took up their stations. 'It's just to make it look good,' opined Zal, coming briefly over to Emma in the shade of the beach umbrellas (Darlene's glare when she had approached the tent had been as expressive as a *Do Not Disturb* sign). 'They'll be lucky if they get one shot in that scene before the light starts changing, and they'll have to set up all over again tomorrow morning anyway. And then the wind'll be different and they'll have to throw out whatever they shoot today.'

In addition to the abrasions of the sandstorm and the dust in his beard, he simply looked exhausted, his eyes red behind the lenses of his glasses, lips split and chapped from the heat. Above them, the beach umbrellas tugged and swayed against the ropes that lashed them down against the gusts. The little staging area had been carefully situated downwind of the battlefield; still, Emma could imagine how easily a single cartwheeling umbrella could destroy an entire afternoon of shooting.

'Pugh's been sheepdogging Larry to show how busy we all are,' Zal went on. 'We've had six of the Queen's Guard go out with the heat, 'cause we're working on through the days now instead of taking a break at one.' He glanced up at Emma with a gleam of suspicion in his eyes. 'Any word back in town about the ransom?'

And when she didn't reply: 'He got another ransom note, didn't he?'

'He instructed me – specifically – not to speak to a soul about the reasons that Mr Fishbein had me drive out here this morning.'

Zal opened his mouth – probably, Emma thought, to say something considerably more vulgar than *putz* (whatever *putz* meant) – then closed it.

She went on, 'So whatever I said, he – and Mr Fishbein, and goodness knows how many other people who work at Foremost – would deny it. And what good would it do, at this point? What good could any of us do? Miss Sutton left Doctor Plaister's sanatorium sometime in the small hours. Goodness knows what she's going to do, who she'll talk to or what will come of whatever it is she says.'

'Zal?' Gren Torley came from the direction of the battle lines, as haggard and sand-damaged as Zal, and looking as if he hadn't slept in several nights. 'Palmer's yellin' for you.'

'Palmer can—' Zal stopped himself. He was one of the few people, Emma knew, who generally didn't blame directors for passing along the abuse they got from higher up the ladder. 'Palmer can take a nerve pill,' he finished, and lifted himself slightly on his toes to kiss Emma. 'God knows he needs one. Sit in the shade and drink a Coke for me.'

But moments after Zal returned, like Achilles, to the battleground (*'Now perish, Troy,' he said, and rushed to fight* . . . in the words of Mr Pope), his assistant Herbie Carboy came to the little cluster of umbrellas with the news that Mr Palmer was looking for her. 'That stuff Zal and Chip took of the blow yesterday was so good, he wants you to write in a sandstorm so we can use it.'

Emma decided it was time to take the dogs for a walk. She had settled them in the shade just outside the stars' tent (in which a love scene worthy of D.H. Lawrence was apparently in progress). Now she unfastened their leashes from the tent ropes – although the Evil Queen Zahar was being coached, a hundred feet away, on when she was to appear on the crest of the dune with sand swirling around her, Emma was willing to bet that the clash of armies would not take place that afternoon. But the vicinity swarmed with extras, and she turned her steps away from the place (despite Black Jasmine's eagerness to assist in marshaling the troops). By the time she returned, Miss Golden and Mr Bandog should have concluded their rehearsal for *Romeo and Juliet* (or *The Lustful Turk*, she reflected), and she could retreat to the tent's greater shade and comfort.

From the top of a small dune, she looked back at the shooting camp – three tents, a half-dozen trucks and the camel lines, small now against the yellowish waste. Dust plumed around the milling gangs of extras and rolled gently away to the southwest. Bright chips of signal-flag color flickered in the muslin-hued air, and the wind tugged at the wide brim of her hat like a sail.

A shadow passed over her. Shading her eyes, she looked up, wondering if Mr Palmer had had the dramatic instinct to film the circling vulture overhead. *Or is that a buzzard?*

More than one, whatever they were. Presumably, on the watch for extras keeling over in the heat . . .

The wind shifted.

She knew the smell.

At the same moment that all the dogs – silky ears cocked and eager to prove themselves wolves – leaned against their leashes and began to bark, Emma thought, *Cow. Poor creature . . . Or antelope . . . Nobody would run cows out here where there's no water . . .*

But she hadn't seen antelope, either.

The smell was one she'd smelled when she'd worked helping unload the wounded from the hospital ships at Southampton: the men who had not survived the crossing.

You will find Susy's body sometime the following week, the note had said. *I mean it.*

Damn them . . . 'Just routine . . . no report filed . . . just wants to cover his ass . . .' She remembered, too, young Bobby Franks, whose kidnappers had not even waited for the ransom demand to be met.

The dogs dragged her towards the spot where the dark birds circled. A gully, Emma saw as she got nearer. All the dogs, even timid Buttercreme, yanked on their leashes, barking wildly as the birds rose like sinister angels out of the dry trench.

Looking down from the gully's edge, Emma first saw the dilapidated brown Ford. It leaned, nose down, on the opposite side of the gulch, as if it had been driven or pushed over the six-foot drop.

The body was half buried in blown sand, ten feet from the wrecked vehicle. Most of the face had been torn away, but Emma recognized the checkered shirt.

It was Burt Sutton.

There was no question, now, about *Do we call the police?*

But what events, wondered Emma, shivering with apprehension in the hot shade of the tent reserved for the lesser actors, would the arrival of the forces of law trigger?

The first thing Frank Pugh did, when Herbie Carboy had clattered off in one of the trucks to the main camp to wire the San Bernardino County sheriff, was to take Emma aside behind the tent again.

'We don't know what's goin' on here.' His heavy face was set like wet concrete. 'We don't know who's in on this, who's on the take, who's behind this or what Selina had to do with any of it. We don't know who's tellin' lies and who's tellin' the truth.'

Including yourself? she had the wits not to say, thinking of the fragile curls of Little Susy's hair, spinning unnoticed away in the wind.

'It's like they say in court,' he went on. 'The truth an' nuthin' but the truth. An' *nuthin' else.* You don't bring up why you came out here this afternoon, or what Fishy might have handed you back in town. You don't pipe up that Kitty got a look at that telegram I got Thursday morning. As far as you're concerned, that telegram never happened. I've already talked to Kitty and I'm gonna have some words with Rokatansky as soon as he gets his camera packed up.'

'Some words' containing the sentence 'If you mention that telegram to the cops, I'll see to it that you never work in Hollywood again'?

Given the way rumors spread, it wouldn't be difficult to put about two or three stories of theft or union sympathies among the studio heads to guarantee Zal's permanent unemployment.

Possibly, to facilitate his arrest.

'You tell the cops what you saw down in that gully, and that's it. Nuthin' about the Santini broad seeing Selina this morning. Nuthin' about going to the studio yesterday.'

'A lot of people saw me,' pointed out Emma quietly. 'I can't very well deny it without making someone on the police wonder what else I might be hiding.'

Pugh rumbled unwilling assent. 'OK, you stopped by the studio to pick up somethin' for Kitty – perfume or some shit like that. You came back out here because she was lonely for those little anklebiters of hers.'

'May I tell the police how long Burt had been missing? The last time I saw Burt was in the early hours of Monday morning. He left his car at Kitty's: Kitty and I sent him home in a cab. A clever reporter might even trace the driver. But Mrs Santini told me that he was gone Monday morning, so I assume he returned in a cab the minute he sobered up. The police are going to want to know how, and when, he came out here.'

She could almost hear the click of wheels under the heavy thatch of his black hair, almost see the glint of turning gears behind the bulging eyes. And indeed, she thought, it would take some well-planned choreography to both telephone instructions to Mrs Santini and keep an eye on Messrs Bandog and Goldman, to make sure neither of these gentlemen heard or said anything untoward.

'OK,' he said after a moment. 'I want you to . . .'

On the other side of the tents, a car door slammed, and a moment later, three men appeared around the corner.

One of them was Chip Thaw's assistant, plump and sweaty Sy Borden.

The other two were brown-uniformed San Bernardino County sheriffs.

Behind them, a police ambulance van rumbled down the dirt road into camp through the grimy haze.

Sergeant Cord Brinkmanhoff walked with Emma out to the gully, listened to her story of finding the body, but took very few notes. One deputy and a man from the coroner's office accompanied him to look at the car *in situ*, but the sergeant himself gave poor Burt's body only the most cursory of examinations before signaling the deputy to help dig him out of the sand. The deputy had brought a stretcher; he and Sergeant Brinkmanhoff carried the body back to the ambulance. Emma heard the sergeant say, when Neil Bandog pushed past the deputy who stood outside the stars' tent to meet them, 'Goddam bootleggers.'

'Bootleggers?' Emma stared at the bull-like law man, startled. 'He was hunting for his daughter's kidnappers!'

The hard little blue eyes were like glass in the sun-damaged face. 'And he ran into goddam bootleggers,' explained the sergeant, in a voice that brooked no argument. 'They bring booze up from Mexico all the time,' he added, with an attempt at patient softening in his voice. 'Booze, coke, smack. First thing we're gonna do is check that car for secret compartments. All the rum-runners get them put in: fenders, doors, behind the seats. Even if there aren't hideouts in the fenders, there were seven empty bottles in the back seat. The man's lucky he made it this far out from LA without running into a wall.'

Extras, gaffers, property men were being loaded into the studio's rented trucks, Emma now saw. The camels were being unsaddled,

Gren Torley stringing lead ropes between them, for the long trek back to the main camp. Brinkmanhoff made a move toward the larger actors' tent, then turned back to Emma, as Zal and a watchful-looking Frank Pugh came up to her. 'You folks might as well go back to Seven Palms, ma'am. My boys will have a look around here, but it'll be tomorrow before we can start taking down everybody's stories for the report.' He didn't sound in a terrible hurry to get the information, Emma thought indignantly.

'It's pretty clear he ran into bootleggers and was shot,' the officer went on. 'One shot to the chest, one through the head, then they dumped him and his car over into the gully.' He shrugged and looked down at the long, desiccated shape beneath the blanket as the men bore the stretcher past them and into the ambulance. 'I'm guessing he was drunk enough to make trouble for whoever he ran into. That true what Mrs Blackstone says, that Little Susy Sweetchild's his daughter?'

'It is,' agreed Pugh solemnly. 'All I can say is, the man had more guts than brains. And like you say, he was probably drunk when he came out here. I heard back in town he's been missing since Sunday night.'

'Fits with the appearance of the body . . .'

'Nothing in his pockets?'

Brinkmanhoff shook his head. 'Not a thing. Ma'am' – he turned to Emma and touched his flat-brimmed hat – 'thank you for your cooperation with this. I'll probably want to talk to you again tomorrow, but you can go have a seat in the shade and get yourself something cool to drink.' He produced a huge white handkerchief from his trouser pocket, wiped his face and gave her a grin. 'If you can find anything cool out here. All I ask is that you don't talk to anyone about any of this, until we've reviewed the details and give you leave.'

'Of course.' *Aren't you even going to ask who saw Burt last? Or why his body wasn't in the car?*

Zal took her arm and led her back to the stars' tent.

'Burt's body was half buried in sand,' protested Emma in an undervoice, as they entered the shelter's thick shadow. 'But his car had scarcely a dusting over it. Surely they can trace who had his car – and who might have seen it . . .'

'Albert Marco and Joe Ardizzone both have distilleries making booze out here in the desert,' replied Zal quietly. 'Like I said the other night, half the isolated ranches have buildings on their land – Jake Dragna's outfit runs sugar out here by the truck-load to make the stuff. I'm guessing Sergeant B's got orders not to go poking around any more than he has to, whatever his personal feelings are. And he's sure not going to make a fuss about some poor bastard, who everybody in town knew was a drunk, getting himself shot.'

The same heat rose through her, the same queasy rage, that she'd felt two weeks previously, in the gray street of that artificial Wild West town, with Kitty holding her arm and whispering, *Don't* . . .

She wanted to scream at them all, *Can't you see that child is in danger of her life?*

She knew they were right. Don't scare the horse. Don't raise a fuss with Mr Pugh. Don't call the Society for Prevention of Cruelty to Children.

And meanwhile, that little girl was sitting alone in a locked room somewhere, trying to feed her cat through the bars of its cage and praying . . .

No. Probably not praying. *What events in her life would lead her to think there's a God?*

'Here you go, darling.' Kitty – resplendent in jeweled finery more suggestive of Little Egypt than an Arab princess – pressed a paper cup of more-or-less cool Coca-Cola into her hand. 'Come sit down. You'll feel better.'

'All right.' Emma took a deep breath. 'But I swear to you, if Mr Pugh comes in here and tells me it's more important than ever that I produce a happy ending to *Tiny Miracle*, I will stab him to death with Kitty's dagger.'

'I'll help you, darling,' agreed the Evil Zahar. 'But I doubt you could. It isn't terribly sharp.' She drew it from her belt and angled the blade – which had clearly started life as a letter-opener – to the light from the tent doorway.

'Sure you can,' pointed out Zal cheerfully. 'Pick a soft target like the belly or the side under the ribs, brace your back foot, keep your elbow tight and drive your weight from your hip – you can do damage with something like that. It has enough of a point on it to scare Marsh Sloane.'

'Marsh Sloane,' retorted Kitty loftily, 'is scared of . . . of Gren Torley's *tiger*, and even *Buttercreme* isn't afraid of *him*.'

She retreated then to the back of the tent, stopping by the icebox to dip a cup of chilly water from the drip pan to pour into the bowl provided for the Pekes, who lapped it thirstily before running to the ends of their leashes in an attempt to get out the entrance and into the action outside. Mr Goldman – who had been watching in stony disapproval as Darlene Golden shared the contents of her flask with Mr Bandog – leaned from his seat on one of the cots to ruffle Chang Ming's fluffy mane, and said something comforting to the little dog in what was probably Yiddish.

Kitty, kneeling on the other side of the water bowl, looked up and responded in the same tongue, and the theater owner laughed. It changed his whole face.

'You OK?' Zal came and sat beside Emma on the other cot. He looked like ten miles of bad road. (After driving all morning, Emma could have told him specifically which ten miles.)

'We work for monsters.' Her voice was quiet, and she meant the words with all her heart.

'Lot of people do, Em. You think Burt picked up his car when he sobered up Monday and drove out here? He could have remembered the house at Desert Light. He may even still have had keys to it.'

'And the following day,' said Emma, 'someone – a woman – telephoned every fan magazine in the business and told them that a woman in Seven Palms was claiming a ransom note had been delivered to Pugh and that the money hand-off was going to take place in the desert. Someone wanted to force Pugh's hand.'

'And ended up forcing the kidnappers.'

Outside, someone yelled, 'Zal? Zallie?' and a shadow blotted the tent door. Herbie Carboy, veiled like a southern belle in pith helmet and gauze against the glare of the late-afternoon sun.

'Zal? When you've got a minute . . .'

Which, Emma knew, in the young assistant's vocabulary meant, *We really need you right now.*

Zal said, 'Shit,' and turned back to Emma. 'I didn't get more than a quick look at the corpse,' he went on quietly. 'And that was a pretty stern blow we had here last night. But it's obvious Burt was dead for a couple of days – maybe since Monday night – and the car wasn't there that long. Tomorrow I'll try to come back out here and have a look inside the engine, see how much sand is in there – not that it'll do us a hell of a lot of good. The question'll still be, are the San Berdoo sheriffs going to care?'

Somebody outside yelled something that caused Herbie to turn away, then turn back . . .

Zal swore again. 'But by tomorrow night they may have phoned Ardizzone and got instructions – if Ardizzone or one of his buddies haven't been behind the whole snatch all along.'

He kissed her hands, then her cheek, and stood. 'I know you're sick of hearing it, but we can only do what we can do.'

She sighed. 'The Greeks called it *kerostasia* – the golden balances of Fate. And you are right on both counts.'

No man alive, garrulous old Nestor says in the Iliad, *can fight the will of Zeus.* There was always something else going on in the background that the heroes didn't know about, from the squabbles of goddesses over their favorite champions, to the inexorable law of destiny. Emma closed her eyes as Zal left, listened to the noises of the camp being broken, the camels setting off for the larger camp to the south. Darlene giggled and murmured responses to Mr Bandog's opinions about films and the lives their stars must lead – which he had clearly gleaned from the columns of *Screen World* and *Film Fun*. Mr Goldman said, his gruff voice quiet, 'My wife has dachshunds, the most loyal little souls – and brave like tigers!'

'Does she travel with them?' asked Kitty interestedly, and their voices sank again.

No man alive can fight the will of Zeus.

That doesn't mean we can't try . . . And from Hector son of Priam before the walls of Troy, to Jim Blackstone and all those young men she'd driven from the train stations to the hospitals, they had tried. With difficulty, Emma put from her the sinking dread of whatever repercussions Selina Sutton's actions could trigger, whether she was one of the kidnappers, or merely desperate enough to try anything. *What does she know about the police that we don't? What does she know about the kidnappers that she won't tell anyone?*

Did she see Burt killed?

Why can't I be like Kitty, and Zal, and wait upon events?

She drew her handbag to her from where she'd laid it down on the cot, fumbled for a handkerchief. *Drat it!* Her fingers touched the smooth, expensive leather of a wallet – *The Araby will have a postal service . . .* She'd meant to package it up this morning and have Mr Shang take it to the post office – *Was that only this morning?* – but the call from Mrs Santini had distracted her.

Digging in the pocket of her skirt, she encountered the rest of the items she'd taken from Wilson Dravitt's unconscious body. A handkerchief, a comb, various scraps of paper (*Natalie LY-4906 – Frankie S. AN-3022* – Kitty's address and jotted directions to the house, rather to her amusement), an empty envelope. There was no addressee's name, but the return address had been typed in the corner.

    Post Office Box 2142
    Los Angeles, Calif.

And she realized what had seemed familiar about it, when she'd seen that same address earlier that day.
    The typewriter was almost certainly Mitch Sandow's.

SEVENTEEN

'Wilson Dravitt told me his father's financial manager is in debt to some of the gangsters in Los Angeles.' By the time Emma had found Zal in the thinning confusion in the camp, Darlene and her wealthy suitor had departed from the stars' tent, and Mr Goldman had also taken his leave. The sun was sinking over the San Gorgonio Mountains. The rising wind, rippling the canvas covers of the remaining trucks, promised another blowy night.

'He said the man was his father's cousin,' Emma went on, looking from Zal's face to Kitty's in the dimness of the now-deserted tent. 'And that he also worked for "movie stars." Mr Dravitt told me he'd gotten the man work with his "friends," which could include his former brother-in-law, Frank Pugh – or whoever Pugh thought needed a financial manager.'

'I forgot Pugh was married to Sponny Dravitt,' said Zal reflectively. 'Well, that was two wives ago . . . And Mitch Sandow has his own office in Selina Sutton's house, doesn't he?'

A trifle stiffly, Emma replied, 'It looked to me as if he ran a good deal of his business there – if nothing else – as well as managing all of hers. He has his own telephone line.'

'And since she didn't wake up from her swoon Wednesday screaming, *It was my financial manager*,' concluded Zal, 'I'm guessing she was in on it from the start. Or *at* the start, anyway,' he added. 'She may have changed her mind when he shot her husband.'

'Oh, come on, Zallie.' Kitty sniffed, cradling Black Jasmine in her arms. 'She'd have shot Burt herself if she thought she could get away with it.'

'Where would they take Susy,' asked Emma, 'if they had to abandon Desert Light? I assume the blood we found was Burt's. They had no way of knowing who Burt might have told, once he recalled that his wife had access to that house.'

'And why call all the reporters in creation?' added Zal. 'Yeah, it could have forced Pugh's hand – though I don't think anyone knew he'd have B, L and G out here that day. But it would also have concentrated a search on this part of the country. Cleghorn Lake is only about fifteen miles from where Selina turned up. And where would she have called them from? That would mean she'd have to have a confederate in LA, or she drove there herself Tuesday. Even if she drove to Banning she'd risk someone recognizing her.'

'Oh, not if she made herself up ugly,' pointed out Kitty. 'Yes, darling,' she added, kissing the black Peke's silky ears, 'we'll go back to the hotel soon and you can get your dinner . . . You don't have to be Herr Volmort to make yourself not look like yourself, you know. Especially if you go early in the morning to someplace like the post office or the railway station, where people aren't expecting to see a movie star.'

Emma said, 'She's right, you know,' remembering what Charlie Chaplin looked like out of costume, and the one time she'd encountered the Gish sisters in Bullock's, when they were wearing sunglasses and big straw hats. Mostly, even when off the screen, film stars held themselves – carried themselves – in a way that said, *I'm a star*, courting recognition.

Kitty produced a cigarette – it still amazed Emma that she could conceal anything so large as a packet of Sobranies in the few square inches of her costume – and fitted it to a holder. (*And where did she have* that *hidden? Much less a lighter . . .*) 'And anyway she hasn't been in front of a camera for three years. *I'll* bet they fought over money.' The flicker of the lighter's flame made all the jewels of her costume twinkle.

'The original demand was for a hundred thousand dollars,' agreed Emma. 'That's the amount Mitch Sandow embezzled from Doyle Dravitt, so it's probably what he borrowed from – whoever he borrowed it from.'

'Add twenty percent to that,' put in Zal grimly, 'for interest, if I know folks like Ardizzone and Page.'

'Since he's a *businessman*' – Emma couldn't keep the sarcasm from her voice – 'he'd have guessed that he couldn't get much more than that from Foremost Productions. But the minute Miss Sutton's relatives started suing for custody of Susy, she'd have realized she wasn't going to be able to parlay the publicity into better contract terms for her daughter. She'd have to have something for herself. That second ransom note – the one for two hundred thousand – was left at the studio Tuesday, remember. I think Miss Sutton drove back to Los Angeles early Tuesday morning – probably in Mr Sandow's car – dropped the note at the studio, called the journalists from the nearest drugstore and quite possibly arranged for someone to bring her back to a spot where she could conveniently stagger to Camp Turpitude Wednesday afternoon.'

'By which time Mitch has guessed what she's up to, burned all the evidence he could, driven to Banning in Burt's car and sent off a telegram to Foremost saying the second note is a fake.' Zal nodded. 'It fits. But where he took the kid after that . . .'

'It's only a bit over a hundred miles to the Mexican border, isn't it?'

'It is, but the San Berdoo sheriffs will be watching the border. Unless he took the kid on horseback . . .'

'No!' Kitty sprang to her feet, arms still full of Pekinese. 'He'd take her to Maya Pearl's, silly!'

'There were papers in his files at Miss Sutton's,' said Emma. 'I think he brokered the purchase of a house for her.'

'You get the address?'

Drat it, thought Emma. *Drat it . . . We could have gotten it from Selina's house in Palm Springs . . .*

'It's on Pinkham Canyon road' – Kitty gestured impatiently with her cigarette – 'about fifteen miles east of Indio. We can't miss it; there's pretty much nothing else out there.' She set down the cigarette, tucked the protesting sleeve-Peke into his carry-box, then gently lifted Buttercreme. 'The highway isn't paved past Indio, but . . .'

'Whoa!' Zal raised a hand. 'What's this "*we* can't miss it" you're talking about, Your Highness? "We" are driving into Twenty-Nine Palms and calling the sheriffs.'

'You think they're going to raid Maya Pearl's ranch?' She stowed the little blonde dog into her box. 'Everybody west of Bakersfield knows Iron Joe Ardizzone runs a still on Maya's property and brings in cocaine and heroin from Mexico to store in her barn . . .'

'And you think that's going to make it safe for us to sashay in there and heist Susy out of the back bedroom at gunpoint?'

'Well,' pointed out Kitty as she did up the box latches, 'Maya's obviously not going to be holding parties if she's got Susy stashed in the back bedroom. The only other time there's anyone around there is when the boys from LA are making a pickup, and all we have to do is scout around to make sure—'

'All we have to do,' said Zal firmly, 'is let the sheriff know that we have no intention of even *looking* in the direction of those buildings out behind the house, or peeking at the fenders of any vehicle on the property.'

'And they'll phone whoever their contact is, and their contact will try to get hold of Ardizzone, and by that time it'll be ten or eleven o'clock, and meanwhile if Selina *does* track Mitch to Maya's place, then Mitch is going to know the jig is up and cut his losses.'

She straightened up, her beautiful face deathly serious in the shifting reflections of the lights from the entry. 'He can't risk Susy recognizing something, even a voice or a sound. The kid's got a memory like a steel trap, Zallie. She's the one who remembers what the director told all the other actors about the scene, from the first take on.'

'All the more reason we need to quit arguing and get going,' retorted Zal. 'You' – he jabbed a finger at Kitty – 'stay here. I should be back in half an hour, with or without the law.'

He ducked through the flaps of the tent, Emma at his heels. Though not strong, the wind lent a flickering weirdness to the darkness, dragged at Emma's hair and skirts. 'Could you at least see if the sheriffs can keep an eye out for Selina's car?' she asked. 'Mrs Santini said it was a' – she closed her eyes, fished in her memory –'a Phaeton, I don't recall who makes them.'

'Lincoln,' said Zal. 'Hers is shiny gold with red trim, and that's a good idea. The thing's hard to miss. And speaking of cars . . .' He strode over to where half a dozen trucks were still parked, being loaded with camel saddles, water barrels, prop rifles and gaudy prop jezails of the kind still used – her father had said – among the Bedouin tribes. A little way off from them stood Kitty's yellow Packard. 'While I'm in town, I'll make sure somebody tells the Border Patrol to watch out for it. I'll try to get the license number from Mrs Santini, if you've got her number.'

As he spoke, he flipped open the Packard's hood, removed the key to the electrical system and handed it to her. 'Hang on to that.'

Emma took it, dug in her pocket and jotted the Shadygrove number on the back of one of Wilson Dravitt's romantic *billets-doux* – keeping an eye, as she did so, on the flaps of the actors' tent. 'Sandow wouldn't really . . .' She hesitated. Then, 'He *knew* the little girl. He'd worked with her mother for two years. He was living under their roof.'

'While he was embezzling a hundred grand from Cousin Dravitt and negotiating with Iron Joe Ardizzone to cover his butt while he raised the wind.' Zal turned his head, signaled to one of the increasingly indistinct figures moving about among the trucks and cars in the twilight. 'Dave—'

The man came closer, as one of the prop men lit the acetylene lanterns on the nearby truck. Emma recognized the ranch hand Dave, who had come to look after rancher Art Parsons' ten camels.

'Five dollars to let me borrow your truck for an hour.' Zal fished in his pocket. 'Em told me something she heard in town about the Sweetchild kidnapping, that I think the sheriffs ought to know about. If anything comes of it, I'll cut you in on the reward.'

The young man said, 'Sure thing, Zal. Lemme help you get her started.'

Zal turned back to Emma. 'Of the ten biggest kidnapping cases in the past sixty years,' he said quietly, 'only one child was released unharmed. One. Our kidnappers . . .'

She noticed that he was careful not to speak Sandow's name, though Dave the Camel-Driver was already strolling off through the gloom toward the big flat-bedded wagon with its load of hay and empty water barrels.

'. . . may not have intended to harm Susy when they snatched her. But the longer she was missing – the longer she was around them – the more time she's had to learn something that could get them sent up the river for a long time. They're real close to the point where it's not going to be worth it to hang on to her. I should be back in an hour – longer if I get a flat. Try to keep Kitty from doing anything stupid. Sit on her clothes if you have to.'

The truck's engine coughed a couple of times, then roared into life.

Zal caught her hands, drew her into a quick, hard kiss. Then he dashed off after Dave, and she saw him clamber into the truck's cab as Dave lit the old vehicle's lanterns, and the creaky equipage jolted away into the dusk.

Kitty had evidently lighted the hurricane lantern in the tent as darkness fell: a slit of orange light beckoned Emma as she hurried back. The murderers of Bobby Franks, she reminded herself, had never intended the boy to be returned. But so many others she had heard of, the fate of the victims was simply unknown. *Selina can't possibly have let that happen. The woman may be vain, and stupid, but surely she would have had some plan to prevent her accomplice – if it was Sandow – from panicking . . .*

'Zal's on his way to town in one of the trucks,' she said, ducking through the tent flaps and into the dim glow of the lantern. 'Even if he can't get the sheriffs, we can get Mr Pugh . . .'

But Kitty was gone.

EIGHTEEN

Fifty square feet of black silk cloak lay draped over the cot, edges fluttering gently in the wind that leaked into the tent. Emma told herself, 'The latrine tent.' The dogs scratched impatiently at the wicker grillwork of their boxes. She glanced automatically at her watch: it was nine o'clock.

By ten – when Ned Berger and the few prop men who remained came to strike the tent – Emma knew. Few of her sister-in-law's on-set romances lasted longer than an hour.

And in her heart, she knew that Kitty had been too angry to be distracted by even the most comely of extras.

She guessed her beautiful sister-in-law had slithered under the shelter's back wall, while she and Zal were talking outside. When Ned said, 'We're clearing out, Duchess. You want to follow us back to the Araby?' Emma nodded and produced the Packard's electrical key. Her heart pounding, she followed the Two Neds – Ned Berger and his assistant Ned Devine – through darkness and blowing dust to where the crew bus, the smallest of the trucks and the Packard stood in the moonlight, amid a scrimmage of men loading tent, cots, the icebox and the remaining costumes and food supplies.

'Can we stow these reflectors in Kitty's car?' asked Ned the Greater, bending over the big car's engine to reactivate the electrical system. 'Doc'll have a fit if one of them gets broken. Pugh, too – it'll mean another day's delay shooting.'

'Yes, of course.' Emma stepped aside as Ned the Lesser opened the rear seat and lifted the three dog boxes in, then carefully lashed the stalky skeletons of the reflectors over them, the sail-like squares of fabric furled tight. It would mean, she guessed, stopping at Camp Turpitude before returning to the Araby – surely Zal would know that if he were delayed, they would rendezvous at the hotel? But the thought of trying to drive back to Seven Palms alone, in the dark, over the unpaved roads, was more than she could bear. Frenchie's obliging assistant had returned on the first bus to Camp Turpitude . . .

'You should have heard Pugh when he found out somebody's

borrowed his Pierce-Arrow.' Ned's boyish grin flashed in the lantern beam as somebody kindled the bus's headlamps. 'I thought he was going to work himself into a stroke! And that Bandog feller looked like somebody asked him to hitch a ride back on a garbage truck, when Pugh broke it to him he'd have to sit in the bus with actors.'

He waggled his hands in mock terror and bulged his eyes, a muscular young Apollo who had neither the slightest desire nor the smallest talent for acting, but who loved the minutiae of putting together a set. 'I had to walk away so I wouldn't get fired for laughing. You want me to drive back with you, Mrs B?' he added. 'If you came out from town this morning, you've probably had it with driving for the day.'

Emma had indeed had it with driving for the day, to say nothing of fixing flats. She suspected that Zal's borrowed truck had experienced at least one such misfortune on the way to or from Twenty-Nine Palms, and as the Packard jolted carefully over the stony trail in the wake of the bus, she scanned the darkness ahead for the gleam of the truck's lamps. It was now nearly eleven. Or had Zal insisted on accompanying the sheriff and his crew to Pinkham Canyon? Just to make sure, she reflected uneasily, that they actually *went* to Pinkham Canyon, rather than spending a suitable time in the nearest speakeasy: *Oh, sure we checked, nuthin' there* . . .

If he was returning at this hour, he would surely guess the crew had returned to the Araby.

Was he waiting for her there even now, with the news that . . .

That what? That Susy Sweetchild had been found unhurt?

The gruesome details of the kidnap-murder of young Bobby Franks in May, of the little Chicago girl – Elsie something? – twelve years ago, of the child Fanny Adams that her grandfather had told her about years ago . . . surfaced in her memory like corpses weeks drowned. *If Zal isn't there, I'll speak to Mr Pugh, and to those backers of his. We can surely get up enough men from among the crew* . . .

It seemed hours before she smelled, above the dust plume thrown by the bus (the truck behind them had suffered a puncture and been left to catch up), the murky pong of horse lines and camel pens. Only three tents glowed dully with lights inside the canvas, tiny against an infinity of blackness and stars. With every lurching mile, her anxiety had grown: for Susy, for Kitty (surely she'd have returned if she found nothing in Pinkham Canyon . . . wouldn't she? Or was she somewhere in the darkness, fixing a flat of her own?)

Was she lost somewhere in those night-drowned hills? Would she try to come back here . . . ?

Would she try to get to the Araby to telephone the sheriff's department?

You can't do anything about any of it, she told herself, as she had told herself six years ago, at every headline concerning the fighting in France. Through every endless night of staring at the ceiling. *All you can do is wait.* Zeus's golden scales would come down as they would.

The fixed decree which not all heaven can move . . .

And that waiting had ended, she recalled, with that kindly letter from Jim's colonel telling her she'd waited in vain.

Stop it! Everything will be all right.

As the bus turned before them and its headlights swept the low canvas walls, she saw the rancher Parsons' small truck sitting outside the telegrapher's tent.

The tent flap was shoved aside, and Zal strode out before the bus had even stopped. Men came out of the nearby stores tent, catching their caps before the wind. Emma heard Ned the Greater calling to them that yet more costumes, props and food supplies were on the way in the truck, and watch out for those reflectors in the Packard . . .

She herself was already out of the car and nearly running to Zal's arms. A swift, hard embrace, and then he was hurrying her to the shadows behind the wireless tent, looking back toward the car . . .

'Kitty's not with you?'

'No. I think she must have taken Mr Pugh's car.'

Zal swore, heartfelt oaths with the weight of rage behind them.

Her own anger – her own fear – rose up through her from the soles of her feet to her scalp. To her own surprise, her voice sounded calmly level. 'What reason did the sheriffs' department give for not going out to Pinkham Canyon?'

'They had to get authorization.' Like her own, his voice was quiet – Zal never yelled – but taut as twisted rope. 'The *verkakte* son-of-a . . . he sort of implied he had to telephone the San Bernardino County sheriff, but the one he really had to phone was Joe Ardizzone. Gren Torley says he knows the way out there.'

Emma glanced back in the direction of the men unloading the bus, then toward the dim gold rectangle of the nearest tent.

'Pugh and the Panjandrums all went back to the Araby on the first bus,' said Zal. 'Arguing all the way – I was standing here, watching for you and Kitty to turn up – about could the kidnappers be talked back down to a hundred thou or even less? You shoulda heard Frank being all solemn and worried about Selina being on the loose, and what if Foremost paid up and Selina did something to piss off the baddies and they killed Susy anyway? Bandog was all, "Yeah, that's something we've got to think about." I didn't know whether to puke or go over and commit aggravated assault.'

His breath was still coming hard with anger. But he saw the direction of Emma's gaze, counting the men around the bus, and he shook his head. 'We don't need an army,' he said. 'What we need to do right now is get out there and find Kitty before she tries to do anything stupid – and we need to find out what she's learned. The more men we've got, the more chance there is that we'll be spotted.'

She said, 'All right.'

'Stiletto,' he added quietly, recalling his words to her about dealing with Pugh and the earlier danger from Vic Duffy. 'Not a battleax.'

Movement in the darkness caught Emma's eye as the men bore reflectors, costumes, props away to the locked palisade – formerly the den of lions – just outside the camp. The white blur of a man's face, then the compact shape of Gren Torley manifested itself, a gas can in one hand, and one of the guards' shotguns in the other.

Behind him, another short, sturdy shape materialized into the broad, pale countenance and sinister eyes of Herr Volmort, a shotgun in each hand. 'You know how to handle one of these things, Madame?' he asked Emma, in the half-whispering voice of a radio villain.

She shook her head. 'My father was going to teach me,' she said as Zal took the gas can and crossed to where the Packard now stood solitary in the cold starlight, the dust of the bus's departure swirling about it like rags of colorless silk. 'We'd planned to dig in the Apennines in 1916. He was concerned about bandits. But by 1916, even if we'd had the money, we couldn't have got the men, or the mules, and of course there was no way of telling when the Italians might be driven back and northern Italy overrun.'

'As ill-supplied as we were by then,' remarked Volmort quietly,

'I doubt we could have overrun Palm Springs, let alone any portion of Italy. But your father was a wise man. Like this.' He demonstrated the action of the gun, for a moment the soldier he had been. 'Hold it tight to your shoulder – so – or the kick will break your arm. *Und jetzt . . .*'

He gestured her before him toward the car.

The moon had set. The desert lay cold and weird under a silver uncertainty of starlight, and the bare rock hills rose up around them as they drove, coarse spikey growths of sagebrush and windwitch alternating with the bizarre shapes of the Joshua trees. Thin dust lines streamed across the stony trace of road. 'Couple of the goldmines are still being worked, north and west of here,' provided Zal. 'Though you probably can make more running a couple of stills . . .'

If Kitty had come this way – in Frank Pugh's borrowed Pierce-Arrow – there was no sign of her.

The road narrowed further as it kinked its way into the Cottonwood Mountains. But it was graded, graveled and better maintained than anything Emma had seen east of San Bernardino – presumably kept that way care of Mr Ardizzone and the staff of his illicit distilleries. (*Can't have those shipments of sugar delayed by flats, now, can we?*) At length, Torley said, 'There, up ahead,' and Zal, who was driving the Packard (dogs and all), slowed and turned up a side road that seemed, if not paved, equally well maintained. (*And presumably the upkeep of these tracks has completely escaped the notice of the San Bernardino County sheriffs . . .*)

An owl passed overhead, voiceless as a ghost. Far off, a coyote howled; others took up the chorus.

Nearer, sudden in the night, the sharp crack of a gunshot, like a stick breaking.

Zal cursed again.

Then dark against the knees of the mountains, a speck of dim light.

'Better turn off here,' said Torley. 'You stay with the car, Volmort. When we come back, we'll call out: *You there, Pete?* If we call out, *You there, Sid* – or anything else but Pete – don't you believe a word we say after that. Mrs B, you stay close. You know Miss de la Rose best; you watch for any sign of her that we might not see, or watch for anything fishy. Here.'

The shotgun he handed her as Zal stopped the car was the same type of pump-action Remington that her father had promised to school her in. Nineteen thirteen, it had been. *Igitur qui desiderat pacem, praeparet bellum,* he had said. But the fifteen-year-old schoolgirl she had been then could not imagine actually pointing it at anyone and deliberately pulling the trigger. She had hated even being taken out, once or twice, on 'shoots' at the country place of her grandfather's well-off friends.

If Zal's life was at stake? she wondered now.
Kitty's?
Susy's?

It weighed in her hands like a bar of lead. She felt as if it were hard to breathe.

In starlight, it was almost easier to navigate, without the sharp, velvet-black shadows of the moon. The ground was rough, rising toward the pale shape of a house, a sprawling adobe with one American-style wing and one in the fake-Spanish style one saw all over Los Angeles (including on the Foremost lot). Balconies and arches, wide windows on the upper floor, looked down on a tiled courtyard enclosed by the wings. On all sides, a well-manicured but savage-looking hedge of cactus defined the immediate grounds. The huge outcrops of rock on three sides of the property sheltered it from the wind, and Emma could smell, mingled with the dust scent of the desert and the darkness, the tarry, malty reek of fermenting liquor.

Are there trucks – men – invisible in the blackness in that direction? Against the darkness of those encircling rocks, she could make out – barely – the low bulk of what looked like a barn, the steely glint of chimneys. Behind her, the soft ticking of the Packard's cooling engine seemed loud as gunshots. She could barely see the spiney balls of sagebrush and Russian thistle that she felt scratch at her skirt. Only movement to her left and right, Torley leading the way a little ahead, Zal watching and listening . . .

Sudden brightness as a car swung around the corner of the cactus hedge, blinding. A hand grabbed her wrist, yanked her back into deeper darkness, something spiney and evil raking at her legs. She didn't need Zal's urgent whisper 'Down!' to be already dropping to a crouch.

A bright gold car, like an ambulatory ingot. Zal hadn't been exaggerating when he'd said it was hard to miss.

It swung around another corner of the hedge and disappeared into the courtyard, the glow of the headlights visible above the six-foot palisade of saguaro and Spanish dagger. By the time Zal, Torley, and Emma had darted to the wide gate of the courtyard and peered cautiously within, Mitch Sandow was emerging from the house, the body of a woman in his arms.

Emma put her hand quickly over her mouth. The woman's head hung down over Sandow's elbow, her dark hair bobbed, barely longer than her jaw.

Not Kitty, she thought. *Selina* – in the moment before Sandow stepped into the reflection of the Phaeton's headlamps and the yellow gleam slithered across the blood.

'OK, Wise Guy.' A woman silhouetted against the dim lights from within the house – Kitty's height, Emma thought, but thin. The headlamp gleam flashed across the round lenses of glasses. 'Anything in the car saying where she took the kid?'

'She didn't *take* the kid.' Sandow's voice grated with exasperation. 'You heard her. She came here yellin' about *me* takin' the kid . . .'

'Yeah,' said the woman – presumably Mrs Pearl – in a voice that despite its rough speech, held the echo of a well-bred childhood. 'And if I'd grabbed Little Susy and you knew who and where I was, I'd wait for you to find me before I said, *Oh, what, who, me?*'

'And if I'd grabbed Little Susy, you think I'd have come all the way out here to stage a scene like that screaming for fifty percent of the loot? If I had her on ice someplace already?'

'If she knew you were the one who knew where the money was going to be handed off, and she didn't? You betcha, soldier. She knows Pughie, and she knows Bandog and Goldman. She knows that after three ransom notes, somebody in that outfit is going to say, *Fuck it, go ahead and kill the kid if you can't make up your mind*. They're not going to believe Note Number Four. We'll be lucky if they pay out on Number Three. She needed a cut of that.'

The man made a growling sound, angry at her point. Then, 'Help me get her in the car.'

Maya Pearl crossed to the Phaeton, opened the door of the passenger's side. 'Where's the gun?'

Whether it was the change in the angle of that gleaming door, or some trick of shadow as Sandow crossed the glow of the headlamps to heave the former star's body into the seat, beyond the car – in the darkness near the corner of the house – Emma caught the glint of jewels. At first, she thought it was the eye of some desert creature, but an instant later the pattern resolved itself: jeweled belt, jeweled hair-ornaments, the jeweled hilt of that ridiculous prop dagger.

Kitty had crouched herself down between the house wall and one of the big ornamental pottery jars – like a smaller version of the oil jars in the illustration of Ali Baba and the Forty Thieves – that stood close to the open door.

Emma felt as if her heart froze for an instant. *They'll see her. Even in the shadows* . . .

Maya Pearl came around to that side of the car as Sandow stepped back, thrust one of Selina's legs more fully into the vehicle, flopped the dead woman's arm inside, like throwing a broken branch.

'Get hers, too,' she said. 'The last thing we need is some cop matching up the slugs from Burt's body with his wife's rod.'

As he went into the house, she called after him, 'And I suppose you want me to come with you?'

He called back, peevish, 'How the hell do I know where the goddam mine is?'

'Idiot,' she muttered. And, louder, 'You know who she might be working with? Or where she's got the kid stashed?'

'If she *did* take the kid,' asserted Sandow stubbornly. His dark silhouette blotted the lamplight of the door again.

'Who else would have? Who else would know she was here? Or guess where you'd take her, when the silly bitch ducked out to make her own deal? That sister of hers?'

'That'd be my guess,' agreed Sandow. He stepped out into the courtyard, a gun in each hand. 'Except she hates that sneaky witch. And after all the slang Sis has spit in the newspapers trying to get the kid away from her, I can't see the two of 'em working together to put out a house fire if they were both locked inside. Ditto for the old man. But I can't see any of her big-time johns going along with a kidnap, either. If they would, she'd have teamed with them from the first, rather than . . .'

He stepped around the front of the car, and Maya Pearl rose and moved back, half closing the door.

And the jewels flashed on Kitty's costume like the stars of desert heaven.

NINETEEN

Mitch Sandow was in the act of turning, gun in hand, toward Kitty when Zal snapped, 'Drop it!' Even as Sandow swung around, Emma knew Zal wouldn't shoot, since Kitty, half risen beside the urn, was in the line of fire. Evidently, Maya Pearl guessed this, too. She grabbed the other pistol from Sandow's hand, flung herself sideways so that Zal couldn't cover them both and fired at Zal in the shadows, missing him by a good three feet. Though Emma had learned in the past months that it is much more difficult to hit a target while running than most films made it out to be, she took no chances and leaped aside.

Zal dodged back, too, and Kitty lunged to her feet to run. Sandow caught her around the waist, pressed his own pistol to her head.

'Drop your—' Sandow began, and swung around in shock as hooves ground on the gravel outside, and the yellow beams of electric flashlights spilled into the courtyard. Maya darted into the house and was in the act of slamming the door when Sandow, his arm still clinched tight around Kitty's waist, sprang after her, shoving his accomplice aside in the confusion of light and shadow in the aperture. He dragged Kitty through; the door shut with a bang.

'Surrender or we'll shoot!' Sergeant Brinkmanhoff dropped from the saddle, but though he had a shotgun in one hand, he made no move to aim it at the house. Two deputies leaped down after him, the horses flinging up their heads in alarm. 'Throw down your weapons and come out of there, Sandow! The house is surrounded!' (By the sound of hooves out in the darkness, Emma guessed this wasn't entirely true yet.) 'You can't get away!'

From within, Sandow shouted back, 'Come one step closer and I kill them both!'

'Who's in there with him?' The sergeant looked from Zal to Torley, who had emerged from the darkness, holding his shotgun by the barrel out at the length of his arm – presumably, reflected Emma, to make sure nobody made any mistakes. The deputy who was holding the horses took the weapon and held Torley at gunpoint.

'He's with us,' said Zal. 'Sandow's got Camille de la Rose and

Maya Pearl – Mrs Pearl was helping him get Selina Sutton's body into that car . . .'

The other deputy went over to the Phaeton and shone the flashlight inside. 'Christ,' he said.

'If he tells you he's got Susy Sweetchild in there with him, he's lying,' went on Zal quietly. 'From the way they were talking, she was snatched by somebody else – maybe Selina, or somebody working for her—'

'Jesus,' said Brinkmanhoff, appalled. 'Poor kid! Anybody else in there?'

'I don't know,' said Zal. 'We just got here a few minutes ago. It sounds like Sandow shot Miss Sutton, about a half-hour ago – we heard the shot on the way here. Probably went to get her car.'

Sandow's voice came from the house again, hard and desperate. 'I want you all to get away from the car. I've got de la Rose and I swear I'll blow her brains out. The kid, too, I swear it . . .'

Brinkmanhoff growled, 'If he hurts de la Rose, that'll really cut it for your friend Pugh.'

'No friend of mine,' returned Zal, and the officer traded a quick glance with him, unreadable in the darkness.

'I mean it!' Sandow called out again. 'I got nothing to lose! You get away from the car – get right out of the courtyard – and I'll— *Gaaah!*'

The gun fired within the house, shattering one of the windows. The door slammed open, and Brinkmanhoff yelled, 'Hold your fire!' as Kitty stumbled out, bloodied dagger glittering in her hand. From within the house, two shots were fired, Kitty springing immediately to one side and out of the line of fire, everybody else in the courtyard scattering.

Silence then. No shadow moved on the illuminated curtains at the windows. Emma rushed forward, circling to avoid (she hoped) getting anywhere near the door, and grabbed her sister-in-law in her arms. The two women retreated, fast, along the wall to the farthest corner of the courtyard where no stray shot from within the house could possibly get them. The moment they stopped, Kitty turned and hugged her, tight.

'Darling, thank you! Thank you! That fucking four-flusher—'

'What did you do?' Emma was aware of hot wetness soaking through the back of her blouse where Kitty's hand pressed, Kitty's hand still fisted tight around something hard.

She stepped back and looked. And, yes, it was the Evil Zahar's ruby-hilted prop dagger – Kitty was still resplendent in the black silk salwars and jewel-crusted brassiere of the Lady of the Crimson Desert, tousled dark hair glittering with chains of gems.

The dagger – and Kitty's hand – glistened with blood.

Before Kitty could answer, Brinkmanhoff raised his hand in a signal, and the five men – Brinkmanhoff, his two deputies, Zal and Torley – charged forward and into the house.

'Zal was right,' explained Kitty, looking around for something to wipe her dagger on that didn't have to be returned to wardrobe in the morning. 'If you brace your feet and put your whole weight behind it, you can do an awful lot of damage even with a prop.' She led the way – cautiously at first, then, when nobody in the house fired a shot, with her customary light quickness – along the wall, around the urn and into the house.

The front room was empty, though blood splattered the carpet near the outer door. Another puddle, larger, glistened near an archway into what looked like a dining room as the two women hastened past, through another arch and into a still-larger room behind.

In that arch, they nearly collided with one of the deputies, the man striding past them without a word. Blood on the tiled floor and on the wall amply showed how much damage Kitty had done with her prop dagger. 'I stabbed him in the stomach,' Kitty explained, as matter-of-fact as a child. 'I pulled his jacket aside, so there'd be less cloth to go through . . . Oh,' she added, 'see?'

Brinkmanhoff and Torley knelt beside Sandow's body in the back parlor, the officer wadding handkerchief after handkerchief – from Zal's collection of lens wipes – against what was clearly a deep puncture wound in the financial manager's abdomen, just above the stylish alligator-leather belt. Zal took one glance at Kitty's hand and dagger, and passed her another square of white linen. 'We've got a car parked about a quarter-mile back towards the road,' he said to Brinkmanhoff.

'Oh, me, too,' provided Kitty. 'It's Frank's. We can put couch cushions on the back seat, in case he springs a leak on the way to Indio – is there a hospital in Indio?'

'Nothing closer than Banning.' Brinkmanhoff spoke over his shoulder. 'Somebody get me something to put under his—'

An engine roared in the courtyard; tires ground gravel. The officer half rose, bit off what was clearly a violation of the second commandment ('He must be a Mormon,' Kitty surmised later) and returned to his efforts to staunch the wounded man's blood. The second deputy appeared like a jack-in-the-box from a door leading into one of the house's wings; his chief grunted, 'That'll be Pearl. Anybody else in the house, Young?'

Young Mr Young shook his head. He was barely twenty, freckled, fair-skinned and barn-red from sunburn. 'No, sir. There's blood in two places in that front parlor, sir, and a lady's handbag.'

Torley came in through another of the big room's several doors, a blanket over one arm and a syringe in the other hand. 'It was in the pantry,' explained Torley, seeing the sergeant frown. 'Morphine. Needles and ampoules. Other stuff as well.'

Emma, who had gone immediately to kneel at Sandow's side, rose quickly. 'Let me see.' She felt prey to a weird sense of déjà vu: *Didn't I just do this with someone else who was trying to kill me?* Sandow's shallow breathing labored, and his pulse, under her fingers, had been fast and thready, his hands like ice. Zal took the blanket and spread it over the wounded man, then made a circuit of the parlor – which was in reality, Emma now saw, probably a screening room: eight or ten small couches oriented toward a pair of thick, red velvet curtains that would undoubtedly cover a screen. (*They must have a generator somewhere out back*, she thought. And then, *Of course they do, if Mr Ardizzone is running a distillery on the property* . . .)

While Brinkmanhoff piled the cushions under Sandow's legs, Emma followed Torley back to the kitchen, in a short rear wing of the house. Behind a pair of red-painted swinging doors, the pantry was enormous and reminded her of the drug storage room at Bicester Hospital: boxes of ampoules, boxes of syringes. Anonymous cardboard or brown-paper packages, some stoutly taped shut. Yellow tins marked with red Chinese symbols. Chafing dishes, opium pipes, condoms, handcuffs. A green cardboard box containing a sinister-looking device with a small electric motor and a tangle of cord. A black leather hood, such as a hangman would fit over a culprit's head. An arrangement of rubber and straps that Zal told her later was a ball gag. Bottles of medicines: digitalis and phenobarbital, cocaine, epinephrine – Mrs Pearl clearly did not want anyone perishing of shock under her roof – and a serum whose name she associated with followers of that famed renewer of male vigor, Dr Serge Voronoff.

A box lay on the counter, open. The label was that of a well-known American firm of medical suppliers – she knew it from her days driving for the hospitals in the War. The ampoules within were sealed. *At least we won't kill the poor man by injecting him with heaven only knows what* . . .

Back in the screening room, she administered fifteen grains of morphine to her patient, and while Gren and Kitty walked back to where they'd left their respective cars, Zal took one of the flashlights and conducted her through the whole of the house, checking each room as Deputy Young had done before them. They found no more than he had in any of the dozen heavily curtained bedrooms, save the reek of incense that covered a stale pong of sweat and sex. In one room only, the heavy perfume could not quite mask the smell of cat, and going in, Emma saw by the flashlight's weak beam the dusting of sand and ashes in a corner.

Three black Ford sedans – none of them bearing a license plate, Emma observed – roared up that well-maintained road just as she and Zal emerged from the house. The cars zoomed past the courtyard without stopping and made straight for the barn, and Emma saw men spring out of them and fan out around the dark building. Flashlight beams flickered over the stout walls and locked doors. One man crossed to the house, flashlight pointed at the ground, his features impossible to make out under the shadow of his hat. Brinkmanhoff went to meet him, big hands tucked into his gun belt. A short conversation followed.

'Presumably,' Emma remarked in an undervoice, 'reassuring the gentlemen that none of us so much as turned our heads in the direction of the barn . . .'

Flashlight reflection splashed across the lenses of Zal's glasses. 'Private detectives, I'm guessing,' he murmured, his hand gripping her shoulder reassuringly. 'Hired by whoever runs the stills – which I assume was the reason for the three-hour delay.' He watched the two men in the moonlight for a time, the shadowy shapes of the armed 'detectives' around the distillery. 'I guess now is when we find out if Maya Pearl was in on the original snatch.'

Feeling through his arm the tension in his body, Emma was reminded of the absolute isolation of this place – of the fact that nobody knew where they were. She saw again Burt Sutton's body, torn by scavengers and nearly buried in sand.

Bootleggers, Brinkmanhoff had dismissed the crime.
Who would even ask?

But the sergeant returned to them alone. 'I'll take your statements at the sheriff station in San Berdoo. And I'll have to ask you – for the sake of the ongoing investigation into the kidnapping – not to discuss anything that happened this evening with anyone.' His voice had the dry note of a man repeating what he's been ordered to repeat. 'There's no telling what information is going to get back to who. We'll get men out looking for Pearl, but I'm guessing she's heading out of the country for good.'

The stiffness of his delivery told Emma that this was probably going to be the last anybody heard of the whereabouts of Mrs Pearl. She wondered if that was going to matter.

'Young? Hobart? Get Sandow into the car – Young, you get the horses back to the station . . .'

'I can help with that, if you don't need me,' volunteered Torley.

'Thank you. I appreciate it.' Brinkmanhoff's glance softened as it returned to Emma's face, moved on to Zal's, then to Torley's, Volmort's and Kitty's as they came hurrying over from their cars. 'We'll find the kid,' he said, more quietly. 'If we have to turn over every rock in this desert, we'll find her.'

TWENTY

'Did you hear anything of what happened?' Emma asked Kitty, on the ensuing, seemingly endless drive to San Bernardino. They cramped uncomfortably together in the small rear seat of the Packard, kneeling on the floor while Emma kept Sandow as steady as she could on the seat itself, her fingers on the pulse of his wrist. The men in the front were no more comfortable, Zal driving, with Sergeant Brinkmanhoff sharing the other seat with the boxes containing three uneasy little dogs. Now and then, the sergeant would speak comfortingly to them, but Emma was conscious that he was listening, over the growl of the engine, the whine of the tires, the thin snarl of the wind.

Still better, she reflected, than riding back in the roomier Pierce-Arrow, with the well-wrapped corpse of Selina Sutton, and Volmort – a non-driver – sitting silent beside Deputy Hobart.

After a moment, she went on, 'I heard Mr Sandow and Mrs Pearl arguing about someone kidnapping – *re*-kidnapping – poor Susy from under their noses. Who else would have known she was out here?'

'Beats me,' said Kitty. 'Who knows who Selina talked to, after she scrammed out of Desert Light? She showed up on Maya's doorstep about a half-hour after I got there – when I got there, the delivery trucks for the distillery were just loading up, five-gallon barrels of bourbon and rye – and I will say, if it's Ardizzone who runs this outfit, he makes a pretty good product. They'd come in with a tank truck full of water and another one of gas . . .'

Emma knew already about the gas. They'd had to borrow five gallons from the 'private detectives' to get the Pierce-Arrow back as far as Indio.

'. . . plus I guess a couple of tons of sugar and whatever was in those compartments in the fenders. And say! I need to get some of those put into the Packard—'

Emma nudged her sharply, glanced meaningfully at the dark silhouette of Sergeant Brinkmanhoff's head.

'Oh. Oh, yeah. So anyway, I had to hang back before I started snooping around, and I guess that's what Selina was doing, too, until she saw them leave. Once they're gone, she drives into the courtyard and bangs on the door with a gat in her hand, and asks Mitch, "OK, how much are you asking, and I want half of it." Mitch says, "What the hell? You're the one who grabbed the kid yesterday—"'

'Yesterday?' As she spoke the word, Emma heard like an echo from Brinkmanhoff: 'Yesterday?'

'You mean Friday?' asked Emma. Behind them the desert stars were losing their brightness against the ashy blue of coming dawn.

'I guess.' Kitty frowned, ticking off events on her fingers. It had been a very long night for everyone. 'He said yesterday. He said, "You think I'm gonna help you set up the drop after you ran out on me?" And she says, "Somebody had to light a fire under Pugh's fat behind . . ." And then the penny sort of dropped and she said, "Somebody else grabbed the kid? You mean after *you* snatched her and left me hanging out to dry? Don't give me that shit about somebody else snatched her—" And then they went in the house.'

Kitty shifted her weight. Years dancing in the Follies had given her an almost double-jointed flexibility (and the stamina of a brewery horse); in addition, Emma reflected enviously, she was wearing the silken bloomers and soft riding boots of the Lady of the Crimson Desert. West of Indio, the highway was paved, the scrub of the desert giving way to orchards of almonds and oranges as the gray dawn took shape. Far off on a hill, a white house looked down on the highway at the end of a long drive; a light went up in one window. Mitch Sandow's face seemed to have sunk in on itself through the long night.

If he dies, thought Emma, *we'll have nothing to go on. Nothing.*

More quietly, Kitty went on, 'I sneaked up and watched them through the window. Selina kept the gun on him – if she was smart, she'd have come up with some story about, *If I don't check in with A Certain Somebody by X time, they're gonna call up Iron Joe Ardizzone and tell him you dragged the star of the country's biggest kidnap case to the place where you've got a thousand-gallon still going* . . . That's what I'd have done, anyway. Maybe Selina wasn't that smart.'

She raised her head to look back at the black shape of the Pierce-Arrow, the only other car on the highway, gleaming like a hearse as it bore Selina's body back to civilization. 'Anyway, they got to shouting at each other, and Mitch was walking back and forth around the room, I think because he had a gun stashed in the cabinet and he wanted to put Selina off her guard while he went for it. If that's what he was doing, it worked. He took out a cigarette, did the whole pocket-patting routine like he was looking for a match, went to the cabinet – with her just standing there yelling at him, I think probably about money – opened the drawer with his back to her and whipped around with the bad news in his hand. She shoots and he shoots, and Maya comes in with a shotgun and she is *not* happy about the whole thing . . . And that's where you came in, I guess.'

To their right, a train steamed eastward behind the orchards. Ahead, the low houses and dusty trees of Banning draped the feet of the San Gorgonios like a green-and-white shawl. 'Turn here,' directed Brinkmanhoff, and guided them to the first hospital they had seen in fifty miles, a modest sanatorium (though still larger than the ones in Palm Springs and Seven Palms), from which the sergeant telephoned the Riverside County sheriffs and the Banning police, to put Mitch Sandow under guard while he was in the doctors' hands.

From there, they drove on to San Bernardino.

Other telephone calls had gone out from the Banning Sanatorium as well. By the time the yellow Packard reached the offices of the San Bernardino County Sheriff, Frank Pugh was there ('Bet he sells the Pierce-Arrow,' Zal whispered to Emma), with Irv Goldman in full Puritan Father mode. Pugh enfolded Kitty in a grateful bear hug – immortalized at once by two bright young gentlemen from the *San Bernardino Sun* and the *San Bernardino News Index* ('Wonder who called them?'). Emma thought the studio chief, beneath his exclamations of relief and gratitude, looked harassed and a little put out.

And why not? she thought. The story that Kitty would tell the sheriff – even the portions of it that the bootleg organizations deemed acceptable for release to the *San Bernardino Sun* and the *News Index* – would force the issue of the ransom. Foremost Films, under the eyes of the entire nation now, would *have* to pay up.

'But pay up to whom?' she asked softly, seated beside Zal on the bench in the station watch room, full daylight now and every electric fan in the building going full blast to little avail. The sergeant at the desk had raised objections when Emma had uncrated the Pekes to walk them; Mr Goldman intervened with an offer to do so and had just returned to the station bearing three hamburgers from the diner down the street, wrapped thickly in newspapers, for their breakfast.

'It is not the little ones' fault they came on this adventure,' he said gravely, breaking up the meat. (Frank Pugh, seated on Emma's other side, pretended to read a newspaper but eyed the burgers enviously. The sheriffs hadn't let him go for a walk, either.)

Watching Goldman now – at the other end of the bench – trying to coax Buttercreme out of her carry-box again to eat, Emma went on, 'That's what I keep thinking. If Miss Sutton escaped from Doctor Plaister's sanatorium Friday morning, she would have stolen a car to do so. Or she may have hidden Mr Sandow's Bugatti somewhere in Los Angeles and paid someone to drive her back to the location on Wednesday. Either way, she could have driven to Mrs Pearl's house and retrieved her daughter under cover of the windstorm Friday afternoon. The house is big enough that Mrs Pearl and Mr Sandow may very well not have heard anything going on in the other wing.'

'God knows she'd have known where the place was,' remarked Zal. 'So she brings the kid back to LA. Why not? Susy may not have known Mom was behind the whole thing. She switches cars Saturday morning—'

'Why come back to the house?' Emma interrupted. 'It's not as if that Phaeton is inconspicuous. If she left Susy with someone, she could have changed cars then—'

'Could be traced,' objected Kitty.

'Like the Golden Chariot couldn't?' Zal shook his head. 'Either way, she knows by this time there's a good chance the courts are going to hand custody of the kid over to Sis or Dad when this is all done, so she wouldn't take her to them . . .'

'What if she didn't take her to anyone?' asked Emma softly. 'What if she just . . . left her locked up someplace? She could have brought her with her in the Phaeton. All those deserted mine workings you and Kitty were talking about the other night, the abandoned ranches in the mountains . . . My mother worked all her life with the Society for Prevention of Cruelty to Children. I don't know how many stories she told me, of going into flats where the mother and the older children worked in factories and had nowhere to leave the younger children in the day. They'd give them a few spoonfuls of laudanum tincture and leave them sleeping, locked in the flat for nine hours – eleven hours sometimes . . .'

Her voice tightened, as she thought of Kitty saying, *God knows what's being hidden in some of those old mine buildings . . .*

Of a terrified, hungry, thirsty child holding her cat in her arms, watching the daylight fade in the cracks of some boarded-up window . . . At what point would she begin to wonder, *What if Mama doesn't come back . . .?*

She forced the image from her mind. Forced her voice steady. 'What if Miss Sutton simply assumed that she'd be back to pick her up in a few hours? What if there is no one to pick up that ransom? No one who knows where Susy is hidden?'

'They'll find her.' Zal's hands tightened over hers, and she saw in his brown eyes the innate cynicism of a man who's been around Hollywood far too long to believe a word of what he said. She could almost hear him ask, *Who'll find her, in twenty thousand square miles of deserts and mountains? Half a dozen guys on horses?*

But Mr Goldman stood up and came over to her, looking down with grave pity in his face. 'She will be found, Mrs Blackstone. I cannot imagine a woman would leave her child alone as you describe – and I cannot imagine a greedy woman would not have made some provision at least to keep chance strangers from discovering the hiding place, and that means at least a guard. Only an imbecile would have left the child alone.'

As Goldman turned away Zal murmured, 'The man obviously never tried to have a conversation with Selina . . .'

Or saw her, thought Emma, *on the set of* Our Tiny Miracle *telling her daughter that almost being killed by a frightened horse and a drunken stuntman was actually nothing to worry about.*

But at that moment, the station's outer door flew open to admit Foremost Productions' lawyer Al Spiegelmann – looking, as usual, as if he'd been pulled out of the bottom of a laundry bag – followed by Neil Bandog (shaved, immaculate and defensive), an exhausted Larry Palmer and detective Colt Madison, coruscating with energy like the hero of a Boys' Own Adventure novel. Thelma Turnbit and three other reporters attempted to follow them inside and were promptly corralled by the officer at the desk. This would have worked had not the inner office door, with cinematic timing, disgorged Sergeant Brinkmanhoff, Sheriff Shay himself, a clerical officer and Camille de la Rose, still gorgeous in black silk, bare midriff, and jewels – she smiled dazzlingly upon the Fourth Estate, posed and winked and shook back her midnight cloud of hair before an explosion of flash powder and journalistic inquiry.

It was fifteen minutes before Pugh, Goldman and (after a hasty and vehement conference in a corner with Goldman) Bandog (Lutz would probably be informed later, guessed Zal) made the statement – for the benefit of the press – that no expense would be spared, and no effort stinted, to save Susy Sweetchild.

At which point Ardiss Tinch and her husband, followed within seconds by Mr Foy Snoach, stormed into the station waving signed declarations from the late Mr Burt Sutton transferring to each of them sole and exclusive guardianship of his daughter Susy.

Buttercreme and even Chang Ming retreated under the bench for safety. Black Jasmine yanked on his leash, braced his feet and barked.

Taking refuge themselves on the bench, Emma held Zal's hand and watched the confusion with cold foreboding in her heart. In time, Kitty scooped Black Jasmine into her arms ('To prevent him from savaging them,' whispered Zal) and joined them. 'Frank wants to take me back to town with him,' she said. 'He's told Larry – hush, sweetheart, I'll let you bite those bad men later . . . He's told Larry to shut down production for a week – the sheriffs are going to want to talk to everyone in the company, and Larry says they'll be all over that area and we can't *possibly* keep them out of the shots – so you can get the train back with the rest of the cast, when they're done with you here. Just wire the studio when to have someone pick you up. Is that all right, sweetheart?' (This to Emma). 'You can get something to eat first, and sleep on the train . . .'

And dream of a gray cat crying in the darkness?

'That's fine,' she lied, too tired to disagree.

'Sweetheart . . .' Kitty reached down to stroke Emma's hair. Looking up, Emma saw the genuine concern for her in her face.

'It's all right,' Emma said again, and meant it, this time.

'I'll make Frank give you some dinner and taxi money . . . They say the Kong Zong Garden on Third Street is *really* good. Look after her, Zallie . . .'

His hand tightened on Emma's. 'Always.'

The word, thought Emma, was a beautiful one. It made Hollywood almost worthwhile. She closed her eyes.

'And that *adorable* Deputy Hobart just told me Mitch Sandow is still unconscious at that place in Banning,' Kitty went on, fishing for another cigarette. (Three deputies sprang forward with lighters.) 'They're doing surgery, but I guess I stabbed him pretty bad . . . Not that he didn't deserve it, the *momzer*. They found Selina's car near Chiraco summit, but no sign of Maya Pearl. She's probably in Mexico by this time.'

'Then let's hope Goldman was right,' said Zal quietly. 'About even Selina not being stupid enough to just lock the kid up someplace nobody knows about and leave her.'

'And what' – sudden bitterness gleamed like a ruby-hilted prop dagger in Kitty's voice – 'would you be prepared to bet on that?'

'Not a plug nickel.'

In the event, Zal would have kicked himself for losing a fortune by such faint-hearted prudence. The following afternoon, a yellow envelope appeared on Frank Pugh's desk – no one knew from where – containing a single sheet of brownish newsprint paper.

It bore the typed words: *Remember: No cops!*

TWENTY-ONE

The Southern Pacific deposited Emma, Zal and the dogs at Central Station at quarter past eight that evening – the rest of the cast and crew still being questioned in Seven Palms by the San Bernardino County Sheriff's department – and a studio car transported them to Ivarene Street. According to Mr Shang, Kitty and Mr Pugh had arrived in the Packard around noon and had lingered only long enough for Kitty to take a bath (assisted by Mr Pugh) and renew her make-up. They had then departed again, presumably to have lunch (it was by then four o'clock) and buy Mr Pugh another car. Emma wondered if the new vehicle would include secret compartments in the fenders.

Guessing that Kitty wouldn't return until well past midnight and be damned to the activities of the previous twenty-four hours, Emma likewise took a bath (assisted by Zal) and they both then fell asleep. It had been a very, very long weekend.

They were wakened at one in the morning by the dogs' excited barking, and Zal, after a number of kisses, made a Romeo-like departure down the back stairs as Mr Pugh was unlocking the front door for Kitty. If the studio chief did not wish to see his inamorata's respectable sister-in-law in his love nest, he certainly had no wish to encounter studio employees there either. Zal, Emma knew, would discreetly walk down to Vine Street and thence to hail a cab on Franklin.

Thus, Emma was startled, early the following morning, to look up from feeding the Pekes in the kitchen to see Frank Pugh in the kitchen doorway. 'Mrs Blackstone,' he greeted her, with what was almost a little bow, 'might I beg some of that coffee that you're making?'

The smell of it graced the kitchen. Emma did not believe in such American products as Washington's Powdered Coffee. She always ground and brewed fresh coffee, to be ready whenever she would hear Kitty first stirring – an event not due (she glanced at the clock) for another three hours. (*Good Heavens, they're not going to be filming* today, *are they?*)

'Of course.' She fetched a cup and picked up Buttercreme's half-eaten food, as the little dog had taken refuge in the pantry at Pugh's appearance, and both Chang Ming and Black Jasmine would have polished off the sauteed shreds of tongue and chicken within seconds. She set the dish in the pantry, and shut the door, glad that at least she'd dressed in her usual tweed skirt and plaid cotton shirtwaist, instead of coming downstairs (as she sometimes did) in her dressing gown. In Kitty's household, there was no telling who you might meet.

'I want to thank you for all the assistance you've been.' Pugh, uninvited, took a seat at the table (he had after all, Emma reminded herself, bought the house) and spooned sugar into the coffee she set before him. 'And for going after Kitty, once the two of you figured out that it was Sandow and Selina who were behind poor Little Susy's abduction. Conrad got a call late yesterday afternoon from the hospital in Banning. Sandow's still alive but in a coma. The gun they found in Maya Pearl's living room with Sandow's prints on it was definitely the weapon that killed both Selina and Burt. And Susy's prints were found all over that back bedroom in Maya's house.'

He paused, frowned thoughtfully for several moments at one of the shortbread cookies that Emma set before him, then put the whole thing in his mouth and swallowed it down with a crunch. Mrs Shang made these two or three times a week with the casualness of a woman buttering bread.

'And that leads me to a favor I want to ask you.' He studied – then consumed – another cookie. Kitty maintained two covered Ming porcelain dishes in the living room filled with his favorite candies; it was one of Emma's duties to make sure these were topped up after his visits.

She poured herself a cup of tea and sat down across the table from him.

'Tonight I'm going to Daisy Dell to deliver the ransom,' he went on. 'The original note said that Susy would be returned the following day. But in case they bring her tonight – simply to leave her in the car, for instance – I want to have someone she knows, someone she'll feel safe with, along with me . . . as well as Doctor Plaister, of course. Is it true what Kitty says, that you trained as a nurse?'

'Not exactly,' said Emma. 'I was an ambulance driver, taking wounded men from the Oxford train station to one of the several military hospitals in the area. Sometimes we'd be sent down to Portsmouth to help get the men on to the trains as well, if there'd been a major push on at the Front. We were taught things like dressing wounds, and what to do if one of the men went into shock or stopped breathing.'

She looked aside, feeling again the bitter chill of those gray mornings, those terrible jolting journeys. Recalling what it felt like to look at some of those chalky faces and sunken eyes, and know that a man wasn't going to make it as far as Oxford.

'They needed all the trained nurses they could get at the hospitals. I did get fairly good at it.'

'Would you come? Plaister's a good man, a very competent physician . . .'

(This was not what Emma had heard from any number of Kitty's colleagues.)

'. . . but I think a child – especially a child who's been through what Susy's been through in the past two weeks – needs a woman . . . and I mean an actual woman and not that zinc-plated harpy Ardiss Tinch. I don't know if the poor kid even knows she's an orphan yet. I need somebody who'll be with her when she hears that. Somebody whose face she knows.'

Emma said, 'Of course,' surprised – and grateful – to hear that, unexpectedly, Frank Pugh could think of a child's heart.

And at the same moment of time – *I really have been in Hollywood too long!* – wondering what the studio chief's real motive was.

'Darling, I understand why Frank wouldn't want that rat-mouthed pocket-twister Sister Ardiss Tinch to come with him,' Kitty guided the Packard through the studio gates and across the plaza to the hacienda through the warm blaze of late-afternoon light. 'Did you read what she said about her father in this morning's *Examiner*?'

'I did.' It had been obvious to Emma that neither the Tinches nor Grandpa Snoach had wasted an hour, upon their return to Los Angeles from the San Bernardino sheriff's station, in filing papers to adopt Little Susy Sweetchild. In the newspaper interviews which had accompanied these announcements, father and daughter had roundly denounced one another as sexual perverts, thieves and possible accomplices in the deaths of the child's parents.

'But I don't see why he didn't ask me to go along as well. I mean, I know you're a nurse . . .'

Emma opened her mouth to correct this misapprehension, but closed it again.

'. . . but I could help. And we're obviously not police.'

'I think,' Emma surmised tactfully, 'that because it will be pitch-dark out there this evening – the moon won't rise until late, and the dell is completely surrounded by hills – all anyone will be able to see is how many people there are with Mr Pugh. Two won't frighten the kidnappers away, if they see them at all. Three, or four, might.'

And she hoped, as Kitty drove away and left her on the porch of the old adobe, that Zal would be able to talk her friend out of trying to hike (*Kitty? Hike?*) over the hills to watch the ransom pickup through binoculars . . .

She could almost hear Zal's hoot of laughter at the thought of Kitty hiking anywhere. (*Does she even possess walking shoes?*) But she couldn't dismiss from her mind the image of Kitty stealing Mr Pugh's car and roaring off into the desert in silken salwars and a jeweled brassiere. *Ought I to telephone Harry Garfield and have him lure her out to dinner with promises of some truly scandalous piece of gossip? Or bribe handsome Jack Lee – who must be finished with* Burning Gulch *by this time – to take her out for drinks at the Ship Café and keep her – er . . . occupied . . . until dawn?*

Selina Sutton's green Vauxhall Velox had been brought down from Benedict Canyon that afternoon and locked in one of the Foremost Productions garages. Frank Pugh arrived moments after Kitty's departure, in his brand-new cream-and-black Isotta Fraschini. (Wrapped as Selina had been, she had leaked blood – and the inevitable other fluids of mortality not usually shown in films – on the Pierce-Arrow's rear seat.) Solemn and worried-looking, he bore a briefcase filled with packets of twenty- and fifty-dollar bills, which Emma and Conrad Fishbein helped him transfer to cotton sacks of the kind sugar was sold in. These, Emma and the studio chief carried to the garage, and stacked them on the floor of the rear seat of the Velox. As Emma had previously noted, the vehicle had no trunk that some enterprising law officer could hide in.

'Plaister's going to follow us up to the dell,' said Pugh, glancing around the dark of the garage as if he feared they were being overheard. 'We'll leave his car on Highland and walk back, if you don't mind, Duchess. I'm assuming someone's going to come up, drive the Velox away and – just possibly – leave Susy sitting on the ground, and that's where we're going to come down and scoop her up. I don't want her panicking and trying to walk anyplace by herself.'

'No.' Emma thought again of that child clinging soundlessly – tearlessly – to Vic Duffy's arm as the angry horse bucked and fishtailed in the dust. Of the child who had loaded her cat – the only creature she felt safe to love unreservedly – into a cage and tried to run away from home carrying him . . .

And are they – whoever they are – going to leave poor Mr Gray beside her in the dark of that deep vale in the hills? Or did the animal get accidentally killed, or left somewhere to starve?

Hold on, Susy, she thought. *Hold on. We're coming to get you* . . .

'Mrs Blackstone?' Grayish light sliced into the garage as the outer door opened a crack, blotted by Conrad Fishbein's rotund silhouette.

Emma crossed the oil-stained concrete to join him.

'I meant to ask you back at the hacienda,' said the publicity chief. 'I've been on the phone with Larry – he's still in the desert, organizing the clean-up, and when he gets back, we're going to have to start the filming again immediately. That whole sequence in the camp with Ken and Kitty – We need to have it rewritten so that it takes place at an oasis rather than out in the desert. That way we can finish the filming on the backlot, and won't need to go back out to location in August. Larry said to tell you we have lots of footage of the camel trains crossing the dunes. We can cut that in with close-ups of Ken on a camel in chains, and Kitty on a camel looking evil, both shot at a low angle from the ground, so all you can see behind them is the sky. Can you do that?'

In between rewriting the ending of Tiny Miracle, *in case Susy doesn't get left sitting on the ground in Daisy Dell?*

In case Susy has been dead for two days already?

We have no reason to think she hasn't been.

She said, 'Of course. When would you need this?'

'Everybody will be back to town tomorrow, so could you get us at least a couple of scenes Wednesday morning? Oh, and if you can write in a scene with a sandstorm . . .'

'Of course.' She felt quite proud of herself for keeping her anger out of her voice, but her weariness was palpable. And what, she thought, would be the point of anger? Her voice a little tight, she added, 'I will want some time to sleep tomorrow, after tonight's expedition.'

'Oh, of course, of course.' Fishbein took her hand and bobbed like a venal Kewpie doll. 'Larry's going to have the extras out at the new set on the backlot at eight.'

He started to close the garage doors, but behind her, Mr Pugh must have signaled him, for instead he stepped backward, swinging the doors wide. With a low, lethal purr, the Velox pulled up beside Emma, Frank Pugh at the wheel. Mr Fishbein opened the door for her. 'Good luck,' he said.

I really will have to find out what the word putz *means.*

By the way Kitty used it, it could not have signified anything good.

Daisy Dell lay a little ways into the Hollywood Hills, where the ground began to get tumbled and steep. A short canyon led into the hills just past the junction of Highland Avenue and Cahuenga Street, amid groves of oaks and eucalyptus, and hillslopes thick with agave, smelling of dust and sage. The sun had set, but the sky still held daylight as the green Velox, trailed by Dr Plaister's very shiny black Cadillac coupe, wound into the deep, almost cup-shaped valley in the hills – a perfect natural amphitheater in which piano concerts were held in summertime for picknickers on the hillsides.

Pugh turned the car around so that it pointed toward the graveled track again, helped Emma out and led her across to the coupe. Plaister – small, thin and oleaginous – gave her a clammy smile and drove back through the canyon and a short ways down Highland Avenue, concealing the vehicle in the wooded driveway of a pseudo-Spanish hillside mansion. Emma would have bet a percentage of the payment for rewriting the end of *Tiny Miracle* on Mr Pugh's inability (or unwillingness) to hike half a mile over the scrubby hillside in the fading evening light and, like Zal, in his hypothetical bet on a further ransom demand, would have lost her money. The studio chief produced a pair of well-worn boots (and thick, clean socks) from the coupe's trunk, put them on (puffing as he bent over) and, with astonishing lightness for a man of his bulk, led the way up over the ridge to the hillside above the dell itself.

Emma, who regularly walked up and down the slope of Ivarene Street and down to Franklin Avenue to catch the streetcar, had no difficulty keeping up, but Dr Plaister labored to follow. He had not, Emma guessed, had the forethought to provide himself with appropriate footwear. Although few trees graced the steep slopes of the dell, the scrubby flora of the California hills was thick, especially near the crest. Pugh had also thought to bring a rolled-up Mexican blanket, a thermos bottle of Foremost commissary coffee and two Foremost commissary cups, as well as a pair of expensive Swiss binoculars. He spread the blanket, pointed out to Emma the square shape of the Velox at the bottom of the dell and then swept the surrounding hillslopes with the glasses.

'Madison's keeping an eye on the road in, from the other side of Cahuenga Street,' he said. 'I doubt our friend's going to show up before it gets fully dark. And right now I'm less interested in catching the bastard – or even seeing who he is – than I am in getting Susy back, poor kid. That's gonna be a mess when it gets to court, and personally, I'm not looking forward to dealing with either that shyster Tinch or a greedy crook like Grandpa Snoach.'

He handed the binoculars to Emma, pointed out again the Velox, now barely visible as night drew on. 'Find something to sight on – that little peak there'll still be visible even when it's full night, and the car's straight down below it. I'm guessing he'll have a flashlight or a lantern with him, but if it's late enough, he may just have the moonlight. The road is over there. He'll have to have headlights on for that, but he may leave the car further up the road and hoof it. When I'm watching the car, you watch the road. All right?'

Emma said, 'All right.'

The night grew cold. Bats fluttered above the hills like a startled handful of blown leaves. On the higher hills to the west, coyotes began to howl.

Dr Plaister complained of the roughness of the ground and the small size of the blanket, to say nothing of the quality of the coffee, until Pugh said, 'No noise.'

And Emma: 'He may be coming over the hill as we did, and pass within feet of us.'

Pugh glanced at her – as much as she could tell of his expression, with night closing around them fast. But he said nothing, and for the next seven hours, none of the three spoke. They only passed the binoculars among them and watched, through pitchy dark, the spot where a car would appear from the road. Emma and Mr Pugh watched: Dr Plaister fell asleep almost immediately, a help rather than a hindrance in Emma's opinion.

As children, Emma recalled, she, her father and her brother would go walking at night, when the family went on holiday to Dorset or Wales. Her father would inevitably take cottages near some Roman fort on the Downs, or what might (or might not) have been a prehistoric stone alignment in Cornwall. His abiding love had been the Etruscans, but the dwellings and lives of any ancient peoples enthralled him. When darkness fell, he would teach his children the lore of the skies, pointing out planets ('The Babylonians and the ancient Hebrews associated Venus with disasters . . .') and telling the tales sealed forever into the patterns of the stars.

Even now, seeing the crooked square of Hercules, she could hear his voice, explaining the ancient hero's periodic bouts of derangement and the tasks he would undertake to expiate the damage he had done. ('Sounds like the poor chap was what they call a manic-depressive,' her brother had said, and their father had replied, 'I daresay. But it all had to be paid for, you see. The strength and the glory were only one side of his story. I daresay mockers flocked to the court of Queen Omphale solely for the bragging rights, that they'd seen him all dressed up in a frilly apron winding wool. It was their laughter that was his punishment, not the labor itself. For all he knew at the time, he'd be a has-been for the rest of his life . . .').

The stars are still there. The stories he told are still there.

It was like touching his hand, to see them, no matter where she was.

Ancient as the stars, the wind breathed the scent of the hills across her cheeks: the smell of sage and the distant sea. Below them in the vale, nothing stirred. Not lights, not a hint of movement near the solitary car (*Not that such a thing could be seen in the starlight . . .*)

And here I'm spending this magic night, this magic time, with Mr Pugh instead of Zal . . .

When the late-rising moon stood only a few handsbreadths over the hills, the stars seemed paler. Venus, fiery herald of wars and passions, burned, then seemed to fade before the steadier music of Apollo's coming. With it, the sense of her father's presence – her brother's presence – faded too, blending back to waking daylight.

Stiffly, she got to her feet, Mr Pugh clambering carefully upright with the assistance of his hands. In the pink fulness of dawn, they walked down the steep slope.

'I didn't see a thing,' Pugh reported, holding out his hand to steady her over a particularly steep patch. 'No lights before the moon came up' – he glanced at the white, gibbous shape that was almost transparent now in dove-colored heavens – 'and nothing stirring after.'

Emma shook her head. 'Me neither. So what now?'

How will we find her in time?

Half a dozen deputies for twenty thousand square miles of desert . . .

'I swear they can't have seen us,' he said decidedly. 'And I gave orders to Madison to scram out of there as soon as dark came on. And if the goddam police had their own boys up someplace keeping an eye on the car, I swear I'm gonna—'

He yanked open the rear door of the Velox.

The money was gone.

TWENTY-TWO

HOLLYWOOD WAITS FOR LITTLE SUSY
POLICE COMBING SAN BERNARDINO
COUNTY FOR CLUES

And in the film sections of several newspapers:

LITTLE SUSY'S FAMILY GOES TO COURT

The headline in the *Examiner* – CHILD'S BODY FOUND IN KERN COUNTY NOT SUSY'S – caused Emma to wonder, sickened, whose body it *had* been. What mother in Kern County was weeping that day, uncomforted by the knowledge that, *Well, at least it* wasn't *poor Little Susy Sweetchild, thank heavens!*

In a way, it helped to have Larry Palmer telephoning four times on Tuesday (twice before she'd even woken at noon after the night of watching in Daisy Dell) begging for scenes to get the Evil Zahar to a backlot oasis for her initial confrontation with her captive ex-lover, so that at least they could begin filming . . . *Oh, and about that sandstorm . . .*

Rearranging the puzzle pieces of scenes 312–382 – and going to the studio screening room for Zal to show her all the multifarious footage of camels crossing the dunes for her to choose transition shots – kept her from obsessively wondering if, and when, and how, that brave and terrified child would be returned . . .

And what waited for her when she got back.

To tell the truth, conditions in that household were a nightmare, Ardiss Tinch reported in an interview in *Photoplay*. *Of course our mother never would – and still never will – admit that our father did the things he did. She went right along with him when he said that locking us down in the cellar was for our own good, that our 'souls' had to be 'purged' from sin . . . We were children, for God's sake! I was nine; poor Selina was barely five. And of course Mother swore – and will still swear – that there weren't rats in that cellar . . .*

Selina did her best by the child, deposed Foy Snoach in the *Times*

Hollywood column. *And I think in many ways she was led on by that husband of hers. But her sister was nothing but a slut. She was the one who started setting poor Selina up with cheap crooks who'd promise a girl anything, and I shudder to think what poor Little Susy's life would be like in that home . . .*

And if nothing else, the need to begin shooting on the backlot the following day forced even Mr Pugh to recognize that Emma couldn't, under the circumstances, be expected to concoct a happy ending for *Our Tiny Miracle*. Sam Wyatt was still wrestling with the rewrites on *Toot-Toot Tootsie* and had been handed a novel called *Shining Bright* which Neil Bandog – still enraptured by Darlene Golden – swore was going to be the next nationwide bestseller and which must immediately be transmuted to a film vehicle to showcase Miss Golden's charms.

By the time Zal walked Emma across the dark plaza to the commissary on Tuesday night after the screenings, she didn't know whether to weep on his shoulder or ask for discreet recommendations for someone to murder Frank Pugh.

Or murder Larry Palmer, who pursued them to the commissary, snatched up the pages Emma had written, cried, 'Brilliant! Brilliant! I owe you, Duchess!' and went loping across the dreary glare of the big hall's lights to inform Ned the Greater and the men from the construction gangs what sets they'd need for tomorrow's shooting. Emma wondered how they planned to bring in the requisite number of camels from Sixth Morning in time.

Or should she simply inquire of God if there were any possibility for a Gomorrah-sized blast of all-encompassing fire and brimstone?

No. Her hand closed around Zal's. *No* . . .

Even a telephone call earlier in the day from Julia Denham had barely lightened her anxiety. 'It was Hal Partington,' the historian exclaimed in exasperation. 'The wretched man confessed to me that he'd helped himself to pottery shards – and to those two fragments of that Egyptian votive of Osiris – from Professor Wright's office after the police left on Thursday, to bolster his own claim of trade routes through Naples in the fourth century. The pages you sent me – the ones Will Dravitt's hired plagiarist copied from Wright's article – described fragments that I knew I'd seen in Partington's office. When I confronted him – and pulled the rest of the things out of his desk drawer – he said they were sitting on the edge of the desk, when he went in to help himself to the books.'

Ego in arcadia, reflected Emma, wasn't simply an aphorism about Death. The theft of contradictory evidence was the University version of behavior she'd seen in Hollywood a hundred times.

'I heard from Eando Willers that Mitch Sandow's conscious,' reported Zal after a time, stirring what could have been either noodles and cheese or the leftovers from the food-fight scene in *Boffo Boys!* scraped up from the floor of Stage Three. 'He's so doped up he's not making a lot of sense, but apparently he swears somebody broke in through the back of Maya Pearl's house late Friday afternoon during the sand storm and snatched Little Susy – and her cat – while he and Maya were at the other end of the house. *Somebody* sure knew that the way to keep the kid quiet was to take a hostage.'

Emma's fists clenched at the thought of what that responsibility – that added horror of trying to keep her pet from harm – day in and day out, for weeks now – would do to a child of seven. *There has to be someplace special in hell for people who would do that . . .*

Zal's hand closed tighter around hers. Outside in the glare of the plaza lamps, Mr Pugh's driver brought the Isotta Fraschini up to the steps of the hacienda, opened the rear door. Pugh clambered out, then Kitty; the studio chief bent his head to kiss her hands.

Emma sighed, glad above all things that in this garish Illyria she had found a friend who was not masquerading as someone else. 'Anyone could have known that,' she said wearily. 'The same way anyone could have known Miss Sutton had a Vauxhall Velox. Anyone who talked to the servants, the family – anyone who was on the Foremost lot, from Vic Duffy to Herr Volmort to that riding extra Kitty made such a spectacle of herself over last week. Mrs Pearl could have set it up herself, through one of her bootlegger friends. What I'm trying to figure out is, how did they get the money out of the car at Daisy Dell? It may be we'll hear from them, after all, now that they have it . . .'

'Well,' said Zal quietly, 'I've got a theory about that, Em. I don't like it,' he added. 'But dark as it gets in the dell before the moon comes up, I don't see how anyone could have come in, found the car, trousered the dough and scrammed . . . not with you and Pugh watching. And the cops had men in a lot closer than you were.'

Emma stared at him, aghast at this disregard of instructions.

'Of course they did,' confirmed Zal wearily. 'They just didn't tell

Pugh. But he knew they'd be there, because Chief of Police wants to score big headlines for catching the kidnappers and saving Susy Sweetchild, even if he has to kill her to do it. But I think Pugh took it.'

'Mr Pugh?'

'Think about it.' Zal prodded at the mess in the dish before him. 'He knew that third note was on newsprint paper in a yellow envelope. So Selina's dead, Mitch is out for the count and probably has no idea where the kid is anyway, and Maya Pearl's halfway to Guadalajara . . . That yellow envelope with the newsprint note turns up on Pugh's desk, nobody knows how. What a surprise. I'm betting Selina had that Velox fixed up with compartments in the fenders or behind the seats or wherever – and I'm betting Pugh knew it. Hell, he's the one who paid for the car. Pugh gets you to go with him as a witness – you're probably the one person in the studio who, even if she did see something a little fishy, wouldn't try to blackmail him. And while he's putting the dough in the back seat, he tells you he dropped his hankie back at the office and would you go look for it . . .'

'Or has Mr Fishbein call me to the door of the garage,' said Emma grimly.

'That works, too. And while Fishy's keeping you in conversation – with your back to the car – Pugh slips the cabbage out of the back seat and into one of the hollow fenders. You – and the cops – sit there all night keeping an eye on the car, and in the morning, Pugh takes the car back to Foremost – it's still in the garage here – and clears it out the minute everybody's back is turned.'

'And meanwhile' – Emma's ears felt hot with rage – 'Susy is locked up somewhere, without food, without water, in this heat, nobody knowing where she is . . .'

'They're looking for her.' He abandoned his dish, laid his other hand over hers, as if by the physical act of contact he could bring her back to the moment. 'If another ransom note turns up, from Maya Pearl or Joe Ardizzone or whoever, Pugh can say, *Dang it! Somebody must have heard about the car in the dell and sneaked in oh darn, I guess we'll just have to pay up again* . . .'

His grip tightened on hers. 'They can't not,' he pointed out. 'Not after all this publicity. And if that doesn't happen . . . They're looking for her.'

'Darlings!' Kitty swept into the long room, looked around and made a beeline for them, a dragonfly in iridescent green silk and flashing with . . .

'Aren't they gorgeous?' She held out her wrists. Each of her new bracelets (Emma kept an inventory of Kitty's jewelry and these weren't on it) was an inch and three-quarters broad, flexible bands of solid diamonds. Had the light in the commissary been slightly better, the glitter would have blinded the room. 'And earrings – see?' (They could scarcely help doing so.) 'And more than that—'

She dropped into a chair at their table, took Zal's coffee cup, added to its content from her flask and took a gulp, before lowering her voice. 'He bought me *land*.'

'You planning on building a city?' Zal inquired.

'Not *me*, silly.' Kitty smiled dazzlingly. 'But Mr Crain tells me' – Ambrose Crain was the elderly land-and-oil millionaire who took Kitty out to dinner whenever Mr Pugh wasn't around – 'that in about five years, mansions in the Santa Susannas' – Emma recalled these rugged hills bounded the San Fernando Valley on the northwest – 'are going to be renting for a *fortune* to people like Tom Mix and Doug Fairbanks, who want to be able to keep horses and ride the western ridges and still drive into Hollywood for lunches at the Montmartre. And Frank says that the property can be rented to studios as a location, and if *I* own it, I can kick back some of the rental money to *him*' – she dropped her voice as she described this piece of financial chicanery – 'only I'm not supposed to tell anybody that. Isn't it *marvelous*?'

'Sure is,' marveled Zal in a perfectly conversational tone of voice. 'Frank buy land for himself, while he was out shopping?'

'Oh, *oodles* of it, darling! Only I'm not supposed to tell anybody that, either.' She produced her amber cigarette holder and a brown Sobranie, and inhaled a revivifying draft of extremely expensive smoke. 'Fifty acres in Lankershim – which is developing like *crazy* – and another fifty north of the river in Reseda. He bought some for me because, he said, he's so grateful I'm willing to do the reshoots at short notice tomorrow. You don't mind, do you, Zallie?'

She regarded him with sudden concern. 'I know you said you were looking forward to a couple of days of quiet, before the tents were all set up at the oasis . . .'

Zal sighed, and reached across to take her hand. 'It's all in a day's work, Kit,' he said. 'But I expect you to take me and Em out to dinner.'

'Darlings, *of course*! There's a *wonderful* place in Santa Monica, if you're tired of the Biltmore . . . And when this is all done, you and Emma can drive down and spend a weekend in San Diego at the Del, and I'll pay, to thank you. Frank gave me enough to—'

'Thank you,' said Emma quietly, and took her sister-in-law's hand. And wondered, as she did so, if this would be before or after Frank Pugh demanded finished revisions of *Toot-Toot Tootsie* and a new, happy ending for *Our Tiny Miracle*. The thought of it made her sick.

'Thank you,' confirmed Zal, rescuing his viscid dinner – whatever it was – before Kitty could dribble ashes into it. 'Gosh,' he added thoughtfully, and glanced beside him at Emma. 'Wonder where he got the money?'

In the event, the issue of what Zal actually felt about the immediate resumption of reshoots on the Foremost backlot became quickly otiose.

Gren Torley must have worked all night, bringing a dozen camels down to Hollywood and having them saddled, caparisoned and ready for action on the following morning – Wednesday, the twenty-third – when Ken Elmore (in his suitably torn shirt) and Camille de la Rose (in her suitably skimpy brassiere, salwars, riding boots and cloak) stepped from the studio truck which had conveyed them from their dressing room to that portion of the former barley fields that stood in for countryside in every venue from Scotland to Korea.

Which was precisely the problem.

'We used this area,' pointed out Zal, disembarking from his own studio vehicle.

Larry Palmer stared at him as if the cameraman had taken a Macedonian sarissa from his pocket and impaled him.

Emma, following Kitty down the steps of the truck with Buttercreme in her arms (and Chang Ming and Black Jasmine wild to resume their interrupted careers as camel herders), looked around at the gently rising scene of shaggy grass and scrub oak.

'In Reel One,' amplified Zal. 'Those scenes where they're getting ready to go hunting at Fairfax Hall? And the scene where Margaret chews out Kitty for being un-ladylike? And then the scene with—'

The director blasphemed with great feeling.

'You're right,' agreed Kitty, much struck by the recollection. 'And then we shot the meeting with Marsh over there by those trees. And that scene that you did with Darlene, Ken, that they shot day-for-night? That was right over there by the . . .'

* * *

'Screw 'em,' said Zal cheerfully, when new plans for the afternoon were announced: Gren Torley and his camels dismissed, the extras given half their day's wages (but denied their box lunches) and an expedition to the wilds of the Santa Susanna 'mountains' organized (*They're hills*, protested Emma, silently – coming west last October from arrival in New York, she had *seen* mountains) to find an area that sufficiently resembled an oasis in the desert to permit reshoots. 'We can follow Pugh's car up there . . .'

('*No*, Chang! *Sit*, Jazz!')

'. . . and while he and Larry are looking around for something that looks like the Empty Quarter of Arabia, you and I can take the celestial cream cakes back down the old stagecoach road to the ocean and drive back along the beach. There's a café at the fish market below Los Leones Canyon that serves a damn good lunch, and from there we can drive along Sunset through the hills. Or down to Venice,' he added, with a sidelong glance, 'if you'd like.'

Zal's cottage in Venice, beside one of the little stage-set canals, was tiny, but at least one didn't have to worry about meeting Frank Pugh in the kitchen.

'I'd like that,' Emma said. The idea of being anywhere but in Hollywood beckoned like – the simile grated on her, but it was the only one that sprang to mind – an oasis in the desert. (*A* real *oasis in a* real *desert* . . .)

Accordingly, when Kitty grew bored with following the studio chief and the director from gully to hillslope in the wildly beautiful fifty acres of wilderness that were now her personal domain, she welcomed the invitation to accompany Zal, Emma and the dogs back to town. ('I can telephone Mr Crain from the Canyon Café and he can take me to dinner in Venice!') Since she had dressed for the expedition in pleated silk of bronze and turquoise with delicate T-strap heels to match, this decision hadn't taken long.

Crowded as this made Zal's Bearcat, with the Pekes standing on Emma's lap to face into the wind, Emma was glad of her sister-in-law's presence. She herself had been silent all day, since the news relayed to them when they'd arrived at the studio early that morning had not changed. Half a dozen Los Angeles police, and several Los Angeles County sheriff's deputies, had joined the San Bernardino County forces (such as they were) in their search, but so far, to no avail. Detective Colt Madison had reported that his 'contacts' among the Los Angeles bootleg and gambling underworld had all sworn they knew nothing – and had heard nothing – of Little Susy's whereabouts. The Tinches and Grandpa Snoach evidently still believed the child to be alive because court dates for the custody fight had been set.

Dear God, Emma prayed, as the Bearcat negotiated its careful way along the winding track that led toward the old stage road from the San Fernando Valley to the sea, *let the Tinches have her hidden somewhere in their house . . . or one of those empty properties in Long Beach . . . Let Maya Pearl be hiding her in some bootlegger's hideout . . .*

When she had slept last night, she had dreamed of the child sitting in shuttered darkness, in a prison that no one knew about: a mineshaft, the cellar of a deserted house in the desert. Clinging to her dying cat, dying herself of thirst. Waiting for her mother to come get her, knowing by this time that it wouldn't happen.

'Of course, I *never* would gossip,' chatted Kitty at her side, to Zal, 'but Clara was *absolutely* right about him in bed! And I understand there's a *divine* fellow over at Metro, except for those ears . . . Like a car that somebody left the doors open . . . Oh!' she added suddenly. 'Oh, Zallie, do you mind? I'll bet nobody's thought to tell Gren Torley they won't be needing those camels until Friday, and then they'll only be back up the road a few miles – Do you mind? Gren will be at the studio still, and Mrs T can phone him . . .'

'Em?'

She opened her eyes. Ahead of them on the right was a white gateway, of the sort that many ranches had, only this was closed with stout gates of white-painted boards. SIXTH MORNING was painted on the boards above. Behind a five-foot railed fence along the track, green grazing land was visible, dotted with trees and an occasional water tank. Horses grazed, and a small herd of black-and-white ostriches. In the distance, beside a water tank, three elephants were engaged in gravely spraying water over their own backs.

'If it won't be disturbing them.' *Mr Torley has just lost his brother*, she thought. The family would be on the rack of grief and fear, over the fate of his niece.

A boy of ten, with Burt's long chin and tourmaline eyes, came out of one of the long barns as the Bearcat came into the open quadrangle between the house, the barns and a line of workshops. Peacocks, geese and guinea fowl promenaded gravely before the house, causing Chang Ming and Black Jasmine to lean against their leashes in a noisy ecstasy of atavistic savagery. Socrates, the immense and uncharacteristically gentle bull elephant, turned his head in his pen beside the barn to regard the newcomers as Zal went to speak to the lad: 'Your mom here, Buzz?'

Evidently, she was. Broad-shouldered, muscular rather than stout in her faded calico dress, Ronnie Torley emerged from the house, embraced Zal as a friend. Emma turned back to help Kitty out of the Bearcat – the low-slung little car had no doors and passengers had to step out over its sides as if exiting a bathtub. Kitty held Buttercreme tucked under one arm, and when she caught the high heel of her shoe on the edge of the running board, Emma grabbed to rescue the little dog, and Chang Ming – usually the most polite and obliging of canines – uttered a gruff bark and dashed away to assault a very large, very fluffy frost-gray Persian cat that dozed on the nearest hay bale.

The cat appeared to be sound asleep, but few cats, Emma well knew, are ever *sound* asleep. The gray cat sprang up, arched his back and swatted Chang Ming soundly on his flat nose with one white paw. Then he dashed, tail fluffed to the size of a cricket bat, into Socrates' pen, and scaled the elephant's thick hind leg as if it had been a tree, to take refuge on the pachyderm's back.

Socrates turned to regard Chang Ming with deepest disapproval, and the Peke skidded to a stop on the safe side of the corral's fence.

The cat sat down on his high perch and proceeded to wash with an unspoken, *So there* . . .

Emma looked up at the cat, then across at Zal and Kitty, in conversation with Mrs Torley by the ranch-house door.

Thoughtfully, she crossed the dusty yard to the barn.

In the barn, it was warm, without the noon glare and heat of the yard. Stuffy with the smells of hay and dust. One end was stacked high with bales of fodder. The other three-quarters of the dim space comprised about a dozen loose boxes for horses, with doors opening into a big corral that faced out on to the rising hills. The rest of its length was a single long pen, which gave – again through a wall of folding doors open to admit the steady wind that was a constant at that end of the Valley – into another corral. Pen and corral were both inhabited by a dozen monstrous tortoises, as big as medium-sized dog houses, creeping about on thick-muscled, scale-armored legs.

A little girl was emptying a basket of kitchen greens – lettuce hearts, carrot tops, chopped-up corn husks and broccoli stalks – on to the thick heaps of hay along the inner edge of the pen. The huge reptiles crowded up around her, nudging her knees, and the edges of the basket, with blunt dust-colored noses.

Among them, the big gray cat picked his way, regarding the monsters with disdain as he went to their water pond and lapped.

Emma said, 'Susy?'

The child turned, regarded her with solemn dark eyes. 'Mrs Blackstone.'

Emma started to say, 'Thank Heavens you're safe!' but couldn't. She only dropped to her knees, held out her arms, weeping with relief as the child ran to her and hugged her tight.

'Don't tell anybody,' whispered the girl. 'Please don't tell anybody. Please don't make me go back.'

TWENTY-THREE

'I don't want to go back.' Little Susy Sweetchild – Susy Sutton – born Susy Torley – clung to her uncle's fingers with one hand, the other arm around Mr Gray, now purring and kneading with his paws in her lap. Her aunt, Ronnie Torley, and her ten-year-old cousin Buzzy, sat on the edge of the tortoise pen, the tortoises grazing contentedly among the hay and vegetable scraps. Emma noticed now that the pen contained about a dozen smaller representatives of the breed, varying in size from serving platters to washtubs, as well as two *very* large lizards who also appeared to be enthusiastic vegetarians.

Outside, the dry wind brought the smells of horses and camels, of hay and the sunbaked Chatsworth hills.

'I'm sorry about Daddy,' the little girl went on softly. 'But he would never stop Mommy from being mean to me – and I couldn't stop *her* from being mean to *him*. I loved Daddy.' And in a slightly stifled tone, she added, 'I loved Mommy. I really did. But . . .'

Tears collected in her eyes, and she blinked them back, as she had long ago learned to do.

'Daddy would run away and be gone for weeks. Even when he came back, sometimes he wouldn't come out of his house, and Mommy would grab me and drag me away when I knocked on his door. And *I'll* run away if you make me go back to Grandpa or Aunt Ardiss and her awful husband.'

'No one's gonna make you go back, honey.' Torley returned her grip.

(*I will never give up my fight for my sister's poor child*, Mrs Tinch had declared in the *Herald*, the *Examiner*, *Photoplay* and *Screen World* that morning.)

Emma looked over at the animal keeper. 'It was you who broke into Miss Sutton's house – into Mitch Sandow's office there – and stole the keys to Maya Pearl's place, wasn't it?'

'When Burt stayed here last month, sobering up, he gave me keys to his cottage,' said Gren. 'I went through all Burt's papers there. I'd heard of Maya Pearl. Pretty much everybody around the studios has. Back when he owned Magnum, Burt was a pretty steady boyfriend of Maya's – that was when she was tryin' to get into pictures herself. He helped set it up with Mitch to broker buyin' that house of hers – she used to have a smaller place just outside Indio. But she had the chance to hook up with some gangster or other, to run a distillery on her land, and Burt gave her the money for it. Then when you rode with me back to town Thursday, after Selina showed up again on the set, and you said you'd found cards an' invites from Maya at Selina's, I sort of put it together, where Mitch would take her if Selina tried to double-cross him.'

From the corrals, the voices of the younger Torleys – Nelly was nine, Ollie, eight, and Jay, five – chimed like the calls of distant birds, mingled with Pedro the Great Dane's barking as he dashed madly around playing chase with the Pekes.

'I knew Mitch pretty much worked out of Selina's house this past year, after he screwed up a couple of stock trades and lost his office downtown. And it made sense that he'd hang on to a set of keys to Maya's new place, after the sale. He was that kind of man.'

When Gren Torley had returned from Hollywood, half an hour previously – at the head of a caravan of camels loaded with all their caparisons and props – he had borne the news that Mitch Sandow had relapsed into a coma. Still too weak to be moved to the San Bernardino County jail, the handsome financial advisor had begged the officers who came to question him to put a guard on his room at the Banning Sanatorium. He had even offered to confess to kidnapping and murdering Susy Sweetchild if they would do so: 'They're after me,' he'd whispered desperately. 'Those guys I borrowed money from – you don't stiff those guys.'

'I went down to Selina's place that same night, Thursday,' Gren went on after a time. 'Rico Santini's just a little hard of hearing – the windows of that basement room were shut, and I could still hear *The Gold Dust Twins* on the radio, from the other end of the garden. I coulda blown those drawers open with dynamite and they wouldn't'a heard. I got the spare keys out of the file, and drove straight back out to Indio before daylight Friday.'

'And because Mrs Santini didn't go into Sandow's office,' said Emma, 'she naturally thought Miss Sutton had broken into the files while there to get money and her clothes.'

'Figures,' said Torley. 'Drivin' out there in the dark, the wind was already comin' up; I knew it was gonna be a hell of a blow.

By noon Friday, you couldn't see your own nose, and dark as twilight in winter. You seen Maya's place: it has about eight doors to the outside, in case they get raided. I knew none of the bootleggers would be coming out in that wind. From Mitch's papers, I knew what wing the bedrooms was in, so I just counted windows and stayed clear of the rooms where I could see lamplight. I wrapped up Susy in one blanket, and Mr Gray in another, and hiked back down the canyon to where I'd left my truck. Drove all night, bringin' her back here to where Ronnie could take care of her, turned right around and went back out to Twenty-Nine Palms, and I don't think I even missed the sleep I lost, feelin' so happy, like I'd just drunk sunshine. Happy I knew she was safe.'

'Don't make me go back.' Susy turned her gaze towards Emma again, and then on to Zal and Kitty, sitting on a hay bale beside her. 'I just want to stay here and feed the animals. I wish I was ugly like Uncle Gren,' she added. 'I wish I had a big nose and bumps all over my face, and crooked teeth. Then they wouldn't keep me locked up in a closet if I tried to see Daddy, or say they'll hurt Mr Gray if I didn't say what I was supposed to, to the reporters and the lady from the school, or make me sit all naked in ice water for forgetting what the director wants me to do.'

There was long silence.

'You know,' said Kitty thoughtfully, 'that could probably be arranged.'

SUSY SWEETCHILD FOUND!
CHILD STAR'S TRAGIC ORDEAL!
SWEETCHILD CUSTODY BATTLE
SCHEDULED IN COURT MONDAY

'She was found by immigrant Mexicans,' explained Zal, his voice low as he adjusted the shut curtains of the farmhouse at Sixth Morning. Unlike the hacienda at Foremost Productions, the new living room, bedrooms and porch had made no effort to mimic the original Spanish style of the adobe. This room was part of the American portion, which had simply been tacked on in the 1870s. Generally sun-flooded – and alive with the fluttering of two caged parrots and a toucan ('You'd be surprised how many directors wants something out of the common,' had said Mrs Torley) – it was now dim, and very quiet. The birds had been moved out – along with four protesting dogs, a cage full of trained mice, and three cats (including Mr Gray). The whole house was hushed.

'It sounds to me like they were smuggling liquor. It would explain why they haven't come forward. She said they found her, out in the desert, but she doesn't remember a lot about it.'

'I wonder they returned her,' sniffed Mrs Tinch.

Her husband added, '*If* they're telling the truth—'

'That I don't know.' Zal crossed to open the curtains that looked out on to the deep shade of the front porch, giving the illusion that the room was reasonably well lighted when in fact it was filled with a melancholy brownish gloom. Nine-year-old Nelly Torley came in with a tray of teacups and a pot, which she set tactfully on the small occasional table between the sofa (where the Tinches sat) and the wooden kitchen chair insisted upon by Mr Foy Snoach.

'And they didn't demand a ransom themselves?' Tinch's eyes narrowed with suspicion.

'I don't think they could have,' said Emma, pouring the tea. 'Not if they were bringing in illegal liquor. Thank you, Nelly.'

Mr Snoach half rose from his chair and examined one of the empty teacups as if he suspected it had been at some point in time used as a birdbath. He then held it grudgingly out to receive the tea (which he noticeably didn't drink), refused one of Mrs Torley's very excellent oatmeal cookies and returned to the chair, sitting as if trying not to come into contact with either the seat or the back. He had refused the armchair originally offered him, after inspecting it for fleas.

'For one thing,' Emma went on, 'they didn't know who she was. She said her name was Susy, but . . .' She hesitated, trying to follow Kitty's dictum of pretending what she'd feel if what she was saying was really the truth.

She almost couldn't. The men she'd driven from the railway station to the hospitals had told her enough about what happened in war for her to know that people actually did such things to children. Let such things happen. She couldn't imagine how she would have dealt with that truth.

She took a deep breath, and tried to steady her voice. 'We don't know what actually happened,' she forced herself to say. 'The doctor we took her to says it looks like acid of some kind.'

She sneaked a glance at the three faces opposite her and saw alarm in all of them, and shock.

'Who'd do something like that?' demanded Snoach, as if he'd been defrauded. 'And *why*?'

And Mr Tinch asked, 'How bad?'

Emma looked aside. How could you answer those questions? *Isn't anyone going to cry, 'Oh, poor child!' Or ask, 'Is she still in pain?'*

Zal stepped in gravely. 'The doctor says when she's sixteen or seventeen – and her face has stopped most of its growing – they can probably do surgery to deal with the worst of it. And in ten years, who knows how surgical techniques will improve? We had her to an eye doctor too,' he added. 'He said there's a good chance that most of her sight probably will come back in a couple of years.'

The Tinches looked aghast. Snoach's brow blackened with cheated rage.

'How do they know these greasers didn't burn the girl themselves?' he demanded, and Emma had to bite her lip not to utter the first retort that crossed her mind.

'I don't know why they would have.' Zal kept his voice calm and reasonable. 'But again, we don't know. They brought her back from the desert and turned her loose near here Wednesday afternoon – I guess she said something about her uncle having a farm with camels and elephants, and they knew about this place. Mrs Torley found her asleep on the haystacks near the elephant pen, with her cat – Mr Gray – beside her in a little cage.'

The room's inner door opened, and Gren and Ronnie Torley led their niece in from the adobe kitchen beyond.

Kitty followed them, but Herr Volmort, Emma was glad to observe, kept himself – and his make-up kit – well out of sight.

The light was better in the kitchen, but Zal had screened it carefully as well. Just enough fell through to highlight the horror that thrown acid – or a wickedly skillful make-up man – could produce.

There were enough bandages to suggest worse mutilations unseen, across cheekbones and under the lower lip. The awful, corroded skin of the forehead extended around to Susy's left temple and above the hairline, so her head had been partially shaved, the remainder of the lovely brown curls clipped short. Around the ersatz sores, and visible at the edges of the bandages, the skin had the horribly convincing red flush of second-degree burns. Emma wondered, looking at the artistic speckling of medium-sized blisters near the largest of the bandages on the scalp, what the gentle Herr

Volmort had seen on his side of the Western Front, that he reproduced to such sickening effect.

Susy whispered tentatively, 'Aunt Ardiss?'

Aunt Ardiss set her teacup down just in time to prevent herself from dropping it. Tea splattered into the saucer. Aunt Ardiss, observed Emma through the semi-concealment of the shadows, was hard put not to leap to her feet and run all the way to her husband's car.

Almost worse than the ruin of the child's face was the movement of her head, turning here and there, with that aimless, pitiful motion of the near-blind.

'Grandpa?' Susy twisted her little fingers out of Torley's hold, extended her hands towards Foy Snoach – whose chair was positioned in the best lighting from the kitchen door – and took three careful steps towards him before her shins collided with the occasional table and the teatray. She staggered, tears flooding the sightless eyes, but she blinked them back unshed . . .

'*Wow*,' whispered Kitty, awed, into Emma's ear. 'She's *really* good! I'll have to use that . . .'

'I'll write a scene for you into *Shining Bright*,' Emma promised, in a murmur like the stir of a leaf. She knew that Kitty, who couldn't act to save her life, would be completely unconvincing as a blind girl, but it was the least she could do.

'It's OK, honey.' Ronnie Torley stepped up to steady her tiny niece, since Grandpa Snoach showed no sign of reaching out to the blinded, mutilated child who was clearly going to be an expensive liability for years to come. And of no value to anyone thereafter. 'Come sit down here.' She led Susy by the hand to a strategically placed chair in a shadowy corner. 'Would you like some milk, sweetheart? And a cookie?'

A whisper. 'Yes, ma'am.'

Mrs Torley had to guide her fingers to the sides of the glass, kept a watchful hand beneath the tumbler as she drank. (Rondara the Jungle Princess knew all about making a scene work.)

Into the appalled silence that filled the dim room, Gren said, 'The eye doctor says she can probably get about with dark glasses to protect her eyes. Next year, when her face starts to heal some, I figure we'll start her in school over in Chatsworth. She'll probably have to wear a mask of some kind, but I know the teachers there, an' they'll keep her from bein' teased.'

'Of course they will.' Grandpa Snoach's relief at the thought that someone else was willing to step in to take care of his disabled granddaughter rang like happy church bells in his voice. 'Why, she'll be just fine. Won't you, Susy?'

Susy's hand – after one artistic grope in the air – closed around Torley's. 'I'd like that.'

Hands were shaken all around. 'Please call me about helping with the doctors' bills,' said Kitty, and though Emma knew the offer would have been genuine (had any doctors actually been required), she also saw Kitty's sidelong glance at Grandpa Snoach and the Tinches – all three resolutely mumchance.

'Any bets on which one contacts their lawyers first to drop the custody case?' Zal closed the front door against the cloud of dust thrown by the speedy departure of the guests.

Torley stroked Mr Gray, who had appeared from nowhere to climb up his back and settle around his neck like a stole. 'I sure hope nobody gets in a wreck roarin' back to town to pull the plug.'

Listening to the howls of delighted laughter from the kitchen, where the four Torley children were watching Herr Volmort scrub the damage from the giggling Susy's face, Emma felt that this was a very charitable hope for the animal keeper to express. Certainly more charitable than anything in her own heart at the moment.

But Hollywood, she reflected, had its uses after all.

The two hundred thousand dollars ransom which vanished on the night of July twenty-first from Daisy Dell was never recovered, though in the month that followed, Frank Pugh bought property in Beverly Hills and Santa Monica, and several more pieces of expensive jewelry for both his wife and his mistress. Weeks later, having found herself alone in Pugh's office for a few minutes, Kitty brought home all four ransom notes, abstracted from his files. Although all four were on cheap pale-brown newsprint paper, the first three, Emma determined, had been typed on the machine in Mitch Sandow's office at Selina Sutton's house on Shadygrove Terrace. The fourth – *Remember. No cops.* – was in typescript identical to that of the machine in Frank's office.

Since all of Little Susy Sweetchild's films were re-released and attracted enormous audiences, the studio did not lose. Thanks to 'block booking,' very little of the profits actually went to Susy herself.

When *Our Tiny Miracle* was released in November, audiences at the premiere gave it a standing ovation, and sixteen-year-old Delia Terry – who had played a bit-part as Rosebud Mary's crippled sister in *Crimson Desert* – was outstanding in her portrayal of 'Older Susy' happily reunited with her parents. She was given a three-year contract by Foremost Productions, and a few years later went on to a moderately successful career in the talkies.

Both Ardiss Tinch and Foy Snoach withdrew from the custody case, and the following year, uncontested, Gren and Ronnie Torley adopted their niece.

With dark glasses and bandages reapplied, Susy Sweetchild was interviewed by *Photoplay*, *Film Fun*, *Motion Picture News*, *Screen World* and nearly every other film magazine in the country, and had nothing but good to say of Foremost Productions, her parents and the 'dear, kind Mexicans' who had found her in the desert: 'I didn't understand anything they said but I think they were smuggling liquor. They were so kind to me and made sure I got home to my Uncle Gren.' (Emma was proud of this particular piece of her script.) No photographs of Susy in her bandages appeared in any publication in the country, only attractive stills from her films. Whether this was the result of good taste (Emma doubted it) or threats from the Foremost Productions legal department, Emma never learned.

Emma herself, when she visited young Wilson Dravitt in the hospital a few days after Susy's return, encountered not only his father but a young Viking who turned out to be Al Paine there as well. Paine returned to Emma all the papers they had found in Wilson's room, allowing her to complete her work on Professor Wright's research. Julia Denham arranged for Wilson to receive an 'Incomplete' in Classics 102 – to be made up when he recovered from the effects of his concussion – and for Al Paine to receive the lowest 'C' grade ever recorded in the history of the University of California (Southern Division) and so remain on the football team, where he led the Grizzlies to a rare victory against the Trojans in the September exhibition game.

Since Mitch Sandow mysteriously died in hospital in Banning ('We just stepped out for a cup of coffee!' protested the men supposedly guarding his room), nobody cared unduly about the results of the game.

And when Dr Leon Wright's article 'Four Painted Tombs: A Comparison' appeared in the *Journal of Archaeology*, its credits included 'Edited by Emma Blackstone.'

'That's my girl,' said Zal.